THE PACT

THE BLACK HIND'S WAKE II

To Rhianne

J E HANNAFORD

The stone shook, the world shook.

Bristol con.
29-10-2022

Copyright © J E Hannaford 2022

Chapter Art Copyright © Carina Roberts 2022

Cover design by www.trifbookdesign.com

J E Hannaford asserts the moral right to be identified as the author of this work.

All rights reserved. No part of this publication may be reproduced or transmitted in any form or by any means, electronic or mechanical including photocopying, recording or otherwise, without the prior permission of the publisher.

PB ISBN: 978-1-7399213-3-0

EB ISBN: 978-1-7399213-4-7

Edited by Diana James.

This book is a work of fiction. All characters, and events portrayed are entirely a work of the author's imagination and any resemblance to actual events or persons, living or dead, is entirely coincidental.

For Janet Hannaford.
Dear Mum, in a book filled with families, you are the inspiration in ours. You are a true force of nature.

THE LANDS OF THE BLACK HIND'S WAKE

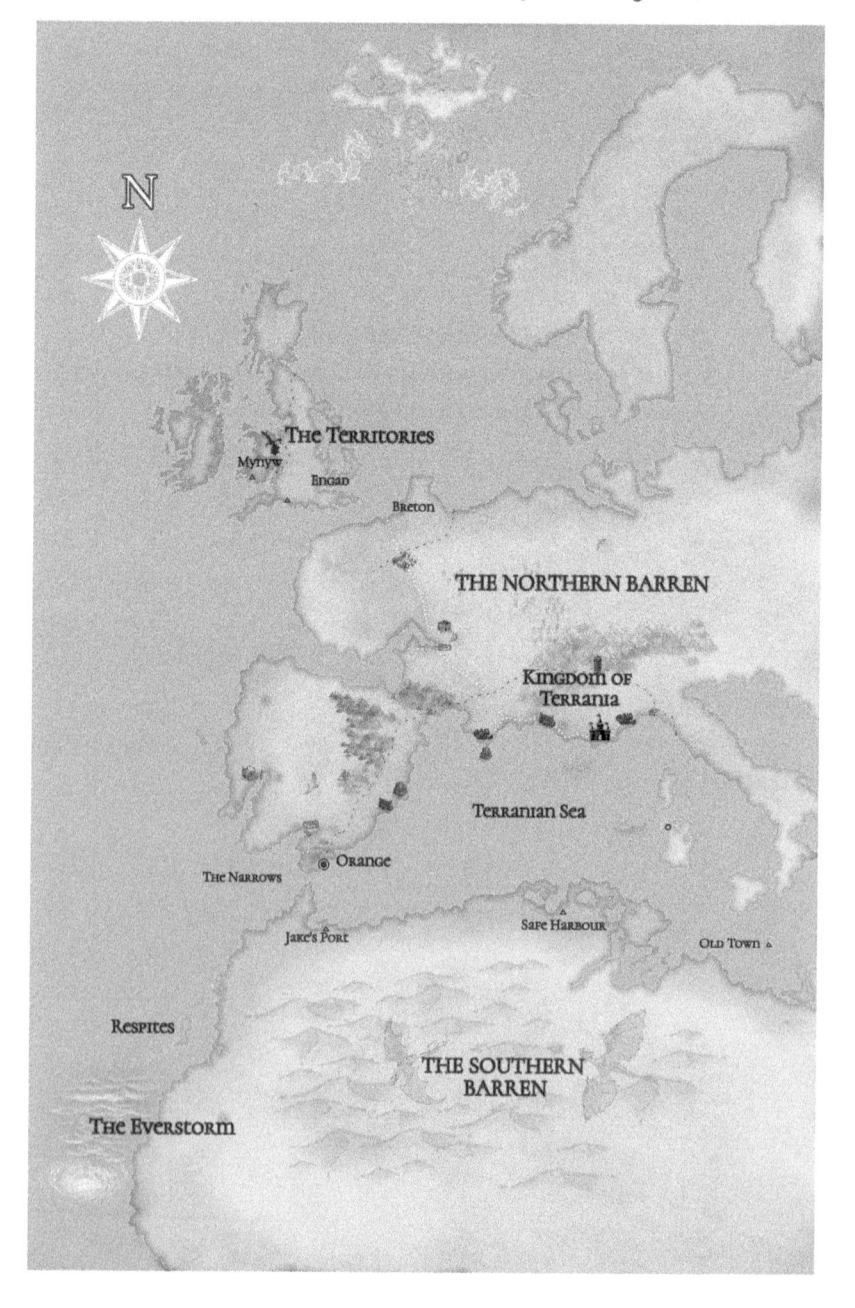

The Territories
Mynyw
Engad
Breton

THE NORTHERN BARREN

Kingdom of Terrania

Terranian Sea

Orange
The Narrows

Jake's Port
Safe Harbour
Old Town

Respites

THE SOUTHERN BARREN

The Everstorm

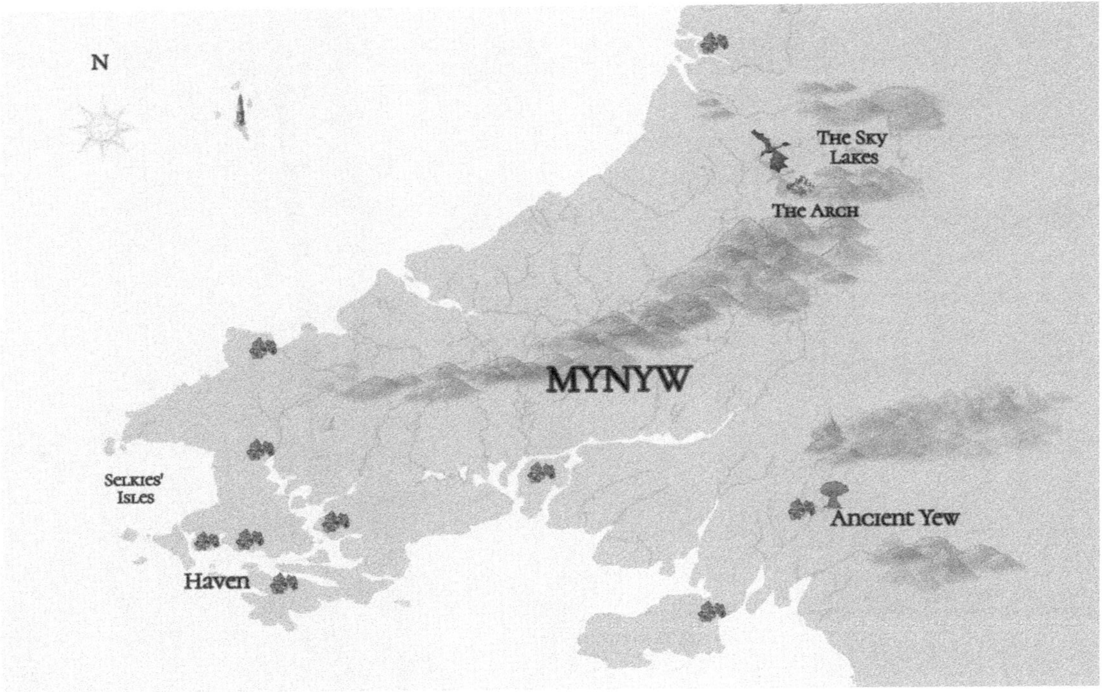
N
The Sky Lakes
The Arch
MYNYW
Ancient Yew
Selkies' Isles
Haven

'The Pact has indeed been broken. A rift between mankind and the Tylwyth Teg could be mended given time, marriages, and magic. But, in this time, in this world, where they do not believe in us? Where their so-called science rules, magic may be of little use, for none remain with enough belief to wield it. A Pact breach involving Lord Flame would destroy our lives as we know them.'

— THE LADY

1
WHAT ARE WE LEGUAAN TO DO?

TELLIN

Thumps resonated through the door as the creatures on the other side threw themselves against it. Barnacle shards, what was wrong with the stupid key? I wriggled it from side to side, pushing and pulling, until, finally the lock gave way.

I thumped the door hard, hoping to scare the room's inhabitants back.

'Ready?' I put my shoulder to the door, struggling to shift its solid weight as it cracked open. The two huge reptiles were hunkered low to the ground, their forked tongues flickering at us, tasting the air.

Zora let out a gasp. 'Tellin, why are you hiding water leguaan on *Barge*?' She stood in the open doorway, staring at them. She recognised them – it was a start.

'Can you feel them?' I asked, trying to urge her forward.

'Why in all the god's names would I want to *feel* them?'

I walked towards the leguaan. Their gaze fixed on me, twin sets of eyes studying every step, their presence as powerful as the white hind. My safety relied on them being undernourished and the chill air of the room slowing their movement. I reached out to stroke the side of the closest. A familiar tingle of power sparked from its skin. 'Zora, I'm sure they're guardians. Feel them.'

A brief frown, a tilt of her head, then Zora followed my lead. She placed her hand on the leguaan, and her eyes widened as she released a pained moan.

'It feels like home used to. I didn't realise it no longer felt this way. I'd simply assumed the gaping hole of emptiness was my grief. Tellin, I know exactly where these leguaan should be, and we need to get them home. My land will be dying.' She removed her hand from the leguaan, shaking, but I said nothing. She'd already helped me so much. Here was something I could do to thank her – to support her in return.

'We can transport them in *Black Hind*. Sal has no work for us right now.'

She nodded. 'Most of the way. If I can get a message to someone at home, they might take them the remainder, or at least allow us to.'

'Your family?' Zora rarely discussed her home, and tended to change the subject when I mentioned it. I expected the usual dive away from the topic.

She shook her head. 'Eden's.'

The name seared through me like a rip current – I doubted there would ever be a time it didn't. I'd watched Eden fall from the rigging, knowing they should never have died, that it was at the whim of the aria. I still couldn't share the true circumstances of that day with Zora, and I suspected I never would. It would remain the one secret I withheld from her.

Meeting any member of Eden's family would open the wound further, but I quelled the rising tide of emotion and pulled myself up tall. The guardians needed to be returned to their homes urgently. They were still staring at me. I stepped back a little, leaving Zora still mesmerised by their presence.

We'd sail as soon as we could get underway, I decided. Then most of the creatures King Anard had brought to us would have been returned to their homes.

He'd agreed to temporarily keep and care for the vulture. There was no point in releasing the bird until its flight feathers grew back. I had a feeling that the pull of its territory would be sufficient to guide it home without our help.

The dragon egg was a different story and we both agreed it couldn't be left in King Anard's care. Oceans, it couldn't be even known about. Whoever sent it to Anard's father had known its value; those who received it on the old king's behalf knew it existed. It needed to vanish, and Anard trusted me to make that happen.

'Shall we let Theo know that he's going to have to leave the incubation in someone else's capable hands while we return them?' I asked.

Zora shook her head. 'He's not going to like it.' During the redistribution of items from Jake's crews, Anard ensured the dragon egg had accompanied the leguaan in their transfer to *Barge*. Theo took careful delivery of it and, if I was honest, he was quietly obsessed.

From the moment he realised what it was, Theo had dredged Sal for information. But Sal knew as little as I. So, Theo had resorted to books – and not for research. At that moment, he'd be in the room next to mine, sitting near the egg, monitoring its temperature, and reading to it.

We pulled the door shut, and I wrestled the lock closed.

Zora stared, as though still looking at the leguaan. 'Feed them before we transport them. They'll be less likely to attack if they're full.'

'Should we bind their jaws?'

Zora shook her head vigorously. 'They are guardians. Let me feed them, then let me talk to them.'

'Do you think you can?' I'd hoped she might be able to. Success in that would make the transfer of them to their home much safer – for all of us.

'I might be able to.'

It would have to do. I pressed the key into her hand. 'Do whatever you need to. We'll get them home,' I urged.

We parted ways at the next junction as she headed towards the kitchens, and I wound my way towards my rooms. *Barge* was busier as I rose higher through the decks to those carpeted in plush fabrics, where our staff attended their clients' every need with solicitous care and attention.

One particularly well-dressed man, dripping with wealth, almost walked straight into me, he was so engrossed in the attentions of his companion. They threw me a smile, and I slipped past, wearing Georgie's face, unknown to the guests.

I rehearsed my speech to Theo as I climbed the stairs to my suite. How I would break it to him gently that we would need to leave the egg on *Barge*. I didn't want to but couldn't see a way around it. We'd have to ask Sal to look after it, and with his other commitments, it was not likely to get much attention. My gentle knock on the door was answered by the bushy, bearded face of Theo, holding a finger to his barely visible mouth. I nodded understanding, and he swung the door open.

Ria sat alongside the egg, her face screwed up in concentration, and her hands pressed flat against the shell. I waited at the doorway.

'How long has she been trying to feel it?' I whispered.

'A few minutes. She's sure she can almost feel something.' Theo's eyes sparkled. A sign of life would be as much of a difficulty as a wonder. While the egg remained unviable, it was merely a status symbol. A hatched dragon was a danger to us all.

Ria withdrew her hands from the shell and opened her eyes.

'What are you two staring at?' she laughed. 'You can stop whispering too. it's not as if talking would stop me feeling a life.'

'So?' I leant forward, eager for an answer.

She nodded. A sharp intake of breath and a few strides took Theo to her side.

'Really?' he asked, his large frame bursting with pup-like enthusiasm. Coiled and ready to explode with excitement.

'It's faint, but definitely there. Something lives inside here.'

I reached for the leathery case of the egg, running my hands over it with reverence. Each crack and crease, each tiny imperfection, hiding something so utterly precious. I was touching a dragon. A spinning-eyed, golden dragon. Sure, there were others, once, but all Old Ones knew they'd gone. Slept or dead except for the desert dragons.

'What do we do now?' Theo stroked his beard as he studied his egg.

'Honestly, I don't know. Ria, was it faint as in new life, or faint ... unwell?' I asked.

'New, I think. It would explain why I haven't been able to pick anything up until now.'

'Then we need to get it away from *Barge*. As much as I love Sal, I don't want him becoming a target for raids or attacks should word get out that it's here. We need to hide it, and it needs to be as good as lost to Terrania.'

Ria shrugged at Theo with her palms upwards, and he nodded. Clearly, I had missed an earlier conversation.

'We already thought that might be the case.' Ria said. 'Theo, I'll let you explain your plan.'

He coughed. It was unusual to see the big man so nervous. 'I want to take it to my mother. I told you I was born of the sea – I'm from a sea-folk family. It will be safe hidden in the flotilla.'

The only sea-folk I knew of were aboard Barge. 'I don't understand, I thought we agreed that we're trying to get it away from Sal.'

Theo gestured helplessly at Ria, who shrugged. 'Maybe there are no sea-folk flotillas where Tellin is from.' She turned towards me. 'When the waters rose, a number of communities took to the water. They live their entire lives on the water, living from the ocean. Many refuse to set foot on land, blaming the humans who remain there for the damage wrought to those of us outside that community. Humans who live on land treat them as outcasts – there are even rumours of witches in their number. The community on Barge are from these flotillas.'

'Where's the flotilla based?' I asked.

'This is why I think it would work as a hiding place,' replied Theo. 'There are ways to track them for one who grew up amongst them – signs and signals we leave each other for the next market or social gathering, but to untrained eyes, they are unnoticeable. The entire community is mobile and has no loyalty to any but themselves.'

Theo must have sensed my uncertainty.

'Tellin, they believe in you. They believe in sirens and dragons. As a boy, I remember sitting at the feet of an old man on a rainbow boat, listening to tales of the Old Ones …' He paused, his eyes glazing over, momentarily lost in the memory. 'My mother always used to warn me that the sirens were no friend of mine, as though she thought I was too young to remember how one almost stole my father. Families like ours, sea-folk are the voices that kept the tales alive. If there are forgotten tales of dragon eggs – of hatchings – we'll find them amongst our elders. It's the best chance this egg has.'

'Where will they be at this time of year?'

'I don't know where they are, but I do know where to start looking for them.' Theo's face split in a wide grin. 'It'll be nice to see my mother. Tellin, if – when – we find her, can you show yourself to her, please?'

I was not about to make a promise like that until I'd met the woman, no matter how much I trusted Theo. After all, the chasm of difference between Anard and his late father demonstrated how stark family differences could be.

'Start working out how we can transport it,' I replied instead. 'The hold will be carrying other passengers, and we may need to return them first. Zora will be dealing with their needs.'

'She recognised the lizards?'

I nodded. 'More than recognised. They're from her area. She thinks we need to get them to a friend of hers, to get them home.' Urchin dung, I couldn't tell him who it was yet. Let him look forward to his own reunion first. 'I'm due to meet Sal for supper, so best Gina behaviour.'

Ria winced in sympathy. 'No planned guests, I hope? Just for visibility?'

'Only Seren and Gar.'

Theo laughed. 'Enjoy your family meal. Make sure that boy is eating enough.'

I entered my own rooms through the joining door. The

huge wardrobe beckoned me with its promise of gauzy dresses, all in shades of black and red, and an array of impractical footwear. I quickly selected a pair of calf-length soft trousers and a floor-length split tunic. I wasn't in the mood to deal with roving eyes. In Gina's guise, much as Georgie's, my glamour hid my face and allowed me to cloak my innate magic that caused so many problems otherwise.

Theo had learned to live with it, but I would never expect other humans to accept me without wanting to own me – the eternal curse of the selkie.

I stared into the mirror and checked the illusion carefully. I wore it so often aboard *Barge* that it was as comfortable to hold as breathing. Though, when old clothes fit that well, it is always worth checking that their seams are still held together.

I crossed the Ocean Bar slowly, breathing in salty air circulating from the central open pool and trailing my fingers through the water as I joined the family at our table. Sal was teaching Gar to count jellyfish, and Seren sat protectively nearby, yet still had her eye on the entire length of the bar.

Since Cor and Eden's deaths, a little of the closeness between her and Sal was creeping back in. Sal knew what he wanted, finally – he'd even stopped taking clients, aside from a very select few – and Seren was trying to look past our duplicity in passing for humans. When she was ready, she'd see Sal for who, not what, he was again.

Seren waved me over, sliding me a drink. 'We received a gift of some mussels from a guest today.' She nudged me gently in the ribs.

'You know me too well! I'd love them tender, not chewy...'

She grimaced. Most of the kitchen staff put my preference

for barely cooked fish down to the fact that I had grown up a long way from Terrania. With Seren's guidance, they had grown better at tweaking recipes for our palettes since she'd discovered our truth. Ever efficient, she ran *Barge* so that every resident had exactly what they needed, including the selkies who owned it.

2
ARROW IN FLIGHT

MADDOC

The yew tree towered over the ruined church, its ancient trunk twisted, warped, and split. To a casual observer, only its outer sapwood remained. The gnarled yew looked past its prime, fading and ancient beyond mankind's written history.

In truth, the heartwood had long gone, and what remained was a ring of sibling outer trunks like sentinels guarding the central hollow. The tree had been there at the founding of the country and would be there long past its fall. It was his yew.

Maddoc ran his hand over the gnarled trunk, caressing twisted branches with the intimacy of one who knew every single whirl and knot. He stepped over the crumbling retaining wall, placed there centuries ago to help support the trunks – instead, it merely confined them. The yew had burst through, and bricks had fallen willingly, tumbling with abandon to allow the yew to grow, to be unrestrained by mankind's walls. The air between the trunks was thick with ancient power, and he drank it in greedily. The previous guardian told him to be sparing, that it would consume him, but Maddoc never felt that way. The old man had been a mere human, not part Tylwyth Teg like himself.

He stretched his arms upward, and had anyone other than rabbits been observing, he would have appeared to vanish.

In the chamber below the tree, from whence endless roots departed to knit together the lands of his home, Maddoc checked each root, whispering words passed down to him by his mother. Too long had humans guarded the tree. Too long had it been left without the protection it needed. He smoothed the trunks where passing burrowers scratched them and curled new rootlets into the ground.

The roots were strong, but their hold on the country grew tenuous in places. Maddoc paused to crouch by the speckled root extending out to the West. At the extent of its reach, a new island had started to break free, and salt water damaged the root. Soon, that island would be abandoned to the Ocean and her caretakers. Humankind would still call it part of this country, but he'd know better.

Maddoc stroked the speckled root gently. He'd follow the trail and cut the root as his predecessors had done many years ago. All who mattered knew he tried his hardest, but sometimes it wasn't enough.

He finished his circuit of the roots. Just one final check to make before he could return to his cottage and maybe a cheese sandwich. Some days he didn't bother with the last chamber. After all, it had been thousands of years since the arrow was shot; thousands of years that it hung there, untouched in the air. A symbol of the peace and cooperation of the races who called the land home. A symbol of the ties that bound them from harming each other.

Maddoc wandered absently into the arrow chamber. He

tried to take the usual three steps from the door to where the arrow hung, except that it didn't. Maddoc came upon it almost a full step closer.

He tried to touch it, but as ever, his hand slid over, unable to connect with the arrow. The toxin that would kill the tree, finalising the breaking of the Pact remained unreachable, unremovable. He walked back to the trunk. Maybe he'd miscounted.

'One, two.'

It had definitely moved on his watch for the first time, and if it hit the tree, the Pact would be irreparable. How long had it been since he last checked it? A week? Maybe two?

Maddoc scratched a mark in the soil directly below the tip. Time passed strangely down there, and he needed to know if it was a one-off or if the fate of the land was on a timer.

He ran his hand over the trunk again, wondering if he could rig something up to deflect the arrow, or a barrier between the tree and the toxic tip. He must have something in his cottage.

Maddoc passed back through the portal to the surface and sat in the hollow with his back against a trunk.

He did not rest, and he did not move. As static as the trunks around him, Maddoc waited in position for a full day. Once the sun returned to peeking between the same branches as when his vigil began, he descended into the chamber, his heart hammering with a fear he was unused to.

Maddoc studied the mark. The arrow had moved closer. If it continued at the same speed, he had maybe six weeks until the Pact was broken.

He couldn't think down there; the pressure and enormity were too much for his slender shoulders. He was a caretaker, a guardian, not the saviour of his country. Surely, that was the job of the Tylwyth Teg; it was time to visit his mam – after he'd had that sandwich.

Maddoc stared up at the gently rising foothills of the Black Mountain. He hadn't been to his mother's home for many, many years. His life wasn't with her. Like those before him, Maddoc straddled the divide between the human and the Tylwyth Teg. It was a role assigned every few hundred years to a new half-breed when one of the Tylwyth Teg would find some worthy human and give them a son.

A son who would eventually be taken from them to guard the tree. Maddoc had enjoyed as much life with his father as his mam had allowed him. He knew she indulged him, let him have far more freedom than most of his predecessors – certainly longer than she should have. When he finally reached the yew, the old man, who was the child of a previous guardian, was barely able to pass on his knowledge before his spirit crossed over to the Otherworld.

Maddoc washed his plate, left it next to the sink to dry, and tucked the remaining lump of cheese in his bag. It was time to leave.

Dust spiralled in the sunlight, and spiders scuttled to new hiding places as he prised open the cedar chest. He reached under the old blanket to reveal his mam's gifts. Being cloaked in the cedar's preserving magic kept them safely hidden from passing or overly curious eyes.

He hung the leather thong around his neck, its long scale-coated feather tucked inside his shirt. It was no more ornate than the totems carried by most humans in The Territories, but his *worked*, and without it, Maddoc could not be granted access to his mother's realm. The shimmering blue cloak cast rippling shadows around the room where light passed through it, much as water does on the bottom of a pool in sunlight. He wrapped it around his shoulders and fastened it with his brooch carved from the old heartwood of the very tree that he now guarded. A smile played on his face as he watched the tiny leaves move with the ebb and flow of his breath. That was the entry to her home sorted.

Before that, he had to overcome the far more human task of getting to the top of the mountain. He had a few weeks, and the journey up and back should take no more than a few days, dependent on how supportive the family was. While there were other ways, it had been a long time since he'd used them, and Maddoc preferred to keep his feet firmly on the ground.

Without knowing why the arrow moved or what had caused the Pact to weaken, Maddoc was unsure what he'd find in the city under the lake. He stuffed a few pairs of thick socks in his bag and slid stout walking boots on. Their eyelets were old and slightly rusted, while the discoloured leather hugged his feet with the support of an old friend. Maddoc glanced down and grimaced. The outfit was too conspicuous to leave town in. Humans didn't wander around in cloaks anymore, a mistaken choice in his opinion. Still, he wrestled a more modern jacket over the top, that he could remove at the last minute.

Maddoc picked up his bag and flung it over his shoulders, then stepped from his small home into the bright light of the low, morning sun.

The route was treacherous, steep in places, boggy in others. The weather could change in an instant, stream beds filling close to overflowing and clouds dropping like a blanket. For the moment, it was a calm day. Small fluffy clouds scurried across the sky, but Maddoc frowned. He knew all too well that the weather was a fickle mistress, and it paid to be prepared for her moods. They usually reflected the mood of the under-city.

Winter in the territories was usually wet, and that year was no different, so he'd be able to follow the stream along the lower foot hills. He'd hiked up the mountain hundreds of times over his extended life, and if he went direct, he should reach the top of the scarp by nightfall. It would've been easier to walk the old roads skirting the mountain range, and going over the top meant he'd miss the incredible view of the mountain towering over the lake. Maddoc sighed. He did love that view, but he didn't have the luxury of time.

Instinct rather than eyesight led him to the Black Mountain's peak on cloud-shrouded hills. Wind snatched at his coat as he removed it, threatening to rip it from his grasp. Maddoc sat at the top of the sheer drop and opened his bag. He set his meal out and, though he grew damper by the minute, ate until he could consume no more. Sated and satisfied that he would not be tempted by offers of food from any but his own mother – and even then, he'd probably say no under the circumstances – he tucked the coat and his boots into the bag. Then, he lay on his stomach, edging over the cliff, and tucked the bag into a well-hidden hole just below the rim.

He glanced down at the old clothes and shimmering cloak. The contrast between the mundane and magical was never more apparent than near his mam's realm. Maddoc swallowed down nerves, then walked along the cliff edge until he found the small rocky protrusion. In the cloud, he doubted anyone would see him, but he checked around anyway before dropping the hood of the cloak over his eyes, and lifting the scaled feather charm to his lips, he stepped off the escarpment.

Maddoc stared intently through the cloak, placing his feet slowly and precisely on the slender Path, careful to step only where the air did not shimmer. The Path into the lake sucked magic from the air to sustain its self, and the feather key gave him permission to walk it, while the rippling cloak hid him from mortal eyes. The Tree only knew what a human would think of a flying man over the lake.

Step after step, he descended towards the lake as the Pathway curved down in a spiral. Birds flew past, heading to their roots in the cliff face. In the fading light, he could make out the wind-mottled surface of the lake, and then his foot met the surface, sinking through it to rest on the Path. Maddoc took a last breath of over-land air before proceeding deeper. As the water closed over his head, the Path fell from his feet, and he fell into the under-lake, losing consciousness as he did so.

As he had every time he could remember, Maddoc awoke from slumber, resting on a mossy bed near the misty entrance to the under-city. A ring of curious faces stared intently at him, one hand retreating from where he presumed he had just been prodded. Young Tylwyth Teg, who'd probably never seen a half-breed before, poked at his clothes. One particularly eager one even tugged at his toes. Maddoc released a low growl, resisting the urge to snap at the intruding fingers. There was no point in inviting trouble. Someone would claim he'd eaten offered food, and the whole ridiculous cycle of forty-two years ago would repeat. He didn't have time to wait out the hospitality again. Not with only six weeks until the land as he had always known it, and the peace they enjoyed, would end.

The growl did the trick, and the youngsters edged away from him, standing warily in a circle as one or two glanced down the pathway to the city.

She was on her way; he'd known she'd feel his arrival. His mam always did. Maddoc sat up and made himself comfortable. There was no point in leaving the landing pad until he was invited. He crossed his legs, checking to see if his feet were dry yet. The whole wet feet dry clothes thing intrigued him, but his mam just laughed at his confusion whenever he tried to address it. Maddoc stretched his arms above his head, enjoying the ripple of responses it generated from the youngsters.

Follow the rules. Even his mother couldn't help him if he broke one. He sighed. So many rules, so little time.

While the small Tylwyth Teg watched him warily, a much taller figure clarified from out of the mist. The Gwraig Annwn of the Underlake – his mam.

She approached with her arms open in welcome and shooed his attendants away with a single gesture. Maddoc rose to embrace her.

'It's been so long!' she chastised. 'I've missed you.'

'Only about five years.' Maddoc laughed. 'You've gone much longer without meeting, and if you were desperate to see me, you could always visit.'

'You know I cannot,' she replied, releasing him and stepping back to study his face. 'You have an extra wrinkle.' She reached forward as though to wipe it away. Maddoc stayed her hand.

'Wrinkles let me live unnoticed, Mam.' he squeezed her hand gently before releasing it. 'Leave them well alone. I'm sorry I'm not here for a social call. The arrow moved.'

'Are you sure?'

'Yes, or I wouldn't be here.' He stopped. Oh, that wasn't the right thing to say. Maddoc cringed. 'Obviously, I'd come to visit you at some point ...'

Her laugh rang through him like the trickling of a hundred tiny waterfalls, musical and lyrical. Tylwyth Teg were known for their strange humour. They cried at weddings and laughed at funerals; her mirth did not surprise him. Endings were something he knew she had a particular fondness for.

'It is ending. Our peace may be over.' She smiled at him. 'Come, Maddoc. We need to discuss what this truly means and what, if anything, we should do about it. A breach between your father's people and my own has been inevitable these last few hundred years. I am only surprised it was not sooner. Someone, somewhere, has triggered the end of our land.'

3
IT'S A FAMILY AFFAIR

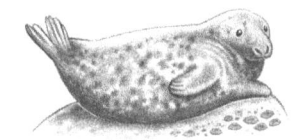

TELLIN

We skimmed along the coast, the dragon-wing rig straining in the wind, as *Black Hind* flew on the breeze toward only Zora knew where. She stood at the helm, her black curls teased back from her face by the wind and her eyes fixed on the land.

The low-lying coast was decorated with beaches, gilded crescents surrounded by a million spears of marram grass, and slices of golden sand gleaming while the heat-shimmer rising off their surface was visible against struggling trees behind. Earlier in the day, we'd passed huge swathes of arid land, burnt and dry from the intense heat of The Southern Barren. The warming had truly decimated much of the region between Safe Harbour and here. Maybe in time, it could recover, although I couldn't imagine this coast as lush and verdant as the North.

'Lift the keel,' Zora called, and we bent our will to the task.

Theo pointed toward a small headland with an eyebrow raised. Zora nodded.

'I'll take her in,' he said as he strolled to take the helm. 'You call us through.'

Zora flashed me one of her grins, and I couldn't hide the smile that began to grow. I peered over the side, trying to spot more of our destination, more clues to Zora as a person. She was taking us to her home, a new world of people I hadn't yet met. A place where sea witches and bird-speakers came from. I would be taking them all to meet my own family soon, and having lived with humans for so long now, I doubted that meeting Zora and Eden's relatives would be as strange to me as meeting my selkie family would be to them. I hoped they would accept me.

I squashed down the worry as the boat shook with a thud from below deck.

The leguaan knew we were getting close to their home – maybe they felt it calling them. Getting them into the hold had been difficult, and we all bore the wounds with good nature. Their well-being was more important than ours. I'd healed my wounds already, but Theo still had a red mark on his forearm, and Zora's trousers hid the laceration on her ankle from the tail that whipped around and caught her. Getting them out was likely to be worse. After all, if they were like their northern guardian spirits, they would be feeling the hurt inflicted on their land in their absence. I just hoped it was a short enough one that the pain was minimal – for all of us.

Theo swung the bow into a narrow passage between the headland we'd just passed and a gently sloping rise on the other side. Short, stubby trees rose as a dense carpet, and the remains of once-white buildings crumbled into the sea. A lack of wind as we slipped into the shade of the western cliffs lent the entire river a solemn and profound depth of stillness.

But it wasn't a river. We sailed along it for a short distance, its wide sinuous path meandering away from the Terranian Sea until it opened up. The sides retreated, and tree-covered hills rose all around. Crystal-clear water lapped the hull in welcome as we glided into the middle of a place like no other I had ever seen.

Islands dotted the huge lake, and around each, far from the outer periphery, were small settlements. I wondered if the settlers of Orange had taken their designs from the lake-bound inhabitants or if it was the opposite. Homes grew from the ground. Woven from living trees, they boasted water pipes curling through upper branches. Unlike the homes in Orange, these were truly wild, the community fully intertwined with their surroundings. I could see why people would want to reproduce the serenity.

Children playing at the water's edge of the closest island waved as *Black Hind* drew close. I supposed they must have seen the boat before when Theo returned Zora home after Eden's death.

Zora waved back enthusiastically, but we kept sailing. Deeper and deeper into the lake we travelled, each island we passed vibrant and busy, some with a few boats bobbing just offshore, others none. It would be a peaceful place to live, and I wished I could explore the lake in my skin, dive beneath the waves and play in this unspoilt place.

After rounding a large island, we turned back on ourselves towards a wide bay. Rocky crags offered homes to sea birds, whose raucous calls were louder than the laughter echoing from the rocks.

As we'd seen on many islands, a group of young children played on the gently sloping beach. Several boats were hauled up on the sand, and for a moment, I thought we would join them. As we drew closer, it was clear that the outwardly green land was suffering the throes of death. The dark green shade was not rich pines, but curling leaves. The woods themselves were unsettlingly quiet.

A tall, slender woman stood knee-deep in the waves, playing with the children. Her hair was as green as tide pool seaweed, and when she looked up, my throat caught the exhaled breath.

If I hadn't seen Eden die, if I didn't know better... Theo stared at her, his mouth briefly hanging agape, and the colour drained from his cheeks.

'If you ever wondered what Eden looked like,' I whispered to Ria, 'that woman is as close as it will ever get.'

The woman saw us gliding in and strode into the deeper water, calling up to Zora. 'Child, why are you back so soon?'

Zora grabbed the bow rope in one hand and gracefully leapt from the bow, plunging into the water. She emerged near the woman and embraced her.

'Zora, we can't pull her up the beach. We'll never get off again,' Theo called.

'We won't. I'm tying us onto a boat-weight,' Zora shouted back, and we saw the dark skin of her legs as she dived with the rope, emerging a few moments later without it. We finished dropping the rig and let *Black Hind* swing in the wind from the anchor. 'Come ashore.' She gestured at the beach.

I didn't need a second invitation and leapt overboard, swimming to join her, followed closely by Theo. He dived as cleanly as I had ever seen a human cut through water, and once again, I was reminded that his life was as aquatic as the rest of us, in his way.

The woman regarded us silently as we approached. I rose from the water, uncertain how to greet her.

Theo had no such hesitation. 'I love your hair,' he said immediately. 'I once told a friend I dreamt of dying my beard that colour, but sadly, they will never be able to show me how to.'

Zora smiled gently. 'Theo, Tellin, may I introduce Eden's mother, Jena.'

Theo blushed, his weathered cheeks growing even brighter than their wind-kissed normal. 'I'm so sorry, Jena. That must have appeared so insensitive.'

Jena took a step through the water and offered Theo her hand. 'If Eden promised to teach you, then I will honour that promise in their stead.' Her dark eyes fixed on Theo, studying him as he accepted the proffered hand. 'You're older than I would have expected one of Eden's friends to be,' she observed. 'But then, my child was ever accepting of everyone. Is this boat their work? I recognise their hand in the rigging.'

Zora offered a gentle smile. 'This is *Black Hind*, Jena.'

Jena looked away from us as tears welled in her eyes. Grief is a slow process, a wound that scars permanently. For even as the wound heals, the eternal silver line of grief remains, running through the soul, and, as fresh as the wound was for us, the pain of hers would be ever deeper.

Zora gestured for me to follow, and I waded after her onto the beach. I thought Theo had followed, but on reaching the shallows, I realised I couldn't hear the water movement of his passage. I turned to find Jena talking quietly, still leaving her slender hand in Theo's large, coarse sailor's grip.

We left them to wade in behind us. Further out in the bay, *Black Hind* swung slightly on her boat-stone anchor; Ria sat on the deck, watching us head ashore. Zora's wariness around her made it easy to decide who stayed aboard while we arranged access. We needed those guardian lizards released, but no one wanted to loose them in the wrong location.

Zora led me past the outer vegetation rimming the cove. The children skipped along with us, chattering in a language I couldn't understand. Zora laughed with them. One pointed at me and giggled.

'What's wrong?' I asked.

Zora shook her finger at the child and laughed back.

'She says you are as pale as the ghosts. I replied that it was because you are one, and she should watch what she says.'

'Thanks, I think?' I muttered. 'I'm not about to start dragging sheets of darkness over myself for their amusement.'

A frown gathered on Zora's brow. 'No, please don't. An actual selkie might be a bit much for my father. He doesn't have a lot of time for the Old Ones. He respects them but has no desire for their close acquaintance. He was hurt too badly by my mother.'

I could understand that. This was Zora's home, and she'd invited me in. I resolved to do nothing that could bring difficulties for her.

'I thought we only needed to see Eden's family?'

Zora grimaced. 'Jena can take us. It's fortunate she was here, but we still need my father's permission. He's seen as a sort of community guardian himself, since my mother ...'

Zora stopped talking as we broke through the tree line to see a ring of houses built around a mound. The thrumming of wild power filled my senses. Zora gestured to a tiny, wizened tree on the crest of the hill.

'It's that shrivelled-up old thing. No, it makes no sense to me either.' She sighed. 'Come on. Let's do this.'

Unlike the shoreline homes, these were old, had survived the ravages of weather and time, and were beautifully maintained. Vines were painted around the door frames in as much detail as Sirena could have achieved. Would they have been real before the warming? Garlands of scent and fragrance? I was so engrossed in imagining the past that I almost fell over a chair positioned in the hot sun against the wall.

Zora closed her eyes and took a deep breath, exhaling it slowly before she knocked on the bright blue door. Why was she so nervous?

A deep voice called out, 'Who's there?'

'It's me, Zora.'

The tapping of wood against stone grew louder. A stooped man cracked it open, his ageless face betrayed by his bent and twisted body. He leaned heavily on his stick and stared openly at me.

'Who is this?'

She glanced at me, her eyes meeting mine for a second before she replied. 'This is Lady Gina. Lord Sal's Daughter.'

Urchin guts, if I'd known that was her plan, I'd have dressed accordingly – or at least switched glamour. I bowed deeply, very slightly altering my cheekbones and the tooth towards those of Gina's glamour before I stood back up.

I placed a hand on my heart in greeting as I met his direct stare. I felt sure he was looking through me, trying to work me out.

'I see,' he said. 'You'd better come in. I have no pleasures or extravagances in my home, but you're welcome anyway.'

He turned away, hobbling ahead of us, the tapping of his stick leading us into his home. Zora gestured for me to follow. The house was arranged around a courtyard, each room opening into it. Burned-out candles gathered dust on tall holders at each corner. Zora's father lowered himself onto a sun-soaked bench and gestured at the ground in front of him. Zora sat, and I copied her.

'Why are you back so soon?' he asked. I liked his directness. It left no room for a wrong answer.

'Have you heard that the old king is dead?' Zora began.

He shook his head. 'It matters not to us who reigns in the North, as long as they do not trespass on our waters.'

'I know. But have the waters been more fragile? The trees less abundant? The crops weaker? Have usually calm animals turned, and the predators become bolder?'

He leaned forward then, resting both hands over the carved wave atop his stick. His eyes narrowed. 'How did you know?'

I sat as unobtrusively as I could. There was more distance between Zora and her father than there was between myself and Sal.

Zora clasped her hands in her lap. 'Before he died, the old king was gifted a selection of creatures beyond price and rarity. Amongst them were our guardians.'

He sat back. 'I hoped I was wrong, but no one has seen them for months. This is grave news indeed. Where are they now? Are you here to gather warriors and reclaim them for us?'

The formal mask cracked, a break in his voice leaking through the composure. Zora reached forward to place her hand over his. 'No, Father. I'm here because we have brought them home. They are aboard our boat in the harbour. Lady Gina has made it her mission to return the lost guardians to their true homes and help the world heal.'

'Why would you care about us?' he looked at me more gently, like a moray eel sitting calmly before the attack. A proud man, he wanted no part in charity.

'I do not help you alone. My father and I care for our home and all who live on its shores. By returning stolen guardians, we heal both lands and inhabitants of the Terranian Sea.'

He nodded acceptance of the answer, and I relaxed slightly.

'Do you give us permission to sail into the leguaan lake?' Zora asked.

'If you take Jena as witness so that the people know your

companions did not defile our sacred waters. I am too old to travel there now.'

'Thank you.' Zora rose to her feet and planted a gentle kiss on her father's head. His face didn't move a muscle until she turned away from him. Then, a softness and a small smile crossed his face. Pride? He showed it not to her, but for a split second, I saw behind the mask.

'Shall I make tea?' Zora asked.

'If you wish to. I'd not have it said that I lacked the basic hospitality to Lady Gina. Even if I lack the balance to pour it myself.'

Zora left me alone with him, and we sat in an awkward silence. Lady Gina was always prepared for meetings, ready for conversation primed with topics by Seren. I was a shellfish caught with my shell open on an outgoing tide.

'Thank you for your kind hospitality,' I ventured eventually.

'What do you know about the leguaan?'

'Little, I am afraid. I have no connection to these creatures, and they do not choose to share anything with me. I respect that. I'm not from these lands.'

He caressed the wave on his walking stick as I talked, inviting me to fill the silence. Wary of betraying Zora's trust, I bestowed him with my most serene Gina smile.

He leant forward, his eyes narrowing as he whispered, 'Do you know what my daughter is?'

I kept my face still as I deliberated a response. I'd promised to keep her secret. If I denied knowing and it was the wrong answer, then at least she would know that I held her truth sacred.

'She is so talented,' I gushed. 'The best captain I have ever sailed with. She reads the tides and the weather like no other. We are lucky to have her aboard.'

He sat back, eyeing me warily, but the tension in his grip released. 'It is good that you recognise her value.'

He changed the conversation then, and when Zora returned bearing a steaming tray of drinks, we were discussing the changes in the lakes, the decreasing numbers of fish, and how one child had even been attacked by a flock of local warblers. The small birds had done him significant damage before they were chased away.

We drank tea companionably until the sun slid off the end of the bench. As though it was a signal, Zora rose to clear the tea away.

'Thank you for the welcome.' I offered.

'Look after her. She is all I have,' he replied.

'I will, I promise.'

When Zora returned, she kissed his hand once more, and he rested a hand on her head.

'Be safe, Daughter. Will you return here before you return to Lord Sal?'

Zora shook her head. We had the egg on board as well, carefully stored in the larger bunk space. It needed to get to the sea-folk as soon as we could travel there. His mouth twitched downward at the corner, resigned, and he escorted us to the door.

Zora didn't talk on the way back. Meeting her father left me with more questions than answers, but it certainly explained a little of her occasionally distant nature. Together, we swam out to *Black Hind*, and Ria pulled us aboard.

'Is Theo back yet?' I asked. 'We need Jena to take these leguaan back.'

Ria pointed to the beach, where a green-haired woman

accompanied a green-bearded man toward *Black Hind*. I hid my smile behind my hands.

'Jena, we need you to accompany us to the leguaan lake.' Zora shouted.

'We're coming,' she replied. 'Theo was telling me all about your struggle to get them aboard. I hope I can coax them out more gently for you.' Theo reached *Black Hind* first and scrambled up the boarding ladder.

'I'll set us free,' Jena called, then dived to untie us before hauling herself aboard as nimbly as Eden would have done. She stood alongside Theo, looking every bit as though she belonged aboard *Black Hind*. Theo stroked his beard, turning his head from side to side and showing it off.

'What do you think?' he asked.

'I love it,' I replied, no longer bothering to hide the smile.

'It suits you.' Ria's gaze flickered from Jena to Theo and back again. 'I just need to check on something.' She vanished below deck, leaving the rest of us to prepare *Black Hind*.

'No sails – it's too narrow,' Jenna said as I started to rig. 'That way.' She pointed along the coast, and Theo started the engine.

The leguaan lake was dark-green with vegetation, but a stench of rot filled the air so thickly that it made my stomach roll with a breaking wave of nausea. The narrow entrance was so well-hidden that I couldn't believe any vessel had sneaked past all the villages and entered their most sacred site without the population noticing. We pushed through plant matter so thick that it mounted in piles to either side of our bow.

'We can't go too much further,' Theo muttered. 'We'll get entangled.'

I peered over the stern. We had a narrow trail of clear water in our wake, but he was right that it closed behind us.

'How far do we need to go?' I asked.

Zora gestured to a higher green patch ahead. 'We'll need to take them to the island. They can't swim in this.'

Jena nodded. 'I agree. Unload them at the island. Hopefully, they will aid a fast recovery. Something's not right about this whole situation. There's no way they were removed by water – someone would have seen. Can we circle the edge of the lake before we leave?'

'How quickly will they work?' Theo asked. 'Because we'll be stuck in here with them until they can heal the lake if we do the entire perimeter.' He glanced downward, and I knew he thought of the egg.

Jena grimaced. 'I'm sorry, I don't know. But if someone took them once, they might be back. I need to know.'

Theo stroked his green beard, his eyes crinkling at the corners. 'I'm sure we'll find a way out if we need to. Zora?'

'If we have to, I'm sure we can work a way out.'

I suspected Zora wouldn't want to use her power in her own sacred lake, but had to hope that our task was important enough to override any rules her community had. Her earlier words about defiling the lake returned to me, and I winced.

When we cut the motor alongside the shrub-coated island, Jena descended into the hold alone. Ria offered to help, but her gesture was brushed aside.

'You met my Eden. Trust that I can get these leguaan out,' was the response.

Ria opened her mouth, but at a glare from Zora, she swallowed her reply and stepped aside.

'How in all the Oceans is she going to get those creatures out of there without the ramp?' Ria whispered.

I didn't want to imagine how she'd get them through the

cabin. Up on deck, Zora had already opened the deck hatch. Jena flung the end of a rope up, and I relaxed a little, then Zora wrapped it round a winch and calmly wound the handle. A calm leguaan dangled in a knotted cradle on the end. I rushed to help, but Zora gestured for us to move back.

Reluctantly, I allowed her the space she asked for. The leguaan waited on deck as they brought the second up.

Jena returned to the deck and murmured quietly to the creatures as she worked around them, loosening the knots. The cradle dropped to the deck, and the first leguaan slipped over the side of *Black Hind*. Where it swam, the water cleared – a small but immediate change. It scrambled onto the island, touching its snout to a small bush, which dropped dead leaves as though shaken by the Everstorm. The leguaan remained in position until green buds appeared, then moved to the next bush.

It was a demonstration of both how much the guardians changed and how much they did to maintain an entire region. It was no wonder the white hind in Terrania had struggled alone. The second leguaan slipped into the water with a gentle splash and swam from the island towards a shoreline.

It turned and looked directly back at us, then swam away before turning again, returning to *Black Hind*, then finally, heading away from us.

'Follow it!' Zora shouted.

We chased it through the slush as it cleared a narrow streak of water. On the lake's edge, the green wall of trees was broken. Trees were missing, and all that remained were occasional branches hauled to the side. In the void where they had once grown, wind-blown sand filled the heavy scars of a vehicle's tracks.

'You were right,' Zora said to Jena.

'I wish I wasn't. Who has the resources to do this and why?'

Jena gazed out at the barren. 'I need to get back to the island. We'll set a patrol up around here. Thank you all for returning the leguaan to us. Our people are in your debt.'

Theo gently turned us around, and we hummed back out of the lake.

4
SEASALT AND SPRAY

TELLIN

As we hummed between the narrow headlands and out into the Terranian sea, I watched the cliffs appear to close up. The entrance to the world of crystal-blue waters and seaweed-green islands hidden from cruising vessels; a treasure of a place tucked so close to The Southern Barren. Zora had graced me with a glimpse into her life away from *Black Hind* and Sal. Maybe, in time, I could visit again. I'd love to see the lake in its full glory once the leguaan had restored it. I turned to ask her. Zora stood in the bow, watching the waves, and something in the set of her shoulders and tightness of her posture halted my tongue. There was time enough to ask another day. I suspected that with what we had discovered, Zora would wish to tap Sal's resources and soon.

I moved forward, ready to shift my weight around at Theo's call, to keep us flat as we headed for his home, still wondering about the leguaan. Who had the means to pull off such a raid? No one I knew of, but Sal's contacts were wide. His reach extended throughout the routes his fleets travelled.

I was still grappling with the many people of influence in Terrania, let alone outside the borders. My mind slid to Icidro. Could he have arranged it? He had the money, and certainly some connections. No, he liked his prizes too much to share them, even for a chance at some unknown deal. My thoughts whirlpooled downward as I struggled to make sense of the situation.

'Hey, I'll trade a fish for your thoughts,' Zora said, her eyes staring into my soul and her gentle smile calming the waters. I laughed her concern off.

'Oh, I was just thinking about how we find Theo's elusive family,' I lied.

'I suspect that will be an adventure of its own. I've never been to a flotilla.'

Zora took the helm as Theo, Ria, and I raised the sails. Having chosen to tie my fate to my new family of friends, it felt natural to meet their extended families – their own blood ties. Yet, so close together, it felt strange, unsettling. A reminder of how my blood family left me on an island, and how I had expected them to. How they accepted my fate, how easily they consigned me to their memories. Soon we'd meet them again. Only then, I'd see them through different eyes. How sheltered their simple lives were, so far removed from how I'd come to live. Sal had become as much a father figure in my life as my natural parents.

I enjoyed the feel of the wind and the taste of the salt spray as we gathered speed. Ria sat alongside me, wrestling her long hair back into a thick braid.

'You'd think I'd know better than to come on deck unprepared,' she laughed as she finished.

'Do your family still live?' I asked as I licked spray from my face. She winced.

'In their own way, I suppose they do.'

Too late, I realised that maybe she had taken her own family's souls. And therefore, held them amongst the great weight of past lives she carried.

'Did you…' I began, but she shook her head.

'No, not what you're thinking, but it's definitely a tale for another day.'

We were skimming the waves half-a-day's sail from Zora's home when Theo called out with excitement.

'I know where they are! We need to go north.' He half ran towards us, his newly green beard bouncing with each step. As he caught me looking, he raised his hand to stroke it. 'She did a wonderful job, didn't she?'

I scanned the waves, looking for some clue that gave away his sudden awareness, but saw nothing. I wondered for a moment at the wistful smile that played on his lips. Maybe the green beard would help in his own healing journey. I doubted it would do much for me, but then, I did not share his very human senses of attachment.

I missed Eden's company, and I felt guilt for my secret part in it. Although it was not my doing, I had brought the aria aboard – the aria that saved the rest of us at Eden's expense. I was sad that they had gone, but such are life and death. We live our brief time, and then, we all leave. As the tide laps the shore, we are replaced by others in our wake. Few, such as the leathergill, lived long enough to see the changes, and though my lifespan was longer than that of a human, it could be extinguished as easily.

Theo moved swiftly to the bow of the boat as land receded

behind us. We tacked into the wind, slowly travelling through the open waters of the sea. Soon we could see no land on any side of us, the horizon blue all around.

'Keep going,' Theo called. 'I'll take a turn if you need a break, Zora. We'll be travelling through the night.'

Zora gestured for him to take over. 'I'll make some food before I catch a sleep then.'

'I'll help you,' offered Ria. 'Someone needs to be up overnight with you, and I'm due a night watch.'

Zora nodded, and they descended into the cabin. Before long, the scent of food wafted from below.

We ate while we worked, and as the others rested below deck, Theo and I sailed by the stars towards the flotilla.

'Do you know where you are?' I asked.

'Always. You're going to love this. Do you want to wake the others or not? I think my people would rather we were in and out quickly. The less traffic and people who know their location, the happier they will be.'

'Theo, your customs, your choice.'

'Look to your right then.'

I crossed the deck to gaze over the rail. Lights began to resolve – points of colour bobbing with the waves. A scattered few soon became clusters of smaller ones, and those in turn split again as we drew ever nearer into single mast lights and bow lamps.

'Light the bow light,' Theo said quietly, 'and shutter it in a one-three-one-two sequence, then pause and repeat. Keep doing it until I tell you to stop.'

I hurried to do as he asked. Focused on the pattern, I settled into the repetition, over and over again.

'Look up,' he called.

In front of us, a number of boats repeated it back to us. It was beautiful.

'They are welcoming a family member home.' Theo said, with a catch in his voice. 'It makes my heart ache to stay every time I see it. Drop the sails. We'll go in under motor.'

I rushed to bring the sails down, leaving them in their grooves, ready to rise again. I tied them off carefully while awaiting his command.

'Tellin, I need you to take us to the boat with the purple toplight. Over there.' He pointed at a small light bobbing to the side of the central group. He didn't often ask me to helm, nor did Zora. I took *Black Hind's* helm and concentrated as well as I could on navigating through the flotilla as Theo descended into the bunks, presumably to retrieve the egg.

By the time he emerged, I was weaving through ocean-gardens on pontoons, floating around boats that were more homes than transport. Washing hung from rigging lines, and wind sculptures glistened in the lamp lights. Curious faces peered through cabin windows and cheery greetings waved from decks.

I had no idea of the correct protocol, so I just waved back and hoped it was okay. We closed on the purple-lit boat. Unlike the others, little decor festooned the vessel. The deck was shining clean, and the sides of the boat had no green skirt to illuminate. It was a craft used to being sailed, not anchored amongst the flotilla.

Theo passed me the egg and took over, gently bringing us alongside. He held us in place as he called across.

'Seaspray ... Mother. It's Timothee. Please catch our lines.'

A shadow emerged from the cabin and called back.

'Timothee Maritim, it's about time you paid me a visit. I've missed you.' Her voice was thin but it carried well enough.

She tied the lines off, and the shadow stood still at their rail, waiting for our approach.

'Others sleep, Mother. I don't wish to give your location away to any more folk than I had to.'

The shadow nodded and gestured Theo closer. 'What do you have there, Timothee?'

'I sail with Old Ones and dragons, Mother.'

She gasped and stepped back. I knew that was my cue, and though I was uncertain of her reaction, I trusted Theo. I held the lamp up near my face.

'Madam Seaspray Maritim, I am honoured to meet you,' I said in Gina's most carefully practiced phrasing. 'I do you the honour of revealing my true face, if not my name.'

I allowed my glamour to drop, and again I heard the sharp intake of breath.

'Timothee Maritim, did you entrap this poor selkie?' she chided.

I spoke quickly. 'No, I am not trapped by anyone. I am here purely by choice, and because Theo insists you are the best person for this task. Theo would never do such a thing.'

'You come here to take me away?'

Theo had stepped inside the circle of my lamp, carrying the huge egg. 'No, Mother. We need to give you this. It needs to be hidden and safe. It needs to be cared for.'

The shadow approached, hopping lightly over the rails of our boat. She was strong and broad – nothing like the thinness of her voice. Seaspray was dark with the sun and freckles speckled her skin. She looked almost eye to eye with me as she reached towards the egg.

'Why?' she asked.

'We believe it is a dragon egg. Theo says that if any still hold the key to hatching it, they will be flotilla.'

'Timothee is right,' she replied. 'How long must I protect it?'

'Until we return.' Theo said. 'There are two other crew on this boat, but I ask that you only return it to myself or—' he looked at me hesitantly.

'Georgie,' I said. 'If it's me, I will reveal myself once again to you. You must not let any knowledge of its existence leave the flotilla. It would not be right for any one person to possess this. It needs to go home, as soon as we can find out where it came from.'

'What if it hatches?'

'Let it fly free as soon as you can,' Theo said. 'Don't let it imprint on anyone.' It was the right thing to do, maybe it could find its own way home.

We carried the egg and all the heating equipment onto her deck. I left them then, returning to *Black Hind* to close the cabin.

Zora peered around the curtain. 'We've stopped.'

'We have, but please – I am so sorry, but Theo wants as few eyes to see where the flotilla are as possible.'

She hissed in frustration. 'I *know* its's the right thing, but I really wanted to see it!' she muttered.

'I'm sorry. I'll tell you about it later?'

Zora narrowed her eyes at me before returning to her bunk. I heard heavy huffs of frustration as she pulled her covers over.

I returned to the deck, pondering her behaviour. I suppose short lives drive humans to fill them with experiences. The fear that they may miss out on something was always present, a driving force. Zora knew it was right for the egg to be hidden, and that the less people who knew where or which flotilla it was on, the better. But still, she was upset that she hadn't seen bobbing lights in the darkness.

Theo's silhouette intertwined with his mother's in her

cabin light as he embraced her. 'Start her up,' he called, springing onto the deck, lighter than usual.

We motored back out of the flotilla, watched by the silhouette of Theo's mother. The egg was safe. It was time to return to *Barge* for some well-deserved rest and to plan our next move. Gar was not well enough for a trip that far on *Black Hind* yet, so we probably had a few weeks to recover. Well, the rest of the crew did.

Sal would have me – as Gina – back at work soon enough.

Theo and I sailed an erratic path away from the flotilla. His determination to hide the location of the egg from even Zora and Ria surprised me. When he could barely keep his eyes open, he pointed *Black Hind* head-to-wind, and I kept watch as he went down to wake the others. The star-studded sky was different from where I grew up, but I amused myself by finding the same stars patterns – the eel and the fish swam close by each other, while the whale sang as ever at the centre of the sky.

Zora stretched as she wandered towards me. 'Which way home?' she asked, rubbing sleep from her eyes.

'Head between the—'

'Just point. I'm too tired to translate constellations tonight.'

'West,' I said. 'I'm sorry.'

She patted me on the shoulder. 'It was his call. It's the right call.'

Ria emerged to take my place and asked the same question.

'Between the fish and the eel,' I said quickly 'That's where we need to head.'

Zora laughed. 'Go, sleep. We'll keep in that direction till sun-up.'

I awoke to the noxious scent of something baking in the cabin. I couldn't understand the appeal of the bread the others seemed to treasure so much. I wandered in to join them as Theo dumped a raw fish on my plate unceremoniously.

'Morning,' he sang. The visit home had done him so much good. His verdant beard bounced with as much energy as he did that morning. 'We should be near *Barge* soon, so I thought we'd anchor up and eat before we get aboard and Sal has a million and one jobs for you.'

'Thank you.' I chewed on the fish gratefully, enjoying the snapping of bones and the squish of flesh. I sighed with contentment. Ria did not look quite as delighted with her breakfast when a chunk of tail flew off and landed on her baked thing. She nibbled around the offendingly fishy bit before leaving that section on her plate.

I finished first and peered out of the cabin. It was cloudy and dull, with little wind, and the clouds promised a high chance of rain.

We pushed on through the showers to find Anard's ship alongside *Barge*. Not the king's huge whale of a ship, but the graceful one we had used to visit Lady Rene before he became king.

He was supposed to be at home, ruling Terrania. My guts tightened, and the ocean began to rise in panic. Something was wrong.

We anchored a short distance from *Barge* and awaited the shuttle boat. I pulled Georgie's glamour on with a sigh. It had been nice to be myself for a while.

'I'll stay aboard.' Theo frowned at Anard's vessel. 'Something isn't right, and I don't want to leave *Black Hind* unattended.'

The scents of *Barge* overwhelmed me as I climbed the staircase from the back deck, my brain whirring. I needed to be Gina, or Georgie? Who would Sal need most? Who would King Anard need? It was easy enough to switch and claim Gina had been aboard *Black Hind*.

We wound through the passageways of *Barge* towards the Ocean Bar. We'd get word to Seren, then she'd let me know what to do and where to go.

Blue light filtered up the stairwell as we descended into the deepest part of *Barge*. Slowly swimming shoals of fish reflected the bar lights, and the salty scents always refreshed my thoughts. Ria gently restrained me as I moved to enter the room.

'Don't panic. It will all be okay. He's hardly been in power more than a few weeks.'

Zora threw me a tight grin, and I entered the room ahead of them. Sal saw me first. He glanced across and gestured me over.

King Anard had his back to me, his familiar stress-tapping of the table audible across the room, and his hunched shoulders telling me more than his words would.

Zora slipped to the bar, and Ria melted into the shadows nearby as I approached the table.

'Cousin, King Anard, the leguaan and ... the other item have been safely returned and hidden.'

Anard turned slowly. Dark circles rimmed his eyes, and his sallow skin implied a serious lack of sleep.

'Ah, my Siren rescuer,' he said, hope flickering. 'Your timing is impeccable. I am afraid I may require your services again.'

Sal caught my eye. The worry lines in his own brow reflecting Anard's mood. So much for a rest.

'How may I help, Your Majesty?' I asked.

He sighed. 'I barely know where to begin.' Steepling his fingers, he continued. Anard always kept a very direct eye contact, so I was prepared for his intensity. 'When I returned to the Winter Palace, I found significant disarray. News had reached us that Dottrine had finally succumbed to her own poison and passed away. In the wake of her passing, the tower where she was imprisoned underwent some sort of madness. People swearing they saw things in the shadows, screaming voices causing pain to all in the vicinity. There are even rumours of possession and dark spirits.'

In the confusion, a small handful of her closest advisors left. They were last seen travelling north into The Barren. There are a few oases, and if they were to follow the shortest route, they could reach the coast soon.

'Good riddance to her,' I muttered. 'Why would this be a problem? It seems they solved their own issue by leaving.'

He nodded. 'You would think that. One of the kitchen staff who returned to the Winter Palace – the one who delivered the news – said there had been rumours of an army massing in the Territories, that in her last days, Dottrine cried equally for death and for her daughter to take the throne.'

'Her daughter?'

He nodded again and slumped his head into his hands. 'It appears I have a half-sister. Dottrine had been in the palace for at least fifteen years. A hidden, illegitimate child could be entirely possible and would have given her the leverage to gain her position. I will search for proof here, but I need your help.' He glanced at Sal. 'We both know it is easy enough to hide a child in the North, don't we?'

A hidden daughter, an army, possessions. So much for a rest.

'What exactly do you want my small crew to do against an army?' I asked.

'I want both of you to help.' Anard replied. He sat straighter, his poise returning as he made his request, the mantle of kingship resting more clearly on his shoulders.

'Sal, I would like you to take *Barge* north. Ply your trade in the Territories, collect what information you can – find out about the truth behind this threat. Georgie, I want you with him. If the threat exists, I want it … removed, or brought onside if you think it might be possible. It would also do me good to be seen to rule alone, to have your influence distant, especially with the nobility.'

'If we leave in the next few days, we might beat Dottrine's loyal retainers. Can Seren get us restocked in 24 hours?' Stocking *Black Hind* was one thing, but *Barge* would be another challenge. Sal might need to visit Safe Harbour first.

'It will take a few days to get *Barge* ocean-fit. It's not a quick process,' Sal responded, 'but yes, *Black Hind* could be underway by nightfall.'

I shook my head. 'Morning. We've sailed all night. The crew need a night's sleep if you want us to take a straight run to Fort Isle and the Territories.'

Anard laughed. 'Fort Isle? There's no such place.'

Sal grinned. 'Let's call it code then. The small matter of payment needs discussing, Your Highness. A favour may not recompense me for several months of lost trade, should the Territories prove sparse and frugal.'

In truth, we had gone through great pains to put Anard on the throne, and we would continue to support our choice – even if he didn't know it. But a sudden volunteering of our time and resources for a cause not aligned with the ones he knows we have might just raise his suspicions. Taking *Barge* north would allow Gar a chance to travel in more comfort too.

Had I worn Gina's face, I would have stayed to help Sal negotiate, but as his cousin, it would not be appropriate. I made my excuses about preparing the boat and left to search for Seren. We had a lot to do before nightfall.

5
FIRE UNDER THE LAKE

MADDOC

Maddoc followed his mam through the misty pathways of the under-lake, as myriad varieties of Tylwyth Teg peered at him from between bushes and hidden amongst tree tops. He loved the place – its beauty was unmatched in the land above the waters. Ancient granite carvings sparkled by the light of thousands of glowing beetles, all clustered on small shelves and posts. Small pots rested there, filled with food they loved, enticing them to rest. One of many ways the Tylwyth Teg worked with nature to create this beauty. He was drawn back from his admiration of a favourite rabbit sculpture by his mam's voice.

'If the arrow has moved on your side,' she sang, 'then has the flame remained fully lit on ours? After all, the Pact is a four-way agreement and bond.'

He trailed along behind her. She was right. He'd been so worried about the human-Tylwyth Teg Pact, that he had forgotten the beacons of the ocean folk and Lord Flame.

'Surely, had the flame gone out, your guardian would have told you – as I rushed to inform you of the arrow?'

'You'd think so,' she replied. 'But, in honesty, I can't even remember whose job it is this decade. It's not as if there has been any change in it before.' She shrugged, the silvery-blue fluid fabric of her dress rippling. Sometimes Maddoc felt he owned more responsibility and accountability than the entire Tylwyth Teg population.

The street, as he thought of it, opened up into the central square, and his mother ascended the stairs to a high plinth, reaching upward to ring the bell suspended from an ornate, wrought hook. The wooden bell rang out, sonorous and deep. It vibrated through every bone of his body as he felt, rather than heard, its summons.

Small, golden-haired individuals fluttered close as moths to a light, while taller annwn gathered behind them. Other members of the community hung from trees or peered from behind carvings, their wrinkled faces screwed up in disgust at having to heed the summons.

'Who is Guardian of the Flame?' his mam called out, her voice carrying into every house and every tree.

Faces turned from side to side, each Tylwyth Teg casting accusing glances around the gathering, searching for someone to offer to her. Finally, a small figure stepped forward, its legs shaking. Hair drifted forward and the tips quaked like leaves in a breeze.

'My brother is ... but he is playing at being a changeling this winter.'

'So, who is checking the flame?' His mam's voice had become silky, slippery and smooth. Maddoc held his position near the base of the plinth, his stomach knotting in response to her voice. As a child, he'd encountered it more than once, his tongue would tie. That irresistible tone could drag truth from even the most unwilling lips.

The small figure clamped their hands over their mouth, eyes bulging as they tried to hold back the answer. 'No one has checked it for months!' they blurted eventually.

One finger. That was all it took. One finger that grew into a silver sword and sliced the unfortunate bearer of the news into two. The hush was physical, the air thick with fear. His mother laughed.

'An end well met,' she called out. 'Who will take on the role and actually carry it out?'

No one moved. The annwn around the edge pressed in tighter, ringing the smaller Tylwyth Teg in. One of the tree climbers fell.

'Thank you for volunteering.' His mam gestured at the unfortunate individual. 'What is your name?' The creature stared from The Lady of the Lake to him, stuttering wordlessly and pointing at Maddoc.

'You don't want to say it in front of my son? My half-human son, who has taken more care over his responsibilities than any of you have in your entire centuries? My son who has risked coming here to tell us that the arrow has moved? And I find we have not been guarding our own Pact?'

The creature gulped. 'Ddôl,' it replied.

'Then, Ddôl, let us go and see how fares the beacon.' She descended, and the crowds parted for her. Ddôl followed dejectedly. If they were named after their usual home, Maddoc could see why the idea of living in a cavern was so distasteful. Meadows were bright and flecked with life.

The informal procession grew behind them as they closed on the beacon cave. The oldest cottages near the edge of the community were carefully patched with a variety of materials – moss and woven grass on some, whilst others were patched with a red soil from the southwest. Not one looked alike. Maddoc resisted the temptation to run his fingers over the tactile walls. As delicate as the houses were, the courtesies he needed to pay were still more fragile, so he stuck very close to his mother, following a pace or two behind at all times.

The beacon cave was past the last houses, the yawning maw reminiscent of the Pact holder it represented. Tiny, carved dragons climbed around the entrance, and long spiral fangs hung from the midpoint of the archway to the huge chamber. The central flame burned with no fuel, as only dragon fire can.

Once it was lit, Lord Flame had retired to his own cavern. Deep underground, he'd slumbered for a long time. As last of his kind to hatch in thousands of years, he saved his energy, leaving the land above to the humans and in the care of other Old Ones.

Every surface of the cave was carved with illustrations of life amongst the Tylwyth Teg from the perspective of the centuries of flame guardians. The previous owner's tools lay abandoned near the entrance. Above them, a half-finished image of a small human child surrounded by dancing Tylwyth Teg. Maybe he had inadvertently inspired himself. As he looked carefully, Maddoc could see other incomplete carvings, signs of a guardian passed before their own contribution was complete.

In the huge bowl central to the cave, the beacon blazed. To Maddoc's eyes, it was healthy and glowing, but a small gasp from one of the crowd packed into the entrance implied that he was entirely wrong.

His mam knelt in front of the bowl with the briefest of motion of her shoulders, which rose and fell in a sigh. Any show of emotion aside from joy was rare from her.

He saw the flash in her eyes as she rose and turned to address her subjects. 'The Pact has indeed been broken. A rift between mankind and the Tylwyth Teg could be mended given time, marriages, and magic. But, in this time, in this world, where they do not believe in us? Where their so-called science rules, magic may be of little use, for none remain with enough belief to wield it. A Pact breach involving Lord Flame would destroy our lives as we know them. Whatever this is, I want it found. I want these lands scoured for the source of the disturbance. Take changelings if you have to! Keep all ears open and all eyes wide. We must find the problem in enough time to fix it. From The Guardian's calculations,' – she gestured at Maddoc – 'we have forty-two surface days to find a solution, or the damage will be irreversible.'

'I will travel to the sky lakes and sit in vigil there,' an annwn volunteered. They bowed deeply and melted away through the crowd.

'Maddoc, my son, you must travel to the island. We need to know if the Pact between the ocean folk and the dragon holds.'

With the Tylwyth Teg hunting for the source of disturbance and the problem handed to his mother, Maddoc steeled himself for the assignment, hoping he could depart soon. His stomach began to rumble as awareness of his hunger grew urgent. It was easy to see how humans became trapped there – the passage of time was so much faster. His brain was fooled, but his digestive system less so. He'd learnt over time to trust his gut, not his thoughts and sensations.

The disconnect between the two worlds was hard for any mortal to cope with. Idly he wondered what it would have felt like as a human. Did the Tylwyth Teg appear to move slowly? Did their speech sound incomprehensible?

The Tylwyth Teg faded away to their homes. Forty-two days was time for them to not worry. In the span of their lives, it was a mere blink – but a slow one.

'I need to eat soon, Mam.' Maddoc murmured once the crowd dispersed.

'Let's get you out of here.'

Maddoc glanced at the flame. 'How much smaller is it really?'

She gestured upwards. 'It should reach the roof.'

The flame was nowhere near the roof – its tip flickered about twice his height from the ceiling. If it had shrunk so fast, were his calculations wrong?

He considered it all the way back to the mossy landing pad. They clasped hands, and he took a deep breath before they ascended through the water, stopping just below the surface of the lake as his mam checked for human presence.

Confident that the way was clear, they emerged, Maddoc dripping wet, and his mam all grace and beauty. The sun rose over the mountains in the east, rays slicing the morning sky and welcoming his return.

'Take the wind stairs and, Maddoc, use our pathways – they will save you days,' she said before kissing him and leading him to the first step. Maddoc dropped the hood over his eyes and began the ascent.

He reached the top, shivering in the cold air as all heat was whisked from his body, then flattened himself against the cliff edge to retrieve his bag.

As he sat atop the curve of the cliff, he saw movement below. Someone was running down the trail from the lake to the town.

He considered chasing them – a younger him would have, but his mam's words rang in his thoughts. Maybe some belief in magic needed to be cultivated. Let them tell their tale. There were only days before they could deny its existence, once Lord Flame awoke.

6

ALE AMONGST WOLVES

TELLIN

'Where do we even begin?' The southern coast of the Territories blurred the horizon as far as we could see. Ria waved her hand along the endless coastline. 'Do we start here? Or in the east?'

I shook my head, as at a loss as she was. Anard had sent us on a mission to track a splinter of rotten driftwood in the length of an entire strand line. There would be other rotten branches and other shorelines to search, so how would we find the right one? I spat out a strand of hair as wind blew it across my face, increasing my level of irritation.

'Debris arrives on the tide. We should start by looking where debris usually washes up.' Zora pointed to a paler section of the coast. 'We'll start with the southern coast, around the Isle of Wolves. The whole southeast is uninhabitable, and the two other deep-water harbours are to the west – along our previous passage with Sirena – and the far northeast.' She glanced at me then. 'Where are your family, Tellin?'

'No one wants to visit more than me, but they're north of the Territories,' I replied. 'Once Sal arrives and starts gathering information, we'll have time to sail up there. For now, our priority has to be finding King Anard's secretive sister.'

The truth was, the closer it got, the more nervous I grew about returning. My family had abandoned me to the humans. Left me tethered to the shore like an animal. I wanted my skin back, and my love for Eryn was still fierce and strong, but deep down, I knew that had the same happened to me with my current crew – my new family – they would have stopped at nothing to get me back. Not accepted my fate passively and continued to swim with the tide. No wonder humankind thought us an easy, weak target. No selkie army ever rose to avenge their stolen ones. As a society, it was something that had to change, but I was not the one to lead that revolution, not yet.

'Isle of Wolves it is then,' I replied.

'It's not closest to the continent. The shortest crossing is in the east,' Theo called. 'But, for what it's worth, I agree. Let's try the isle. Prepare to tack.'

We scrambled to free the ropes and cross to the other side of the deck, all the while watching for the boom as we changed our heading.

Short gusts made us heel over, then the wind would drop and we'd flatten again. Zora kept her eyes fixed on the water ahead, but the wind was so unsteady, she'd had to join us in keeping *Black Hind* level. Watching for the wind shadows on the water became a full-time occupation to avoid being thrown from our feet.

The blurry horizon became distinct islands, their pale grey

coastlines streaked with gold, and the one Zora identified as Isle of Wolves sloped up gently from where waves lapped its southern shore. Theo had warned us that the tides were fast-moving in the region and kept us on our toes as he wrestled *Black Hind* through them.

We'd be much too memorable if we entered port with the dragon-wing rig mounted, so Theo took us into the shelter of a small island, where we dropped anchor. Ria and I raced up the rigging to loosen the detachable spars and lower them to the deck. We worked best as a team, especially as neither of us had the deftness of hand or natural balance that had allowed Eden to do the task single-handed.

As I fed the ropes back through their keepers, Ria returned to the deck. I remained up the mast head for a moment longer, swaying as we rocked. It was calming. I enjoyed the feeling of motion outside my control; the land had so many limitations compared to the sea. For an area Theo had suggested was one of the busiest waterways, it was quiet, and I couldn't spot any other sails nearby.

I tied off the ropes Ria dragged up, threading them through the pulleys before returning to the deck and raising our white foils. Their stiff material flexed in the wind, the repaired patch so neatly sewn in that it was barely noticeable, but to an experienced eye, it would look like we'd had no choice but to repair, as most vessels did.

'We sail as a normal crew would, stop at night, eat locally, and appear in no rush,' Zora said as we gathered around her. 'We draw as little attention as we can to *Black Hind*. I'll close the covers over the panels – we won't have any motor close to port, nor will we be able to access it for a while once out, but they mark us out as something to watch.'

We resumed our posts, and Zora raised the anchor before

we swung our bow back out into the tide and sailed for the Isle of Wolves.

The waterway grew busier there. We sailed around the sea wall to be greeted by the sight of a surprisingly large – to me – harbour filled with an eclectic mix of vessels. The harbour itself was wide yet shallow, and a quick glance overboard told me that on a low tide, the sandy sea bed would hold us all in her grip.

Years of erosion had created a sand bank on the outside edge which would stop *Barge* from calling. A deeper channel led into the main pontoons, and Theo steered us through, passing between the buoys and waving at other vessels. Wind carried us towards the far end faster than I would have liked. My hands began to sweat as I battled my worries about being so deep in, and potentially grounded, with little opportunity to make a quick escape. Ria placed a hand on my arm.

'I can see you shaking. Be calm. Theo won't put us anywhere we can't get out of easily.'

She was right, of course, and he swung us around at the far end, having taken a good look at the available berths. That end was dominated by old, river barges. Their paint flaked in patches and patched up cabins housed families who lounged on the decks in the wintery breeze. It was a long way from the tranquility of Theo's flotilla and their floating gardens, but I supposed that it was a Territories flotilla of sorts. They did not look welcoming. Children stared and pointed, while adults pulled them away from the boat rails, cloudy anger obscuring their love in a shout.

'This is where we start asking questions.' Ria whispered. The occupants of a boat with *Dolphin* emblazoned in faded gold paint along the cabin stared at us, their heads turning with no attempt to conceal it, as Theo sailed back to the row of weather-exposed berths at the entrance.

'I'll go pay the harbour master, wherever they are,' Theo said as he brought us alongside smoothly.

Zora chuckled. 'I'd rather anyone but you went, Theo. Your green beard, whilst beautiful, is very distinctive.' Without waiting for a reply, she vaulted over the rail and tied us off to the pontoon. Her confident stride carried her towards the ramp before we could argue. Colourful buildings sat on the cliff above us, and while the path from the harbour lead Zora that way, we busied ourselves with securing the boat.

'Theo, come into the cabin,' Ria suggested. 'I'll braid your beard. It will still be green, but if it is not a swathe of brightness, maybe it will attract less attention.'

They vanished into the cabin, leaving me alone.

I leant against the mast, inhaling the scents of land. It was always the same after weeks at sea, and my nostrils reeled in shock at the assault. A faint drifting scent of gorse, and a lot of human, blended with bird guano – delightful. Shrieking gulls clustered around fishing boats in the middle of the harbour, diving on deck to return aloft with a prize. To my great relief, the stinking thieves kept far from us. I turned my attention landward. It was cooler there, more like the weather at home than in Terrania, and flat grey skies threatened to douse us with rain at any moment.

There were no signs of early spring; trees wore winterbare branches with steadfast grace. At least they'd survived. Sal told us that most of the southeast Territories had been eaten by The Barren, but, the lingering threat of rain hinted that the land here was still useable – if their regional guardian survived.

Aside from the huge river barges at the inner wall of the harbour, the boats were a mix of small fishing vessels, recognisable by their stench, and essential transport boats – functional and sturdy. Boats that could handle the sudden storms which raged in the region. No pleasure boats bobbed in these waters. It was a community on the edge of survival, for all the gaudy colours they presented to the world from the clifftop.

Could they raise and feed an army there? I doubted it. But they may have seen the passing of one. More and more my certainty grew, that if there was any large gathering being formed, it would be in the lush, green lands of Mynyw, or the cooler northern reaches of the Territories.

We'd spend a few days there while we tried to gather what leads we could. Maybe, the trading folk knew which way an unusual number of Terranians were travelling – if it was Terranians the supposed queen was gathering.

Ria's laughter bubbled from the cabin as they emerged. I didn't think the braiding had dimmed the colour of Theo's beard very well, but at least its volume had reduced.

'What's our plan?' he asked as he reclined on the deck. I tried to follow his relaxed attitude, but my nerves tingled like sea anemone stings.

'Drink, eat, relax, and listen.' I replied, throwing him a smile I didn't feel.

Theo grinned. 'That sounds like my kind of information gathering. I fancy a real drink this time, though. Not like that last bar we visited together.'

'I'll try not to kill anyone tonight. I'm going to get changed.'

Down in the cabin I shared with Zora, I pulled clothes from the chest, fingering the black skin-suit at the bottom. If I needed the venom capacity of that, we were in more trouble than using it would save us from. I gently replaced it and settled for a loose black shirt with minimal embellishment on the sleeves. We'd all started wearing deep cuffs – it made my venom-filled ones less obvious.

I dipped the needles carefully in the bottles I removed from the hidden panel under the bunk. Left hand in the venom that led to drowsiness, and the right in a paralytic. Carefully, I tightened the lids and placed them back, before sliding the needles into their cases. Two of each should be more than enough. I hoped we'd need none, but no way I was going ashore as vulnerable as a sea-squirt.

'He charged us a gold per night!' Zora's outraged tone carried down to me. Our attempt at using patched sails for cover clearly had not hidden our potential as a cash source. I doubted our food would be at the regular prices either. She was still grumbling as I joined them.

'Four gold he tried to charge me. Four! Even King's Harbour isn't that much for a boat our size.' She stomped to the cabin, checking everything was turned off, as though we hadn't already done it.

'We'll pay the difference you haggled down all night.' Theo muttered, 'This will be expensive ale.'

'Ale?' I tried to link the word to a food I'd tried and couldn't come up with anything.

Theo's eyes took on a misty glaze as he replied. 'The golden liquid they brew here has no match in Terrania. It is cool, and …' he tailed off, blushing with embarrassment.

Zora clapped him on the back. 'You'll be drinking it soon enough! Is all secure?'

I turned the locks in the cabin door and set the trigger for the venom catch we'd installed on it. We couldn't risk our supplies or have anyone see the hidden technology of *Black Hind*. 'It is now. Lead us to the ale, Theo.'

We ascended the ramp to the locked gates, Zora held a tag against it, and they swung open, releasing us to the town. I resisted the urge to check back on *Black Hind* one last time. Anyone poking around would wish they hadn't, and I needed to look as relaxed as the others.

Up close, the houses were salt-smeared, and their paint

flaked like the barges. I listened for voices, for accents from Terrania, but like any port, there were people from all regions north of the Everstorm.

Directly at the top of the ramp was a brightly decorated bar. Its paint was fresh, and its tables were filled with clients chatting contentedly. It was welcoming, and we gravitated towards it. Tall glasses frosted with condensation sat on tables, many filled with a golden liquid.

Theo was grinning widely as we ducked into the dark interior. The sensation of being watched prickled my skin. Someone out there was taking a lot of notice of our arrival.

The man at the bar smiled broadly. 'Welcome to the Dripping Bucket,' he called. 'Inside or outdoor table?'

Few patrons sat in the freezing interior. Those that did clustered around a fire at the far end. An acrid scent hung in the air; only the unwashed and unhealthy lingered indoors.

'We'll take 'em out.' Theo replied, clearly having come to a similar conclusion. 'I'll have four pints of ...' – he took a moment to read a selection of tags on tall levers, then pointed at one with a compass on it – 'Western Wonder.' He grinned as he glanced behind him and winked at me.

They all knew I didn't drink. It had unpredictable effects on my glamours, but I could not be seen to abstain. That would be harder to do in public than a darkened indoors.

'Two gold,' the barman said, looking intently at the drink and not Theo as he pulled the lever, and golden fluid poured into the glass.

I placed a quick hand on Zora's arm as I heard her sharp intake of breath. We knew it would be that way and needed to play along for the time being.

Theo fished out a selection of smaller coins and placed them on the counter. 'Seems a lot, mate,' he murmured.

The barman shrugged. 'Can't make anything round here no

more. Barren's closing in. I have to bring it all from the West now – aside from Seaswill.' He gestured at a well-worn pump and pulled a mouthful into a tall glass before offering it to Theo.

He took a long sniff. 'What did you brew that from?'

'Seaweed. It's a fucker of a process, but it keeps the locals in cheap brew. Without that, I'd be heading west too. Can't have a port without a pub – whole place would fold. The locals drink what I can make, and you visitors keep my roof mended.'

Theo passed the golden ales around, leaning on the bar and continuing to chat as we returned outside.

There was one table left. Frost still coated its planks, and no sun was likely to fall on it soon. I sat with my back to the crowd, letting Ria and Zora observe them. Someone had taken more than a passing note of us. For the moment, I'd hide my face from curious gazes.

'How did he feel?' I asked Ria.

She shrugged as her eyes scanned the crowd behind me. 'No darkness builds there in excess of a normal human. Nothing is drawing my attention out here either. There was something near the barges, but up on the land, no one feels any different to normal.'

Zora narrowed her eyes for a moment as she gazed over my left shoulder. 'Normal they may be, but some of these groups are exceptionally well-dressed for humans teetering on the precipice of having to relocate.'

I picked up my glass, sipping a mouthful of the ale. It was bitter, with a tiny hint of sweetness. A strange play on my tongue. Nothing to compare to Fish's drinks, but if I hadn't been concerned about its effects, I'd have happily drunk the whole glass.

Zora drained half her glass in one go, then pushed hers

next to mine, both glasses hidden by my body from onlookers. She grinned cheekily, then lifted a finger towards them. A small, spiralling tongue of liquid rose from my glass and poured into hers.

'Stop it,' hissed Ria. 'Now.'

Zora immediately let the liquid drop.

'Far table,' Ria said, then picked up her glass to take a mouthful. I laughed, as though she had said something amusing, then checked to see if Theo was headed out yet, and glanced around quickly. That was the area where I'd felt attention from earlier. Theo's silhouette filled the doorway as he strode over to us, taking the seat alongside me.

'One of the women on the far table froze when you started to use magic.' Ria hissed.

'Interesting,' Theo grunted. 'Bar man says they get two to four boats a week at the moment, all small, all headed west. He was really pleased about it. Said that it's a new thing for so many vessels to be sailing in winter, and it had kept the town afloat.'

'More than afloat, looking at the clothes they're wearing,' Zora said.

'Someone was staring at me earlier.' I murmured. 'Same sort of area as that woman. I'm going to tweak a tiny bit of my glamour. Watch her again, Ria.' I moved a tooth – nothing anyone who watched us walk in would notice. Ria nodded.

'Urchin dung. We could do without this.' I quelled the panic as well as I could.

'It might not be bad news,' Zora said. 'Look at me. I just use magic for sailing.'

Theo raised an eyebrow in reply and took a swig of his drink. I had to admit, I shared his scepticism.

He leant closer and spoke quietly, reassuringly. 'Tellin, we can hardly sail straight back out after a single drink. We're next to the water – Ria and Zora need no help, and I'm assuming you have things up your sleeves. Relax. We'll get some food, go for a stroll, and keep our ears open.'

'We know who they are, even if they haven't pinpointed us yet.' Ria added. I tried to settle my nerves. Whoever the individual was, they were seated amongst humans. Were they in human employ? Or like us, hiding in plain sight?

We ordered food from a passing waitress and ate. My tension levels were so high, a small bird landing on our table had me flexing my wrists with instinctive readiness. Zora's fingers fluttered too. Small motions, but I couldn't decide if I was relieved that she was as edgy as me.

Eventually, the far table rose to leave the pub; they chatted amiably about the weather and people as they passed. One was so close to us, that they brushed my side. The frisson of contact sparked through me. I tried to hide it and looked up, trying to keep it casual – just a glance at the person who bumped past me. Her eyes were as blue as a winter sky and her hair the colour of sand on a summer's day. She wore a top that matched her eyes, the material so flowing, it could have been in my wardrobe aboard *Barge*. It did little to hide her broad shoulders and strong arms as it draped around her.

Other than that, she was unremarkable. A face with few distinguishing features. Had I been asked to draw her later that day, I'd have only been able to recall those eyes. She met my searching gaze with a jolt, then pulled her lips into a thin smile, cold and emotionless, that didn't reach her eyes. She inclined her head in an almost formal greeting, then turned and rejoined her group, glancing back one last time before they rounded a building.

She knew – I knew – neither of us was human. But I could not tell what she was. Without that direct contact, I felt nothing. Who was she? What was she?

'Tellin.' I pulled back to the moment. Zora's hand on mine was enough to break the whirlpool of thoughts I was starting to spiral down.

'What happened?' Zora pushed.

I glanced to where the group had gone. There had been no sense of connection like I had with Zora, or even the sense of *other* I had with Ria. It was sheer power contained in a human form. For the first time since we met the leathergill siren, I knew I was truly, utterly outmatched should the creature decide to take offence at my presence.

7
WESTWARD-HO

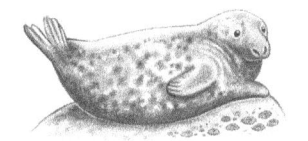

TELLIN

I resisted the urge to follow the woman. We were supposed to be keeping our heads down.

'Whatever or whoever she is, she's powerful,' I said. 'Did neither of you feel anything?'

Zora shook her head. 'Not sea-linked then.'

Ria looked thoughtful. 'We're in the Territories,' she murmured. 'I think you've become too used to the magic-dead lands of Terrania. This close to Mynyw, the lands abound with Old Ones.'

Theo grunted. 'That's a fair comment. It's one of the most whole places left, north of the Everstorm. What I care about now is whether she'll be back and I need to worry, or, can I have one more ale?' He grinned at us all broadly and shrugged. 'Ria has a point. We might bump into anything here.'

I tried to follow his example, to relax, but the roiling water of my insides would not settle.

We were towards the end of our meal when Zora spotted a crew readying their boat for departure beyond *Black Hind* on another guest berth. She was sleek, and the crew slick. 'It's *Wavecrest*.' She flapped her hand at Theo to catch his attention. 'One of Sal's courier ships – I know the captain. They'll pass *Barge* on their route back to Safe Harbour.'

'What are we waiting for?' If we could tell Sal to head directly to the deepwater harbour, he might arrive soon after us. I had Gina's seal in the *Black Hind*. We'd agreed it was the most secure way to communicate if necessary.

We were strolling casually back towards *Black Hind* when I felt that prickling sensation again. I glanced behind, but wherever she watched me from, the blue-eyed stranger was well-hidden.

We closed the ramp gate behind us, and I breathed more freely. Although Ria said she couldn't detect anyone with a corrupt spirit, that didn't mean that one with an entirely different world view would feel wrong. I wouldn't sleep easy while we were there; the potential of becoming grounded – trapped – weighed heavily on my mind. The others could sleep as they liked. I'd be keeping guard.

I slipped the venom lock free to open the cabin. 'You write the letter, and I'll stamp it.'

'I'll tell him we'll see him soon, at home in the west.' Zora suggested. It was a good idea. Sal could work out that we meant his home.

I melted the wax, and we sealed it with a red sea holly. Now, it was up to Zora to persuade the captain of *Wavecrest* to deliver it in passing. She could be very persuasive. I watched her stride along the pontoon, confidence and sexuality oozing with every step. That captain had no chance.

We busied ourselves with checking ropes and the tensions

of ratchets and winches. She paused alongside *Wavecrest*, and a tall individual leapt over the rail and embraced her in greeting. It was clear Zora had downplayed just how well she knew the captain. I tried not to stare too blatantly, but my shoulders lost some of their tension when the sealed note passed from hand to hand.

At least we knew that Sal would go the right way now. He'd told us the western deepwater harbour was near his home, so we had to trust he'd understand what we meant. Zora stayed chatting to the other crew as they prepared to leave, then threw their bowlines over and waved them off.

'I know we planned to take our time.' I fidgeted from foot to foot, glancing back at the shore. Was she still up there? 'If we know there are unusual numbers sailing west, surely we should be heading that way too?'

'She's really upset you, hasn't she?' Theo stroked his beard as he followed the direction of my gaze. 'We could continue our passage west – if everyone agrees?'

'It makes sense to me,' Ria replied, and Zora simply nodded as she re-boarded.

I knew we should stay longer, find more details, but every part of me wanted to be as far from that creature as possible.

We sailed the following morning, watched by a blonde-haired, blue-eyed woman from atop the harbour wall. I tried, unsuccessfully, to ignore the skin-crawling sensation of her focus. Ever since we'd made contact, I was painfully aware of her presence, and it was a relief to be away from Isle of Wolves.

There was a fair wind, and we slipped out of the harbour as the sun rose. Low light reflected from small wavelets, scattered into a rainbow of spray as we cut through them. Out in open water *Black Hind* leapt forward with enthusiasm as wind filled the foils.

We remained close to the cliffs, where seagulls soared on up-currents. Another boat left the harbour and set the same course as us. If the majority of the trade was in the west, other vessels travelling the same route as we planned was a good sign. We relaxed into our usual routine – Ria cooked the meals and worked the winches while Theo and Zora took turns on the helm; the sea didn't need Zora's deft touch or cajoling. I kept watch and worked the winches.

It was a peaceful day's travel. The pale sails behind stayed a constant distance throughout the morning; nothing passed in the opposite direction, and the ocean felt calm. I wished I could trail a hand overboard, feel the water against my skin, and explore the coastline. Around midday, Ria surfaced with food, and we loosed the sails to eat, Zora remaining close to the helm as she tucked into Ria's creation.

'Do you think we should stop somewhere, let them pass, and follow to see where they go?' Theo asked, jerking his head over the stern of the boat. The boat behind was gaining slowly.

'Let them pass us in their own time.' I said as I chewed the dried fish Ria offered me. It had a strange smoky taste that wasn't entirely unpleasant, though I'd never choose it over fresh meat.

By mid-afternoon, green-fringed cliffs gave way to rolling sand dunes; dry and dusty land stretched behind them as far as I could see. Occasional bushes sprouted amongst silvery grass dressing the closest mounds. Even then, the resilience of marram grass flourished in extremity. The Barren kissed the sea, and no human communities could survive on that section of coastline. I was reminded of our first visit many months ago and the ruins clustered along the further western coasts. The difference between the verdant green there and around Isle of Wolves was stark compared to the rest of the south.

The boat behind continued closing in, its tall mast flexed as the foils strained with the wind. That crew was pushing their boat hard as I watched them scurry around like shrimp in a rock pool. Why were they in such a rush? I decided we should try to stick close behind them when they passed us. Theo's hunch could be correct, and they might lead us somewhere useful.

Late in the afternoon, they were close enough that we could make out individual faces. I counted at least six on deck. No, seven. Urchin dung, it was *her* – the blonde woman was aboard that boat.

I kept my voice low and turned to hide my face from her stare, though I felt the pressure of her gaze like a weapon trained on my back. 'I'm certain as the tide goes out twice a day that they aren't rushing to a destination. They've been chasing us down. It's that woman again.'

She walked to the bow of the boat and raised her hands skyward.

'Zora!' I called. She glanced past me, and her expression hardened.

'Theo, take the helm,' she growled and strode to stand alongside me. 'What's she doing? She's no Sea Witch. The water isn't answering her.'

I couldn't feel her in any way either. Her pale face was screwed up in concentration, and her hair blew freely in the breeze. My nails dug into the rail as I gripped it. She frightened me; everything about that woman felt wrong. She drove her crew on – screaming at them to get every breath of power from the wind. A ripple ran down my spine, and sweat beaded on my hands. What did they want? What or who was she after? Was it me? Did she know what I was? Was she a hunter for someone like Icidro?

A noise began to build, distant at first and thin. From the land, a dark shadow grew – flowing towards us. The volume increased. Theo scanned around, searching for the source. His face screwed up in pain.

'My ears!' he yelled. His eyes widened as he forced them to remain open, and his grip on the helm became white-knuckled. The screaming intensified. Loud and unearthly, it flowed over us as the shadowy tide resolved its self into a shoal of ghostly forms. Ria poked her head up from the cabin, drawn by the noise. She looked around and frowned. Her lips tightly pursed as she wordlessly reached towards the shadows. Each one that she touched, vanished.

'She's taking them!' Zora said. 'There's far too many. We need to help.' But even as she spoke, she winced in pain. We would be as incapacitated as fish out of water soon. The darkness fell upon us.

Theo sunk to his knees, one hand still on the helm; his head pressed tightly against that arm to block one ear, whilst his free hand clamped tightly over the other.

What use was an illusion in such conditions? My own ears were in pain, and it took all my concentration to stay upright, even as the boat closed on us. I needed to find some way to protect Zora and let her do her magic. As far as we knew, our attacker didn't know about Zora, so the element of surprise was still ours. If she was able to concentrate.

Ria reached us and gestured towards Zora. She pressed her head close to my ear. 'I'll keep her safe – find something to block out the sound, and fast. I can't take them all in. There are too many, and by all the gods, they're so hurt.'

I ran, half stumbling into the cabin, searching for anything to help us. Oceans, the blankets were too big, the drying cloths too short to tie. I saw them then ... Ria had pulled bread rolls from the oven just before we'd been attacked. They were still moist and soft. I ripped one open and scooped out a handful of the bread, squishing it into soft balls, and ran back up to present Zora with two lumps of warm, squashed bread. She raised an eyebrow, and a particularly loud screech by her ear elicited a wince. With that, she took them and jammed them into her ears. Ria looked sadly at the dough but took a pair too.

'Get Theo some, then hold onto something – tightly.' Zora shouted as she turned to face the ocean.

Theo gave me a strange look, but when I plugged my own ears with bread, he followed my lead.

I stared past Zora to the other ship. None of the black wave of shrieking shadows attacked them, and the smug faces of the crew, all wearing a device over their ears, gave away that this was a tactic they'd used before.

Were they after me? Had they been capturing selkies or other ocean folk? I checked my sleeves; the needles were safe in their pouches. The other vessel was within a boat length of us now. Ria was on her knees with exhaustion. Still, she reached out and captured more souls, but her motions were smaller, the effort needed to lift her hands apparent in the shaking of her limbs.

Zora's shoulders rose then fell – a sign I knew well. She was ready. That last breath was always a big one when she was carrying out a large task.

She grew a wave between our boats, pulling the still ocean into action, building a towering wall of water, then sent it crashing over their bow. I thought that the intensity of sound dimmed for a fraction of a moment, but with the bread earplugs, I couldn't be sure. What I was certain of was that the woman had faltered, her pose slipping for a split second.

Zora saw it too. She sent another wave crashing over their deck, leaving the crew hanging onto rigging and rails. They scrambled to their feet, and the woman leading them climbed part way up the mast. One of the crew had grabbed a rope with a claw on the end. He swung it around his head, gaining momentum, and studying our stern. I crawled closer to the rails as Zora raised the biggest wave yet – under their boat. Over and over it tipped until their sails hit the water. The crew were dangling at this point, or swimming. The boat's righting keel brought them back upright, and the backwash of the released wave caused *Black Hind* to heel over herself. My grip wasn't enough. In moving from one position to the other, I had not reattached myself to the rail, and I slid from the deck into the water.

My first instinct was to cry out in Ocean that I was under attack, hoping that someone or something would come to our aid. My second was to gather the intense power that was concentrated in the water near me and draw it into myself. My skin tingled and I followed its thread back to the source. The woman flailed in the water, and shock grew on her face as the ocean stripped power from her body.

Then I knew. She was in some way related to the Tylwyth Teg. As her power dissipated, a light on the other boat's mast faded, and the crew of her boat froze for a moment. The captain shook his head and stared around; one crew member scratched his head while others gazed around in apparent confusion. Her hold over them was gone.

'For no sea-folk shall cast charms in the Tylwyth Teg's lair while the dragon sleeps fast and the humans are blind.' I murmured. There were no dragons in the Northern Territories, but maybe the old sayings rang true after all. I wondered how many more of my grandparent's tales would prove to hold the truths of packs long past and beings long gone. It appeared she could not cast in our home either. I swum closer to her, continuing to suck in the leached power. I had no need of so much, but better than it going to waste, better than her recovering it in some way. The woman tried to manoeuvre away from me, striking for her boat. Trailing clothes drifting in the water ensnared her limbs, like tendrils hindering her movement. Her freshly awakened crew stared in horror at the dark swarm hovering around their heads. Lost and without direction, I suspected they would take time to dissipate. My earplugs had washed out in the water, but the spirits' screams were tolerable compared to before.

I followed the woman, baring my pointed teeth at her when she glanced back. She was pushed back off the side of her boat with a boat hook as the captain tried to put right his vessel.

'We need that one,' she shrieked, pointing at me. Her accent was strange to my ears, her pronunciation clipped and hard. The crew glanced over at her and dismissed her, turning their attention instead to *Black Hind*. I saw one pass a sly look as they realised that *Black Hind* was still within reach. The one with the hook in his hand drew his lips back in a half smile, half grimace.

Zora must have seen it, too, given the standing wave that appeared between the vessels.

The woman turned and lunged for me, hatred flashing in her eyes. I could take her out now, drag her beneath the waves. If I had my skin, I could have drowned her with ease. I floated calmly as she approached. I still had my needles. Was dead the right outcome? She was still an Old One, even if she was fighting on the opposing side. We needed to know why and who she worked for.

I let her approach, gathering my strength, and as she made contact with me, I grasped her in a tight embrace and cast a full glamour of darkness around us both.

I dragged her under. In pitch darkness, devoid of her magic and unable to breathe, she began to thrash. I held her still until I felt her go limp. We sank together, deeper and deeper. Then, a small, slender hand reached for mine. I took it and let Ria pull us both to the surface. The woman was floppy, our timing crucial. We dragged her to *Black Hind*, where Zora raised us aboard on a small wave.

'I drowned her ...' I gasped for air as I gestured to Zora. 'Can you save her?'

Zora nodded and drew water from the woman's lungs. I had a feeling it would take more than a dunking to kill her. A globe of water splashed on the deck. The woman gasped for air and reached for Zora with a lightning-fast reflex. I touched her and was relieved to feel no tingle of magic had returned yet. Assuming it built as mine did, we would have time to deal with her before she became dangerous again. Zora flicked the woman's hand away easily. Ria sat on her, and the woman stopped moving, staring in horror at her.

'Do you know what I am?' Ria asked. The woman nodded.

'Do you know what she is?' she asked, gesturing to Zora. 'She could replace the water just drawn from your lungs as easily as you breathe. Then, I will take you. Do you wish to join the spirits you loosed on us today in peaceful rest?'

The woman shook her head violently. She valued her own life. At least we had a starting point. Zora took Ria's hint and re-gathered a ball of water in the air over the woman's head.

'If you're all okay, Georgie, then let's get away from trouble,' Theo called across, gesturing to the other sailors who were slowly beginning to appear organised.

I hauled myself from the deck and set the sails.

Zora and Ria had more than enough incentive to get the woman to speak between them.

'Let's start with your name …' Ria said as she adjusted her posture to shift more of her impossible weight onto the woman.

'Diana,' our captive hissed. 'My name is Diana.' I wasn't able to follow the rest as Theo needed my help. Every now and then, the ball of water would lower to Diana's face, or rise again. I hoped they had something useful from the woman.

Theo took us to a small, hidden cove, and we tucked in against the sheltered cliffs to discuss our next moves. Diana had not given us a lot. She was, as I suspected, a kind of Tylwyth Teg, and admitted that she had been aiding the humans but refused to expand on it. Instead, she pointed out that we sailed as a mixed crew and there was no law or treaty against co-operating with other species.

She was right, of course, but that still didn't explain her actions. When Zora asked why she attacked us, Diana laughed. Her laugh should have been beautiful, but instead of sounding like magical waterfalls or music, it cut through my mind with the grating of metal across rocks.

'I did it for the queen's bounty of course. Some shapeshifting female killed the queen's mother. She doesn't know what she's searching for, but from my knowledge, a selkie is a good bet. And there you are.' She grinned at me, a predator waiting to pounce. 'A selkie in a mixed crew.' You can't blame a woman for trying to make a living.

I couldn't – if that was the truth. There were parts of her story which fitted well with Anard's rumours. A self-styled queen whose mother had been killed by a shape-shifter? It wasn't impossible that we had found our target, or at least a way to check the rumours. After all, you cannot be a queen in exile without support of those who believe you to be one.

Ria dragged Diana down to the hold, leaving the rest of us on deck.

'What do we do with her now?' Zora asked. 'She'll regain her powers over the next day or so, and then we're stuck with a trapped fae-kin on board.' She glanced at the cabin frequently as we chatted.

'Dunk her regularly.' Theo growled. 'Drain her! I'll not be screeched at by a hoard of lost spirits again in a rush, thanks very much.' He rubbed his ear. I couldn't blame him; he'd really suffered.

Zora shrugged. 'I'll not stop you if it makes you feel better. But you might want some help from Ria.'

It didn't sit right, dragging an Old One through the water. After all, we didn't know the affiliations of the other Tylwyth Teg. We'd been sent north to prevent trouble for Anard, not start a war he couldn't win, or worse, open war between Old Ones.

I gripped the smooth rail and gazed out at the choppy waves while I tried to tame my thoughts.

'We'll take her with us.' I said eventually. 'If she as much as raises a gust of wind, Zora dumps a wave in the hold.' I turned to face them. Zora was still, calm as a summer sea, while Theo tugged at his beard braid. 'Do you both agree?'

'Aye,' Theo replied. Probably better than dragging her through the water like shark bait.

Ria appeared on deck, brandishing a bread roll. 'Did you have to take a bit from every roll?' she chuckled. 'I was hungry, but all the rolls have holes in them.'

Zora stifled a laugh as we turned our bow into the waves and continued along the coast to meet with Sal.

8
ALL BULL AND NO BEACON

MADDOC

Maddoc gripped the charm tightly. Logic told him that he wouldn't fall to his death any less painfully whether he was gripping it hard or it hung against his chest. But, the human, fearful part of his brain held onto it as though it were a lifeline – a handrail through the Pathways, rather than merely a key.

Hate was not a strong enough word for how Maddoc felt about the Paths. Their disorienting whirls of colour, the way the earth passed beneath his feet – miles at a stride. He swallowed hard. He would not be sick, he would not vomit. Mind over matter. He could do it. It was just that the human part of his body did not cope well with this form of travel.

His next step took him over the first toe of a bird-foot-shaped estuary, splayed across a sandy beach far below. He kept walking, focused through his lowered hood on the clear air ahead, on staying on the thread-like Path.

Another step over green pastureland. Only a few more, and he'd be there. Then, he'd need to rest for a few hours before he could think straight again. Still, it *was* faster than the alternative, and even the best of horses would be too slow. Finding out if any parts of the Pact held was one thing; having the time to mend it was quite another.

He took another stride on the Path. More beaches gleamed in the distance, all golden sand and blue waters. It looked so inviting that he almost stepped off the Path early, knowing that it was just a few days on foot to get to his destination.

No. Each day mattered too much.

Over a ruined castle. The collapsed bridge.

The Path ended on a headland that dipped to the water below his feet. Where once there had been land, tide and time had eroded away the old, soft sandstone, and the newly forming island was breaking free. Maddoc stood on the headland and gazed across the narrow gap, wishing the Path could have taken him all the way to the selkies' islands. They squatted on the sea a few miles offshore. Somehow, he'd have to take that journey by water. He decided to hire a boat – if he could find someone willing to take passengers.

Maddoc wound his way down the steep cliff path; winter gorse and other shrubs tugged at his clothes as he negotiated passage between them. Small boats bobbed at anchor in the bay. Far more than he recalled from his last visit to check the small island calving from the headland – the one the roots had told him was almost lost. The population of humans in the region swelled annually, with people migrating west for an easier life. The increase in boats was likely just that.

Mynyw was one of the last places in the Territories where crops grew reliably, and the land was always green. The blessed rain shadow, cursed by many in the past, yet ever the reason for the living lands of Mynyw, still cast its own form of magic here. The Barren curse was yet to sully his homeland. If Maddoc had to make the choice between migration from The Barren or death, he'd move too.

He broke free of the entangling shrubs fringing the shore as the first wave hit. Boats bobbed frantically, pulling at their tethers. He'd been so busy trying to negotiate the Path and lost in his thoughts that, somehow, he had missed the ship.

It was the biggest vessel Maddoc had ever seen. In his long memory, he recalled childhood tales of huge vessels filled with desperate humans at the rising's peak. Floating cities fled The Barren and the scalding temperatures of the land only to perish at sea. No port would feed a ship that size; no port could cope with the supply needs for long.

Only a few harbours, such as Haven, could still take one so large.

He closed his slack mouth. What was an enormous vessel like that doing there? He studied it more carefully. Were those... *trees* on the deck? It was not in distress – it was polished and immaculate. Another wave from its wake bounced the boats as it passed further into the deepwater harbour. The rear of the ship became visible. It flew a flag he didn't recognise, and was emblazoned with a single word. *Barge*.

Rather than continue up the inviting, deepwater channel as he anticipated, it stopped alongside the old fort. *Barge's* Captain must have known that the estuary waters hid a snarled mass of wreckage from the old docks and jetties. Unless one knew those waters intimately, it would be almost impossible to navigate a ship that size up the waterway. The damaged superstructures remained in part to protect the towns further up from piracy and pillage.

Someone aboard the vessel knew about them, making it even more surprising that he'd never seen or heard of it before.

The babbling of human voices drew his attention. His arrival would be an unmemorable event compared to that; he smiled and let *Barge's* arrival work it in his favour. While they studied the ship, he studied the people on the beach. On the far side, an older woman sat on the sea wall, mending nets. She glanced up occasionally but appeared unfazed by the new arrival. Her hands flashed through the tattered net, weaving and knotting as she worked. Maddoc slipped behind the crowd and joined her on the sea wall.

'Would you like some help?' he offered.

She frowned at him.

'No stranger turns up and offers to mend my nets unless they want something. I can't imagine I'm much to your tastes, young man, so what are you after? I don't need no pity.'

Maddoc quirked a corner of his mouth at the choice of young, but let it slide. The fact that he was probably twice her age was immaterial. He picked up the net, running his fingers across the knots. 'I can see that. Your work is fine and sturdy.' He gave an appreciative nod. 'I won't waste your time. I need passage to the island.'

'Which one?' she narrowed her eyes, taking in his clothes, appearance, and face more closely. 'What do you want by there?' she asked.

'That's my business.'

She stiffened. 'Then it'll be your business how you get there.'

The woman returned to mending her net. Maddoc sat and picked up a section with loose threads, then, selecting a length of twine, he wove and knotted silently. She glanced across and scowled, working faster in response. Maddoc held back the smile as he worked faster. She didn't ask him to leave and didn't thank him, but when she stood, trying to haul the heavy nets down the beach, he quietly took the rest of the weight and aided her.

When the woman began to push her boat off the sand, he helped, holding it steady as she hauled herself aboard. Waist-deep in the salt water, Maddoc felt it eating at his magic. He stood tall to keep his feather charm above the lapping waves. When the old woman was ready, she sat in the front of the boat and stared at him.

'Are you getting in or what?' she demanded. 'We need to travel with the tides, not splash around like wading birds.'

Maddoc pushed them out and sprung into the boat. He took the central seat she had left him and picked up the oars. The old woman nodded once, then turned to stare out at *Barge*, occasionally berating Maddoc for rowing off course or too slowly.

They rounded the headland to see a group of larger boats moored in deep water alongside the new island.

The old woman pointed at an immaculate white-hulled boat. It was old but beautifully maintained. A bright blue cabin perched in the middle of the deck and the mast rose just ahead of it. 'Take us there,' she demanded. He altered course and brought them gently alongside.

'Lift the nets up.'

Maddoc did as he was asked, again with no resistance. If she left him there, he could swim ashore easily if he had to. The salt water would drain him for a day or two, but that was time he couldn't afford to waste.

She'd tied the small boat onto the bigger one. 'I'd usually leave it on the mooring,' she muttered, 'but we might need it.'

Maddoc hauled the large net aboard, careful to lift it over the rail without snagging it. He'd recognised the old-fashioned style of repair work. The holes were deliberate, the threads and knots all designed to break under stress. This woman went to great lengths to only catch her small prey. Whatever that was.

'We'll drop the buoy weight opposite the channel to the islands. You'll help me catch my supper and enough for a few others now, won't you?' She wasn't really asking. He could see the steel in her eyes as she stared at him, so Maddoc nodded.

'Thank you,' he ventured. He'd not met humans like her for a long time – ones who aided him warily yet asked no questions once he'd offered his aid.

She pursed her lips and turned her head towards the open sea as they hummed through the mouth of the estuary, out into the rolling waves beyond.

Once far from shore, the old woman cut the engine, leaving them at the mercy of the sea.

'I'll not have your name, and I won't give you mine. I ask no boon – as you already aided me, I'll return your kindness with a single voyage to the island and back. But don't you think for one moment that if you show me any of your sly magical ways, I'll not just be leaving you there,' she huffed at him before picking up the end of the net and throwing it in.

'How did you know?' Maddoc asked. How much did she know? They had stopped far enough from shore that he had no way back.

'Your eyes are too old for your face. You were able to do net repairs perfectly on a very old net, and you used techniques my grandfather taught me. I've not met anyone else who can do those knots. You were unbothered by that huge beast of a ship. And, you winced at the touch of salt water. Not all our kind have forgotten yours,' she continued. 'I remember Y Plant visiting the markets and their wily tricks. Because I know what you are, I sure as hell don't want to be beholden to you or subject to none of your trickery. You earned this trip with genuine hard work, same as anyone else would've.'

They motored the boat in a circle from the buoy, then pulled the bottom rope tight.

'I don't expect much fish,' she muttered as they hauled the net in, spilling small fish through the over-large holes like a silver waterfall.

When the small creatures had fallen back home, she opened it up. Three fat fish remained.

'That'll do nicely,' she said, then cracked their skulls with a heavy stone. 'Better'n suffocation,' she remarked as Maddoc watched in horror. His stomach churned at the thought of eating them.

The catch complete, they hauled the buoy over the rail and travelled towards the island, staying well clear of the tide race he had seen from the coast many times before.

They closed on the red rocks as seals slipped beneath the waves, spilling from their basking spots amongst the rocks in a wave of silvery fur. The old woman carefully manoeuvred the boat alongside the landing steps. Maddoc jumped out.

'You have one hour,' she called.

Maddoc ran.

He crested the hill, searching for the tunnel he knew should be there, yet as he studied the plants and probed at the area with all his senses, he felt nothing.

A naked male, heavy and stockily built, crested the rise from the other side. His long, mottled hair hung around his body, and his powerful walk was predatory. He closed in on Maddoc, offering him a smile filled with sharpened teeth. His hair was a strange silver tone, with patches of darkness mottled through it. He was twice Maddoc's size, and that smile did not appear at all friendly.

'Why are you here?'

Blunt and to the point. Maddoc had always liked that about selkies. 'One of the Pact beacons is damaged,' Maddoc replied. 'May I check yours?'

'Why would you care? You've shown us no thought or consideration as foreign humans plagued our world. As they harvested our oceans and stole our children. Why should I let you anywhere near the beacon?'

'Because I need to know. We all need to know. There are only days left by my reckoning.'

'Our kind are being stolen, taken by humans. Our agreement with the humans is over. The ties of the Pact have weakened, allowing harm to come to us. War can be declared.' He gnashed his teeth in emphasis, and Maddoc stepped back despite himself. Stealing a selkie was not unheard of, but it hadn't happened for years. Whatever they were up to, the humans were audacious and ambitious. They would break the last bastion of balance left.

They weren't going to let him see for himself, that much was evident. The selkie was as unyielding as an oak. 'I'll carry your message back to the annwn. We must try to halt war before it begins,' Maddoc urged. 'Peace has been good for all our kinds. Give us a countdown time before you begin to sink their ships and steal their women.'

The selkie laughed. 'From one such as you? I bet you are desperate to place changelings in homes once again.'

Maddoc squashed a sigh. His place was to be mediator, not instigator.

'Please, give us time. We'll help you search for your lost children then. I carry the pledge of The Lady of The Lake.'

'We'll see what the next tides bring,' the selkie replied, turning abruptly, then diving from the cliff into the water below, his body slicing through the waves with ease. Several minutes later, a huge bull seal rose to the surface. Maddoc considered trying to find the beacon anyway. Would that make the situation worse? He'd been denied access – that was as clear as lake water. The selkie bobbed in the water, watching Maddoc until he turned and clambered back down the steps towards the boat.

Only once they left the island did he submerge. Other seals watched from ledges and the water until it was clear that they were headed to the estuary once more.

The old woman said nothing about their watchers as they travelled in quiet. She occasionally asked Maddoc to move something or change position, but overall, Maddoc was left to wrestle his tumbling thoughts. What should he do? Go directly home to pass on his findings? He hadn't seen the beacon for himself. And he still needed to visit the new island to check whether the magic had leeched into the salt water completely, finalising its slow but inevitable decline.

He tugged whatever ropes he was asked to, and once back in the small boat, he put his thoughts aside to battle the tide instead, rowing them back to the beach. The huge ship had begun to unfold like an opening flower. Sections previously sealed had dropped to the water, exposing decks and balconies all around the structure. Fabric flapped against the skyline as large, tented structures were erected, and a faint floral scent floated downwind towards them.

Maddoc could just make out figures on the deck. Most ran around, busying themselves with the work of the vessel, aside from two. An exceptionally tall, slender figure, accompanied by a small child. As he watched, the taller figure crouched against the skyline, and he was sure they pointed past him, out towards the selkie island.

'There've been many foreign vessels round here in last few years, but that ship heralds trouble,' the old woman muttered. 'You mark my words.'

Maddoc wasn't sure that a human vessel could bring any more trouble than had already begun, but he bit his tongue. It was not the time.

The beach was far emptier than they'd left it, and he dragged the small boat up onto the sand for the old woman.

She nodded her appreciation. 'I won't invite you in.' The old woman barred her doorway after he carried her fish up the beach to a small home on the edge of the harbour. 'There's a shed in the garden if you need shelter. Most of your kind just vanish off home at night, though, or go causing trouble. We'll have none of that around here, thank you.'

The woman folded her arms, and Maddoc had to hold back a grin that was trying to escape. She was a human force to be reckoned with.

He gave her the fish and accepted the offer of a shed gratefully. If she thought he was fully Tylwyth Teg, it would be no bad thing for his chances of an undisturbed night's sleep. As long as there were none of his mother's helpers truly afoot in the area.

He moved to open his mouth, to say that actually, he was only half-breed, and it was safe for him to come in, she would not be bound ... but her determination to avoid trickery all day stopped him. Let her believe she had tricked and outsmarted a Tylwyth Teg. There was no harm in it.

He bowed deeply. 'Thank you for the trade. All is paid and settled as you suggested. I will not take your offer of the shed – else you would be the one in favour.'

Maddoc then walked back into the bushes on the hillside and climbed to the top so he could better observe the huge ship.

It was a cool evening, and had he felt more secure on it, he'd have been tempted to return to the Path for refuge. As it was, he needed to return one last time – to look at the island. Sliding sideways into it, Maddoc studied the Path's end. He knelt and touched his fingers to the frayed edges where strands hung on to the island. Gossamer-thin, they would not last much longer. It might be in its last days before it became part of the sea-folk domain. He plucked at one of the strands, feeling the vibration traveling its length. It remained taut enough. But insufficient to use, as he had presumed on arrival.

Maddoc walked down to the water's edge. The tide was low, and he tentatively dipped a toe in, feeling the little magic he possessed begin to dissipate as he did so. He shrugged – in for a splash, in for a swim – and waded across to the island.

Setting foot on the rocky shoreline, Maddoc searched for the hut he used many years ago when the damage was new. A grey stone wall half-hidden by brambles hinted at potential shelter. It had been largely reclaimed by the wild, but up close, the limestone walls remained stable. The external walls were deeply shrouded in the vegetation, and the only remaining room had little space for him, but it was enough. He'd have time to inspect the island in more detail the next day. Other islands had broken off numerous times over the years, but that one held on for so long that he had to wonder what else made it special. Why had it not left the tree when the tide cut it off at the height of the rising? It was a question for the morning.

Maddoc stood on the headland for a while longer, feeling the last of the sun on his back as he watched fishing boats heading in for the evening. Three fish was all they caught – it was a lot of effort for three fish. He doubted the boats below were so careful to free the small ones as that woman.

The day had taken a lot out of him, and Maddoc needed a clear head to check the caves. He returned to the hut and laid down in the small room as the night hid her beauty under a blanket of soft clouds. Forty-one days left.

9
SEW FRUSTRATING

TELLIN

Diana escaped.

We woke the next morning to find the hold empty and Theo entirely fuzzy-headed. He sat on the deck, his head in his hands and shoulders slumped.

'What happened?' Zora sat alongside him. 'We saw those other crew. There's no shame in being bewitched.'

'I should have stayed up with you, I'm sorry.' I should have thought, should have had a closer eye on the time.' With Zora and Ria exhausted from the day's exertions, I'd taken the first watch and Theo the second. Diana recovered more quickly than I imagined possible.

'There was a bright light …' Theo raised his head, his eyes remaining downcast. 'It was beautiful and entrancing. I wanted to touch it, to follow it. I knew it was her doing, but I couldn't resist it.' He shuddered. 'Oceans below, she took the small boat, unhitched it, and … and I just watched her. I'm so sorry.'

Ria sat next to him and encircled his shoulders in a small, fierce hug. 'It's not your fault. We know what she is now. You've given us that.'

'Fat lot of use that is when she's out there somewhere!' Theo gestured at the coast.

'How long ago?' Zora stood at the rail, studying the sea. I wondered how far her reach would go if she could catch the boat?

'Hours. More than long enough to get to shore.'

'Then we've lost her. Maybe we'll find our boat on the coast somewhere? We could chase after her.' I suggested. Three heads turned my way.

Ria's eyes glazed, and she stared over the water. 'I think she's an Irrlicht. She will lead Theo astray every time we get near, taking his life but leaving his hollow spirit. I thought they'd all died out. They lived in what is now The Barren.'

'So, she's like you?' Zora said, turning back to us and leaning on the rail.

Ria shook her head, her eyes almost flashing in response. 'I would never do that to a living thing. It's disgusting. What it does mean, though, is that there are creatures not of this land at work for the queen.'

'That's hardly a shock, given Dottrine,' I muttered. 'I'm only surprised she didn't employ Blood Witches once they reappeared in Terrania.'

'Let's not wish any more foulness to cross our path.' Theo pushed himself from the deck. 'We should get under way, but there's just one more thing.' He gestured up at the sail. It had a new rip down its length.

'Urchin's arse, that's going to slow us down.' I sighed.

'Switch rigs?' Ria suggested.

Theo pointed at the clips for the dragon-wing rig. 'I bent

those too. They'll fix easy enough from Barge when we reach it. But we'll have to take it easy until then.'

I tried to hide my frustration from Theo – he was only human after all. 'Ria, can you fix up some food? Theo, go and rest. We'll fix the foils enough to sail to *Barge*.'

We spent the morning stitching a rough patch across the white sail. It wouldn't take high winds well, and the sail flared unevenly, but Zora was confident it was functional enough to get back under way. Ria and I re-rigged it, and we sat on deck eating a breakfast of dried fish and some sort of sweet thing that Ria created for the others.

After that, we sailed in the day, anchoring up in sheltered coves along the coast at night, each taking turns on the watch in pairs. Diana didn't return, and neither were we pursued – openly. Slowly, steadily, we worked our way westward, and the dusty lands of The Barren gave way to ever-greener landscapes. In those ancient lands, with their gods-blessed rain, it might still be possible to feed a large gathering of humans.

Eventually, with the wind rising and the waves building, we closed on the golden beaches and twisted, red-hued rocks heralding the western coast of the Territories and the small island chain where we first encountered the aria.

I gazed northward, searching the waters for a hint of the selkie pack who called the area home, longing for a single, furred snout to break the surface, for a friendly whiskered face. But their attentions were elsewhere. If the tides were kind and the weather favourable, I intended to swim with them soon.

We climbed and surfed down the faces of swelling waves as Theo nudged our bow between green-capped headlands, where lichen gilded the grey rocks at the high waterline, and waves swelled to lumbering mounds as they passed into the estuary mouth. Inside the shelter of Haven, tree branches dipped low to the water and flew tiny, unfurling spring leaves, flags declaring the arrival of spring. A wind shift caught the boom, and I flattened myself just in time to a roar of laughter from Theo.

A single figure stood atop the cliffs to the north, outlined by the evening sun as we entered the estuary; tall and slender, they stood alone. I gazed up at them from the deck, drawn by their presence for a moment.

'*Barge* ahead,' Zora sang out, and I scrambled to my feet. The massive bulk of *Barge* was anchored near a small island where an ancient fort sat solidly against the invading weather. Cables ran across to the mainland, and small boats bobbed on their moorings near a private dock. I couldn't help but wonder what, or who, it had once been built to protect.

That area of the Territories, known by all Old Ones as Mynyw, had a long history filled with battles both magical and mundane in nature enough for it to be either group of inhabitants. For most of its history, humankind had merely been a visitor, settling at the fringes of the wild places. With the spread of The Barren, they had washed up in Mynyw like driftwood.

Our slow passage along the coast meant that *Barge* had arrived ahead of us with enough time to drop the lower decks and attract a shoal of small boats – who floated around *Barge* like wrasse on a shark. Far too many for us to sail up unnoticed.

'How about we drop anchor in that cove?' Theo asked, gesturing to a narrow strip of sand below steep cliffs. A thin, shale-covered path wound down their face.

'Looks as safe as anywhere we'll get around here.' I replied. No one would get down without giving themselves away, and we were in full sight of *Barge's* upper deck. When he was ready, Sal would send a boat for us.

Ria prepared the anchor, and Zora and I worked the winches as Theo brought us into the shelter of the northern cliff. We were close enough to hear trilling bird song carry across the water from the land, but far enough away that seabird calls blended with them. A familiar croaking alerted me to a bronze-backed cormorant racing across the water. It skimmed the wave crests as it sped into the distance, and a pang of loss curled tight in my gut.

The sun sank, lighting up the cloud-spattered sky with flames of promise for a good day ahead. A shimmering shoal of sand eels glinted in the fiery sunset glow. I hadn't realised how badly I'd missed their taste until I saw them. I gestured over the side to Zora. She glanced at the meal taunting me and raised an eyebrow.

'You can't go naked here,' she said.

'Urchin's arse, I can't,' I muttered and stripped before diving into the water.

'Don't go far,' she called over the rail while I chased the shoal into shallow water. Eventually, I cornered some and grabbed a handful before surfacing to eat them. I bobbed close to the side of *Black Hind* as I ate, careful to stay concealed.

'Do you want any to go with your tea?' I asked Theo hopefully, desperate for an excuse to keep hunting, but he shook his head.

'Best you get aboard, Tellin. There's a boat heading our way.'

I scrambled up the knotted rope ladder thrown overboard for me and ducked below deck to dress before the boat arrived.

Seren's flame-coloured hair flew pennant-like behind her as the red boat slowed alongside us. I caught one rope and Ria the other to pull *Petrel* alongside as tightly as the fenders would allow.

Seren boarded, studying the damage to our sails with a deep frown. 'What on the waves did you run into?' she asked, reaching for a tattered rope. She appraised me, too, and satisfied that I was undamaged, turned her attention to the others.

'What happened?' she asked again.

'Would you like a drink?' I sidled toward the cabin.

Seren huffed. 'No, I want to know why you're so damaged and why you were so determined to have us bring *Barge* straight here.'

'We ran into a little trouble, but we're fine, honestly.' Theo slipped into the conversation gently. 'Seren, it is a joy, as ever, to see you.' He offered a charming smile, but this thought-shrimp was not going to get eaten. Seren refused the dangled bait.

'If you won't tell me how, you'd better show me the extent of the damage. We don't want to be too closely associated yet, but you'll need some repairs, somehow.'

I pushed up from the winch where I perched. 'I'll get a bag ready. Seren, I need to come aboard and talk with Sal.'

'Please do. He's waiting,' she called over her shoulder as Theo talked her through the damage.

Zora followed me down to our room. 'We need to be careful,' she said as she stuffed a few dry clothes into a bag.

'I agree. Until we get a feel for the locals, assume every one of them is working with that Diana.'

'I'd rather not.' Ria's voice was strained and quiet through the heavy curtains. 'I need a rest. In my big, comfy bed on *Barge*. All my food brought to me, some time to recover.'

Zora winked at me before replying. 'Of course, your spirit-catcher-ness.'

I felt rather than heard Ria's sigh. I really wished they'd get back to the closeness they had shown briefly before. They wouldn't, now Cor was gone, and Eden with him. Zora had little love for Ria, despite having proved over and again how much she was a part of the crew. Having them both in my rooms on *Barge* would rather spoil the restfulness.

We boarded *Petrel*, leaving Theo happily sat on the deck, relaxing in our absence. We promised him we'd send someone over with supplies. He laughed and pointed at the haven around us.

'I have everything I need. Don't worry. Just get that report in, so I can head ashore for a decent ale soon!'

Seren headed away from both vessels, steering deftly between moorings deep into the estuary. Lights glowed on dusk-bathed coastline as we rounded a headland into a long, thin bay. The tide was out, and a building silhouetted against the skyline between the trees.

Oak grinned over at us from a small fishing boat floating inside the bay. 'All aboard,' he called across cheerily.

We boarded and left the bay in the white fishing vessel to return to *Barge*.

Oak slowed the motor as we came into the shadow of the huge ship, the sun's departure making us little more than silhouettes. He cast a fishing rod from the stern and let the boat drift as he played out the line. We crouched in the cabin, hidden from view, waiting for his signal. Eventually, he gestured to the side, and we slipped overboard. The calm waters wouldn't hide us from the deck of *Barge*, given the amount of light she cast, but we trusted Oak's timing as far as other watercraft were concerned.

It was a long swim underwater. Ria looked comfortable, and Zora struck out strongly. I struggled to keep up with them. Maybe we could have used Zora more effectively, but as

Seren had said, we didn't want to draw attention to ourselves. My lungs felt ready to burst by the time the hull of *Barge* was close enough to touch. I slipped up her glossy sides and quietly swam to the nearest deck; reaching for the wooden boards, I half floated, gasping for air. We couldn't do that every time – it was madness.

Zora sprung onto the deck and reached down for me. I grasped her hand, and she hauled me up. 'I keep telling you to use that skin! You could have done this without attracting a moment's notice.'

She was right, but my sister's pelt was locked in Sal's safe on *Barge*, although none of them knew that. We sat companionably for a while, watching Oak cast and recast his line. Eventually, a whoop of delight carried over the water as he caught a fish. We were too far away to see what it was, but the small flash of red left me suspecting that gurnard would be on the menu tonight.

Had we been in Terrania, this deck would've been filled with laughter and couples as the crew entertained some wealthy individual or another. Instead, I curled my arms around my legs as the chill wind whipped past and eyed the nearest door. *Barge's* warm innards called strongly enough that I uncoiled myself and ran, with Zora and Ria close behind.

'It's cold enough to freeze an urchin's spines off,' Zora muttered as we shut the wind out. I bit back a smile. I'd have them all swearing like selkies soon. 'We can't traipse around like this,' she continued, and moments later, she'd pulled all the water from our clothes and gathered it into a globe. I opened the door a crack, and she flung it onto the deck.

'Right,' I said. 'Now we're all ready, I should go and see Sal. You're welcome to join me. I'm going to try Ocean Bar first at this time of the day.'

'I'm going to wait for Seren,' Ria muttered. 'We need warmer clothes.' I tugged my clothes tighter around me. She was right. Lady Gina's flimsy dresses would be no match for the spring in Mynyw, and our warm deck clothes were all aboard *Black Hind*.

'Zora, are you coming?' I asked.

She shook her head. 'I'll let you have your family reunion in peace. I'm going to go to the common lounges, try to find out if anything has been heard. The rumours of sailors rather than the politics that usually reaches Sal.'

It all reached Sal. I thought about saying that but decided against it. I watched them both go, then started off through the orange-themed hall towards the guest area.

In the resident zones, Ria's and Zora's eyes would be more kindly treated. A bright purple curtain embellished with breaking waves hung across a doorway, ostensibly to make it look as though the door was private and hidden. Many doors on *Barge* were, but that was not one of them. I pushed at the heavy, metal door, and it swung open freely. So close to the decks, it would be a true water-sealed door, and they had to work properly.

The decor was not much easier to bear once through. The scent of flowers drifted through passageways, pumped from somewhere sunnier, no doubt, and my feet left footprints in the deep pile of the carpet.

I passed no one. That alone struck me as unusual on *Barge* – it was usually alive with people. It was enough to make me change course to the top deck, where Sal had first introduced me to the crew.

It was the right decision. Sal stood, flanked by Driftwood at the top of the steps, while many of the residents sat or lounged on the deck below him. His words drifted over to me as he addressed the crowd.

'—we don't, then there could be war.' A murmur rippled through the residents. I sat quietly at the edge as Sal's eyes continued their ceaseless study of the residents. They paused on me for a second, he nodded gently, then picked his speech back up.

'We don't know who she is, where she came from, or how many have joined her. Usually, I'd let you take instructions from Seren, but this is urgent. We need to know what's happening here and fast. These people do not know us, our services, or our kind. They may not be as welcoming as we are used to in the Terranian Sea, but they're the tools we have. I know many of you are sea-folk, and you'll know what these lands represent in your legends. Now you will see their truth. I'll not have a southern army wrecking one of the most pristine regions left. You are sea-folk. Believe your tales of this land, and believe your eyes. Make no bargains, and go ashore in pairs.'

Meaningful glances were cast at others around me as the crowd's emotional resonance changed. He'd worried them. Murmuring voices held notes of concern; people fidgeted in their seats and reached out for friends' hands.

'Rustlers, go visit the shores. Advertise us – carefully. Fill our rooms with noise and laughter. I have never brought *Barge* so far north before, therefore, any who recognise us may need careful observation.'

He waved his dismissal, and the residents melted away to the darkness, preparing for new guests.

I strolled up to Sal, weaving through the departing crowd. He strode down the steps towards me, affection beaming from his face. 'Cousin Georgie! How was your journey? We got your message, as you can see.' He gestured around him. 'Come, tell me all about it.' He ducked under a jasmine arch, grimacing at its already-browning petals. 'This weather is going to play havoc with my plants,' he said.

'I suspect King Anard will compensate you for their damage on return,' I replied.

'He better had,' Sal muttered. 'I suppose stopping a war should be a good price, but it took me years to grow these!'

We descended into Sal's rooms. He held the door, checking the hallway was quiet before locking us in.

Sal flopped into his red chair. 'What did you find?'

I sat on the end of his bed. 'Discontent and poor ale, according to Theo. The land to the east is in a bad way. It is almost as bad as the Northern Barren. There is little growing, and what they do get is coming from this direction. Prices are steep. Rumours abound of a gathering in the west around someone styling herself a queen.' I paused. The room felt wrong.

'Where's Gar?' I asked.

'He's with Seren.'

'No, Sal, he's not. Seren picked us up. She's not back aboard yet.'

Sal sat up abruptly. 'He's always with Seren if he's not here.' He rushed around the room frantically checking under covers and the bed, calling for the pup. His panic was contagious, and I started to check the cupboards.

'Where do you keep his skin?' I asked. 'Could he get out on his own?'

'Only down the back stairs.' Sal opened the tall cupboard. By the light of the pulsing jellyfish, an empty drawer was exposed.

'He's got his skin, or someone else does!' Sal cried, turning from the door and flinging open the back door. He took the stairs two at a time, practically flying down them in his desperation. His fear for the child filled my nostrils, sharp and astringent.

We reached the private dock. The hatch was closed, and only a small volume of water filled the bottom of the area. It was silent.

We stood still, and Sal gestured for me to move around to the far side of the decking. I crept along the wall, searching for any sign of Gar, but as hard as we looked, we could not find him.

Both Gar and his skin were missing.

10
ROW, ROW, ROW THE BOAT

MADDOC

He was wet. His clothes were wet, his face was wet. Hair stuck to his cheeks as he tried to wipe straggling lengths from in front of his eyes. Grateful that his coat had at least kept part of him dry, Maddoc sat up. A small waterfall cascaded to the ground behind him; the roof, which had looked solid the night before, had leaked like a sieve. Maddoc pushed the door – balanced on a single weathered hinge – open far enough to peer out.

A thick blanket of clouds told him that the weather was settled in. Maddoc pulled his boots from his bag. *Never sleep with boots on – keep them safe, and they will keep you safe.* He'd never really understood that old saying of his father's, but over a hundred years later, he still stuck to it. So far, his boots had never had to keep him safe. Was it finally the day? He laughed to himself. The way the next forty days panned out might prove the wisdom of the saying.

He shook the rain from his hood and felt inside him for any traces of magic. A tiny amount had built back up. Enough to use the Path home later – if he could cross back off the small island without getting in the sea.

First, he wanted to look at the root from the side he was on. There was a sea cave down on the shore that went a fair way under the island, but maybe not high enough. If he could get close to the centre and not get salt-wet ... perhaps he could reach out through the rock to check on the root. If he couldn't feel it, then it was time to let go. To cut the root and save the tree; let the seal-folk and their kin have the small lump of land.

Maddoc stuffed the blue cloak into his pocket, the fabric folding impossibly small, and left his bag in the hut. He climbed slowly down the cliff face, his hands seeking out slim cracks, testing each ledge before shifting his weight onto it. He passed over bands of red sandstone and grey limestone flecked with the fossils of sea-lilies long since extinct, until he reached another band of red. The rock decorated the coastline with neat horizontal stripes, giving no hint of the geological turmoil just around the headland.

Gravel crunched under his feet as he landed. The incoming tide would severely limit his time, so Maddoc wasted none. He ducked into the narrow entrance. Light faded ahead of him, and large boulders strewn across the cave floor made for tricky walking. He avoided several, then as it grew darker, his foot collided with one.

It moaned a small, thin cry of pain. Maddoc pulled his foot back to peer down. The lump was not big enough to be a human unless it were a child. It was dark and mottled. He crouched, reached forward, and his hand made contact with fur. The creature stirred but didn't run from his touch.

'Hey, what have we got here?' Maddoc said, trying to keep a friendly tone. He relaxed his arms and tried to look as unthreatening as he could. Nothing that weak and that far into a dark cave could cause him harm. He felt the creature again. It shuffled closer.

'Sal?' it muttered. 'Is that you, Sal? I'm sorry.'

'I'm not Sal,' Maddoc said. 'But I am a friend. Are you hurt?'

'Are you my pack?' the small voice sobbed. 'I want my pack. I want Sal, and I want Mam.'

Maddoc reached down and ran his hands carefully over the creature. Seal-shaped, except – the skin was open. The child was very cold. They must have made a mistake, got their skin wet. Young of any Old Ones often needed much guidance in their early years. Magic was unpredictable, and the pup shouldn't have been swimming alone. He scooped the selkie pup into his arms, holding them close to share his heat before glancing up towards the roots and sighing. The seal-folk had claimed the cave already – even if unintentionally.

Had all been as it should, they could never have gotten so deep. Or maybe that was the problem … maybe that's why the pup was stuck neither in or out of its pelt. Maddoc rushed out of the cave into the open air. The tiny pup stared up at him with huge, dark eyes, then shivered violently.

Bloody rain. Its presence was the only reason the area remained fully alive. Heavy rainfall on the west coast drenched Mynyw and filled the lakes, persisting even as the rest of the country dried out – that day, he could have done without it. The cliffs were too steep to carry the child back up. Maddoc searched the water for seals, for bobbing heads, or the long powerful bodies of this pup's family. Had he drifted from the isle Maddoc visited yesterday? Perhaps returning the pup would allow him access to the beacon.

Out beyond the shore was a group of boats. The old woman's tender bobbed on its mooring. If they could get round the headland, they could reach the small beach he'd seen the previous day. Then, he could leave the youngster on the sand and retrieve the tender. Maddoc thought about waiting for the old woman to return, asking for her help in returning the child to the isle ... but no. He needed to find a way himself.

'I'm going to need to tie you to me,' he said, removing his coat. The limp seal-pup didn't fight as he stuffed it in, then tied the coat-sling to his back. 'We'll go around the rocks. I'll have to leave you for a short while, then we'll get you home, little one. Don't you worry.'

A small whimper was all the answer he received. Maddoc clambered up the cliffs; the smallest height that would keep them above the water line. Lichen-coated rocks made for slippery footing, so he moved carefully. One hand to the right, then the foot, then the next hand, always keeping at least three parts of his body in contact. Always aware of the precious cargo he carried. Slowly and steadily, Maddoc climbed around the cliff. About halfway, the pup stopped moving, but there was no way he could check on it. The tiny beach came into sight. As soon as he reached a safe enough spot, Maddoc jumped down, letting soft sand soak up the impact of his fall. He untied the coat and lowered the pup to the sand. Their eyes were open but glazed, each tiny, gasping breath fainter than the last.

'Hey, no sleeping on me. We've done the hard bit. Now it's just a boat ride home,' Maddoc said, holding the small creature close to his body, trying to warm it as well as he could. The pup blinked slowly.

'Sal, it's cold here,' the pup said.

'I'm not Sal,' Maddoc replied. 'I'll be back soon. We'll get you to your Sal.' He covered it with his coat. As he stepped into the water, he felt the magic drain from him.

Weeks. He had weeks. He could spare a few hours to help to save a life and access that beacon. The remainder of his small replenishment of power drained away as Maddoc struck out for the small boats, swimming as fast as he could. A bigger vessel sat near the tender. It hadn't been there the day before. A man similar to his own apparent age was on deck threading ropes through winches and splicing damaged sections together. The man's green beard and dark tan marked him as a stranger to these lands. Maddoc tried to wave casually as he clambered over the edge of the small boat and untied it from its mooring. The older man's eyes bored into him.

Maddoc tried to ignore it and picked up the oars. His muscles still ached with the mere memory of the rowing he'd done less than twenty-four hours earlier. That boat could get him to the isle faster. There was no way he could ask a human for help, not when that selkie pup had his skin half-open.

He struggled to get the rowboat moving in a straight line, eventually managing to point the front of the boat towards the beach. It would be a long and risky row, so he tried not to over-exert himself, despite the urgency. He was useless to the pup if he was worn out before they rounded the headland.

The bow crunched against sand. Maddoc leapt out and dragged the boat to the shallows; he bundled the selkie into the boat, then leapt in after him.

The coat fell off the pup as he started to row back out. It was lying so still that only the slightest flutter of breathing motion told him it hadn't died. Maddoc wasn't willing to give up yet. He looked at the bigger boat once more. He couldn't lose a selkie pup in his care – not while the Pact was so fragile.

Maddoc swallowed hard and turned the bow of the rowboat for the bigger vessel. The older man stood at the rail, all pretence of not watching him abandoned. As Maddoc grew closer, he heard him call out.

'What's the rush? You climb around the cliffs into the bay, take a boat that's clearly not yours, and now you're struggling with it.'

'I found an injured seal pup.' It was partly true.

'Why didn't you leave it for its parents to find?'

'It's too injured. Can I warm it on your boat? Then I'll return it to the shore unless you could help me return it. There's a seal colony just off shore.'

The older man frowned. There was kindness in his face, but he crossed his arms and stared down at Maddoc.

'Let me see the seal. You could be trying to steal my boat.'

Reluctantly, Maddoc held the pup up. Hiding its open skin against his own body.

The man paled. 'Gar?' he called. 'Gar! You're supposed to be on *Barge!*' He threw the ladder down, his speed belying his age. 'Quick – get him aboard. Where did you find him? What was he doing on his own? Was a bigger seal with him, a black one?'

Maddoc shook his head. This man reached down and took Gar from Maddoc's outstretched hands.

'Urchin's arse, but he's cold!' Without turning back to check on Maddoc, he ran off with the small pup.

Maddoc clambered aboard, tying the small boat onto the rail, and waited on deck for the other man to return.

He wouldn't enter a home uninvited; he had no intention of putting a foot against convention. If the man recognised the pup, was he a selkie too? He looked a little too old, too haggard. Yet his eyes were young, and he moved with more grace than an old human. He didn't smell of selkie magic. All Maddoc could do, was wait.

Maddoc paced the deck impatiently. If they returned the pup to this Sal the child mentioned, his drained power still held him there. He could no more jump on the Path and travel than he could light a beacon for attention. Maddoc ran his hands around the boat, feeling touches of magic absorbed into her structure. It was strongest by the bow, although a gentle hum permeated the entire vessel. He opened his senses to the boat. It reeked of magic. Whoever that man was, he knew far more than an average human, more than the old woman. Maddoc held the rail near the bow, but the magic felt alien to him. Whoever and whatever the user was, they were not of Mynyw – that was for sure.

He recognised the tang of selkie, but that was likely the child. Faint lingerings of other things, too, both old and powerful. Were there others below deck, away from observant eyes? It couldn't be coincidence that such a vessel had appeared at the same time as the *Barge*. The selkie on the island had said that the humans stole their pup. Were these events linked? Could that ship be the source of unrest?

He sat on the deck, wishing that he had even the slightest ability to do more than sense magic, and use it through his mother's tokens. He was about to widen his senses, reach out further to follow the scents on this vessel, when he was interrupted.

'I've wrapped him in blankets. He needs to get back to *Barge*.' Green Beard pointed at the enormous ship. 'There are … people there who can help him.'

'Can you get help from them? Call a boat or something?' Maddoc asked, eying up the distance between the two vessels. Small boats peeled away from it, heading out towards coastal towns and filled with brightly dressed people. 'You have a motor. Can't we just take him on this boat?'

The man looked torn. 'I can't. We can't link the two vessels to strangers. But as a stranger who brought a selkie pup to an unknown boat. I suspect that you are more than you appear.'

'Shall we leave questions un-asked?' Maddoc replied. 'What neither of us know cannot harm the other.'

Green Beard shook his head. 'After the last few days, I can't take you to *Barge* without knowing what you are. Tell me on the way, though. Gar needs help. We'll use the boat you stole.'

Maddoc felt heat rising in his cheeks. 'I planned to return it!'

The man's beard parted in a wide smile. 'Then let us *borrow* the boat a little longer and hope its owner will not take my boat in its stead. Get back in it. We'll wrap Gar up as well as we can. Hold him close against you, keep him warm. I saw your attempt at rowing earlier. We'll never get there if you row.'

Maddoc climbed back into the small boat. Hopefully, they could return it before the old woman came back from wherever she'd dragged someone else out to.

Blankets followed him down, and Green Beard stood at the railing. 'Are you ready?' he asked.

'Yes.' Maddoc held his arms out to receive the pup. He wasn't shivering as much as earlier, but his eyes were still closed. He sat at the back and pulled the child in close to his chest.

Green Beard climbed down into the small boat, untied them, and took up position at the oars. His powerful strokes carried them across the wide estuary much faster than Maddoc could have rowed. Green Beard pulled at the oars, saying nothing for a while, just looking up at the small bundle frequently.

'Georgie and Sal will tear this place apart if that child doesn't get back to them soon,' he muttered. 'Silly of him to try and make it on his own. Such a good boy, you'd have thought he'd know better.' Drips cascaded from the oar blades as he drew his arms back a few more times. Pull ... drip, pull ... drip.

'So, what are you?' Green Beard asked.

'The Guardian of the Pact.'

'Means nothing to me. Why should I let you aboard once Gar is safe?'

'Because the Pact is failing. Because in forty days, Lord Flame will wake, and there will be carnage. Does the owner of the *Barge* know what they've done by stealing a selkie pup?' He could feel the heat rising in his cheeks. More and more certain the boat was involved.

Green Beard raised one eyebrow at his outburst. Waves of calm rolled from him. 'Lord Sal rescued young Gar here so that he could return him home. He is a champion of the Old Ones. I suggest you may not want to enter his home with accusations flying. Whatever you are, wait.'

Maddoc said nothing, staring up at the huge vessel. Human rescuers of selkies? Or, given the number of magics aboard the other boat, non-human. His mother would want to know what was going on along the fringes of Mynyw.

They drew alongside the huge ship. Green Beard took them to a wide deck, where a couple sat in the rain. It wouldn't be Maddoc's choice of location to relax.

They bumped gently against the deck, and Green Beard gestured for Maddoc to get out.

'Oak, Willow, take this man to Sal – or Georgie if she's aboard.' Green Beard called.

A woman unfolded herself from her seat and strolled over

to them. She peered at the man. 'Theo Maritim, I almost didn't recognise you with that beard. It suits you.'

He shrugged. 'A kind of tribute, a promise. If you can't find Lord Sal, then take him to Seren. She'll know what to do. Don't leave him alone.' He waited until Maddoc stepped onto the deck, then pushed off, heading back into the estuary once again and back to his boat. Maddoc held the pup close, fully bundled in blankets aside from his nose, which opened and closed with each faint breath.

'Lord Sal might be a bit harder than usual to find. Why do you want to see him?'

Maddoc uncovered the head of the pup.

'Gods of above and below, the markings match the description! He's had us hunting for that pup all night! Follow me. We'll go straight to him,' she said. 'Oak, make sure you see Theo reach *Black Hind*. It's a long haul both ways.'

'Will do,' the man replied.

Willow led Maddoc through a door and into a gently lit stairwell, then glanced at him more carefully. 'Where did you find it?'

'In a cave on an island. I was trying to warm it when Theo Maritim brought me aboard and rowed me over – said he'd be missed.'

'That's the understatement of the year,' Willow muttered, leading him up some stairs. Maddoc struggled to keep up with her as she jogged through a maze of passageways that became ever brighter and more opulent. Eventually, she stopped at a large door and knocked.

'Enter,' a male voice called. Willow pushed the door open to expose a white room. A tall, dark-haired man sat in a red velvet chair, his face creased with worry. A woman turned toward them, her light-brown eyes narrowing as she studied Maddoc. The room contained more magic than he had felt anywhere, bar his mam's home. Selkie magic, and he was certain some of it was coming from the seated man. The woman strode towards him, reaching for the bundle in his arms. Her nose was crooked, maybe broken in a fight. She held herself with utmost confidence as she approached, and when Maddoc lowered the edge of the blanket, her face lit up.

'Gar!' she cried, reaching for the seal. Her hand grazed his own, and the tiniest spark flared. But she was so engrossed in taking the pup from him that he hoped she had missed it. She was a selkie too? Two selkies aboard a huge ship, mingling with humans.

'He's still alive! Thank you.'

Maddoc mumbled acknowledgement. Trying to keep from attracting any further contact between them. They were a potent combination.

'Theo brought this man to us with Gar.' Willow said. 'He told me to bring them both to you, Sal.'

The tall man turned and stared at Maddoc more intently. He offered his hand in thanks. Maddoc had no real choice; he accepted it and exposed himself, or he declined it, and they would wonder what he was hiding.

He'd been in the water long enough that surely ... He offered his hand. Sal clasped it firmly, and his mouth set in a firm line.

'I'll talk to our guest a while longer, Willow,' he said. 'Please inform Seren that Gar is returned and that Driftwood can stand down.'

Willow left. As soon as the door shut, Sal's friendly visage dropped.

'What do you really want?' he asked. 'Only a matter of days ago, one of my ships was attacked by a fae-kin, and now you come into my ship bearing my lost child!'

Maddoc could feel himself tensing up. His hands curled

into fists, and he had to breathe deeply to release the tension. Two angry bull selkies in two days were far more than he'd anticipated dealing with.

The woman turned towards them and opened her arms in frustration. 'Not now, Sal!' she said. 'He can't go anywhere. Take a seat.' She pointed at another seat in the room, and Maddoc sank onto it. The chair was lumpy and uncomfortable. 'Gar's skin is stuck. We need to get him out. He's got water inside it. Thank the Gods of above and below that he didn't drown. It's no wonder he's so cold. Until we get him either fully in or fully out, he's not going to recover. I vote for out. We can warm him more easily.'

Sal backed away from Maddoc, still casting narrowed eyes in his direction intermittently. As the two selkies gathered around the pup, he saw a growing glow of blue around Sal's hands. The woman started to tug the child from the sealskin. Maddoc averted his eyes quickly. It was one thing to know selkies did such a thing, but quite another to see it actually happening in front of him. That pup was tiny.

The longer he sat, quietly hoping that Sal had lost the fire of that initial contact, the more uncomfortable the chair became. Maddoc was desperate to get up. Standing would be considerably more comfortable than staying put.

His attention was drawn back to the selkies, who appeared to be having a quiet disagreement.

'... hide it from him.' Sal said.

'No. He clearly wants to go home. It's only a short journey. As soon as he's well, we should return him.'

'I know.' Sal's shoulders dropped. Strange that the idea of returning a pup to his home should bring so much upset. Maddoc shifted his weight again. If he could get in on the trip so he could see the beacon, maybe he'd have some real news to take home.

The woman cradled the pup, taking him into an adjoining room as Sal turned back to Maddoc.

'Now they're out of the room, I think we need that chat,' he said, baring his pointed teeth as he strode towards the red chair.

'Who are you, Tylwyth Teg, and why are you *really* on my ship?'

11

SLEEPLESS IN HAVEN

TELLIN

Gar's pulse was weak, his limp form cuddled as close to me as he could get. What had he been thinking? Oceans above, he'd been fortunate to be found. I dreaded to think what might have happened had Theo not escorted him back.

After the pain the fae-kin had caused Theo, I had to assume he hadn't recognised exactly what he had brought to *Barge*. I could hear him in the other room, telling Sal that he had just been investigating a disturbance. That he was only half Tylwyth Teg and no threat.

If he had dived into salt water for Gar, I believed that – at least until he proved otherwise. A failing of the famous Mynyw Pact was a problem.

Gar's breathing was steadying. Dry and safe, he would warm quickly. I gently checked him over, finding no other injuries, then tucked him under the covers to keep him warm.

Sal's cool tones carried clearly from the adjoining room. With Gar resting, it was time to add my own questions to the conversation. I strolled in and sat on the end of the bed. The Tylwyth Teg, who'd named himself Maddoc, remained in the interrogation chair. I begrudgingly admired him. He'd managed longer than I could in that foul thing.

'What do you know about a Tylwyth Teg who can summon spirits called Diana?' I cut in. Ria had been certain she was an Irrlicht, but I wasn't prepared to rule her out as an acquaintance of this Maddoc just yet.

The man's head turned abruptly in my direction. 'That name is unfamiliar. If she's using her powers to attack seafolk, then she's in breach of the Pact, and things are far more dire than we realised.'

'We?' I leaned forward, watching his face carefully.

Sal sat back. A calculating look crossed his face. 'You're the urchin-pricking guardian! Something's happening beneath your noses – the Pact is breaking in Mynyw, and you have no idea why? Whatever happened in Terrania, I've always believed this corner of the world would be safe because of it.'

'Not any more. The arrow has moved, and the flame is reduced.'

'Who's broken Pact with Lord Flame? Please tell me your kind hunt for the traitor.'

'Hunting, but so far failing. From what you tell me of the encounter your crew had ... I suspect you may have found our traitor yourself,' Maddoc said.

'Men in Terrania imprison Old Ones. Tylwyth Teg in the Territories attack a selkie unprovoked ...' Sal rolled his eyes. 'This is why I find it rather hard to trust your kind. Bargains and promises, entrapment and snares, but the most important snare – the one holding us all in its thrall, protecting us from each other – you've let go of the threads.'

'Are you so innocent?' Maddoc raised an eyebrow at Sal, and I shifted uncomfortably.

'I have killed men,' I responded. 'But only those who did harm, and not here. Nor am I bound by the Pact, being not born in its net.'

Maddoc sighed. 'Who are you to judge what level of harm deserves death?' He shook his head.

Had our actions contributed to this? None of the vengeance we carried out affected Mynyw, surely. No pact existed in Terrania – it was in part why they were so desperate and their land fading. I was certain of it. How do you convince a land in denial that they should talk terms with those they do not believe exist? The closest Terrania had to a pact was the tacit support of the Old Ones by sea-folk.

Maddoc's brow creased as he rose from the seat to pace the room. He stopped and gesticulated widely with palms upward, his arms spread in agitation. 'None of this explains the flame! Squabbles have always happened – small checks and balances. But they've never involved Lord Flame. This is much bigger.'

'Diana claimed that she was helping a human queen,' I probed gently. Sal sat forward, resting his elbows on his knees. Maddoc looked thoughtful.

'In my quiet town, I've heard no rumours of queens. The last monarch in the Territories died with the old borders centuries ago. Since then, there has been fragile peace and rule by the people, elected and fair. Human battles outside our borders are not usually our concern.'

'Maybe our interests align,' Sal offered. 'We've been sent to discover if there's truth to these rumours. A new king rules in Terrania. It's in the best interests of all Old Ones to keep him there.'

I watched the guardian, as Sal had called him. His blonde hair shimmered as he moved and stared out the window, deep in thought. I didn't think his face expressed the famed beauty of the Tylwyth Teg. Aside from his hair, I'd have walked past him ashore and thought nothing of him. His nose was slim and pointed, his eyes murky – maybe brown or grey. I didn't want to walk up and study him too much. Wrinkles creased the corners of his eyes, and his cheeks were spangled with freckles. He looked of an age with Theo, old for any Tylwyth Teg blood. I wondered idly what he'd done to get such a long, silver scar across his hand. His clothes were practical, aside from a feather charm, and he was barefoot, his shoes presumably dumped in his rescue of Gar.

That *was* something we could do to thank him. I hit the call button to bring Seren. She'd want to know Gar was back, and I had no doubt that Maddoc would be wearing the finest boots she could conjure up very soon.

'I believe our interests may align,' Maddoc said finally. 'I need to see the beacon on the selkie isle before returning to the Black Mountain. The pack would not allow me access. Can you arrange that?'

'I cannot speak for them. It was once my home, but I've been away so long I've no way to know how they'll receive me,' Sal replied.

'You saved Gar,' I cut in. 'We can ask. For now, rest. Gar needs at least a night's sleep and food before he's well enough to travel.'

'One night,' Maddoc replied.

Sal closed on Maddoc, and I could feel the prickle in the air of selkie magic. A faint blue glow outlined him. 'We will leave when we are ready, and not a day earlier,' he growled. 'I'm not risking Gar before he's ready. I'm not losing him after all he has been through. You said forty days. One or two more makes no difference.'

I'd only seen Sal so fierce when we rescued Gar in the first place ... when I had told him. Oceans, even I wouldn't argue with him in such a state.

Maddoc appeared to reach the same decision. 'When you're ready,' he replied. His hand twitched, his fist clenched with tension. I'd never seen Sal use his power for anything other than illusion, but the way he crackled in that moment, I wouldn't have been surprised if he found a way to use it.

'I've called Seren,' I said, trying to ease the tension. 'Maddoc needs new footwear and rest. Gar needs peace and quiet.'

Maddoc dropped back into the lumpy chair. 'I'll wait quietly until you're ready to leave.'

It was diplomatic and probably sensible, given Sal's mood. Seren knocked, then let herself in – that was new. I was pleased to see it.

'He's in the other room.' Sal gestured through to where Gar rested. Seren didn't spare us a glance, running past to see the child. Gentle murmuring flowed around the corner, and I tried not to listen. Seren may have prayed to gods or the ocean herself. But it was not my place to listen in on her thanks to whoever she needed to give them out to.

We remained silent, kelp fronds pulled towards the open ocean by an outgoing tide, where circumstance and some want-to-be queen had pulled us as one. My head spun with thoughts as loud as a storm.

Seren returned to the room eventually, looking from face to face as we sat in silence. Sal's power slightly diminished by time, but to my senses, entirely present. As the moment passed, I wondered how he'd planned to use it. I sympathised with the need to hold the magic close, recalling my attempted escape from Icidro's and that same feeling of security I sought. I think I had just expected Sal's control to be so much more than my own. He was not going to deal with Gar's return to the pack very well.

'I was told that a stranger brought Gar back to us.' Seren

stared at Maddoc. 'Thank you.' She looked him over, then leaned forward, peering into his eyes as though inspecting an animal. 'Sal, introduce me, please.'

'Seren, this is Maddoc. He returned Gar, who tried to go for a swim alone and hadn't fastened his skin properly. Maddoc found him, Theo recognised him, and they brought him to *Barge*. Maddoc lost his boots in the rescue and will be staying with us for a couple of days before we take Gar to the island. He has asked to accompany us. Once that is done, I anticipate that he will leave.'

Sal's lack of polished manners, his tone, and his face all hinted at the tension running through the room, but Seren didn't raise an eyebrow in question.

She looked at Maddoc's feet and nodded. 'I'll see what we can do about new footwear, and I'll set you up in a room for some rest. Please respect the rules of our vessel. No fighting, and respect for all residents.' Without waiting for a response, she hustled the Tylwyth Teg out of the room.

'Shouldn't you have told her?' I asked. Knowing full well that Seren would be fuming later on if – when – she found out what was really going on.

'I will, eventually. As wonderful as Seren is, I need her to focus on the information coming in without the worry of a Tylwyth Teg on board. He can't do a lot right now anyway, and if he wants to get home, he'll need to save what he has.'

It was fair, I supposed. 'If he's stupid, I'll just chuck him overboard.'

'He won't be. I'll ask Driftwood to keep watch. Send one of them up to me when you leave.'

His eyes drifted to the other room and our sleeping charge. It was time to leave them both to rest, and I decided I should probably do the same. I hoped Zora and Ria had heard the news. None of us had slept, and I doubted any of Driftwood had either.

I wandered the short distance to my room, pausing as ever at the painting of my home. 'Soon,' I whispered to the beach. 'I'll be back soon.' I ran my hand along the frame and turned towards my rooms to await Zora and Ria.

12

THE FOREST OF MEMORIES

MADDOC

The door closed, leaving him alone. Quiet voices chatted outside. While it was too solid to hear the details, he was certain he was the topic of conversation. In Sal's shoes, would he have posted a guard? Probably not, but maybe he was just more trusting; that selkie really didn't like Tylwyth Teg. The way he talked about betrayals and broken promises made his heart sink. There were certainly groups of Tylwyth Teg who pushed the Pact to its limits, ones that the old woman and Sal had clearly had dealings with.

Rest, the selkies had said. They might have been up all night, but he was well-rested. Maddoc fingered his necklace. He wanted to head back and needed to check on his yew, but without the details of the island beacon, he'd be deemed to have failed. And, after the display his mother had put on, even he might not be safe from her mood.

Maddoc paced the room, caged and frustrated. It had simple furnishings, but everything was beautifully made. A soft, blue blanket draped over the bed, and Maddoc sat on it as he took in his surroundings. The flooring was made of some hard, shiny material he didn't recognise and warmed with strategically placed rugs. A small window gave him a view over the estuary. Light flooded the space from gently glowing sections of the ceiling, and warm air caressed him. Not the simple warmth of four solid walls, but artificially warm – as though *Barge* retained the heat of Terrania inside her. He searched the room, following the flow of air back to its source, a gentle jet of warm air above a wardrobe.

The power needed to maintain the ship in such luxury was almost beyond his comprehension. It would make a prize worth fighting for by any standards.

The people he'd seen so far on *Barge* were well-fed, well-dressed, and confident. Not one looked as though they'd struggled for anything in a long time. Life was clearly easier in Terrania than Mynyw.

Sal would soon find that supplying a vessel so large was going to be a challenge in Mynyw. Though he had no doubt the locals would be well paid in coin, money would not fill their bellies or maintain the trade route with the communities hanging by their fingernails to the southern coast of the Territories. If those places received less food, the ensuing migration would be inevitable.

The more he considered it, the more he realised that, by their very presence, Lord Sal and his *Barge* might drive hungry people directly into the arms of a seemingly beneficent queen – if she existed.

Maddoc opened the door. A woman looked up at him from where she sat against the opposite wall. She cracked a half-smile. 'Hi. I hear you found our boy. Thank you. Sorry I have to sit guard. It seems like poor thanks.' The shadows beneath her eyes suggested she'd little opportunity to rest.

'Lord Sal has his reasons, I'm sure.'

She nodded. 'I'm sure he does. Did you want something?'

'I am rather hungry. Can I get something to eat?'

She pushed herself up from the floor, stifling a yawn. 'I could use some food myself. Come on. I'll take you to The Forest. It's not that far from here.'

They continued down the corridor towards the bow of the ship. The decor became more and more muted as they walked. Warmth and light still flooded the space, although the carpeted floor gave way to polished boards of the same material that was in his room. Sparkling reflections glinted underfoot. Then, for no reason that Maddoc could tell, they stopped.

'Sorry again,' she said. 'I can't let you see how to proceed beyond this point. We can't have you returning uninvited later.' She unwrapped a scarf and pointed at his eyes. 'I know it might seem overly cautious, but ...'

Earning her trust was worth a little inconvenience and the information he would gain from whatever lay beyond was worth it, Maddoc decided. He reached for the scarf. 'Everyone is entitled to their secrets,' he replied.

The fabric was soft and flowed over his fingers. It reminded him of one of his mother's dresses. Maddoc tied it around his head. He could see darkness or light, but little detail. What was he doing? In the belly of a ship, run by selkies – and he knew there was more magic somewhere. He'd felt it on that other boat. Were the crew of that vessel on *Barge*?

What kind of people worked for a selkie? Did they know what he was? What both of them were? Blinded and totally reliant on his guide, Maddoc allowed her to pull him forward. He tried to remember the way, to count the steps he took, but as they passed through a door into a smaller passage, the light dimmed, and he stumbled on a sill. The floor sounded dull, and his footing was less steady. His guide stopped him frequently, telling him to step higher over some obstruction. Or to turn him through some narrow space. Then, they were back into lightness again.

'Ocean's above, Ivy, you look about as good as a dried anemone!' someone laughed.

'You're no angel fish yourself,' his guide retorted as she started to untie his scarf.

Maddoc's vision cleared when the scarf rippled away from him. Ivy didn't wait for a reply, but was already walking across a wood-panelled space filled with comfortable-looking red seats, much like the one up in Lord Sal's room. A variety of individuals lounged in the chairs. Some studied him openly, while others chose to ignore his presence. They all appeared relaxed. He wove between the tables, narrowly missing crashing into one with his thigh. No pictures hung on the walls, but they were covered with engraved scenes of the ocean, of creatures of lore and legend. Some were incredibly intricate, the hand and art of a master, while others were far rougher, a mark made by someone with less skill but equal passion.

Ivy returned with two plates of pastries and gestured for him to sit at the nearest table. She followed his gaze as he studied a rough carving on the wall next to him. It appeared to be a woman, her hands raised and a huge circle hovering above her head. It was roughly chiselled, and he could not work out what was inside the circle. If he hadn't known better, he'd have thought it was someone performing a magical act. The image didn't yet have the polished finish of the others.

'That one's still in progress,' Ivy said through a mouthful. 'It's Oak's carving. Every image you see was created by one of us. A record of our service aboard. We pick a moment that we feel defines us or our contribution. This is Oak's.'

'What happened?' Maddoc ran his finger over the rough carving, feeling the circle and trying to make out the shape in the background. It was odd how some things transcended species. The carvings etched into the room's walls reminded him very much of the drawings in the flame-beacon cave down in his mother's domain. The people around him were guardians of some sort in their own way. People who felt the ship, *Barge*, was a place of such permanence in their society that they recorded their lives on her very walls. Ivy gave him a lopsided grin and pointed to a smaller figure on the roof.

'You wouldn't believe the details. Not everyone in Sal's crews is quite as they appear.' She said, as one of the others winked at her. 'The short and long of it is that we rescued some people. Eat up. I can't have you out of your room for too long. If Seren comes back, she'll have my skin as sewing fabric!'

They ate the rest of their food without chatter. Aside from the carved walls, the rest of the room was simple. Everything was well made – solid furniture, all fastened to the floor. It wasn't that the space was less rich than the areas of *Barge* he'd initially seen as much as it was less gaudy. The people had what they needed and no more. It was practical and cosy. Maddoc preferred it to the ostentatious parts of *Barge*; it was lived in, used, and loved. At the far end of the room was another exit.

'Where does that go?' Maddoc asked, not really expecting an answer. After all, he had been blindfolded before.

'To the resident's decks and homes. Where we can close out the excesses of the public side of *Barge* and just relax.'

'Don't the customers find you?'

'No. Lord Sal is very strict about that. Anyone who wants

to get to the rest of the ship has to pass through here, another guard room, or an outside deck. We'd know.' A veiled hint that he wouldn't get back down. He gulped down the last of his food and picked up the scarf.

'Then, should we get back?' he offered. Ivy nodded.

She had stood to tie it around him when noise and laughter preceded the entrance of two women. The first through the door was tall and strong, her muscled arms exposed by a red vest top. A crown of tight, night-black curls framed her dark-skinned face, and she positively hummed with power. Following behind was a petite, slightly built woman. Her own brown hair hung in loose waves below her shoulder. Her eyes were what drew him, though. Deep and endless pools of something ... was it time? It was her power he'd felt through the boat. Her strength eclipsed anything he had ever met, including his mother. She carried it lightly, relaxed and chatting merrily until she saw him.

'Who's this, Ivy?' she asked, approaching him as though he was the wild magic in the room, not herself.

Her eyes passed over him, and he shuddered. Despite himself, he felt judged – the Guardian, under study. He offered his hand to her. Not everyone was what they seemed, indeed! The others in the room ignored the diminutive woman, their attention instead drawn to her companion. Charisma dripped from the black woman, and yet, he felt certain that the most dangerous being in the room stood an arm's reach from him. He swallowed his fear and inclined his head in greeting.

'I'm Maddoc. I found a missing child on a beach in a precarious situation.' Maddoc was sure the women knew what Sal and the boy were, but careful to couch his words in double-talk, he carried on. 'His clothes weren't closed up properly, and he was dangerously cold. I returned him to Lord

Sal, and in return, I'm recovering here for a few days before I return to my work.'

She took his hand as her eyes softened and resolved into something more intimate, more human. 'Thank you. That child means a lot to many, many folk. Tell me, Maddoc, what is this work of yours?'

Maddoc's knees shook as the jolt of contact with her rang through him. He tried to hide it. As much as those people might think they knew what was aboard their ship, he was certain they had no idea what the creature was. A soul-taker. She was much like his mother. A different origin, maybe, a distant part of the world, but the power she held, the ability to take life with a mere touch, was humbling.

'Mostly, I take care of an old tree in a churchyard,' he replied, trying to make it sound casual. Sal had known of him – did she?

The woman quirked a small smile, and an almost-laugh escaped. 'That would appear to be a very easy job. Surely an ancient tree will not travel far or need much care.'

'You'd usually be right,' Maddoc replied, withdrawing his hand from the clasp. With both women staring at him now, the urge to return to the quiet of his cabin grew stronger. 'It was nice to meet you. Ivy, you wanted to get me back before Seren returned?'

Ivy nodded and tied the scarf over his eyes.

'Oceans above, Ivy, if you're having to hide the way in and out of the guard room, should you really have brought him?' the other woman muttered. 'We're headed to meet up with Georgie, so we'll help you get him back to his room. When did you last sleep? No, actually, don't tell me. I'll return him. You go and rest up. One of us can keep an eye on him while the other briefs Georgie.'

'But Seren said—'

'I'll deal with Seren.' The woman's voice carried command and clearly accepted no argument. Within moments, Maddoc was being guided by the newcomers, blindfolded at their mercy.

Barely had the air from the closing door brushed past him when the smaller woman leant in close. 'I'm certain Sal has reasons to allow a Tylwyth Teg aboard *Barge* after recent events, but the good folk of Driftwood, despite their bravery, have nothing at their disposal to hold you in place. Let's return to your room, shall we.'

He was half dragged through the passageway. The Diana creature had certainly made an impression on these people. Maddoc had a feeling he'd have to do more than rescue a selkie pup to win their trust.

When they finally removed his blindfold, he was not in the same passageway where he had covered his eyes previously.

With one woman on either side, he found himself walking down a familiar passage toward his room from the same direction as he'd originally walked with Seren. They stopped at his door, and the soul-taker took a key from her pocket, opening it up and gesturing him in. 'I'll stay with you. I think we could do with a chat while Zora is busy.'

'I'll leave you to it. I won't be long.' Zora strode off without a backward glance.

'Shall we start with proper introductions? My name is Rialta. I'm a spirit-taker. And, thanks to some irritating Irrlicht, I'm overburdened and rather irate right now. Don't try to hide anything from me. I'm not in the mood for your trickery.'

She slumped onto the nearest chair and gestured for him to sit.

Maddoc declined, his frustration simmering to the surface. 'I've already explained everything to your Lord Sal. I'm only half Tylwyth Teg, and I'm the Guardian of the Tree. Diana is a rogue from somewhere else, and I want to know who she is and what she is up to just as much as you do. I was sent here to investigate the failing Pact, found a half-drowned selkie pup, and now I'm stuck here until I have regained enough power to travel again.' Maddoc remained standing and kept eye contact with her until she broke it. Rialta moved her hands as if to get up, then changed her mind.

'Are you sure you won't sit?' she asked. Maddoc shook his head. He felt inside himself to see if there were any reserves. Not much after the morning, but he could get most of the way home by the evening if he had the opportunity. Rialta, however, did appear exhausted. Whatever the event had been with the creature calling herself Diana, it had taken a significant toll on her.

'Why are you here?' he asked as the silence stretched out.

'Honestly? I don't know.' The chuckle that followed surprised him as much as the admission. 'Georgie and Zora freed me from a pretty rough situation, so I stayed with them. What they're doing is big, more important than my personal ambitions. I suppose I thought I might be useful, might be able to contribute too.'

'More important than catching loose spirits – the very reason you exist?' Maddoc couldn't hide his surprise.

'You all have it safe here in Mynyw. Your Pact made these lands a haven. Your country remains fertile in the rain-shadow, and humans are so few that they cause little trouble. They respect their land as much as you do. In Terrania, it's all gone to pieces. The guardians are being taken, collected for some stupid human ideology of status, and these people?' She gestured around the room. 'Sal and his daughter, Georgie and her crew – they're trying to right the balance. To return the lost and captured. They killed a bloody king! There's a good man in his place now, but someone is gathering under a false flag here, seeding rumours of war and conquering – of taking Terrania in their name. King Anard asked us to investigate, and where *Black Hind* goes, I go. For now.'

'Lord Sal mentioned this army too. I cannot believe that an army could gather in Mynyw, and my family has heard nothing.'

'Then maybe it's time your people came out of their seclusion and roamed the world in earnest.' Rialta snapped. 'Help or be caught. Help us, or watch your precious Mynyw go the way of Terrania. This floating city may appear grand, but the people of the land suffer badly.'

Maddoc wandered to the window, looking over the green coast at the small boats that began to flood towards *Barge*. It had hurt to feel that the small island was leaving Mynyw. The idea of the whole land being broken up made bile rise in his throat. Not on his watch would the Pact fail. If the twisted Tylwyth Teg was somehow involved, or Irrlicht as Rialta appeared to believe she was, then the soul-taker was right. It was past time for his mam to do more than watch. He'd visit the selkie island, try and gain what information he could, then head back to the Black Mountain.

'I'll help, even if others of my kind won't. I give you my word,' he replied. A gentle snore drifted from Rialta's mouth in response. Gods, she really must have fought hard. Maddoc considered trying to wrest the key from her and head back out into the main part of *Barge*. He couldn't rule out the fact that the people aboard were involved, that they themselves had also broken the Pact. Could it all be an elaborate ruse?

He gently padded across the room, bare feet silent on the smooth floor. As he reached into the first pocket, someone knocked at the door. He leapt back as Rialta snapped her eyes open. His heart pounded as she stared at him, her head slightly tilted.

She sighed deeply and shook her head. 'I should have let someone else do this. Turns out all I needed was a comfy chair to make me a useless guard,' she muttered. 'Thank you for not running off.' She knew what he had been trying, he was certain.

'I have shoes to deliver for Maddoc,' a male voice called. The handle rattled as the speaker attempted to open the door. Rialta pushed herself to her feet, and, swaying with exhaustion, unlocked it.

'Rupal, thank you.' She reached out to take something. 'Do you need to check the fit?'

'No need. They lace up.' Rupal's accent was strong, almost unintelligible to Maddoc's ears, and he struggled to understand the quick conversation that followed. Rialta ended with a laugh and closed the door, once again locking it.

'No more barefoot sneaking around for you,' she joked as she passed the bag over.

Maddoc took out the soft leather boots. They were beautifully made but wouldn't last two minutes up on the mountain. He'd still need to retrieve his old shoes from the beach somehow, if the tide hadn't taken them already.

He sat on the bed to pull them on, watching Rialta from the corner of his eye. She didn't sit back down again.

'You said that you'd know if there were armies building in Mynyw,' she stated.

'Mhm,' Maddoc replied as he tied the laces.

'But what if those armies were massing off the coast somewhere? Like flotillas in Terrania?'

'In Terrania, your seas are flat. Here, the west winds pound the coast, sending any resemblance of a flotilla crashing to shore multiple times through the winter. It simply couldn't happen.' Maddoc dismissed the idea, even as the old woman's words came to mind. Ships vanishing north – never to return, strangers in the markets. Maybe there was more to Rialta's idea than she realised. A niggling familiarity began to wriggle in his mind, an idea, a memory ... someone telling him a story as a child. He reached for it, but the details were lost, just out of reach. He needed to get home, and soon.

13

HOMEWARD BOUND

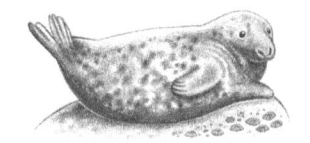

TELLIN

'I see them!' Sal called from his position up in the rigging. 'Swing our bow more to starboard.'

Theo edged *Black Hind*'s huge rudder round as Zora tweaked the sails, and we nosed towards the selkie islands.

'I swear he's lived on *Barge* with its cell engine for so long that sometimes he forgets about the relationship between wind direction and sails,' Theo chuckled. 'We'll have to tack our way closer.'

Sal's excitement was palpable, and the small seal pup snuggled against me for comfort began to wiggle. I could understand it. I'd be returning home soon, too, and Sal's home was our destination. The pack we sought was his blood family.

Sal had been away for a long time, and we knew from Gar that his name had almost faded to memory – a local legend. I hoped, for his sake, that returning Gar to their home was an opportunity for reunion.

In the privacy of Sal's chambers, I'd seen his true apprehension. Would they accept him? Would he be welcome? After all, Sal had changed. He, like myself, was far from the calm serenity of most selkies, no longer content with a passive life ruled by the will of the ocean. He was utterly convinced they would reject him. I hoped not. On our previous meeting, the pack had been approachable – supportive even.

Eryn's silver skin was stored in the inner loc-box on *Barge*, and that's where it would stay. I would not swim with this pack. Sal had his, though, and I hoped he'd have the opportunity to use it. It was stowed safely in the hold, through a locked door, and away from the reach of Maddoc.

We'd spent hours debating the best course of action for how we should return Gar without scaring them. How we introduce Maddoc to them and ask for his access to the beacon. Finally, we settled on simple truth – for without his actions, Gar would not be returning, regardless of what had gone before.

It was typical Territories weather. Thin, grey clouds skimmed above, while slices of blue sky allowed lancing sunlight to strike the sea, leaving glimmering water trails that faded as suddenly as they appeared. Waves lapped the ancient rocks hungrily, casting white spray up the cliffs, and the plump white bellies of razorbills passed us, skimming the water.

'I remember that rock, Tellin,' Gar yapped, waving a flipper at a large outcrop.

'We'll have you home soon,' I assured him. The rocks were certainly memorable, etched in my mind from our previous visit to the Territories. Dusty red cliffs rose from the choppy grey sea, their vertical scars and folds a proud badge of their endurance. Porpoises played in our bow waves, but the seals and selkies remained elusive.

We approached the island slowly as Sal slipped and slithered his way down the mast.

'There's a jetty on the far side – or at least there was,' he said, gesturing around the headland to the north of the island. Beyond it was another island, and further out to sea, another. 'Soon, the gannets will return,' Sal said, gazing towards the far island as we rounded the headland.

We turned our bow into the bay, where an old post protruded defiantly from the water, the last vestige of a sea-eaten jetty. 'It's been a long time,' Sal muttered, scanning around him. 'There's the old landing steps, I suppose, but they won't be very friendly to *Black Hind* under sail.'

'That won't be necessary,' a voice called in Ocean from the water. 'Sal Deepwater, I may not recognise your face any longer, but I know that voice. I recall your scent. You left us for good. "To find better things amongst humans," you said. Why do you come slipping back into our waters now?' The tone carried the pain of hurt and abandonment. Spoken through the emotional language of Ocean, it was threaded with bitterness.

Sal, Lord of the Terranian Sea, owner of *Barge* and the biggest information network in existence, bowed his head towards the female selkie swimming alongside us.

'Stop the boat, please, Theo,' he murmured.

'Again, with the lack of sail knowledge,' Theo murmured as he loosed the main sail, letting the foil flex freely, and turned our bow into the wind.

'Aunt,' Sal replied. 'I found one of our pack in trouble. I came home to return him. I ask no favours, and I claim no ties unless you give them to me.' He looked over his shoulder and nodded. I gently lifted Gar in my arms and carried him within sight of the selkie.

I felt her cry – her anguish and joy; her hurt and her pain. It ran through me like a tidal wave.

'Gar? Is that really you?'

At her cry, other heads emerged from the water, a full pack of selkies to support their matriarch. Youngsters bobbed near the fringe of the group, and as I placed Gar on the deck, a familiar voice rang out. The young female I'd met on my last visit pushed her way through the pack to look up at us. Her eyes met mine, and recognition flashed between us.

'I thought I recognised that boat! You were here in one of the autumn storms then you just vanished. You did it! You found my brother. Thank you.'

Gar wriggled forward to look down at his big sister.

'Ijna! I was really scared, but Tellin found me! And Sal helped rescue me. And I swam in a lake. And then I walked on land! I've been living on the biggest ship you've ever seen with Sal and Seren. She's kind of Sal's mate – but they won't admit it, like you and—'

'I'm so pleased you are safe. Come, swim with us!' Ijna interrupted him quickly.

Gar looked up at Sal with wide eyes and twitching whiskers. 'Can I?'

'That's why we're here,' Sal replied, crouching alongside him, a smile across his face though hurt threaded through his tone. He adored the boy, and we both knew this was the right thing. But Oceans, I'd miss him too.

Gar looked at the drop, and I saw his flipper tremble. Sal hesitated; I didn't. I stripped my clothes off, picked Gar up, held him tightly to my chest, and jumped overboard, protecting him from the water's impact with my own body.

He wriggled out of my arms, letting out squeals of joy at reuniting with his sister. The pack parted to let them play, and the matriarch swam right up to me. She looked at me with her big round eyes, nosing closer as she scented me.

'You are Tellin?'

'I am. I'm sorry he has been belegged. I promise we fulfilled the ceremony as thoroughly as we could. It was to protect him as his captors hunted for a seal.'

'No selkie takes the moment lightly. While his blood family was unable to guide his footsteps, I thank you for stepping in.'

'Sal—'

'Is no longer our family, as he stated himself when he left.' I didn't dare turn around. I couldn't bear to see Sal's face. He'd been so desperate, so determined to save his own blood, despite knowing the pain it would bring. He had hoped ... It was on me to try and mend what I could. Sal had given me so much.

'I could have done none of it without Sal. He took the vow of guidance, and he risked his own life to retrieve Gar. All he does is try to right the wrongs mankind is doing by hiding under their very noses. He may have left for one reason, but the selkie you see before you now does more good for the Old Ones of this world than any of you can possibly imagine. Even now, he is here to aid with the damage to the Pact of Mynyw.'

It wasn't exactly true, but I had no doubt our path and that of Maddoc were entwined. The army was linked to the bigger issue.

A big bull seal pushed through. His powerful head and mottled features reminded me of Sal in his skin. 'What do you know of the Pact?' he asked, his voice pitched low enough that it barely reached me.

'I know that it is failing. I have aboard my vessel, the Guardian. He needs to check your beacon, then return to his own kind to help us formulate a plan. Something is very wrong across Mynyw.'

'Why would he need to see it?'

'To see how damaged it is, to report truth.'

'Hrm.' We bobbed in the water, facing each other for a while. 'Sal ... Does he really help others now?' he asked eventually.

'He freed me from captivity, he freed Gar. He rescued a leathergill siren, a white hind, and was responsible for ending rare creature collecting in Terrania. He has guarded Gar constantly.' I hesitated, but we needed both Sal reunited and Maddoc on the island. 'He guarded him until last night.' I finished.

'Why would he stop?'

'He didn't!' Gar chipped in. I sighed in relief. 'I wanted to get here, and didn't know how far it was. I went for a swim off the back of *Barge* while Sal thought I was asleep. My skin caught on something. I'm not good at putting it on properly without help yet. Then I don't remember much, except I was cold and I found a cave. A magical-tasting man rescued me, brought me back home to Sal and his ship. I need to say thank you to him. Can he look at the wave? Please?'

The selkie Sal had called aunt winced as Gar called *Barge* home. I couldn't help but think that having a selkie accustomed to life amongst humans as part of the pack might be good for the reticent group.

'We need to discuss this. You may tie up on the mooring post while we decide what action to take. Do not go ashore until we return.'

'Agreed.' I climbed up the rope ladder Theo threw down for me, retrieved my clothes from Zora, and relayed our conversation for them, interpreting the context of the words from Ocean as best I could. Sal remained at the rail, gazing down on the pack. Listening no doubt for a sign that they would welcome him.

Ria watched the stern for pups, and Theo gently guided us to the post, where Zora tied us off, dropping a fender against the rocks to the rear of *Black Hind*. All we could do was wait.

They deliberated for a while. Long enough that Ria started muttering about food and Maddoc began to pace the cabin. I joined Sal at the rail, gently resting my hand on his. An incredibly intimate gesture for us. But he needed to know I was there – I was his pack, no matter what the group decided. We waited and watched the clouds break up. A distant sea mist rose, and the scent of the island drifted towards us on the wind. Despite the earliness of the year and the chill weather, there was a floral smell, herbal and fragrant.

'Know that scent, but I can't place it,' Maddoc muttered.

I squeezed Sal's hand and turned to lean on the rail instead. Maddoc was halfway out the cabin, staring towards the island. 'It's as though it were a scent from a dream of my childhood. It's familiar, and yet entirely not. Do you recognise it?'

'No. It's pleasant, though,' I replied. 'Are you sure you want to be up here?'

'I need to move fast if they say yes before they change their mind again.'

'We aren't Tylwyth Teg. No trickery lies in these waters, Maddoc.' Sal's response lacked his usual charisma. Even out of Ocean, his words usually carried power. Right then, he sounded like a mere human. My heart drowned for him.

The bull returned to us, and the tides were not fully in Sal's favour. 'The selkies on the boat, Sal and Tellin, may go ashore to accompany the Tylwyth Teg. You must remain in belegged form at all times.'

It wasn't outright rejection, yet Sal would not swim with his pack that day. I wouldn't let him wallow in sorrow. Somehow we'd win their trust and heal his freshly opened wound – one that only now exposed its raw edges for others to see.

I clambered over the side, hopping from rock to rock as I ascended the path. Sal's light steps followed, his feet as bare as my own and seeking connection with his home. Behind him came the splashes of Maddoc's boots as he tailed us up the path. Rupal's care and finesse would make those boots waterproof – at least, I hoped so. If time truly was of the essence, Maddoc needed to stay out of contact with the water.

It took a while to scramble up the long-unused route. The steps were gilded with lichen and framed in moss. Each slab, hewn from the grey limestone of the mainland, sat out of place amongst the red rock; a relic from when mankind dominated everywhere.

At the top, the view opened up. All the islands in the group seen from above were both as alike and varied as siblings. The half-white outline of the furthest isle gave away the avian presence that dominated there.

We were met by a woman with long, dark hair. She stepped forward with both palms open in selkie greeting toward me. Then, to my surprise, she ran directly past, throwing her arms around Sal.

'My pup, my boy. I thought you lost to me forever.'

'Ma.' Sal's voice broke, and I gestured for Maddoc to follow me. I had no idea where the beacon was, but that was a family reunion I had no part in.

Maddoc joined me, and we strolled to the crest of the island, its gently domed rise giving us an unparalleled view of the horizon. On the top of the hill grew a patch of flowers that looked entirely out of place. They bloomed despite the time of year, and that same heady fragrance that had caught my attention on *Black Hind* was seeping out from under my feet as I walked.

Maddoc froze. He dropped to his knees and ran his hand through the vegetation. Then, he got up to look around.

'What are you searching for?' I asked, checking to see if Sal was coming to join us.

'You see these flowers? Smell the scent from their crushed leaves. Can you find any more patches of them?'

I looked closely. The scent had been strong – surely there must be more than the one small patch. We searched for a while as I hunted out the small flowers. Maddoc let out a yell of triumph. 'I found more,' he said. Then more quietly, 'If there is more than one patch, then we stand on one of their islands.'

'What in all the oceans are you talking about?' Irritating Tylwyth Teg, taking in riddles and half ideas.

'I have a theory, a long-forgotten memory. I'll need to check when we are back on the mainland, but tell me, Georgie, how many islands do you see?'

I stood where he indicated and surveyed the horizon. To the south and west, I could count maybe three more, a small one to the east, and then further north, almost on the horizon, I thought I could make out a dark patch.

'Four, one, and some in the distance,' I replied.

Maddoc nodded slowly. 'That's what I'm seeing too. Which is rather interesting – given that I am certain those islands in the distance show on no map.'

'We've never reached them either,' Sal's mother said from closer than I expected. I tried not to show that she had startled me. 'But the vanishing islands are not why you're here. Let's go and see the wave.'

She led the way across to the far side of the island, where a rocky beach sat at the base of steep cliffs. 'It's in the blowhole,' she said, gesturing to a deep hole ahead of us.

I laid down on the ground, wriggling closer and closer to the edge as I peered down. Maddoc on the other flipper pulled a rippling cloak from his pocket, then draped it over his clothes and pulled the hood over his face. He grasped the feather charm in his hand and walked out onto the air, continuing downward in a spiral as I watched, slack-jawed.

'I thought he said he was only half Tylwyth Teg,' growled Sal. 'If he could fly this whole time, why did he need us?' We watched him until he reached the base. A standing wave of water rising from the sea next to him stood twice his height. 'It's certainly gotten smaller,' Sal said as he looked down. 'I'm sure I remember it almost reaching the top in a storm surge.'

'You remember right. It began to shrink months ago. It's still shrinking,' his mother replied.

'If the wave lies flat, the lie is told, and the land is lost,' Sal muttered, and she nodded slowly at his words.

'Truth indeed.'

'What does it mean?' I asked.

Sal shook his head. 'I don't know – it's just an old saying. I'd always thought it was about the rocks under the cliff edges, the hidden dangers of this coastline, and how they kept human ships away normally. Now, I'm not so sure.'

'It's more than that, but its origins are lost. As a wave-eroded cliff tumbles to the water, so does the meaning of folklore. Remaining in our families as tales for the wary and lessons for the unwise.' His mother almost sang the words.

Was it part of the puzzle? Or a separate thing entirely unrelated to our own mission? The way Maddoc had reacted to the islands in the north implied he knew more than he was letting on about the wave and the whole situation. I suspected the strands we un-wove were merely single kelp growing in a larger forest. And we'd have to swim through them all to find our truth amongst the fronds.

Sal's mum accompanied us to the steps, where she embraced Sal, extracting promises of his return and assuring him that she would try to work on the matriarch in our absence. 'She will let you back in if you want it, in time.'

Sal wouldn't wish to return to a life under the waves, but I knew he wanted the chance to return home, to swim in the sea caves and with Gar and his family. He needed to feel as though he belonged. I knew, because I needed that too. As much as *Barge* was his own empire, and the crew belonged to him heart and soul, some of that was without doubt due to his charisma and the constant leaking of selkie magic in his speech. Humans were drawn to him, and he did little to stop it. A pack – those not affected by his charms and wanting to be with him because he was theirs – would fill the recently exposed hole in his life.

We bade her farewell and carefully wound our way down the wet steps, where we were greeted by Gar and his sister. Most of the pack had returned to their basking spots and hunting, but Gar and Ijna played around and under *Black Hind*; a group of younger bull seals floated nearby, jostling each other playfully. They watched us with open curiosity. Gar would be safe amongst his blood family. His small head bobbed in the water as I descended to *Black Hind*. Gar splashed me playfully with a flipper before ducking under the waves and resurfacing near Sal to repeat the play.

'Are you heading back home?' he called to us. *Home* ...

'We'll return to *Barge* and try to fix what Prince Anard asked of us, yes,' I replied.

'I'll come to see you before we leave Mynyw, Gar.' Sal crouched at the water's edge, stroking the pup's head. 'This isn't goodbye.' Ijna swam up next to Gar to nuzzle him.

'I won't let him out of my sight, Tellin, I promise.'

I managed a smile and mustered the enthusiasm for a

cheery wave as I hopped from the steps into *Black Hind*, followed closely by Maddoc. Sal boarded last, glancing back at Gar. 'It's the right thing to do,' he muttered.

'That doesn't make it hurt less. Come on. We have an army to find, a war to stop, and apparently, a Pact to fix.'

He frowned at the last. 'When did we take on Tylwyth Teg business?'

'When I decided that I think they're all linked. While Mynyw is unstable, it's a tempting target for those of Icidro's ilk.'

Ria started to haul up the anchor, and Zora gently coaxed a few small waves to push us away from the steps. Theo fired up the engine, then we hummed out of the bay, leaving a small selkie pup where he belonged – with his family.

14

CHEESE ABOARD

MADDOC

The islands had gone again. No matter how he squinted at the horizon, Maddoc couldn't see them. Were they too low now, or was it something else? That uncomfortable familiarity grew again – the feeling that he was missing something. Maddoc ignored *Black Hind's* crew as they scurried about him doing boat related tasks. He sat in the most-out-the-way spot that he could on the busy deck and allowed his mind to wander.

He could go home and ask his mam, but Maddoc felt in his gut that the islands were a puzzle he'd be expected to know the answer to – or maybe one that she wouldn't part with the answer too easily. He rubbed his eyes and found himself pacing, his frustration finding an outlet, even there. No yew tree to sit in and calm his thoughts. No cheese sandwich to ruminate over. Maddoc looked back to the distance again, the itch at the back of his mind frustratingly unreachable.

The closer they got to the mouth of the estuary and the

further from the islands, the less the sensation of familiarity with them became. Their importance was fading, the urgency to seek them receding like the horizon into a rolling cloud of mist. If he directed his mind through it – focused on the idea – he could retain the thought of them. But as soon as he let it drift, so did the urgency.

Boats passed them on their way between the towering headlands. He watched one absently. It was crewed by a few small figures; they dropped pots, not in quite the same area as the old woman had taken him. The old woman who had talked about others like him, mer-folk, and the traders going elsewhere.

He hadn't heard of mer-folk in that region before. She'd named them something, but try as he might, the name eluded him. At first, he'd supposed she meant the Tylwyth Teg when she talked about bargains before they visited the islands. But the itch told him there was something – someone – else out there.

Black Hind rounded the heads, passing under the small hut where he'd sheltered and towards *Barge*. Under his breath, he kept a chant going – *find the islands, find the islands*. And, as the small boat pulled alongside and they transferred to *Barge*, he kept it up. Rialta sat alongside him.

'What are you saying?' she asked.

'Find the islands,' he said, slightly louder. 'Don't let me forget it. They are slipping from my grasp, and I don't know why. It's as though they want to remain hidden.'

'It means nothing to me. Will it affect our task?'

'It might,' Maddoc conceded.

'Then we must find these islands.' Rialta looked at him as though she saw into his core, into his soul. She could take his spirit if she wanted to. Rialta scared him, but if she chose to be on his side, he'd gladly accept her help. He wondered if she could navigate the Path with him, if her magic would be compatible.

It was getting harder to recall what was so urgent. He began to panic and glanced at Rialta. She smiled. 'We need to find the islands. It's okay – I remember. Tell me about them.'

They reached *Barge*, and the crew disembarked. It was only then that Maddoc realised Theo hadn't joined them. Rialta said something quietly to Georgie – Tellin? Her name kept changing. The selkies and Zora continued on past, into the body of *Barge*.

The couple he'd seen on his first visit sat on the far side again. They watched him but got no closer. Rialta gestured for Maddoc to sit.

'Tell me all you can about these islands. Then, we'll go in and write it down for you to remember.'

'No, we don't write it down.' Maddoc wasn't sure why that felt like the right decision. It just did.

'Fine. I will try and hold the descriptions for you. I saw no islands. No magic affects my thoughts, so you will just be telling me a story. I can remember a story.'

It was worth a try. Maddoc was certain he needed to get to the bottom of it. 'The islands are north of the selkie islands. I saw them on the far horizon. They were clearest and their pull strongest when I stood amongst the fragrant herbs on the selkie island. When we got back into *Black Hind*, I couldn't see them anymore, nor could Georgie.'

'Did the others see them from the selkie island?'

Maddoc searched his thoughts. Sifting through them grew harder by the moment. 'The selkies who live there said that they can never reach them.'

'Is that everything?'

Maddoc sighed. He may as well throw every thought in here as he went. 'An old woman who lives near here told me that there had been sightings of mer-people – I think – and that strange folk had been seen at market, driving the prices up.'

'That could be our army?'

'It could. It might be nothing, or it could be a piece of the mystery.'

Rialta nodded. Maddoc felt relieved that whatever it was, whatever mystery they had discussed, he had someone to help him with it. He had to get home to his mam about the wave. There was a Pact that needed fixing.

'Why don't you eat before you go?' Rialta said. 'Then we can look at investigating your islands.'

His islands? Maddoc tried to shake the fog in his brain, but it wouldn't shift. Still, food sounded good. Rialta led him up the stairs to the opulent top decks, where local accents sang out in excitement as visitors sampled *Barge's* delights. She took him to the blue fabric tents. Maybe in the Terranian sea, it was a cool shelter from the sun, but in Mynyw, they flapped and strained at their tethers, each thin flap seeking the freedom to float on the winds.

Exotic foods were laid out on a long table, their scent filling the tent. The structure may not have been altered for the weather, but the food certainly had. Warming soups filled with exotic spices, and fruity meat dishes, rich with mouth-watering spices were arrayed on tables. A goblet of hot, spiced wine was offered to him, and he took it gratefully.

'Eat. I'll be back soon. If you need anything, Pine will look after you.' She gestured towards a stocky man. He sat in a huge mound of cushions, looking to all the world like a guest enjoying his visit. But his eyes never stayed still, constantly searching the space. Rialta waved at him, and he gave her a half-smile, raising his glass in response. Maddoc had no doubt that he would be under surveillance as much there as he had been everywhere else on *Barge*.

'I'll be back for you soon,' Rialta said. 'I just need to go and catch up with Georgie and Lord Sal.'

Maddoc sipped at his drink and wandered over to the food. If he was to be left under the watchful eyes of Pine, he may as well enjoy what *Barge* had to offer. After all, he didn't want to enter his mother's home hungry. He studied the spread. The foods looked exciting, but sometimes one just needed comfort food. On the far table, he spotted a selection of cheeses. That was more like it! Maddoc took a warm, spiced roll from a basket and set course for the cheese.

15
SCARLET IRIS

TELLIN

Ocean Bar teemed with life, both in tanks and around the tables, while bar staff floated from table to table, bearing extravagant drinks. I stared into the tank ahead of me, looking for creatures I was used to seeing. Some were missing. I studied the cooler section of the central rock pool, too, finding it mostly empty. None of those juicy starfish I liked. Had I eaten so many?

I trailed my fingers over the rocks as we walked to our seats. 'Sal, where are they?'

Sal grinned. 'They've gone home. I told you – the creatures in my tanks only stay aboard until I can return them.'

Like myself and Gar. Gar needed to live a natural life. *Barge* was no place for him to grow up. I'd made my own choice to stay, unlike those creatures. One particular individual caught my eye as he crawled across the chill tank. 'How long will the Antarctic octopus be with us?'

'Until we, or one of my larger vessels, travels through the

passage to the Southern Ocean.' Sal waved for a drink, taking a seat at our table. Had we been in Terrania, there would have been a steady queue of visitors by then. I appreciated Ocean Bar being open, but preferred a calmer environment to enjoy it, to observe the workings of our home in relative obscurity for once.

Ria strode in, her gaze never settling on anyone for long as she took in her surroundings. She slipped into her usual position behind me for a moment – her role as Lady Gina's maid an automatic reaction in the bar.

Zora looked up her. 'Ria, Lady Gina isn't aboard right now. Sit with us.'

'Gods, but I must be distracted. Sorry.' She pulled up a chair and stared at the bar, then at the menu. Then she got up again, walking along the tank wall.

'What is it?' I asked.

'I don't know.' Ria stopped pacing and stared at me. 'What were the islands like?'

I frowned. 'What islands?'

'The ones you saw amongst the herbs on the selkie island. The ones that Maddoc has been obsessing over ever since.'

'I don't remember any islands.' What was she talking about?

Sal furrowed his brow. 'Always on the horizon, always out of reach. They will fade from my mind too soon enough.'

'I forgot an entire island?' I was growing more confused by the moment.

'An entire group.' Ria sat and leaned in close. 'What if those islands hide the army? What if whoever lives there are those who are aiding the false queen?'

'How do we find islands that fade from the memory and that Sal says, even selkies cannot swim to? If we cannot find them, how does an entire fleet?' Zora shook her head. 'The volume of magic required to do that is almost unimaginable. It would have to be many, many users.'

'I suspect that Maddoc will hold the key to finding them, or at least his family will. I'm going to go with him. He can't remember the islands already without prompting, but I'm certain he knows something deep down. I suspect the source of our magic shares enough in common that I can use his Pathways. It might take me a lot more effort than a Tylwyth Teg, but it's worth a try.'

She exuded determination, and I knew there was little point in trying to stop her. Besides, with Gina officially not on board, she was conspicuous alone.

'Try the markets,' she added. 'Maddoc was muttering about mer-people and how they were pushing up prices locally. I'll be back as soon as I can. Keep each other safe.' Ria threw her arms around me briefly.

'You'll be fine as long as you only eat your own food.' I laughed.

'Not a mistake I plan to make twice.' She smiled and waved at the others before she left.

'And then there were three ... again,' Zora muttered as she watched Ria leave the bar. 'Think she'll find anything?'

I agreed that Maddoc might hold a key, but I wasn't entirely sure that it was the one we needed. Still, even if she eliminated a dead-end of an idea, it was worth it. Maddoc's problem might be linked to ours, but it wasn't the whole of it. We still had an army to locate. And we couldn't assume they were on some hidden islands off shore.

'I don't know. We can't just sit and wait though? Shall we travel along the coastline and start searching for these ships?' I asked.

'We'll need an extra person aboard *Black Hind* if we travel far.' Zora pointed out.

'The easiest solution would be for me to lend you a member of Driftwood – maybe Ivy? You need someone nimble and technical.' Sal sipped at his drink as he looked around the bar. Cypress was around, as he always was. Ever watchful, ever alert.

Ivy ... I liked her. I owed her my freedom. She'd seen Zora at work, so from those people immediately available, she made sense. I wasn't sure I wanted her to know all my secrets, though. 'Oceans, does that mean we'll have to tell her everything?'

'I don't know. You aren't headed out yet, are you?' Sal gestured Cypress over to our table. He strolled across, positioning himself alongside Sal so he could still study the room.

'Seen anything unusual yet?' Sal asked.

'Nothing I haven't seen a hundred times in Terranian waters.' He laughed. 'The far table are reaching their limit and will need to move upstairs soon. The most interesting ones have been the group with Terranian accents, though. I wasn't expecting those. They knew exactly what drinks they were ordering, right from the start.'

Sal's eyes narrowed. 'And you didn't mention it?'

'They've been no trouble so far.' He shrugged. 'I hoped that with enough drink, tongues would loosen. I'm not blind to the fact that they are possibly who we're looking for. Seren has particular rooms and workers lined up for them.'

'Who's allocated?' Sal asked.

'Rose, Nightshade, Jessamine, and Iris.' Cypress replied.

He'd never use their sea-folk names on the public side of the deck, but I knew who he meant. These were some of Seren's best. If there was a secret to get out of the Terranians, we'd have it by morning.

I was woken later that night by Jessamine. Her golden-toned skin was spattered with scarlet droplets, and black rivers of makeup ran from her eyes. She gasped for air as she leant against the wall. Her hands shook. 'Georgie, Seren sent me. Sal isn't answering his door, and she needs one of you, now.'

A pool of dread dripped from my soul as I followed Jessamine through the hidden doors and into the visitor's area. From there, we rushed along the purple corridors belonging to the high-end courtesans and ladies of pleasure. Anguished wails drifted down the corridor. I resisted the urge to sprint, although I prepared my needles and checked every other door in the passageway as we closed on the noise.

'They've all been sent ashore or up to the cool-down tents, Georgie,' Jessamine called. 'Come on!'

She paused at the door. A sinuous trail of drying blood darkened the deep rugs, leading to the bed where Iris's body was laid on lilac sheets drenched in her life blood. A piece of paper pinned to her chest by a dagger fluttered in the air movement of my passage, and on the wall behind her, written in blood, were letters. Oceans, the courtesans would expect me to be able to understand the writing.

'Go home,' Seren muttered, staring at the wall.

'What's on the note?' I asked.

She stroked Iris's hair back from her face. 'I haven't looked. Sal will want to see this as it is. But I can't find him.'

'As much as I care for my cousin's opinion,' I replied, 'I am reluctant to wait. Where are these men? Surely someone heard Iris scream? Make a noise? Anything before they were able to leave *Barge*.'

Jessamine shook her head. 'We heard nothing.'

Urchin's arse, they were all looking expectantly at me. I took a deep breath, the metallic tang of blood filling my nostrils. I sifted through the scents in the room, but the blood was so strong that it overwhelmed everything else.

'Seren – Captain – we need to preserve the room as it is. No one is to move anything. If you picked something up, put it back.'

'Even Iris?' one of the others said.

'No. Let her have the little dignity you have afforded her.' I replied. 'We will find those who did this, and dispense our own justice. You have my word.' I held my hand out towards Iris in a selkie promise. The others would not recognise it. But I meant every word. 'I assume you have tried to call Sal on his alerter?'

Seren nodded. He was rarely without the small device he kept hidden under his clothes. I remembered seeing it that first time at Icidro's. Since then, I'd just taken it for granted. It's familiar blinking when he was being called by Seren was just part of who he was.

'Then I'll check his rooms.' Could he have gone for a swim? He never wore it with his pelt, and it was dark enough that no one would see him slip from our dock. His pelt was as dark as my own. We were the black seals of our respective packs.

'Meet me in his rooms once you've secured things here,' I said. Leaving Seren in charge once again, I ran.

I took the hidden door into one of Driftwood's security rooms.

'Find Zora, send her to Sal's rooms, and send someone up to the Purple. Seren will need your support,' I called as I ran past, seeing uniforms but not stopping to look at faces.

I wove through the residential lower decks, ignoring calls and questions as I pushed past people. Down and down, to the access to Sal's private dock. The deck was open, but *Petrel* was in the hoist, not readied for travel. I climbed the back stairs of Sal's apartment two at a time and let myself in. It was empty. Sal's clothes were neatly folded on his bed. The kelp-whipped idiot had gone swimming. I knew he'd be missing Gar and his pack, but it was reckless given the number of unknown visitors we'd had aboard. I looked in the drawer where he hid that foul, sweet drink of his and retrieved the blinking alerter.

He'd be back soon, surely? He didn't usually go for long, and Seren must have tried for him a while before she called me. I stared out the window, where it looked across the bay to *Black Hind*. The mast lights weren't there.

The door opened, and Sal stood in front of me, dripping with water and holding his wet pelt.

'They've got *Black Hind*,' he said. 'I saw the lights moving. Still had my skin in here from today, so I thought I'd see if Theo was all right.'

'Where's Theo?' I asked. I felt sick. They had killed Iris just to make a point, as we'd killed one of theirs in Orange.

'Still aboard. Tied to the mast.'

'They've killed Iris. Left you a message pinned to her chest with a dagger and wrote "Go home" on the wall in blood.'

'Fucking humans.'

'I've sent for Driftwood and Zora. Seren will be meeting us here as soon as she's secured the Purple. Get dressed. Your people need you.'

'I'm coming with you.'

I looked at my dripping wet friend. The man who had taken me under his flipper, given me safety and a home. I wanted his support and could have used his calm strength, but his people on *Barge* needed him more.

'What if it takes days to get it back? *Barge* is without you.'

'Seren can manage it.'

'Yes, she could, but word will get out. They need you. Zora and I can handle this. Give us some of your least easily startled Driftwood. Oak and Ivy have both seen Zora work before.'

'Take Ash too. Or Cypress.,' Sal said. 'He was watching them until they went to the Purple.'

'Fine. But no more, or *Petrel* won't have enough speed to catch *Black Hind*.'

Pounding at Sal's door interrupted us.

'One moment,' I called as Sal threw clothes on as fast as he could.

'Did you find him?' Seren called.

I swung the door open, and she rushed over. Her arms rose as if to embrace him, then they returned to her sides, and she to business. 'I tried to call you,' she said.

'I'm sorry, Seren. I was having a swim by the dock.' Sal was quick, and Seren glanced at the wet trail of drips from the back door. Her lips tightened, but she let the truth remain buried as others poured into the room. Zora, Ash, and Cypress had followed her in. 'Lock the door behind you, Zora.'

'Right,' Seren began. 'Sal, we've had a murder. I know you said to leave everything in place, Georgie, but I brought the note.' She handed the blood-stained paper to Sal.

'Tell my brother I'm coming for his crown.' He frowned as he read it. 'Brother.' He looked around the room, his gaze coming to rest on Cypress. 'Did you overhear anything we can use? Anything at all?'

Cypress shook his head. 'They talked about nothing of any relevance. Just restocking supplies for their journey home and fastest routes. You know, normal sailor stuff.'

'Did they mention a timeline?' I asked. He shook his head.

'We need to get going, Sal.' How far would the *Black Hind* have gone in the time we spent chatting? How long might we be chasing it? What if it was taken to the islands beyond reach?

'*Black Hind* has been taken.' I gestured to the drawer where Sal kept his poisons, and he nodded.

Zora gasped. 'Theo?'

'Still aboard as far as we know. Cypress, I want you, Oak, and Ivy with us. We're going to get our boat back.'

'With respect, Georgie,' Ash said, 'Take me instead. I'm smaller and lighter, but I can handle *Petrel* through anything, freeing you or Zora to do what you need to. Sal needs Cypress here.'

I glanced at Sal. He shrugged. 'Ash is a good helm. Not as sharp as Zora, but she has a point. You need Zora free to focus.'

'Fine,' I replied. 'Let's go.'

'I'll get the others.' Cypress turned and ran down the corridor.

Ash looked at the back door from Sal's apartments. 'May I?' She gestured to the door.

'Yes, just go.'

She ran through the door.

'Zora, we'll have to tell these guys everything.' I grimaced.

'Whatever it takes to get Theo back.' She chased after Ash.

Sal crossed to his drawer and pulled out a vial. 'Sleep not death. We need to know what they know,' he said through gritted teeth. 'Use whatever else you have.'

I ran down the steps to find Zora and Ash already had *Petrel* in the water, her engine humming with readiness. Oak and Ivy pushed through the other door, laden with weapons.

We shot out from the dock, and under the thick cloak of night, we hugged the coast heading north to hunt down *Black Hind*.

16
LET SLEEPING LIBRARIANS LIE

MADDOC

Rialta was as good as her word, and by the time Maddoc finished his meal, she was back.

'We can go whenever you're ready,' she said, dropping into a seat next to him and placing a large bag on the floor.

'What have you got in there?' Maddoc asked.

'Food. It's a long story. But I only eat what I make myself amongst magical company these days.' She reached for a sweet pie. 'Or food I trust the preparer of.'

Maddoc's lip curled, and he nodded. 'If you trust the chefs here, I'd eat now. I cannot let you eat in my mam's world – if you can gain entry.'

Rialta raised an eyebrow. 'There are those like that in my homeland too,' she said between mouthfuls. 'I'll trust your judgement.'

Once they were finished, Rialta led him through the maze of passageways back to the chilly lower deck. Water sprayed from choppy waves caressing the sides of the platform, and Maddoc stepped back to avoid their reach.

Rialta pressed a button on the wall, and an exceptionally tall, dark-skinned man ducked through a doorway.

'Cypress, can you take us ashore, please?' she asked.

He gestured to the small boat tied up alongside. 'She's ready. Where to?'

Maddoc scanned the coastline to get his bearings. He needed a Pathway point, and the closest was still the one he'd arrived at the day before. He pointed at the hill above the village. 'We need to get up there.'

'I'd like a dry landing point, please,' Rialta interjected. 'We've potentially a long way to travel, and I'd much prefer to do it dry.'

That was good – it would save him having to ask.

They hummed away from the looming shadow of *Barge*, and Maddoc wondered how much wet Mynyw weather it would take before its blooming decks closed like fading petals and the dramatic vessel reduced to keeping its pleasures inside. It was no ship of war, that much was apparent, and he couldn't help but think that even with magic users on board, they would be hard-pressed to win any kind of battle with two vessels and a fleet of small boats.

He wrapped his coat tight, trying to keep every drop of salt water from him as they bounced across the waves and into the bay. Cypress manoeuvred the small boat alongside a pontoon, and Rialta leapt off. Fewer people crowded the shore than on his last visit. He glanced around for the old woman, but neither her nets nor dinghy were in the bay. The sensation of eyes boring into his back set his nerves on edge as he led Rialta through the houses, searching for the bramble-wrapped track.

They reached the top of the headland, slightly scratched, and as Rialta took in the view, he reached inside his pocket to withdraw his cloak. He shook it out, admiring the ripples, and dropped the hood over his eyes. Rialta turned.

'Why do you do that?'

He paused, reaching for the feather pendant. 'I can't see the Path without help.' The faint thread of the Path glimmered. Rialta stood alongside him, and, reaching forward, she plucked the thread. He watched it vibrate at her touch, once again uncomfortably aware of the sheer well of power she must hold to allow her to do that.

'I can't see it, but I can feel it,' she muttered. 'Gods, it's almost within my reach. How do we use it?'

'If we plan to reach my mam in time to tell her about the wave, we have to walk along it.' He rubbed his forehead.

'The islands – we need to ask her about those too,' Rialta prompted. 'Can you hold my hand as you access the Pathway? It might help.'

Maddoc reached tentatively for her.

'I won't bite. Or steal anything you need.' She chuckled. 'I'm quite capable of contact without draining spirits, I assure you.'

He clasped her hand and stepped onto the Path. 'It's narrow – be careful.'

'No, it's as wide as a river. The flow is so broad.' Rialta gasped as she followed him along it. 'It's incredible. I could move armies on this.'

'Let's hope there's no need.' Maddoc felt a pang of jealousy. It wasn't even *her* magic. It was his, and yet she felt more of it than he ever would. He stepped, and the world receded below them. Back they went, closer and closer to his mother's home.

But as they reached the clifftop on the Black Mountain, they were thrown off the Path.

Maddoc shook himself and started to rise when he felt the presence of his mam hovering nearby.

'What are you doing?' Her voice was dangerously low as she glared at him. 'Stay sitting, child.' She turned to regard Rialta, drawing herself up to her full, imposing height, golden hair flowing behind her in the breeze.

Rialta didn't get up. She sat on the floor, outwardly relaxed. She tilted her head to one side and studied the leader of the Tylwyth Teg from under her curtains of hair. To his senses, only his mother bristled with magic. Rialta was quiet, a calm pool of power, opposing his mother's raging storm, where white-capped waves of magic rippled across her body.

'A pleasure to meet you.' Rialta rose fluidly. 'I apologise for using your Path without permission, but it is urgent, and with your entire Pact at risk, I pushed your son into it.'

'What interest do *you* have in our Pact? Who are you?'

'Who I am is less important than the fact that you are under attack. What I am is irrelevant. I came merely to aid Maddoc's memory and seek my own answers.' She stepped closer, unafraid, unyielding. 'How can it be that The Lady of The Lake, annwn of world-wide legend, is so unaware of the happenings of her land that an army masses in secret off her coast? Are you so unbalanced here that the precious Pact fades beneath your gaze, and none of you know why?' She took another step with her chin raised, allowing her to look up into Maddoc's mam's eyes. 'How can you let things fade so far? I had a reason. I had cause since I was limited. You – you just hide in your lakes, playing games. This world crumbles. The last refuge north of the Everstorm is Mynyw, and you have let it fall into jeopardy.'

Maddoc tasted the magic in the air. He wished he was just about anywhere other than next to those two forces of nature.

'I could destroy you as soon as touch you,' his mam spat.

'But you would lose your spirit when you tried.' Rialta remained calm and actually smiled. 'You do have one, right? Are you inviting me into your home, so we can talk like civilised individuals? Or shall we battle it out up here and leave the world one Old One less as a result? We need to work together, as you failed to work alone.'

Every time Maddoc thought it would calm down, Rialta stuck the wound a bit harder. Any moment, he was going to feel the rough side of his mam's tongue. Under normal circumstances, he'd have expected to see a body at The Lady's feet.

'I would hear what you have to say,' she replied eventually. 'But not here. Not on my ground. I will not be undermined in my home in front of the others. Get back on the Path – we head for the Pact stone. You too.' She pulled Maddoc up and gestured for him to go first. 'Lead on, Maddoc.'

They travelled north to the ruins. The tumbled stones hinted at faded, ancient glory; moss-covered tiles peeked out with elaborate patterns from between tiny green stars. Burdock plants grew alongside the barns. Here and there, a carved pillar rose from mossy ground. They stepped off the Path at the Yew marker, and The Lady of The Lake led the way to the Pact Stone. The worn, lichen-patched stone only reached his waist. In a graveyard filled with great extravagance, with the bodies and memories of great poets and princes of a time long gone, the stone appeared inconsequential.

It wasn't. Older than the ruins – older still than the

princes' lost graves, their simple slabs long claimed by vegetation, once humankind stopped caring for this place. At first glance, it was adorned with a simple cross, four holes sunken in the spaces between each arm. Closer inspection revealed the truth. The lower arm tapered to form a blade, and the pommel and guard flared to triangles at their ends. Where the blade met the hilt at the quillons was a deep hole, as though someone had melted it in with a finger. Four others sat around the first, one between each limb of the weapon.

'In the presence of powers greater than either yours or mine, even though he slumbers beneath our feet, let us talk.'

Maddoc sat where his mam gestured. 'The Wave is half-height,' he said. 'The fire is half-height, and the arrow moves, although I have not yet returned home to check how far.'

His mother nodded. 'As yet, I have found no cause, no trigger for the change. Every Tylwyth Teg can be accounted for, every changeling located. None are missing.'

'Yet one with powers of a gwyllion or Irrlicht attacked my ship off the south of Engad not more than a week back,' Rialta parried. 'One with sufficient power to call lost spirits to swarm – to howl like banshees and to keep them at her call.' She briefly dropped her eyes. 'I had to take so many lost spirits that day to protect my crew, my friends.' The moment passed, and the steel returned to her gaze. 'We need to find that creature, Diana – if that's even her name.'

'If she's responsible for breaking the Pact, we'll find her,' Maddoc said. 'Mam, I saw something else on the island, but it keeps sliding from my memories. I know it's there, but hidden. I asked Rialta to come with me, as she hasn't been afflicted the same as I was. Rialta, please can you explain what we saw.'

'Unreachable islands, strong-scented herbs that appear to make the illusion stronger – or the ability to forget about them more intense, rumours of mer-folk, and traders. The selkies can't reach the islands. Have never been able to.'

The Lady frowned. 'That sounds familiar.'

'Familiar? Surely, it's your land?'

Maddoc watched his mother carefully. She was unsettled. Could she be hiding something? She stared at the stone, running her fingers across its pattern, lingering on one part longer than the others.

'I recall a group who lived offshore, but not their details or where they went. They've been absent for a very long time.'

'How long?' Rialta asked.

'Almost seven hundred years. They were around for the first few hundred years of the Pact, but then they just faded away. Maddoc, you need to visit the library – we need the details I can't recall. If they are involved, we need to find out who they are and how to get to them.'

'If others can reach them, so can we.'

'If others can reach them, it would give a hiding place for an entire army just off your shore,' Rialta replied. 'How do we get there?'

'You need the keys,' Maddoc replied. 'We only have three, maybe even two. He looked between Rialta and his mother. I suspect you fit the same lock.'

Rialta studied the stone. 'Five keys, three beacons ... How did you totally forget about the fifth?'

'Time turns – gods faded, and mankind grew. To open the lock, we need three out of the five; Fire, Ocean, Land, Mankind. You need to return to the island. We need an Oceanic Old One or a human to open this lock. Three out of the remaining four should allow us access.'

'What's the fifth hole?' Rialta asked.

'That key is lost to us. The old gods and their descendants no longer walk the Earth.' Maddoc shrugged.

'We need to know what's going on, and now. Get these records, and deal with the issue. Six weeks you said? Five now? We don't have time to walk people up from the islands. Which hole is which? Let me try for the ocean. Maybe being another water spirit will work just as well.' Rialta stood in front of the stone, running her hand across the design.

Maddoc placed his finger in the left upper space. His mother into the top right.

'The one below mine is the one for the ocean,' Maddoc said. Rialta nodded her understanding, then ignored him and placed her hand over the central hole – for the gods.

The stone shook. The world shook. The birds stopped singing and silence fell, a blanket of shock filling the valley. From the hollow of the old yew tree, a groaning noise emanated as the entrance to the library was exposed. Rialta was godkin?

His mam's skin paled. They watched in silence as Rialta skipped across to the library.

'Don't think on it too hard. How else could I collect lost spirits?' She laughed. 'I won't hold your ignorance against you. Coming?'

'Maddoc, go. Remember, it's a one-way route, and you'll come out on the island in Llyn Egnant. I'll meet you there. This changes things.' With that, his mam stepped onto the Path and vanished.

'She took that well,' Rialta chuckled. 'Do you know what we are looking for without her?'

Maddoc shook his head. 'No, but there's someone down there that will if we fail to find anything. This might be the one occasion when it's important enough to wake him.'

Maddoc led the way down tight spiral stairs. The air grew hot and dry – it wasn't unbearable, but it was how he imagined a desert to be. Perfect conditions under which precious manuscripts would be preserved, free from damp. All the magical history of Mynyw was stored in the library. Its true history, not the tales passed down by mankind, whose stories grew ever more embellished with each telling. The human part of him understood the longing for happy endings and the requirement for using the Tylwyth Teg as warnings – even as threats for misbehaving children – but it was far from truth. He stopped at the base of the dark stairwell.

'I can't light the torch,' he muttered. 'I don't have the power.'

'That's not something I can help with either,' Rialta replied. 'There's something bright down that way, though.' He felt the air of her motion but could not see anything.

'Stick to the edge,' he muttered. He knew what that light source was, and it started his stomach churning. Maddoc edged around the room. There was no sound behind him, and he could not hear Rialta. A shadow blocked the source of light for a moment. She'd walked straight in. His breath came short and fast as he hurried through the darkness after her. He tripped on an object. Why was there a fallen anything in there? He pushed the thought aside; he could check that later. He had to get to that next room, fast.

As he stumbled through the doorway, he ran into the back of Rialta.

'It occurs to me,' she said in a low voice, 'that this is one of those things that it might have been good to warn someone about.'

'I didn't think you'd rush off ahead,' Maddoc replied. 'Rialta, did you walk into the room?' On the floor, running past the huge, sleeping dragon, was a trail of footprints.

'No, I waited here,' Rialta whispered. 'How deeply does he sleep? Will we wake him?'

Lord Flame was curled up in the centre of the oval room.

His enormous bulk didn't fill the space as much as Maddoc remembered. 'He doesn't usually wake.'

Rialta moved closer, reaching forward to touch shimmering red scales. 'I've never met a dragon before,' she said. 'I thought all the northern dragons had died out.'

'Not all. Some, like Lord Flame, sleep instead. He guards the hoard of knowledge and his egg.' The egg! Maddoc scanned the room. Why didn't he see it? It was usually on the empty pedestal, next to Lord Flame. Had it fallen off?

'The egg is usually on that.' He pointed at the pedestal where it had always been, then looked down. The footprints in the ash-dust tracked directly across the room. He wanted to run, to check the floor, but he was already certain what he'd find. There were two sets of boot prints accompanied by a set of paw prints larger than any dog he'd ever met. The ash beneath the prints was different, hardened into a thin sliver of rock.

Rialta walked alongside him as they stuck close to the edge, careful not to disturb the tracks. Nausea rose, and Maddoc tried to hold it down. He swallowed hard as they could see the rest of the room. The last dragon egg of the northern dragons – Lord Flame's child – was gone.

'Oh Gods, it's been taken.' Maddoc hoped his voice sounded calmer than he felt.

'If the stealing of selkie children by men wasn't enough to break the Pact, then I presume that stealing a dragon's egg has entirely smashed it open.' Rialta said.

'It would certainly play a part. We have to wake him,' Maddoc replied. It was not what he'd signed up for. He just wanted to find out about ... what was it again?

'Does he know you?' Rialta whispered.

'I doubt he knows anyone alive. I was joking when I said we could ask him about the books. When the Pact was sealed, we removed all true documents, our records, and the history of Mynyw to here. Lord Flame has remained a sleeping guardian of this hoard of knowledge ever since. Can you truly imagine in the times of human dominance that he would not have been killed from curiosity or sport?'

'The southern dragons survived,' Rialta said.

'Yes, the desert had its own protections.'

'So, we are going to have to wake a dragon whose egg has been stolen, who has no idea when and who we all are?'

'That's about it,' Maddoc replied. It sounded ridiculous when said like that. But there was no question in his mind that it was their only option.

'Do you think we could find what we came for first?' Rialta asked. 'I suspect he might not be in the mood to help us research once he finds out someone stole his egg.' She crossed carefully behind Lord Flame and removed a light from the wall; its gentle glow pulsed as they returned to the first chamber.

They illuminated chaos. There was an entire section of shelves where book prints in the dust told the tales of recent movement of objects which had sat untouched for years. Drag marks through the dust showed traces of their passage. Who would move all the records and why? Maddoc had been there before, but had no real memory of what should be in each area. The moved records must surely relate to the egg.

'To get in here, the thieves must have needed at least three individuals to represent the forces behind the Pact,' he said, as he walked the room looking for more drag marks in the dust – clues to the new homes of these records. 'Maybe they used four, to be sure. Those paw prints are like nothing I've ever seen. Whatever that creature is, it's not from Mynyw.'

Maddoc ran his finger across a shelf. The row below showed the trail of his fingers from his initial entry in the dark. A shelf above was disturbed, too, and the dust shadows no longer matched the spines. If he moved that one to the left, and that one, took another one out, then they lined up again. The book he held was faded, and the ink almost unreadable. The suede cover's gilding gave clues to a far more recent origin than many of the other documents. He flicked through the pages and sighed; human-produced records were always fragile. A bookmark fell out, and the pages opened. A few words were legible where the marker had somehow preserved the page.

'Gruffydd, market trader of corn ... visitor ... Rhys Ddwfn.' He stopped. 'Rialta, come here.'

'What have you found?' She peered at the writing. 'Does any of it trigger memories? Markets, you've mentioned before. You told me an old woman was muttering about markets.'

'I did,' he said. 'Markets and mer-folk, it's a start.' He replaced it, and his foot caught something tucked under the lowest shelf. He'd tripped over something earlier. Maddoc reached down and retrieved the metal case, then opened the end, tipping out a tied and sealed document. The seal had been peeled from the paper, a jagged edge of fibres protruding from it.

Rialta took the case as he unrolled it. 'It's a transfer of lands document for the selkie isle. It was taken in payment – can that be right? – From Y Plant Rhys Ddwfn.'

'That same name again! Who are they?'

'According to this, they live on islands off the west coast.'

'Islands you saw. Islands you are being induced to forget about. Whoever they are, they've gone to extreme lengths not to be found.'

'I'm inclined to agree, and if this document is here, then they might be Old Ones. Or at the very least, a group of Tylwyth Teg who have been long absent.'

Rialta glanced around. 'It looks like they've had enough of being absent but don't want us to know they're back yet. What would they have to do with an Irrlicht?'

Maddoc frowned. 'Our closest would be the gwyllion. Luring people to their deaths with glowing portents is hard to do with the death of most humankind, so they've been pretty inactive.'

He turned back to the shelf. What was that section about? None of the books had a theme, by location or date, and the more he looked around the library, the more convinced he was that maybe the books weren't missing, just moved. Some were probably taken, yes, but if they were trying to remove an egg, then they wouldn't have room for as many volumes as were missing from that shelf.

'They made quite a mess in an attempt to hide stuff.' Rialta looked at the huge selection of records. 'I don't know where to begin.'

'Nor me. But at least we have a name.'

17

WALRUS AHOY

TELLIN

'How do we follow if they're heading north to the islands Ria was on about?' Zora called back from the bow.

I knew she'd be struggling to resist flattening waves as we chased *Black Hind*. We left the shelter of the main headlands, where the lighthouse to our north kept up the same regular pattern I'd seen since we arrived. Flash, five-second pause, flash, pause.

'We need speed.' Zora began to flatten the waves, and *Petrel* leapt forward, no longer battling swell.

We'd passed several other islands when we returned Gar, and there were multitudes of bays where a stolen boat could be hidden along the coast. A hundred potential places to dump a body, a hundred places to wreck our boat.

The rock chain where I'd met the aria stretched between the islands and the coast. No sane sailor would traverse those in the dark. Could that mean that they were heading around the selkie island? Maybe they'd had to stop for the night.

'How did they get to *Black Hind*?' Ash asked no one in particular, but she had a good point. We were assuming they'd planned to steal or wreck our boat. In order to reach it, they must have had their own. Could we be looking for two boats? *Petrel* couldn't tow *Black Hind* very fast if she was badly damaged, and *Petrel* was our fastest cell-boat. So, what would they be using?

'Zora, can you *feel* any disturbance in the waters?' I asked in hope.

'Around here, there's so much disturbance, I'd be pressed to pick anything out. It's a fair question, though. Anything you can do to help us in the dark?'

'What are you pair on about?' Ash asked.

I heard Oak's throaty chuckle and was glad the darkness hid my smile. 'Ash, you obviously know that Sal uses *Black Hind's* crew for jobs you aren't sent on,' I responded, still searching the water for mast lights.

'Yeah. I know there's a Sea Witch amongst the crews somewhere.'

'Well, then you already know my secret,' Zora sang out. 'Nice to re-meet you.'

'Ahh, it's *you*.' Ash replied. 'The flat water makes sense now. I'm glad I offered to drive so you could do your thing. Can you capsize the bastards – or drown them if they've hurt a hair on Timothee's head?'

'Sure. Although, I want my boat intact as well as her crew,' Zora replied. 'Do you think there might be any Old Ones around here, Georgie? Could you call for help?'

'Did you already know about this?' Ash asked Oak and Ivy.

'Yeah, Zora did some really awesome stuff back in Orange several months ago,' Ivy enthused.

Zora might be onto something. 'Cut the engine.' I removed

my clothes, for wet clothes are a pain to fight in, and lowered myself into the water.

I sunk below the waves, keeping hold of *Petrel* with one hand, and called as loudly as I could in Ocean for help from any who would aid us. I called of my loss of a friend – Old Ones have little notion of possessions, so a lost boat would elicit no response. The cold was biting, and I surfaced for air.

'It's bloody freezing in here,' I called up, trying to make light of the situation. Early spring waters were too cold for my belegged form. I'd try one more time, and then I'd have to get out and hope I'd attracted the right attention. When I sank beneath the waves, I didn't hear any response.

'Get out, you idiot.' Zora was shouting at me when I resurfaced. 'It's freezing, and you have no pelt on. You'll be no good if you're frozen with hypothermia. Bloody idiot.' She hauled me aboard with help from Ivy; the others stood on the far side to keep the boat level. Zora threw a towel over me from somewhere, and it stank of stale water and metal. I guessed it had been buried in the locker, cushioning the anchor.

'It was worth a try.' I sighed. 'No one out here. Gar's pack might've heard me, but we're a way off them yet.'

'What in all the Oceans was that noise?' Ash stared as I shivered on the deck.

'No guardian creatures like there are in Terrania?' Zora asked, ignoring Ash.

I shook my head, my teeth chattering so much that I could barely speak as I tried to reply. 'No. In Mynyw, there are sufficient Old Ones in numbers – that it is more about balance than it is one single creature. In areas of Engad, I'd imagine there are few left, and the system is more fragile. Here, the problem is almost too many.'

'Gods of Below. Ash, take us north. When you see the lighthouse on the small island, keep it to your right as you navigate around it.'

Ash frowned. 'Once again, what just happened?'

'Georgie is a selkie,' Zora said, shrugging nonchalantly as she passed my clothes.

Ash shook her head as she started the engine. 'An unusual crew indeed. Next you'll be telling me your cousin's a selkie too …'

I said nothing. The wind chill made everything worse, and Zora shuffled me down to the floor, where the pounding hull against rough seas made my spine shudder.

She sat alongside me. I could feel her hands running through the salty tangles of my hair, her gentle fingers unknotting as she removed the water. She continued down my body until the wind still chilled me, but I was dry enough to reclothe myself. 'Don't do that again,' she murmured, enveloping me in a hug. 'Get dressed and warm as quickly as you can.'

'Something moving in the water on the landward side,' Oak said. 'It's huge and heading straight for us.'

'Prepare to fight,' I responded, rippling a small amount of healing through my body in the hope it might counter the chill. It sort of helped, and I felt less shivery.

The creature closed in on us. Its huge flanks were bigger than any bull seal I had ever seen, and our visitor's tusks gleamed in the moonlight.

What in a sea of confusion was a walrus doing in Mynyw? Was it sheer coincidence, or had he understood my call? I leant over the side of the boat. Unafraid despite his size, I reached to touch him and was flooded with images. Death of the ice, green lands where his home had been, the heat of the springs melting in other areas. Not enough food, and finally, dispersal. He'd got stuck in a south-flowing current and needed a way home.

I pictured *Black Hind* in my own mind, trying to build an image like his but struggling with the level of detail. To my joy, he responded. Through his eyes, I could see the sleek hull of our boat and the narrow one of her captor alongside. We'd been right. The accompanying vessel was bigger than *Black Hind*. It probably had far more people on board than we'd been expecting.

'We can't win this alone.' I sighed. 'He's seen *Black Hind* and her companion. There are more of them than us. We need more people.'

'That's not happening,' Oak grumbled. 'I'm happy to go with our earlier plan. Capsize the other boat, then attack those holding *Black Hind*.'

Walruses cruise at a relatively slow speed normally, but are capable of a surprising turn of speed. He swam ahead while we followed with our running lights off. There was little light to see by, and as the moon slipped behind a cloud, we were left using Zora's detection of his disturbance trail as a guide. The walrus swam directly towards coves on the southern side of the island. His call echoed back from the tall cliffs as we approached. Rather than getting closer, he slowed, turning in the water to face us.

Ash cut the engine, and we floated in the company of the walrus. I stared ahead, searching for a reason why we would stop, studying the cliff face.

'There!' Ivy pointed as she whispered. 'There's a light moving from side to side under the cliffs.'

'Well spotted. What now, Georgie?' Zora asked.

It was too close to the cliffs, in the selkies' territory. Starting a battle without warning them would not help endear Sal to the pack. It was at that moment, an utterly ridiculous idea came to me. We could not ask the walrus to aid us in a battle – he had nothing to gain from it. But maybe he'd let me ride with him to the selkies. That way, I could warn them to stay away from the cove and let them know a storm was about to descend on their home.

'I'll be back,' I said and leapt from the boat.

We were too close for Zora to shout at me without alerting anyone aboard *Black Hind*, although her hiss of frustration carried pretty far. The walrus didn't take too much persuasion. Bored and gathering his strength to try returning north, he was happy to help. It caught me out a little when he gathered me in his flippers and carried me below his body, occasionally surfacing to let me breathe. It was much as a mother walrus teaches her pup to swim. He kept me close to his body, and I resisted the urge to grab onto his tusks for stability, instead taking in air when we paused and enjoying the ride.

'No closer.'

I panicked that we'd caught the attention of the thieves, then slowly realised the speaker had used Ocean, and I was underwater.

'A selkie and a walrus? That's a new combination. I see you, Tellin Dark. Why are you back so soon and in such unusual company?'

'I see you too,' I replied. I couldn't, but manners cost nothing. 'My boat has been stolen, and one of those involved in Gar's return and rescue is aboard. I need it back. They plan to take it to the queen's gathered army.'

'Then take it back,' the selkie muttered. 'Why involve us in human affairs?'

'I merely ask your permission and indulgence to allow the Sea Witch on our crew to use the full force at her fingertips to regain our vessel. We didn't wish to cause you or any of your pack discomfort should they be in the vicinity.'

'Then, thank you. I will move everyone toward the beach so we may instead play in the surf she creates.'

He turned and flippered away. I snuggled into the walrus as closely as I could, feeling the cold, despite his attempt to shield me from it.

'May the ocean aid you and the waves crash in your favour,' the selkie called back.

I pictured *Petrel*, and we turned, racing back to her small, bobbing form.

'Whenever you're ready,' I said as they hauled me aboard to a loud huff from Zora 'We know the group aboard *Barge* earlier were four men. We don't know if that was all the mercenaries or pirates sent to investigate. We do know that they knew *Barge* well enough to leave the message they did – they know our links to Anard.'

Was *Black Hind* an opportunist attack? Or would we have to assume there were at least double that many?

'Ash, keep people out of *Petrel*, even if it means getting out of our reach. Zora, how do you want to handle this? Their lights are on, so we won't get close, even under cover of darkness.'

'I need to sink the support ship,' she said. 'I need to see to direct any wave I build. We need Theo in one piece too.'

'As if you'll get Theo out. The moment he's free, he'll help us.' Ash said.

I was counting on it. 'Ivy, I take it you have a dagger up your sleeve?' She nodded, her silhouette outlined by freshly blooming light over the cliff tops. We'd been out long enough that sunrise would soon crack the sky and expose us. 'I have venom that you can use. It's not deadly in small quantities, and we need them alive.'

Ivy took the small bottle and offered cloth. 'A double-edged dagger.' She nodded approvingly.

'I need to know what the other boat is.' Zora squinted intently into the bay. The vessels would remain in shadow for longer than us.

'You should have used the walrus. Although, it might have been a little tricky, keeping us both warm.'

'It is freezing here,' Zora said. By the slim morning light, I saw a grin tug at the corner of her mouth. 'Freezing ... ha! Ash, approach *Black Hind* from the west. Its companion is about to make a new friend.' As the sun rose on our small party, Ash started to bring us closer.

Zora stood in the bow, her arms outstretched, and created a perfectly walrus-sized ice sheet. She sent it surfing across the water until it collided with the other boat. Then, she lowered herself to sitting and grew ice from the platform. The walrus was delighted. He clambered aboard, tipping the vessel towards him. It began to ship some water, which Zora turned to more ice.

'I hope you're going to be quick,' a voice called down from the cliffs. Standing in the morning sun, glowing with radiant power, stood Sal's mother. Though she was many years older than me, the power of her attraction was far stronger than mine. Her mature magic deeper. Ash and Oak were mesmerised. And, if they were, I could only hope that those on *Black Hind* were too.

'She's a selkie,' I barked. 'Don't look at her. Trust me – that's one relationship you do *not* want to get involved in.'

Aboard *Black Hind*, three crew stared at Sal's mum while a female member of their group jostled them for attention. The glow of the selkie's magic, as she enhanced her charms even further, only served to illustrate where Sal's immense powers had come from.

We took full advantage of the chaos; *Petrel* shot into the bay. As we came alongside, Oak leapt off *Petrel*, landing none too lightly on *Black Hind's* deck. Ivy followed, shimmying up the mast, her dagger embraced in an iron grip. I wrapped myself in darkness and slipped aboard, wearing a shadow glamour. I clung to the patches the darkness refused to vacate.

Oak swung his heavy hammer in a wide arc at the sailor's knees. The man dropped to the deck howling. He reached for his gun, and Oak dropped the weight of the hammer on his hand as the others turned to face them. He stood alone on the deck, solid, huge, and imposing – but one man is no match for three gun-wielding mercenaries. I hoped he had something with more range tucked around his person.

A body fell from the masthead. I'd miss-counted, but Ivy hadn't. The noise distracted the mercenaries, who glanced at their companion for just a moment, but a moment was all I ever needed. I slipped behind the closest and flicked my needles into his arm, retreating once more to the shadow.

Two left. One looked up, training his gun on Ivy's fast-descending form, while the other faced Oak.

A crack of gunfire – not from the boat we were on, but the other. It ricocheted off the mast. The walrus roared and clambered further onto the vessel, tipping it and leaving those aboard scrambling for their footing. The shooter turned the gun toward the walrus.

A tide of darkness flowed over the boat. To my eyes, it glowed with magic. A group of young selkie males had joined the fray. Boats were of little interest to the selkies, but humans shooting the walrus must be a step more than they were willing to accept. I left them to it.

'Find Theo!' Zora's voice carried across the water. I glanced at her, and she stood, arms outstretched towards the ice. Thin cracks of ice had started to shear off, and I threw myself flat to the deck, edging towards the hatch. 'Oak, get down.'

'I can't just duck!' he shouted back.

'Do it.'

Shards of ice, thin and vicious, flew towards us. Someone screamed. I dived for the cabin, leaving the scrap on deck to the seasoned fighters.

'What the fuck's going on?' someone muttered as they headed towards me. It was dark in there – they hadn't got the panels working. I flattened myself against the wall, flicking the left hand's needles into readiness. Once they moved within range. I reached for their neck; they turned and lunged for me, catching my arm. The space was too close for a gun.

I raked their face with the needles from my free hand. The man stank of fresh blood. *Theo, I'm coming.*

'You bastard. I'm going to bloody kill you,' he said, pushing me up against the wall. The man was shorter than me, so it would be difficult to hit up at his jaw from that angle. Instead, I raised my knee sharply into his groin. The exhalation of stale, ale-filled breath and loosening of his grip told me I'd hit true. I removed my glamour, and his eyes widened.

'Fuck me,' he said.

'Go fuck yourself.' I bit his ear off.

He screamed. His hand released me as he grabbed his head, his knees buckling as the venom kicked in.

He flailed towards me, and I dived below his grasp to get to the cabins and the main hold.

No one was in our room, and Theo and Ria's were similarly empty. There was still a lot of noise from the deck above. Instinctively, I reached for the boat, running my hand along her bodywork as I strode to the hold door.

'We'll fix any damage. Don't you worry,' I told her. The hold door wasn't locked. Whatever they'd done with Theo, they hadn't decided he needed keeping secure.

'Theo,' I called quietly. Every muscle coiled in case there

were more of them inside. 'Theo, are you there?' A muffled thump came from my left. I ran across the swaying space. Under a heap of sailcloth, I found him.

'Urchin's arse, what have they done to you?' I struggled to keep my voice level. The scent of blood was overwhelming. *Stay calm.* He was curled into a ball, and the big man let out an occasional whimper. I was going to break every last one of them personally for this.

I scrabbled around his body, trying to find what they'd tied him with. What was stopping him getting free? His legs were tied, but they felt unbroken – it was a start. Everywhere was sticky. That arse who I'd dropped in the cabin must have only just done whatever was happening here. I patted up his body, and he cried out, so I untied his ankles and tried to shuffle him to a more seated position. It was still too dark to see details, but even in dim light, his face looked wrong.

The noise from above quietened. A muffled thud punctuated the quiet. The hatch was thrown open, and Zora peered down. In the morning light, Theo's true state was exposed. His fingers had been removed from his left hand. I was glad I hadn't got the rope off his wrists yet – it was so tight that it was likely stemming the blood flow. He lifted his head. His nose pointed sideways, and his left eye was swollen closed. Blood dribbled down his green beard, streaking it.

'Which one of the bastards did this?' Zora shrieked.

'I suspect they're near the cabin door.' I said. 'Theo, I need to get you out of here. We need to return you to *Barge* as quickly as we can.'

'I lost my fingers somewhere,' he said, a grimace giving away the pain of moving his face. 'Maybe Seren can sew them back on.' I winced at that. Seren was many things, but no medic. 'Sorry they got *Black Hind.*'

'If I untie you, I'm worried about blood loss.' Why was I

telling him that? Theo had always been the one who looked after us.

'I twisted them tighter,' he mumbled. 'Don't loosen them. Tellin, I think they fucked my eye up. I can't see out of it.'

'Maybe, Theo. Maybe it's just a black eye.' I tried to reassure him, but Zora's earlier reaction would have blown that, I was certain. A heavy thud landed through the hatch next to me. Ash leant over Theo, breath hissing from her teeth.

'We have enough of them to question. Where is the bastard? No one does this to my family and lives.' I inclined my head to the door and watched her stalk through. I had no intention of stopping her. The question would only be whether Ash or Zora killed the man first.

I had some fingers to find.

18
SLICE OF LIFE

MADDOC

They sat on the floor amidst a pile of records and documents.

'So, all we've established is that they arrive in mist and live on islands that can only be seen when you stand on a patch of special herbs?' Maddoc rubbed at his itchy eyes. The dust and reading were taking their toll.

'One square foot of herbs near one village on the coast in north Mynyw!' Rialta laughed. 'That's a crazy security feature if I've ever heard of one! The only reason you could see them from where you were on the selkie island is that it was part of their home once, but long enough ago that the selkie isles are now visible to anyone.'

Maddoc rolled his shoulders. The ache from all the reading was starting to become a little uncomfortable. He needed a table or his comfy chair at home in his cottage. 'Yes, and they used to come to market.' He put the book down. 'The old woman I met on the coast mentioned that, almost as though they were back. This is an old human record with specific names. Why do we have it? We let them keep the records needed to make sense of the world, you know? Leave enough of a hint should we mingle again.'

'You missed the fact that they speak a language no one else could understand. That could be any Old One dialect, though.'

Maddoc dropped his head to his hands. 'I still don't see how this affects the Pact. Are they affiliated with us enough that our side of the deal has also been broken?'

'I suppose,' Rialta said. 'You need to look at the exact wording of the agreement, or do you know it by heart?'

Maddoc had known that was coming. He'd hoped they could find answers amongst the piles of scrolls, then sneak back out and let someone else wake Lord Flame. But no, it would look like he stole the egg were anyone to see the extra trails they left.

'It's under Lord Flame,' he mumbled.

'Under? Well, we were going to wake him anyway. Now, we have two reasons.' Before he could stop her, Rialta strode back into the room where Lord Flame slept. Maddoc leapt to his feet and ran to catch up. He stopped at the entrance when he saw her.

Rialta sat near the dragon's head and reached forward. 'Sorry to wake you, Old One,' she murmured as she laid a hand on his head. Nothing happened.

'Rialta, move back! He's not called Lord Flame for no reason. The dust is his ash, and the heat is his. At least, move to the side so he'll see you when he wakes.'

'Seeing me might help, yes.' She stepped to the side and reached forward again, gently stroking the neck of the huge Old One. Lord Flame's red and gold serrated scales rippled under the pressure of her touch. Each was large enough to count as a weapon in its own right. 'How are you supposed to wake him?' she whispered.

'I don't know. He's not been woken in my lifetime.'

Rialta closed her eyes and made contact again. She was crazy. A sleeping dragon was bad enough – an awake one with fury in his heart was quite another.

She moved closer, stroking the dragon's cheek, then placed her head near his ear slit and began to sing. It was neither a beautiful song nor beautifully sung, but Lord Flame stirred a little. The language was strange and foreign to Maddoc's ears, sort of spiky. She stroked the neck as she sang.

Having heard tales of Lord Flame's ferocity throughout his childhood, Maddoc kept his distance, his muscles tight and heart pounding, ready to dive back into the next room. Tendrils of smoke rose from Lord Flame's nostrils, and his thick tail began to uncurl. Rialta stepped away, placing her back against the wall, still singing.

Lord Flame's crystalline eye opened. It spun slowly as he lifted his head. His huge bulk filled the room as he stretched out centuries of sleep, then swung his head towards the pedestal.

His sinuous neck snaked around the other side, then Lord Flame roared.

Anguish and loss in his call flooded Maddoc's being, his mind crumbling under the echoing emotions of Lord Flame. Sorrow and hatred warred for dominance.

He wanted his egg.

He needed his egg.

Who had taken it? Where were the creatures responsible for the loss of his only spawn?

Those creatures, slinking around in his den ... he would smash their bones to fragments and stamp on them until they were no more than dust. He would ...

Maddoc curled up into a ball, unable to cope with the barrage of thoughts and emotions flooding over him. He'd not been prepared for the clarity of understanding, the sheer force of rage. It was too much to bear. He fell against the wall to await his fate – utterly certain that Lord Flame would pulverise him at any moment. Maybe the godkin could talk sense into him? Could Rialta survive long enough to let him know that it wasn't them, to speak with him through the red-hot fire of his anger.

Lord Flame turned toward him. Smoke from his nostrils no longer curled in elegant spirals, but billowed out in clouds that filled the room.

'We think we know who took your egg,' Rialta called into the room. 'We're here to help.' Her voice was drowned by the roar. Lord Flame swung his bulk to face her. As he turned, he swung his tail at Maddoc, winding him and slicing through his leg. Blood spurted, as red as the dragon himself.

'Rialta!' Maddoc screamed. She moved closer to Lord Flame until she was under the dragon's head, ducking and weaving from his snapping jaws, impossibly agile. Then, she swung up onto Lord Flame's neck. To Maddoc's amazement, Lord Flame lowered his head to the floor. He let out an anguished roar and started to twist the rest of his body. She'd pinned a dragon down? Her lips moved, and he was certain that she continued to placate him. Maddoc tried to keep pressure on his leg.

Lord Flame's attention refocused on Rialta gave him time to move back into the entrance passage, away from accidents and swinging limbs. Safer inside the doorway, he watched the dragon buck and writhe his enormous body, remaining unable to lift his head. The battle of wills and bodies continued for what felt like hours, and both combatants' sides heaved with exertion – well, the dragon's did. Rialta sat on the dragon's neck, both hands resting on the back of Lord Flame's head as sparks jetted from his snout. She was as cool as his mother at a funeral.

Funeral jokes about his mother – he must be getting light-headed from blood loss. All Maddoc could do was watch and wonder. Eventually, the dragon lay down, curled his tail around his body, and appeared to give in.

'Maddoc, come back in,' called Rialta.

He tried to stand and failed. His leg was agony. Tears of pain burnt rivers down his cheeks as he dragged himself back into the room.

Lord Flame seethed, but his barrage of anguish was muted, as though Maddoc heard it through a thin wall.

'Don't move.' Rialta ran over to him and crouched. 'Did he catch you?'

'No, it was a rogue manuscript,' Maddoc quipped. 'His tail caught me right at the start when you woke him. When he was so loud I thought I would burst.'

'I'm sorry I didn't notice sooner,' she murmured. 'Do you think you'll be able to get us out and to your mother? You need help I can't provide – unless you seek death?'

Maddoc crooked one side of his mouth up. 'No, I think I'd rather like to see this task through. Sort out the small matter of a broken Pact and potential war, then return to my tree and cottage.'

'Glad to hear it. We need to try and talk to Lord Flame about his egg and Y Plant Rhys Ddwfn before we leave – if you think you can hold on that long?'

'You wrestled a dragon. I can watch the outcome.'

'I need to ask ... did you ever see the egg? What colour was it?'

'Is that important right now?' Maddoc groaned in pain.

'Maybe.'

'Sort of beige, I guess, but it kind of shimmered golden-red. Like Lord Flame himself.'

'Could it be?' Rialta murmured. She turned from him, bowing low to Lord Flame. 'The Pact is failing, and there are strange creatures afoot in Mynyw.' She gestured at the melted footprints in the floor. 'I believe those individuals have taken your egg. What do you know of Y Plant Rhys Ddwfn?'

Lord Flame snorted. 'You? Speak of strangeness in Mynyw?' His head snaked towards her. 'What do you do here Godling? Y Plant Rhys Ddwfn are no thieves. They most honourable ocean *Sidhe*. Never betray – traitors die! Traitors are devils to Y Plant Rhys Ddwfn. They all agree – or all die.'

'I don't know,' Rialta said. 'But I am certain that we need to find out whether they have ships hiding in their harbours. Ships that may have taken your egg south as payment to a foreign king in trade for something.'

Lord Flame's tail flicked from side to side, and his wings fluttered. 'Ships? If my egg is wetted, it wakes – it hatches.'

Rialta sat suddenly, her voice wavering for the first time. 'Lord Flame, what will happen if it hatches without you?'

'It will devour the closest thing. If a fool king has it and got it wet, he'll be eaten, then his court. Humans think we imprint like birds.' He spat flame to the side, narrowly missing Rialta. 'Imprinting is legend, spread for time to recover eggs. Hatchling cares only for food.'

'I need to go!' Rialta cried. 'Maddoc, you need to find out about Y Plant Rhys Ddwfn. I think I might know where this egg is. If not your egg, then another has been stolen and received a blessing of salt water. Either way, it's bad news.'

'If a dragon's egg has been stolen, it begins a time of change.' Lord Flame's lips curled, and his teeth exposed. 'Go, Spirit-Catcher. Bring my egg back. Half-Tylwyth Teg, stand where false herbs grow. You will see the islands. Will you know if the ships are part of the grand conspiracy?'

'A lot happened while you slept. I suspect the townships were as flooded as other low-lying lands. Once we find a way to them, we'll go and see for ourselves.'

'I give you until full moon, Spirit-Catcher, or I will begin to hunt, and the world will know my wrath.' He curled back up on the floor, his eyes watching them as they hobbled away. His fury still filled the room, but the overriding emotion Maddoc felt was sadness and loss.

They emerged from the stairs on a rocky outcrop in a mountain lake. The air was eerily silent, so quiet that Maddoc was aware of the noise of his own breathing. Birds flew past, each wing beat audible. The clear waters weren't deep around the island, but it wasn't easy to get off. Marsh filled the gap between the island and the nearest land. Maddoc looked out over the gently rolling landscape, and a smile tugged at his mouth. He loved that place. He sat and waited, confident their arrival would trigger the alerts, and any moment, the Tylwyth Teg would arrive.

If his arrival set the alerts, then surely those who passed through there carrying the egg must have set the detection off too? Was it possible that the thieves could have passed over the sky-lakes of the Teifi Pools and not drawn notice from those beneath the crystal waters? Someone *must* have noticed them passing, even if they thought it little more than a wild animal. He wondered about that set of paw prints. They may have made little impact on the rocks, but might there be singed plant life as part of the trail they left?

'What are you doing?' Rialta asked as he started to study the floor, shuffling to the side to look at the next section.

'Distracting myself by looking for burnt footprints.'

'Hmm, if the egg is where I suspect it is, then it was taken before midwinter, as that was when it was gifted to the King of Terrania. You won't see burnt footprints.'

'Who gifted it?' Maddoc winced as he moved again.

'That's your job to find out. Mine is to recover this egg as soon as we can.'

'How will you take it from a king?' Maddoc thought she had lost the thread. If a king had it, they were battling two armies with those boats. He started to laugh, aware that he was feeling faint. Only he could end up returning from a library half dead.

'We killed him. It's hidden on a boat somewhere I cannot navigate to, in the care of Theo's mother!' Rialta was pacing across the small island, a trapped rabbit waiting to bolt.

Maddoc raised his gaze from contemplating his injury for a moment. 'You know it's been wet, don't you?'

She nodded.

Maddoc sighed. 'Then we need to get it here. Even if it's not his egg, maybe he can restrain it.'

'And if it is, we avert part of the crisis.'

The waters began to ripple as the Tylwyth Teg arrived, rising from the lake en-mass, a guard for the dragon. A line of defence they were obliged to provide under the Pact. Once again, Maddoc couldn't believe thieves had slipped past.

He'd have to have a chat with his mam once he healed up. There was a piece missing from the puzzle. He was leaving a small puddle of red on the stone – how long had he been bleeding? Too long. Maddoc struggled more and more to remain awake. Tiredness seeped through his bones after the climb, and the world was closing in. Darkness encroached on the edges of his vision. An annwn leant over him.

'Maddoc, we've got you.'

'Take Rialta back to Haven,' he managed, then passed out.

19
A NEED FOR MÔR

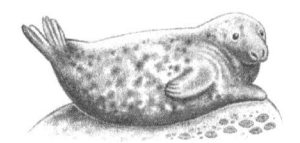

TELLIN

There was blood everywhere, but somewhere down there were four small bits of human flesh. With the hatch open, I began my search.

'Where did they do it?'

'Here. If you hadn't interrupted him, I don't think I'd have either thumb by now.' Theo winced as he spoke.

'Did you see what he did with them?'

He shook his head, muffling a sob.

'May the blackest chasm of the deepest ocean devour their spirits,' I hissed. Less movement meant less blood loss, but we didn't have time to be gentle. I needed those fingers.

'Theo, I need you to move. Can you shuffle away so I can get behind you?'

Oak charged through the door and stopped dead at the sight of Theo.

'Help me move him,' I said, making as much eye contact as

I could to draw Oak's attention my way. He nodded, shaking himself from his initial shock, and between us, we moved Theo carefully onto an area I knew was finger-free.

'There's a medic on *Barge*, right?' I asked Oak quietly.

He nodded. 'Yeah. I guess you'd not need one. Aline is based in the residents' area. Has a skinny-ass apprentice too.'

'How good are they?'

Oak shrugged. 'Before you came aboard, we did all the fighting, and I'm still standing. I have the scars to show for it.' He pulled his sleeve up. Fresh bruising showing from the day's scuffle crossed over faded silver scars. I looked him over more carefully. The blood on his face appeared to be from somewhere – or someone – else, and he was limping.

'Help me find his fingers then.'

We searched the area where Theo had sat, finding three of the four fingers easily. I cradled them in my hand.

'You need ice,' Theo mumbled. 'Have you found them all?'

'Three.'

He sighed deeply. 'That's better than none.'

'Oak, can you stay with him? I need Zora.'

'Yes, I'll keep looking for the last one.'

I hauled myself up onto the deck and stopped in stunned silence at the sight of the other vessel. Zora had frozen the lot, people included. I stared at the frozen figures in horror and awe. 'Zora did that? I'm surprised she's still standing.'

Petrel was alongside with Ivy at the controls.

'We need to get Theo back urgently. He's badly injured. Can you and Oak keep the other vessel secure if Zora, Ash, and I take Theo back? I'll send others to recover you.'

Ivy shrugged. 'Sure. Leave *Petrel* with us in case we need to get away fast. You go get him back. We'll see you later.' She gestured at the pack of selkies who still swam around the boats. 'Would you mind having a word with them first, though? Don't fancy our odds against a pack with teeth like yours and charms like hers.' She gestured up at where Sal's mum had stood.

'Of course,' I replied.

'I see you,' I called over the water.

'We see you too, Tellin Dark.' There were no false names with the selkie pack – another thing to explain later. I sighed inwardly. 'I need to take this vessel back to the haven – there's an injured man aboard.'

'Can you not help him?' the larger of the pack asked.

'How? I'm no medic.'

He blew across the water, his whiskers making tiny waves in the wind shadow alongside us. 'I thought you Northern selkies still had the old magic, the ability to heal. I'd hoped you could teach us.'

'I've never seen any of my pack heal anyone but themselves,' I replied. 'I wish I did. I have the same as you, just the same old self-healing and curse.'

His eyes widened. 'You still have the curse? We've lost that.'

'Maybe our magic just works in different ways. I've always found Sal much more powerful than me. You should see how intricate his illusions are! Once all this is over, I'll come back, and we can talk more, maybe?'

'I'd like that. Do you have enough people to sail the boats? There aren't many of you.'

'We can do it in two trips. Can you keep my friends safe?' I gestured to Ivy. 'I'll take the Sea Witch with me. That iceberg might melt once she's out of range or sleeps.'

'I'll keep them safe,' he said. Then, more quietly, 'Do you think, maybe, Sal might let another couple of selkies visit his ship if we do? I know the elders weren't welcoming, but we aren't all like that. Can you tell him Môr would like to visit?'

'I'll ask him. But right now, I truly need to go.'

Ash and Zora emerged from the hatch, blood-spattered and dragging the corpse of the man behind them.

'Throw him overboard!' Zora said.

'No! I needled him. Don't poison the fish,' I called. 'We'll have to take him back to *Barge*.'

'Zora, I need more ice. I have three of Theo's fingers. He says to freeze them.'

She stared at the small, pink objects I cradled, then took them from me and carefully encased each in a layer of ice. 'Only three?'

'So far. I couldn't find the last one.'

She looked exhausted. Her legs shook, and I helped her to a sitting position before she passed out.

We needed another set of eyes or hands, after all. 'Ash, can you go and sit with Theo a moment? Let Oak come back up so we can get underway. The last finger must be aboard. We'll find it somehow.'

Oak jogged onto the deck and helped me check our prisoners. We ensured the two sleeping crew members were safely tied up, and the groaning heap of broken-legged mess of a man that Oak had left on the deck was not going anywhere fast. Once he was happy, he joined Ivy, and they sped off to the other boat in *Petrel*.

Ash could helm while Zora slept off the exhaustion she

was wrestling through, but then we'd have no one to support Theo.

'I could use one more set of hands,' I called across the water. 'If one of you truly wishes to visit *Barge*, now's the time.'

The selkie who had spoken earlier swam close. 'I will.'

'Can you trust another to take care of the bachelor pack?' I asked, knowing he would have fought hard for his position.

'Yes. While the walrus remains, he must be protected.'

Môr swam powerfully towards me, and I could smell his excitement on the wind. 'Please, glamourise your face before you board,' I said.

'Naturally.' He placed a veil of wrinkles and sun spots over his flawless face after he removed his skin.

A gentle snore reached me from the bow. Zora had lost her battle with wakefulness.

'Stay here so I can explain your presence. While Ash is at the helm, please stand wherever she tells you.'

'I heard you are missing a finger? Maybe I can help scent it out?' he suggested.

It would be easier to sail *Black Hind* between myself and Ash. I hesitated for a moment, then agreed. 'Let me just warn Theo.'

Theo gave me a half-smile when I told him that another selkie would be joining us to get him home.

Ash shook her head slowly. 'I'm gonna need a big drink tonight,' she muttered, then went to collect Môr from the deck. He came down, cradling his pelt and entirely naked, aside from his thick, waist length hair which was a pale, dusty brown. It wasn't an unpleasant sight, but did need dealing with. I retrieved some of my looser clothing from my cabin and left him with Theo.

Back on deck, I pried the anchor chain from Zora's

exhausted hands and, with Ash's help, gently moved her sleeping form.

I lifted the anchor, and *Black Hind* rocked gently as I wound my way around the captives and back to the cabin to release the panel shield. 'Panels up, and engine on,' I sang out, and Ash took control, turning us away from the selkie island and back towards *Barge*.

20

HOW MANY FINGERS AM I HOLDING UP?

TELLIN

Once we were underway, I headed down to the hold. I didn't want Theo uncomfortable and battered while he couldn't stabilise himself. His bed was messed up, and his stuff strewn all around the cabin he shared with Ria. I rummaged around and found an untouched blanket on one of the other beds to take. Back in the galley, it was clear that those who stole *Black Hind* had no idea how to work the panels. Dried food packets had been opened, their contents scattered around the floor. I found a small stash of Zora's chocolate at the back of the shelf; she was as predictable with her hiding places as a tompot blenny. She wouldn't begrudge him when she woke. It was way too sweet for my tastes – chocolate made my tongue hurt – but I knew the rest of the crew enjoyed it. Maybe I could persuade Theo to eat some.

Theo was still in the corner. We'd had to close the hatches, so the hold was dimly lit, but now that the panels were running, he looked so uncomfortable. Môr rushed across as soon as he saw the door open.

'I found it!' He held out the last finger.

'I'll get it to the others as soon as I can. Thank you, Môr.' I flashed him a true smile before crouching next to Theo and attempting to coax him out of the hold. 'Please, at least will you come to your bed? Or maybe the table if you won't lie down,' I cajoled wrapping the blanket around him, breaking some chocolate, and placing it on his tongue.

'Where I would be in the way? No,' he mumbled through the chocolate.

'Theo, if you don't move of your own free will, I'm getting Ash down here to help carry you.'

'Ash wouldn't force me. She respects me too much. She was always a tearaway kid – I tried to take her out on trips, get her to love sailing, but she always preferred big ships. Likes to poke around in technology – and places she shouldn't be. But she won't go against my wishes.' Theo struggled for breath.

'Too much talking, not enough breathing, Theo.' I tried to hook an arm through his. 'Come on. Let's get you somewhere warmer. Don't lie to yourself. You need to get out of here, and Ash would rather upset you than lose you. Môr will support your other side.'

'Fine.' The big man shrugged. 'To the table – a seat. I don't want to lie down. It would hurt even more.'

Hurt? He'd lost the fingers on one hand, and I didn't want to tell him how bad his eye looked. There was brave and stupid, and Theo was pushing past the first into the territories of the second. I should have got Zora to give me some ice for his eye before she passed out. Theo leant heavily on me, curled slightly to one side. I wouldn't be surprised if they'd done something to his ribs too. His breath was snatched and shallow as we walked slowly to the table.

I propped him up carefully. 'I'll be back soon. I need to go and check Ash is alright. There are quite a few captives up there.' His shoulders moved with a brief laugh, but the noise stilled before he could release it, slipping into pain.

'Captives on the deck and another selkie in the cabin. Go. I'll be okay.' He leant over the table. Gods of Below, his arms looked painful tied like that. I swallowed and looked away; he mustn't see I was concerned. It wouldn't help him.

'I'm going to try and get us back to *Barge* quickly,' I reassured him as I left the cabin. Above deck, Ash stared fixedly at the water while Zora still slept.

'He's going to be okay until we get him back?' Ash's words were more a spell of desperation than a true question. I knew the feeling of that emotional whirlpool, and all I could do was throw her a life raft.

'He's strong, Ash. Now, let's get back there faster. I'm going to try and wake Zora.' I negotiated the bodies and people on the deck to reach the bow. I shook Zora, but she was in deep sleep, and with all the will in the world, she wouldn't wake soon. I found the small collection of frozen fingers she'd curled around, protecting the spell with her own body, and added the last one to the bag. Then, I took up a position on the upper edge of the deck. We'd centralised the captives as best we could, but we still heeled more than one selkie's weight could help with. I could use Môr up top as we went through the headlands where the wind shifted.

'Môr,' I called into the cabin. He appeared shortly after.

'He's sleeping, and I've packed him in. Can I help?' he asked.

I shrugged helplessly. 'One of my closest friends is down in the cabin with his eye smashed in and his fingers cut off. I suspect broken ribs too. Another is asleep on the deck from expending the energy to free him. Without Sal's mother and her distraction early on, we could never have done this. You've already helped. I need your weight over here so we can try to pick up some speed.' I wilted slightly as I continued, moving to stand at the rail alongside him while Ash coaxed *Black Hind* to give us a little more. 'I wish there was truth in your rumours. I wish I could heal him.'

'Tales get churned and intertwined,' Môr replied. 'Tell me a tale I don't know. How did you end up travelling with my cousin?'

'He rescued me, as he has rescued many others. Sal does a lot of good.'

He let a smile dance over his lips, grasping for the rail as we crashed through the waves. Ash was not as smooth a helm as Theo, and she was pushing us hard.

She called for adjustment of the sails, and I did so quickly. Ash raised a hand as they reached her desired position, and I clamped the rope into the cleats.

'The people aboard *Barge* know me as Sal's cousin.' I looked directly at Môr as I spoke. He didn't flinch as I continued. 'My skin was stolen, and Sal helped me find it. He gave me his protection at my most vulnerable.'

'And in return, you give him what?' There was a humour in his tone.

'Dead bodies and rescued Old Ones. It's a little more complex than that, but that's all you need to know. Should you hear his daughter mentioned, don't worry that you have missed more family news – that's me too. I'm sorry.'

'Living amongst humans requires a level of deception,' he replied. 'I did it once. It was fun but had certain ... challenges. What's your daughter name?'

I was taken aback. The pack's hostile rejection of Sal led

me to believe that it was something they hated. One of the captives groaned, reminding me that we were far from alone. I kicked each in turn, checking they were still under the effects of my drug. Ash might have been listening, but she stared so deliberately away from us that I felt confident enough to continue. I leaned in close to whisper, 'Lady Gina.'

Ash brought us in against a different deck than I was used to. It led to the resident's area; it was less gaudy and the boards more worn and weathered than those at the stern of the vessel. The relaxed familiarity of the women who tied *Black Hind* alongside their deck – and the reaching for hidden weapons when one of the captives stirred – identified them as Driftwood.

'These guests need escorting to the double-walled guest rooms, please,' Ash called across. One of the women gestured for Môr to follow her, and I shook my head.

'This one's with me. Take the rest of them, please, and fetch a medic urgently.'

The smaller woman, thin-nosed and wiry, glanced along the deck. 'Is that Zora? She looks pale.'

'It's not for Zora,' Ash growled. 'It's for Timothee Maritim. These bastards fucked his hands up and possibly his sight.'

The Driftwood kicked the nearest captive, who didn't move. 'The tide-cursed on the deck can say there.' She spat, turned, and ran.

The other nodded slowly. 'We care for our own first.' She approached Zora, crouching near her. It had been several hours, so there was a chance Zora might wake – and she did, slowly sitting upright. She picked up the precious bag, checking the fingers were still frozen.

'You found the last one! Well done, Georgie,' she said. 'Did he make it?' I nodded. 'Then let's get him above deck so the medic can get to him.' Together we descended, and with a mix of cajoling and reassurance, we managed to support an exhausted Theo to the deck, where he promptly collapsed again. He regarded the tied-up captives with hooded eyes and nodded.

'Good job. Who did the kneecaps?'

Ash crouched. 'That was Oak. Timothee, you've had an eye on me since I was a barely salt-wet kid. It's time for me to return the favour. Rest, and get better. I'll clear it with Lord Sal to look after your boat until you're ready to sail her again.'

Zora shot me a glance, her eyebrow raised. Those two really did go back further than we realised. 'I'm exhausted, Georgie. Do you mind if I sleep the rest of this off?' she asked quietly.

'Go. We've got this.'

Zora's steps lacked their usual bounce, and she stumbled as she left the deck, crossing paths with the woman who had run to collect the medic. A small figure bustled onto the deck shortly afterwards. Her grey hair was coiled atop her head like a shell. Small, dark eyes peered intently at Theo, and she chewed her lip as the large bag she dropped to the deck opened with a click.

'Shoo. All of you.' She glanced at the large man with broken legs and then back to us. 'Am I supposed to deal with that too?' she muttered. 'Always a mess when Driftwood goes out.'

'No, we'll deal with them,' Ash growled. 'Don't waste your medicine on them.'

The two Driftwood gestured at Ash. 'Shall we get them secure?'

'Yeah, I'll give you a hand.' Working as a team, they lifted the first captive, vanishing into the passage with the limp body hanging between them.

Shell-hair looked up at Môr enquiringly. 'Give me a hand until my apprentice arrives, would you?' She didn't wait for a reply, but looked to me. 'Do you have his fingers?'

I passed her the bag. 'It took us a lot longer to find one than the rest.'

'Urchin balls,' she muttered under her breath, staring at his hand intently. 'Timothee, I'm sorry.'

I sat next to him and wrapped my arms around the big man's shoulders as he let out a gasped sob. 'Gods, Aline, if you're saying that, it must be bad.'

Aline and Môr busied themselves behind him, their whispered instructions covered up by Theo's cries of pain.

A skinny youth ran onto the deck, followed by residents bearing some sort of bizarre object between them. It looked almost like a chair but had no legs. 'I'm here, Aline,' the youth said through curtains of hair.

'I see that. We'll move Timothee to the warmth.'

I was gestured away, and between the residents, they lifted Theo and placed him into the device. He was strapped in with his legs dangling loose and borne from my sight.

'I'll look after him. Don't you worry,' Aline said. 'You can come see him this evening. He needs rest until then.'

With the deck empty of casualties, Ash sat heavily on a winch block. 'Fuck me,' she muttered. 'You guys really do pull different shit than us.'

'Talking of Driftwood, we need to get Ivy and Oak back here,' I said.

Ash glanced back out to sea. 'I'll arrange that. You need to get your guest aboard before people start asking questions. Don't worry, Georgie, Tellin, or whatever your actual name is – my lips are sealed. I promised Theo I'd look after his boat, and that applies to her crew too.'

I was about to reply that *Black Hind* was mine, but thought better of it. Some things didn't need saying.

Reluctantly, I left my boat in Ash's care and took Môr inside *Barge*. 'Stay close,' I murmured. 'What do you want to see?'

'Everything! Will Sal be able to show me around?'

'That depends on which areas you visit.'

Sal could hardly parade round an old local man without attracting attention, though it was best that he stayed unremarkable. The glint in Môr's eyes shone through his glamour as we wound our way through the resident's quarters.

'You'll have to stay overnight now. We can't get you back tonight.' I saw him try – and fail – to hide his grin. 'Everyone knows each other down here, so I'll have to hide you in my other rooms. They have a shared private corridor with Sal's suite that will allow you to slip in and out, as well as access to our dock, where the red boat will return later. No one aside from the crews you met today knows Sal or I are selkies, and they know nothing about Zora's power.'

'Or Timothee's?' he asked.

'What do you mean? He is an incredible sailor, but that's his only secret. We know everything there is to know about each other on *Black Hind*.'

He glanced at me as though to check my honesty.

'The scrapes we've been in, he'd have used anything he had,' I continued as we passed along another small passageway and into a Driftwood checkpoint.

They looked at me and raised an eyebrow at Môr.

'Wrong side of the walls,' one muttered.

'Young Gar's grandfather.' The idea sprang fully formed from my lips. At that, they relaxed.

'Nice kid. Glad we could help get him home to you. Sorry about the blindfold, but you can't see the way through.'

I'd expected as much and took it quickly from the outstretched hand so that I was the one fitting it to Môr. Then, I gently led him through the hidden maze of passages connecting the resident's area and the opulence above.

No one passed us, and as soon as I was confident that we'd not be seen, I removed the blindfold. 'This really is an adventure,' he enthused.

'We have a lot of guests, who we keep above deck. Our residents need somewhere to call home away from all – this.' His eyes widened as he took in the purple paint, the velvet wall hangings, and the deep carpet.

'I want to feel it on my feet. It looks so incredibly soft.'

'It is, but let's get to my rooms. You can feel it there!' I held back a laugh as I rushed him through. We descended towards the painting of the northern Territories and into the calmer colours of my little area of *Barge*.

'Is that your home?' he asked, his hand pausing a finger's width from the frame, much like I did almost every time I passed.

'Yes, Sal had it painted for me soon after I arrived.' I passed him and strolled to Gina's rooms, opening the door and peering in to check they were as empty as I expected. We strolled in, and almost immediately, Môr slipped off his shoes and curled his toes into the sandy carpet. Age, experience, and power – it appeared we selkies were all equally fascinated by softness underfoot.

I was rummaging in my closet for something Georgie-appropriate when I heard the door open. 'Don't go out without me,' I called.

'Too late,' Ria answered. 'Why are you in here? Who's that?'

She looked exhausted. There was blood on her clothes, and she flopped on the bed.

'You look like urchin dung, Tellin,' she muttered. 'No wonder you're rummaging in there. Whose blood is that?'

'Theo's. He's alive,' I followed up quickly as the colour drained from her face. 'I could ask you the same thing.'

She looked down. 'Oh, I suppose it must be Maddoc's. He's going to be fine. He's with the annwn. Theo though ... that could be a problem.'

She stared pointedly at Môr. 'You're another selkie.'

'Pleased to meet you. Why is your friend's poor health a problem?' he asked, taking a seat in my chair as though it was his room, not mine.

'Ria, get yourself cleaned up. I'll take Môr to Sal's rooms for a bit. Maybe he can show Môr some of *Barge*.'

'Thank you,' she said. 'I need a word alone. It's quite personal.'

We exited through the back of my suite and navigated the passage to Sal's room. I knocked before entering. It wasn't my normal practise, so I hoped it would warn him that it wasn't a normal visit.

'Come in,' he called, and I opened the door. Sal was sat in his red chair with a book.

'Sal, you have a visitor.'

He set the book down. As he looked up to see his cousin, I caught the flicker of a smile, a breath filled with hope.

'Môr.' Sal rose to his feet, the book discarded.

'I'll leave you two alone.' I said, and left quietly.

21

HERBS AND KNIFES

MADDOC

There was too much light. Maddoc threw his arm across his face. His mouth was as dry as the Barren, and he was so hungry that his stomach felt knotted. He tried to speak, but his tongue stuck to the roof of his mouth.

'Where am I?' he croaked. 'Can I have a drink?'

'The Lady said nothing to eat or drink.'

'Call her!' Maddoc lowered his arm and tried to work out where he was, as the attending annwn hadn't answered.

A shimmering dome of water sparkled above him, and a passageway deep to the lands beneath the waters spiralled past, almost close enough to touch. He reached for it; he could just find her himself. Maddoc pushed himself off the mossy bed and stared at the whirlpool passage.

No, he would wait. While he was protected from the sight of mortal eyes at the sky-lakes, they hadn't taken him into their home, instead keeping him in a sort of mid-way place.

He smiled as much as his parched lips would allow. It was rather apt for a half-Tylwyth Teg.

He laid back on the soft bed and reached for his wounded leg. It was still there – that was a good start. Maybe one of them had deigned to use magic on him.

Fish swam over his head, shadows darting from one side of the sky-lakes to the other. Other faint shadows graced the surface, small birds going about their hunt with no regard for those beneath the waters.

It was as quiet below the water as it was above – an unearthly stillness that he never truly found down the mountains. He could see the top of the mound from there – the library's exit on the island in the lake. Anyone appearing on it wouldn't be able to hide. It made him certain there was someone amongst his people who knew about the egg theft.

The annwn who sat nearby said nothing while they were alone. Maddoc twisted to see them staring at the island too, a guard for the guardian of secrets and legends watching to ensure Lord Flame's slumber remained undisturbed.

Except that he knew Lord Flame was awake. Maddoc reached for his leg again. 'Did my companion get back to Haven?' He twisted himself to look at the watcher.

'Yes, we took her back.'

Short and to the point. Rialta would be on her mission to retrieve the egg she knew of. The time scale set by Lord Flame was almost impossible, even with a fast boat.

How long had he been down there? His insides told him at least a day. What was that floating past his head? He chuckled as the feet were replaced by a beaked face, and a duck reached towards him. At the water's edge, a feral sheep, its overly thick fur heavy and dragging in the water, drank deeply.

Slowly, Maddoc bent the dragon-slashed leg. Pain lanced through him as the wound's edges pulled apart, and the muscles beneath it threatened to rip further. He laid it back down, bending the other enough to let him sit up. He could see through the water-wall, down the stairs, and into the mist from whence the tall silhouette of his mam appeared.

'You survived the night,' she said. Was that a pang of disappointment in her tone? Her joy over death, over endings in general, was disturbing. He was grateful that part of her personality hadn't been passed on.

He offered her a smile. 'I'm hungry and thirsty,' he responded. 'Can we do something about that before we speak? I have urgent things to share with you but am afraid my hunger will distract me from the details.'

'Of course. I'll have something brought up for us.' She reached over him and swept Maddoc up in her arms as though he was still a child. With no further words, she carried him out of the lake and set him on the island once more.

'Why not the shore?' he asked.

'This was closer,' she replied, lifting a curl of wet hair from his cheek. 'What did you find?'

'Betrayal, theft, and fire. If we don't find Lord Flame's stolen egg, then the fire will spread. The betrayal will cut the Pact to shreds, and the thieves will steal a crown in addition to the egg. I didn't care about the crown, but maybe we should.'

'Who stole it?'

Maddoc shook his head. 'I don't know, Mam. There were booted prints of varied sizes, but the strangest thing was the paw prints.'

The Lady leant forward, eager for details – he could see the hunger in her eyes. Nothing of interest had happened since the Pact was sealed, and her enthusiasm was palpable.

'Paw prints of a beast both huge and so hot that it melted the ash that settled on the floor of the library. Perfectly melted prints ran around Lord Flame's chamber – until he awoke and scattered them.'

'Melted paw prints? I've not heard of a creature with that trait? It must be one far from its origins or displaced by the Barren.'

Food appeared, floating on a small boat-like tray towards the island. His mam reached down and retrieved it. 'I didn't want to risk snaring you when we need you up here. I'm sorry for your hunger.' She didn't look sorry, but he accepted the words and food regardless. A small loaf of bread and some cheese were soon demolished, and, finally sated, Maddoc sat back and looked more directly at his mam.

'Can you think why all the records of Y Plant Rhys Ddwfn might have been hidden? All of the deeds and stories – bar one from a human that someone clearly decided was not valuable – and a land deed.'

'Hidden? I never ordered anything moved. In honesty, I thought Y Plant long gone. When the warming happened, their islands would have flooded. I'd presumed that all those who could not take another form were drowned, and they were a race long lost. With their islands now resurfacing, maybe they return to the land. What was the property they gave away?'

Maddoc sipped slowly at the clear lake water. It was so typical of his mam. He'd asked her about those islands before she sent him into the library to find out about them. Then he mentioned them again, and she was suddenly full of knowledge. If he dared to roll his eyes in her presence, he would have.

'The island now inhabited by the selkies has partly broken whatever charm existed. After all, I can recall seeing some islands, but they could have been nothing more than mere lumps on the horizon, not the gilded images I had in my mind.

If that charm was strong enough to take, could they be back? And if so, what interest would they have in stealing Lord Flame's egg?'

Her eyes widened. 'Does he know?'

'Yes, and to complicate things, there's a chance that Rialta already has knowledge of where it is. She knows the location of one for certain. An egg sent as a bribe to a Terranian king. She also said it got wet.'

'Then she needs to rush. You did the right thing sending her back without waiting for me. If someone like her can't get it back, then we have no chance. We need to figure out who took the egg.'

The way Rialta sat on Lord Flame's neck to pin him down had certainly been impressive, but he failed to see how she could travel fast enough. 'We'll need to set a watch for her return. Someone who can whisk her back here as soon as possible,' his mam continued. 'In the meantime, we have a few things to investigate. Can you stand?'

There may be two weeks in Lord Flame's time scale, but he had his own. They needed to fix things before the veils of the Pact faded; before it was too late and the restrictions it placed on their ability to harm each other were so thin as to be useless. He struggled up, and to his surprise, his mam offered her arm as support. 'We're going to go and visit Y Plant,' she murmured. 'Hold on.'

One step and they were over the mountains.

Two steps, and he could see the coast in the distance.

Three steps. His mam stepped from the Path. Maddoc collapsed, his exhausted legs struggling to keep him steady. His nostrils filled with the heady waft of the herbs he'd smelt on the island. As he lifted his hand, the freshly crushed herbs sprung back to life, their twisted stems and crunched leaves graced the air with aroma.

'There,' his mam said, pulling him close so they both fitted into the small patch of herbs. It must have been barely longer than his forearm in both directions.

'They're back. And that's a lot of ships.' Maddoc looked out at the islands crowding the horizon and the sea of masts around them. He stepped to the left as his legs grew unsteady, and the islands vanished.

'They've gone!' he cried.

'No, you're off the only spot in the whole of Mynyw where you can see them. Step back on the herbs.'

Maddoc tried to erase his frown and hobbled closer again.

'Bloody gods and wildfire! I can see them.' He moved on and off the spot several times as his mam ignored his amazement, staring out to sea instead.

'I don't think those boats are from around here,' she finally declared.

Maddoc bit back the sarcasm brewing on the tip of his tongue and nodded. 'I agree. But how will we get to them if every time we step off this spot, they vanish?'

His mam smiled, and the world recoiled. She bent down and murmured something. A dagger of pure energy appeared in her palm, growing from a tiny spike to a weapon with a blade as long as her hand. It glowed with gently pulsing white light and its own cloud of mist. It wasn't the first time he'd seen her do it, but each time, he felt inadequate. After a moment, the pulsing slowed, and the dagger solidified.

She crouched on the ground, digging the weapon into the soil around the edge of the herbs. 'We'll take it with us.' Within moments, she'd marked out a square. From the seaward side, his mam peeled it from the clifftop. Maddoc crouched alongside her, holding the edge that she'd freed. His leg pulled, the wound threatening to reopen. As she continued to slice out the herbs, he wondered why she hadn't created a spade – it would have worked so much better. Slow slice after slow slice, they removed the herbs from the clifftop, taking as much rootstock as possible and attempting to keep it stable. The ground was moist, and the soil was bound well by the woven roots.

They placed it to the side of its original location, and Maddoc stepped on it once more.

'I see them.' It was not the spot but the herbs that allowed the sight of the islands. 'If we see them by removing this ...'

His mam nodded slowly. 'Then they are providing sections of herbs for each of the ships navigating to them. We need a boat.'

'You're not seriously thinking of going yourself, are you?' Maddoc spluttered. 'If they invade here or come back to the library, you need to be here. You need your power. One dunking overboard or a large wave, and you'll be useless.'

'That's why *you* are going. You'll take a group of Tylwyth Teg and find someone who can helm. You must have found someone of use on that trip to the island.'

Theo? No, he'd have to take *Black Hind* south to get that egg back. Zora could helm; he'd seen her steering the boat. But – no, they needed to reach the egg. There must be others aboard *Barge*. A ship that massive with all its attendant craft must need people to sail it.

'What would you offer a human who took the risk?' he asked as an idea came to him. She'd probably say no – tell him to clear off – but he knew where there was a boat and an old woman not afraid to tell a Tylwyth Teg what for.

'Beauty? A long life?' his mother mused.

Maddoc choked back a laugh. 'I don't think she'd be sold on that. Nets that never need mending, maybe.'

'That easily pleased? I'm sure we could do that.'

22
FORWARD TO THE GALLEY

TELLIN

I rushed back to my rooms, where Ria waited, dressed, calm, and ready. Nothing ever appeared to ripple her still waters.

She watched me gasping for breath. 'No rush will change what I have to say. The few minutes you need to breathe won't make a difference in what we need to achieve. I need to speak to you alone, without Theo, for now.'

'Theo is very unconscious right now. He won't hear you even if you shout,' I replied.

Ria did suck a breath then, just a short inhalation but loud enough that I heard.

'What has your meeting with Maddoc's mother have to do with Theo?' I sat on the bed and kicked my shoes off.

'Everything and nothing. You remember all the treasures gifted to the late king of Terrania?'

'How could I forget? We'd only just returned the lizards when Anard sent us out again.'

'I think I've found the person responsible.'

'It's this mystery queen, isn't it? What does it have to do with Theo?'

Ria clasped her hands and leant forwards, her voice taking on a solemn tone. 'Deep under a ruined abbey, in a magical place between this world and the Other, lies a magical library. Its entrance only opens by individuals from different aspects of the Pact working together. We were able to open it with three of us.'

'What did you represent?' I asked. I couldn't imagine her powers would open any magical lock keyed to the selkies.

'That doesn't matter.' She flapped the question away like it was a strand-bug on her meal. 'What matters is what's in there. Deep underground slumbers a northern dragon. The Tylwyth Teg refer to him as Lord Flame. Tellin, I thought they were all gone. Yet there he was, slumbering in his hidden library filled with magical books and records. It was incredible.'

'Theo?' I pushed, sensing the possibility that she was going off track again.

'I'm getting there. Lord Flame sleeps in the library, as he has done for many hundreds of years, along with his egg. But it wasn't there. It had been stolen. The way Maddoc described it – right down to the golden sheen – makes me certain it's the one we left with Theo's mother.' She stood, raising her hands with palms upwards as she paced. She stopped, spinning to face me. 'Tellin, we left a northern dragon egg in his flotilla. When it hatches, it will eat its way through everyone.'

'If it hasn't hatched for so long that we thought they were extinct, why are you worried?'

'Because it got salt-wet. Do you remember when Anard transferred it to *Barge*? It got sprayed and splashed by the rowers on that small boat. When I unpacked it, it wasn't responding, remember? But it *was* definitely wet. Lord Flame has given us two weeks to find and return the egg, else he will emerge from the library and go hunting for it himself.'

'Why's that such a problem?' I thought it sounded an excellent idea. He could get to his lost egg a lot faster than we could, and Theo's mother would be saved.

'Because he's the last one. Because to lose him and his egg would be the end of the sirens and the dragons. It would mean that when the current guardians die out, they would be the last – the north left unprotected and the ice even more vulnerable. The waters might even rise again.

'It would also mean the Pact of Mynyw was irrevocably broken. The Tylwyth Teg and the dragons have only survived by hiding from human eyes – much as you did. For Lord Flame to grace the skies once again would expose every last one of us as a truth, for if you believe in dragons, then everything else is a smaller step. Old Ones would be forced to defend themselves from inevitable attacks as humans fought over us as trophies, and the only possible outcome is a magical war against mankind – who are mostly too stupid to see that different doesn't mean bad.'

'You really mean this. We have to go collect this egg. What happens if the egg hatches aboard *Black Hind*?'

Ria laughed. Nervous, rattling – pebbles of noise dropped in a dry rock pool. 'I'll sit on it. If I can pin Lord Flame down, I can weigh down a hatchling.'

I wasn't convinced by her bravery, though I knew she was capable of it. I felt her to be a friend, but I didn't like the idea of Ria having to weigh our lives against that of one of the last Old Ones. There were plenty of selkies. And, even if I hadn't met any, Sirena's comments about Sea Witches as we rescued her from Prince Ulises implied that there were more out there somewhere. No, getting the egg back unhatched would have to be the priority.

'We'd better leave as soon as we can get *Black Hind* provisioned.' I said and slipped my shoes back on.

'What's wrong with Theo?' Ria asked.

'There were a group of Terranian mercenaries, pirates – whatever they call themselves – aboard *Barge*. They killed Iris, then fled, stealing *Black Hind* on their way.'

I rose to grab some food from my tank, forgetting that as Gina was away, her tank would be empty. Urchin's arse, I wasn't in the mood for faking enjoyment of human food. I hovered my hand over it, trying to decide whether or not to pull out the last fragments of seaweed that had encrusted the rocks but thought better of it. Ria stared at me.

'They cut his left-hand fingers off and hit him so hard in the eye that I'm not sure he'll see out of it again.' There, I'd said it. It felt no better once the words floated from my mouth. Why Theo? It felt so unfair.

'Where is he now? Did you find the fingers?'

'Yes, we gave them to Aline. She wasn't sounding hopeful when I left her, though.'

'He can't sail.' Ria sank to the chair. 'The only way we can get there is if we sail non-stop, and Theo can't sail. We can't expect Zora to remain awake for two weeks, and with the best will and meant kindly, Tellin, you aren't skilled enough to do long periods. Nor am I.'

'Ash. We'll have to take Ash,' I replied. 'She keeps muttering about Theo being family, maybe the same flotilla. At the least, she can get us there.'

'Ash it is.' Ria agreed.

'Theo won't like this.' I shook my head, knowing that trying to keep Theo where other medics could keep an eye on him would be hard – on all of us. He was as much family to me as Sal or my blood family, if not more.

'I can't see Theo until this evening, and Zora needs to rest until then. She froze an entire ship – it was amazing! Shall we get food?' My stomach was growling, and despite the lack of sleep, food would need to be addressed first, even if it was human food.

'Shall we head to Forward Galley?' I asked. 'I don't fancy the Ocean Bar tonight.'

Ria nodded. 'We'd be better sleeping in our other cabin in the residents' section anyway.'

'I'll meet you there. I need to see Seren about the supplies.' Ria didn't wait for dismissal; she just left. I liked her straightforwardness. It was a refreshing change from human niceties.

Seren was easy to find. Given the recent situation, she was in the Purple, looking after the women who chose to work there. Despite outward appearances, no one was ever asked to do a job on *Barge* they didn't choose. The clothes, status, and gifts those women had access to, as well as the power of their patrons, afforded them a higher level of comfort than many other residents. The carpet's deep pile sank under my feet as I strode towards Seren's drifting voice.

'No one entertains a Terranian alone. Do you all understand? There may be others who try to board. From now onward, unless you know them and they're a long-term resident here, do not be alone.' Let Pine know if you take anyone from the tented area below deck, and he will arrange an escort.

Her care for the women was evident. There was no real level of status on *Barge*; everyone worked to keep her running, to keep money and information flowing the right way.

I stopped by the doorway to Rose's room. 'Seren, can I have a word?'

'Georgie, of course. I always have time for you. How did it go, and how can I help now?'

'It feels like today has been a week,' I muttered. 'Seren, we have to take *Black Hind* back south.' I looked meaningfully at the women chattering around the over-indulgent room. One by one, they slipped from their silken pillows and retired to a room nearby.

'What aren't you telling me?' Seren shuffled closer.

'We need to collect something we left in the care of a flotilla.' I sat in a pile of cushions, sending them sliding everywhere. Once they finished slipping all over the floor, I carried on. 'Do you remember the animals Anard brought to us?'

'Yes.'

'There was also an egg. A huge one, shimmering gold, and Ria is convinced it needs to come here.'

I relayed the entire tale as quickly as I could while Seren sat back, soaking it all in.

'So what you're saying is that you need three weeks of food for six people? Medical supplies and the internal doors and hold of *Black Hind* re-enforced and made fireproof, by yesterday?'

'Six?'

'Yes.'

She frowned, and I could see her fingers counting off items as she spoke, multi-tasking as ever. 'You'll be taking Ash to helm and someone with medical experience to look after Theo as he recovers. Maybe Aline will let her apprentice go. He needs some time to develop real sea legs.'

'Theo's staying here to recover. It's only two weeks.'

'You want to tell him that? I want to be a fly on the wall when you tell him his mother's life is in jeopardy, and he has to hope you find her and retrieve an egg in time. I've met her numerous times, and I can tell you right now that Seaspray will not part with that egg, unless he's there.'

'But his hands?'

Seren sat back. 'Fresh dressings and whatever Aline has done will mend in its own time. Not letting him do anything aboard will be a bigger challenge. I've seen him recover from big injuries before.'

Recovering injuries was one thing, but deliberately letting Theo jeopardise himself was quite another. 'How quickly can you get *Black Hind* stocked?' I asked.

'I'll get someone on it right away. Go and rest – you'll need it.'

I nodded. She was right, as usual. 'Thank you, Seren.'

'It's his choice, Georgie,' she called as I walked away from her room.

Two weeks. It sounded almost impossible. The only thing in our favour might be the early spring weather since the last strong winds hadn't yet dropped away. I was trying to calculate times and distances when I walked into a wall of noise. Forward Galley was busy. The cushioned bench seating around the walls was packed, and all the tables had been pushed back from the middle to leave space for dancers and performers. The room pulsed with energy and life. There were as many bodies in there as any fancy gathering in Terrania, yet somehow it felt warm and welcoming.

Ria waved at me from a stool at the long bar that ran the width of the room. People shoaled in groups, moving in small masses from table to bar and bar to table with steaming plates of food in their hands. The scents turned my stomach, setting it to churning like water in a draining tide pool. It was sweet and spicy. Another table assaulted me with fresh bread and fragrant meats. I tried to ignore it and aimed for Ria. She liked to eat there, and I knew Seren would have ensured there was something I could digest on the menu.

We ordered our food and wandered away to a quiet corner where we could watch people dancing to the beat of a small drum and sea-pipes.

A slim, long-fringed figure scuttled across the edge of the cleared area, all legs and arms. They appeared to be looking around, but through the curtain of hair, it was hard to tell. Midway across the room, they changed course to head straight for us. As they grew closer, I recognised Aline's assistant. Presumably, the same one Seren was suggesting we take aboard *Black Hind*.

'Your friend's awake,' the lad muttered. 'Aline says you can see him if you want to.' He turned and walked back out of the room, joining the flow of bodies funnelling through the door and back to the residences.

Our food arrived soon after – the fish was cooked but edible, and once we'd eaten, I followed Ria to the pristine white medical area that Aline presided over with the same air of authority that Seren held elsewhere on *Barge*.

'I'm coming with you.' Theo said after we'd explained what was happening. He was propped upright in his bed, his hand heavily bandaged and his eye cleaned but still swollen shut. He saw my glance at his hand and waved it at me. His fingers rigidly fixed under the dressing.

'Aline reattached them,' he beamed. 'They may not be perfect, but if Aline can't fix them, then no one can.' Ria reached for his hand, and Theo withdrew his arm; he winked as he spoke, but the wince of pain showed his truth. 'You can't have their souls yet. I'm not letting you have any part of me until I'm done with it.'

Ria laughed. 'I was just curious. Human medicine is such a strange thing. Surely you need to rest them, though, not charge across the ocean with us. Ash knows where the flotilla is.'

'Ash isn't me! I know the fastest routes, the best angle to sail *Black Hind* at for speed, and every buck, twitch, rope, and winch. She can't grow that close to her in a day or so. You need me.' He looked at me with his good eye. 'I put my mother in a danger far more imminent than I realised. I need to relieve her of that.'

'Not on your own, you don't.' Aline sailed in, tailed by her assistant. 'You only go if you agree to regular dressing changes and not to get your hand wet.' She produced a bag and a roll of tape from behind her back. 'You will wear this at all times above deck to stop your hand getting any wetter than necessary, and you do everything that Alex says.'

Theo growled at the skinny lad. 'Only if it impacts my hands or eye.'

'Of course. On the subject of the eye ...' She pulled out a highly decorated eye patch. Embroidered on it were blue crested waves breaking on dark purple leather. 'You need to wear this too.'

Theo took it and turned it over in his hand. 'Never thought I'd be wearing one of these,' he said.

'Could you?' I took the patch from his hand and gently positioned it.

'Arrrrr,' he growled. 'Do I look like I should be aboard one of Lost Jake's boats now?'

I bit back laughter. 'Ash and Zora will helm while you sit out on deck and direct us. But surely you need more work on that hand? Need to be under Aline's care.' Alex shuffled from foot to foot as he watched. He'd clearly been volunteered. He smelt of fear and nerves; it was sharp and tangy, his discomfort evident even for those without my enhanced sense of smell. I offered him a smile.

'How long will you be away?' he asked, a slight tremor in his voice. I pitied the kid. If his sea legs weren't good on a smaller vessel, we might end up looking after him rather than the other way around.

'We'll be back with the puffins,' I replied. Urchin spines, but he made me nervous just watching him. I hoped he could contribute more than patching Theo up once a day.

Aline checked Theo's hand and huffed an approving sound as she repositioned a turn of the bandage. 'He can't have anything else done for six weeks and needs to keep this on.' Theo opened his mouth, but she cut him off with a wave of her hand. 'I know what you're going to say. Don't waste your breath, Timothee. I'll pass this on to Georgie and Ria in your hearing or out of it.

'Georgie, we reattached all his fingers, but one was not as fresh as I'd have liked. There's a chance it could go bad. So, regardless of what Theo wants, Alex will be coming with you. If a finger starts to fail, someone will have to take action. I can't ask you to do it, and Theo's other hand won't do. Alex has performed amputations before and has the skills to do them. I'm sure Theo can guide him through it if necessary, and Alex will have whatever medical supplies I can spare in his bags.'

Beneath the floppy fringe, the skin paled. Poor Alex ... I

had no doubt that we'd be struggling to stop Theo performing his own surgery if he had concerns.

'If you're sure?' I checked one last time with Aline.

'Yes. Get him out of my space! He'll drive me crazy. Bring him back when you return so I can check his progress.'

'I'm still here, you know!' Theo chuckled. 'I've lost my sight on that side, not my hearing.'

Aline gestured for us to follow. Once we were out of Theo's hearing, she picked up a small bag from a white unit so clean it almost shone with its own light and pressed it into my hand. 'He's only this cheerful because he's full of drugs. When they wear off, he'll be in agony. Get him out of here by then. If he's distracted and busy, he'll cope better. For all the legends that follow in his wake, Timothee is still flesh and bone.'

I tucked the pouch into a pocket. 'As soon as *Black Hind* is ready, I'll collect him.'

23
A MAGICAL CREW

MADDOC

'You're not looking all that great now, are you? Tell me you haven't been up in that old hut for the last few days! Surely one such as yourself has means at their disposal to be in less of a state than this.' The old woman stared him up and down, a deep frown creasing her already weather-wrinkled face. 'No, you haven't. That wound has been treated, your clothes are changed, and you're dry.' She sat heavily on the sea wall and looked out over the water. 'Why are you back? I told you I want nothing from your kind, and you'll get nothing from me.'

Maddoc chose the sand instead of the wall, sat in her eyeline, and ran his hand over her nets, checking for damage. 'How would you like it if you never had to mend these again?' he asked.

'No, thank you. Mending them gives me a reason to be out here. It keeps my mind and brain busy. Why would I want perfect nets? What do you want from me? I've no children for you to steal and no crops for you to buy.' She looked at him then. 'I'm not bargaining with any of the folk.'

Maddoc bit his lip and continued knotting the net quietly.

'I'm not taking you back to the island,' she continued. 'Heard bad things about a walrus and strange sailors with foreign accents out there. Some idiot even claimed he'd seen a walrus resting on an ice-encased boat. No, out by there is not a place I'm headed anytime soon. So, you're mending my nets for nothing.'

Maddoc glanced around, ensuring they were out of range from other ears. 'I'm not from the islands. I'm not from the sea at all. But those who were lost are re-found, and they harbour foreign queens and warriors. They steal what is not theirs, and they break the Pact.'

She dropped her net. 'Look at me come over all cack-handed. You're speaking a load of capswabble to me now.'

Maddoc grinned. 'And you're using language many have forgotten. You're born and brought up here, as were your family. You must know these waters as well as the rocks on this beach.'

She snorted. 'Sweet talk gets you nowhere. Why should I care?'

'Because your cosy home, one of the last places on this planet almost untouched by the warming, is about to become a battle zone.'

She shrugged. 'Fight somewhere else then.'

'I have no control over where dragons fight.'

She stopped still, placed her net on the floor, and crouched close to him. 'The last dragons died out thousands of years ago.' But there was hope in her eyes, a light he hadn't seen before. She held his gaze, waiting.

'You ever wonder why the symbol of this land was a red dragon, long after he vanished?' Maddoc teased her, and she bit.

'Because he sleeps, but that's no truer than claiming that Bedd Arthur is the true grave of King Arthur. It's a legend, a metaphor for something else.'

'It's a truth, no metaphor. Lord Flame sleeps between the old abbey and the sky lakes. He dreams of revenge on those who stole his egg. If I cannot prove that the folk – Y Plant Rhys Ddwfn – took it, then he will come hunting, and last I saw him, he was pretty mad.' Maddoc gestured to his bandaged leg.

'Screw the nets. What do you need from me?' Her hands shook slightly, and Maddoc reached for them.

'I need your skills, your expertise, and I need you to sail your boat to the islands of the folk, so I can check they do not have Lord Flame's egg. You need only take us there.'

'If you are not *them*, then who are you?'

She was excited by dragons. Legends and myths were clearly the way into her favour. 'I am the only son of the annwn you know simply as The Lady of The Lake.'

'When you've lived as long as me, you stop getting surprised.' She shook her head. 'Now, you've done it twice. I'll sail you to a land of legend sunk beneath the waves if I can meet one of the legends you speak of first.'

'Sail first,' Maddoc suggested, and she shook her head.

'Meet one first. The other afterwards – assuming I survive. I'd be sailing a boat full of magical creatures to a place full of other magical creatures. It's a bit of a risk, don't you think?'

He wasn't sure this was a deal his mother would approve of, but it was the best he could get.

'One other question.' She picked up the net once more,

though her hands shook so much that it rattled its fibres against themselves. 'How do you propose we see invisible islands?'

'That bit, you can leave to me,' Maddoc replied. 'Can I ask you one more thing? Do you think you've met any Y Plant?'

'Aye. I've seen them ashore, flicking tails in the water and wandering through the market. They look different, and they speak different. But you can always tell.'

'If they're in the market, how did you recognise them in a crowd?'

She shrugged. 'You just can. They do things *different*.'

'Meet me at the top of the hill at first light,' Maddoc said. The old woman nodded her head, a small smile playing on her thinned lips. She rolled up her net, then walked off, whistling.

An old white building set back from the beach was busy with people, and the scent of food drifted out on the breeze. The sharp tang of onions and spices coiled up his nostrils, and Maddoc decided that eating before his return may as well be done there in the warm and dry, else he'd be too hungry.

A handful of patrons perched atop bar stools like seagulls on the roof outside, hunting for scraps of gossip, not food. Looking at a few of the skinniest, he couldn't help thinking that more food would help them too. Maddoc scanned the specials board; it all sounded delicious. He was so hungry for a hot meal that anything would do. The cawl might have been in the pot a while, judging by how thin it was in the bowl next to him, but the bread roll looked crusty and fresh, and it would be quick. As delicious as a freshly prepared meal would be, he needed to get back urgently. Ready food would do.

The steaming bowl arrived, chunky parsnips and vibrantly orange carrots mingled in the broth with lamb so tender he could barely catch it on his fork. The crusty roll and chunk of old-fashioned crumbling cheese finished it off beautifully. Maddoc inhaled the steam, knowing he was smiling like a moon-touched fool. But he really didn't care. It tasted every bit as delicious as it smelled.

While he enjoyed his food, Maddoc worried at the task ahead. He had a ship and a helm, so he just needed to bring a group of Tylwyth Teg down from the end of the Path and into a boat as though it was the most normal thing in the world. Oh, and persuade his mother to attend and do her party trick to pay for their passage.

The locals passed occasional glances his way but nothing overt, nor did they appear unduly concerned by the arrival of a stranger in their village. With so many travellers passing through and trading in the area, maybe it wouldn't be so bad. Still, for appearances sake, he decided to actually stay in a room for at least part of the night. He could use a proper rest on an actual bed!

He returned his empty bowl to the bar and hopped onto a seat. 'Thanks for the cawl – it was delicious.' His compliment was met with a broad grin from a soft-faced woman. She leant across the bar and took his bowl, her dark curls bouncing as she moved, and her ample curves filled out her loose dress. It had a delicate pattern around the neckline, twisting and knotting like something he'd see in his mother's home.

She coughed gently. 'I'm not for sale like the cawl.'

Maddoc felt redness creep up his cheeks. 'I'm sorry. It was just your dress ... the pattern is so unusual. Can I get a room for the night?'

'Just one night?'

'Yes, please.'

She reached under the counter and produced a wooden tagged key, marked with a large float. They weren't taking chances of it getting lost in anyone's pockets. 'Top of the stairs, on your right. Sorry, I've only got the hill-view room left. Breakfast is served from six.'

'Thank you.' Maddoc took the key and headed up the stairs she indicated. The room was small, and the soft bed looked incredibly inviting. But before he could rest, he needed to set the rest of his plan in motion.

Maddoc locked his door and opened the window. It was no drop at all for him, and he quickly slipped out of the back and headed into the darkness. The brambles caught on his clothes, and his injury hampered his movement, every step a personal challenge in the darkness. Eventually, he reached the Path. Lifting his hood over his head and holding his charm in his hands, he stepped back onto it, heading for the Black Mountain and the lake.

He stepped off at the top of the cliff and ran down the stairs into the lake, not at all surprised to find his mam waiting for him, a mixed group of Tylwyth Teg arrayed nearby.

'Do we have a boat?' She leant forward eagerly.

Maddoc gasped for breath. 'We do, and a bargain that needs your presence.'

'Fine, whatever. Did she want eternal youth after all? To be loved by everyone?'

'Heh, no. She simply wants to meet you before she will sail anywhere, and Lord Flame on her return.' A collective murmur rippled around the assembled Tylwyth Teg. Maddoc ignored it and approached his mam. 'We'll need a human to re-forge any Pact. One that is willing. Those Terranians who sail with the selkie may know what we are, may be willing to help, but they are not of this land, and they hold no sway over the magic that rules here.'

The Lady of the Lake raised her hand for quiet, her head

tilted to one side as she regarded him. He could taste her power in the air – coiled and ready to use if anyone should push her. Assembling volunteers must have been more challenging than they'd hoped.

'I will meet this woman. How many can you get aboard her vessel?' Maddoc rubbed his neck as he thought. The tension was building, and his muscles were tight. 'It's not huge. Maybe six,' he suggested.

'I need six volunteers. You might die.' Her laugh first filled the area, then faded away through the mist as though it had run away of its own accord. 'Should you volunteer for the scouting mission, I may look kindly on your assignment in any upcoming stand-off with Y Plant Rhys Ddwfn. If you have ever met with them before, if you know anything about their customs, please offer yourselves up now.'

Maddoc watched the group shuffle as individuals rated their chances of survival and willingness to leave their closed world for adventures of their own. Two annwn offered themselves first, kissing the outstretched hand of his mam before moving to stand alongside him. Both were tall and slender, with long golden hair typical of their kind. Their sculpted faces were identical, and the hard edges of their bone structures were reflected in the set tightness of their lips. The twins. Much like his mother, they found death fascinating and joyful, but their inhuman beauty would be hard to hide. Still, he knew they had certain talents, and every skill helped. He forced a smile, and they bowed together in response. Maddoc bit back the shiver that ran along his spine. His elderly human friend would not like the two of them at all.

A small changeling skipped and hopped forward, shifting in and out of his Tylwyth Teg and changeling forms as he did so. A human child would not be entirely out of place on a boat or likely to be questioned should they get close enough to put him ashore. Yes, he could work with that.

He leant closer to his mam. 'Two changelings would be even better,' he whispered. 'The most human-looking you can persuade.'

She shot him a look. 'Volunteers only, my son.' Maddoc retreated to scan the group.

A small and exceedingly misshapen individual stepped forward. 'I'd like to join you if you think I could be of any use,' the coblynau offered. 'I'll work hard all the way and do whatever is needed.'

'Your help is accepted.'

Maddoc sighed. He was never getting the Tylwyth Teg to the boat unnoticed. All that was missing now was a ... oh, great.

A wrinkled, elderly gwyllion pushed through the rest. Mist hung around her. He had no idea how they would navigate with her aboard, but at least compared to the rest, she looked human.

'Few folk wander the mountains in the winter. I find myself in need of more sustainable lives to take.'

'You promise not to take that of the woman who will sail the boat?' Maddoc asked, feeling rather protective of the woman who refused to share the power of her name with him.

'I do.'

'Then it appears you have your crew.' His mam turned to the remaining huddle of Tylwyth Teg. 'Go. I will need you all soon enough.' They flooded away like the receding tide, leaving just the eight of them.

'My son leads you. No matter your station, you defer to him. We will leave just before sunrise to meet him at the land's end, where he has secured you passage on a vessel to the lands of Y Plant Rhys Ddwfn. We have no certainty of what you will find, but some of you must return. Our peace depends on it. Mankind may wane, but there are still many who would see us as sport, or wish to use you, no matter how ridiculous it sounds.'

It was time to wear his guardian's role with pride and remember his place in the world. Maddoc pulled himself upright and smiled at his new companions. 'If you need to bring anything, collect it now. I'll meet you at dawn. We will be on the water for a good few days, if not longer, as we try to sneak into the islands.'

With that, he bowed to them all and turned to ascend to the surface.

The coblynau called out, 'Is it true that Lord Flame's egg has been stolen?'

Maddoc nodded. 'I saw the empty pillar with my own eyes. In his fury, he lashed out and caused the injury I bear on my thigh. It's also true that there was some creature amongst those who stole it whose very footprints melted the ash of Lord Flame's breath into solid glass.'

'What if we don't find the egg?'

'We'll deal with that if it happens. You all know the consequences of Lord Flame leaving his lair and flying in full sight of the humans. Let alone the chance of him killing to regain his egg. We need to find the foreign creature and learn why Y Plant would turn-coat and act against the Pact. For creatures so utterly averse to the concept of traitor, it makes no sense for any of them to act so ... irrationally. Even if they've had more dealings with humans in the past than many of us – except coblynau – turning against us makes little sense.'

Silence dropped as his new companions contemplated his words. The gwyllion spoke. 'We'll see you at dawn, Guardian.'

Maddoc nodded. No matter he was half-breed, it was good to remind them who he was. He dropped his hood, surreptitiously searching for the first step as the group began to break up. A mist rolled past his feet, outlining the first steps clearly for him. Maddoc turned to thank the gwyllion, but found them all departing. The old hag turned back and winked before she hobbled after the group.

24
STORM BOUND

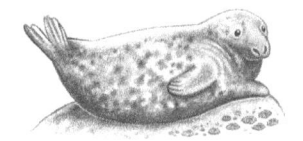

TELLIN

The wind rose, clouds scudded across the sky, and *Black Hind* climbed and surfed through the waves, as she tended to do. We'd left the Territories the day before to race south under the limestone-grey skies with the wind on our seaward side. Theo sat on deck, resting his back against the mast foot and watching the foils like a hungry gull. Occasionally he'd call something back to Ash, who, in turn, would raise a bemused eyebrow at one of us. The rope would get loosened, or the heading tweaked, and Theo would relax again. The winds were strong enough that we weren't willing to risk the dragon wing rig without his experienced hand on the helm, and so the blue sails graced our spars.

Zora stared over the bow, her black hair tightly braided away from her face in neat rows. She wore extra layers, and her waterproof coat flapped like swan's wings on take-off. She would likely remain there most of the day, looking for trouble and coaxing particularly unruly waves to flatten themselves for our smooth passage. She performed no huge works of magic. She might need those for the storm-rich bay we'd cross in the next few days.

There would be no stopping for anything but an emergency – that was the plan. Since we left *Barge*, Alex had mostly hidden below deck, occasionally venturing out to offer his weight to a steep heel. Wind whipped his curtains of hair into twisted threads the colour of sand. His eyes, having nowhere to hide anymore, were even more fidgety. Under the hair, he was older than I'd guessed. Probably a good thing, given he was potentially in charge of cutting Theo's finger off when things went wrong. He was maybe twenty summers old and reminded me of a hermit crab I'd met once. He'd scuttle across the deck, trying to be inconspicuous, then once spotted, he'd pop back into hiding, curling himself inward to try and avoid our notice.

We were three days into our journey when the wind started to howl through the rigging, and the crashing of waves against our side grew intense. I'd crossed the bay several times before and worked my way around the deck, checking all the winches were secure and each rope was where it should be.

'That one's tangled.' Theo pointed past me to a pile of ropes snaking through each other. He was right. I shouldn't have let them get that bad. 'I'd help, but …' He shrugged and waved his bag-covered hand at me.

'It's okay.' I started to untangle them, and he stayed close by, watching. 'How does it feel?' I asked. *How does it feel to have your fingers cut off and be left with stumps, then have them sewn back on, and held in a fixed shape onto a splint?* What was wrong with me? I kicked myself and hoped that the wind had stolen my voice.

'It hurts like nothing else,' he replied quietly. 'The worst is that one of them's going dark. I don't think Aline could save it.

Alex will likely have to do surgery. I know she gave you something stronger than she gave him. Do you think I could have it? The next few hours will be rough.'

'As soon as I've untangled these, I'll fetch some.'

Alex's quiet voice cut through the waves, all tremor gone for a moment. 'The white tablet only.'

Theo leant in, his uncovered eye closest to me. 'He is sneaky quiet, and his bedside manner needs some work,' he whispered. 'I hope his surgical skills have more confidence than he does.'

'If we can find a siren, maybe we can speed things along? You've said that you saw southern sirens as a child. Maybe, we'll come across some on this trip.'

'Maybe, but I'd not stop for the most beautiful woman in the world until Mum is safe. If you find one afterwards, I'll gladly douse my eye and hand in its vomit, but for now, we keep going.'

A wave crashed over, and the sluicing water caught Theo off guard. He instinctively reached for the rail, but his hand didn't grip. He thudded down to the deck. I grabbed for him, trying to break his fall slightly, and stopped him sliding any further.

'Right. You're going below deck until we're through the bay.' I had to shout over the rising wind.

'For once, you might be right, Tellin. I'll head down and strap in for the ride. Ash will be okay.'

'Ash will be down there with you,' I responded. 'Zora, Ria, and I have got this. Wake Ria and send her up.' If Ash and Alex were below deck, we could use Ria without upsetting the humans. They might not know what she was, but just in case, the sight of a small woman flattening a boat with the weight of thousands of souls was best left far from their imaginations.

With all humans safely below deck, Zora and Ria worked

their magic, and *Black Hind* sailed the smoothest path through the storm that we could manage. Occasionally, we'd see another vessel, and at one point, I caught a glimpse of a familiar three-hulled ship cresting a wave on the landward side.

Zora spotted it, too, and adjusted our course through some unusually tall waves. Given that we didn't have time to run from Icidro as well as race to the flotilla, I was grateful for her intercession – even if she feigned innocence when questioned about our incredibly lucky route through the storm.

We passed out of the bay late that night, and I wandered down to ask Ash to take a turn on the helm.

Rather than resting, they were sat around the table. Alex wielded a very sharp knife over Theo's unwrapped hand, and Ash held it still. Theo himself had mildly glazed eyes.

'What are you doing?' I rushed toward them. If he lost his fingers, Theo would never be able to sail *Black Hind* solo again.

'He's developed a fever,' Ash said. It wasn't the response I wanted, and she knew it.

'Then give him some of the medicine Aline gave me! Don't just hack his fingers off. It took you ages to sew them back on.' *Humans!* Theo's fingers were swollen, and the one they were concerned about was purpling and looked thin – far less healthy than the others. But it wasn't dead yet. It was as stubborn as Theo.

'What should we do? What can we do?' I asked. Ash looked pale and, in the lighting down there, a little green. Alex looked confident. The usual tremors were gone, and a hard determination glinted in his eyes as he studied the fingers.

'I'm not happy with this one. If it doesn't come off, there's a chance that this infection might spread to the others. If we were on *Barge*, I might give it a little longer before making the decision.'

I dropped to the seat next to him. 'Then give him a little longer now? What do you need from Theo to buy him that time?'

'Sing like a bird on the wing, a sign that we are near land.' Theo sang, waving his good arm around.

'He's had a heavy dose of the painkiller. Should fall asleep soon.' Alex glanced at Ash. 'I can't have people nervous around me while I work. It makes me anxious. Please go above deck.' Once Ash had stomped upstairs, muttering unhappily, Alex raised Theo's hand and sniffed it. 'It doesn't smell bad – yet,' he conceded.

I could have told him that without sending anyone away, but he was the medic.

'Sing little flying fish, sing a song of the sea ...' Theo was still singing, though words trailed off as his head started to drop, and before long, he was asleep.

'What he needs is to stay bloody still, dry, and to stop trying to help you all,' Alex said, his face flushing red.

'I can try to reason with him once he is between doses,' I said. 'But short of someone sitting on him to keep him down here, I'm not sure how much more we can restrict him.'

'If he doesn't, he'll lose more than one finger. I'll give him another day, with the medicine and your promise to watch him. I'd rather cut his fingers off than return a corpse to either his mother or Aline.'

'Have you tried asking him yourself?'

Alex snorted. 'Me, tell Timothee Maritim what to do?' He shook his head. 'The man is a hero, a legend—'

'Theo is as human as they come. Get your head out the kelp and see him for what he is, not the mirage you have built.

He is a friend, a son, and a dear companion. He is also not as young as he was then.' I rested a hand on Alex's shoulder as I stood. 'He is a very dear friend. Stop hiding in your shell and be the medic you were trained to be. Help me move him to his bunk.'

We roused a sleepy Theo, and shuffled him awkwardly through the narrow space to their bunk room. Theo stumbled, struggling to stay upright as he was supported between us. We unloaded him onto the closest bunk and secured him in place with tightly wrapped blankets.

'Get some rest yourself, Alex.' I whispered, closing the curtain before I headed back to the cabin. With the sea's temper calmed, I flicked the switch to raise the panels. Hot food would do all the humans good after the last few days. I didn't understand it, but guessed it made the food feel like freshly killed prey, and that wakened some comforting instinct in them. I truly couldn't comprehend a logic for hot vegetables, though. The panels would be ready for sunrise and whatever meagre light we would get.

Ash refused to meet my eye as I emerged into the moonlight. I clipped onto the upward rail and shuffled along next to Zora. We stood in silence, watching the moon-dappled waves cast silver glints of light on an otherwise black sea.

'Why does Ash look like a flatfish trying to bury in the sand?' she whispered.

I explained the situation. She rubbed her hand around the back of her neck and grimaced. 'She's known Theo since she was a kid. It's not surprising that panic for her friend's life won over logic and patience. I'll talk to her.'

She wandered off, and I stared alone into the moonlight, wondering where the wind would blow us and if we'd reach the egg in time.

25
CLOUD OF DESPAIR

MADDOC

Maddoc rose before dawn to tiptoe down the creaky stairs, trying not to disturb any other residents. He expected to find some of last night's drinkers asleep on their stools, but the bar was empty. Small flames licked the logs in the fireplace, rising as slowly with the morning as he did.

'Ouw!' a loud clang rang out from somewhere behind the bar as he presumed someone dropped a pan. Maddoc scraped a stool across the floor and called a greeting. 'Good morning. I wanted to pay for my room and maybe some food?'

'Not so certain about the good, but it's definitely a morning,' a man grumbled as he shuffled into the bar. 'I was making some pancakes, but the batter just went everywhere. If you give me a few minutes, I can start fresh.'

Maddoc offered what he hoped was a sympathetic smile. 'I'm okay. Something easy and fast would be great. I have to be somewhere, urgently.' Bird song trilled through windows as the dawn chorus awoke; he needed to be at the top of the hill before the old woman. He scanned the bar, his gaze landing on some dried fruit packs. 'I'll just take some fruit and a biscuit to get me on my way.'

The old man gratefully grabbed both, wrapping them in a cloth and handing them over. 'You can drop the cloth back later.'

The scent of freshly baked biscuits seeped through the cloth, and they warmed his hand. Maddoc had come off well from the exchange, he decided. Pancakes could be a bit of a false promise. All taste and no filling.

Maddoc munched on the food as he left, circling round the building to a path he had trodden more times in the past few days than in his entire life.

The thorns pulled at him less that day. He wondered idly if he'd already pulled most of the vicious barbs off on his previous passages. Once he reached the top of the hill, Maddoc reached for the thread of the Path – it positively thrummed with power. It wouldn't be long before his mother arrived. A small patch of mist coalesced on the far side of the small clearing, moving away from the Path.

Twigs snapped, and Maddoc turned to find the old woman marching up the hill towards him.

'You are here then,' she puffed.

'I am, and The Lady will be here to visit you as you requested, along with a party of Tylwyth Teg.'

The hum grew audible, a storm-surge of power transmitting so strongly that Maddoc was surprised the old woman didn't acknowledge its presence.

His mam stepped off first. The others backed away several steps behind her, as wary as the old woman was of them. That was no bad thing – for everyone.

'I believe you wanted to meet me.' The Lady approached

the old woman, gliding across the ground and glowing with power. She was out to make an impression.

'Are you really her? Lived so long ago and now roaming our lands again? Are we in so much trouble that legends come to life before my own eyes?'

'We might be,' The Lady replied. 'That's what I need you to take my people to find out. My son says you are one of the best.'

He'd said no such thing, but Maddoc plastered a smile on his face.

'She can handle her boat alone, and she knows the waters.'

'And has a healthy respect for Tylwyth Teg,' his mother finished for him. 'So why did you want so badly to meet me?'

'Is Arthur really buried up there?' The old woman pointed in the direction of the bluestone-capped hills rising to the north.

'How would I know? Once his spirit passed from our world, I had no idea where his mortal shell went. Nor did I bother to find out.'

The old woman folded a little. Had she thought to find the answer to a great secret? The Tylwyth Teg cared little for the dead once their spirit was gone. The answer would exist, recorded in the hidden library, as it pertained to his mam's own legends. Maybe she'd be more blown away by the library than Lord Flame himself.

'How do I know it's really you?'

As though prepared for the question, The Lady of the Lake raised her arms and allowed her hand to glow, creating a knife of pure power from her own source. She offered it to the old woman.

Her eyes widened in shock. 'But, I'm no queen or princess.' She bobbed a curtsey to his mam, and Maddoc held back a smile. He'd almost forgotten the human obsession with that one sword she'd made. It had taken a lot out of her, and she swore not to do it again. But, small knives and daggers – she'd made more of them than he could count. They were practical when you were sensitive to iron and still needed to cut things.

The old woman took the dagger in her wrinkled hands, turning it and staring in amazement. 'Thank you, your ladyship.'

'Think nothing of it. May I know the name of the one who holds my boon and will be carrying my only son in her care?' his mam asked.

'My name is Julia.' The words slipped out almost unasked, and even Julia looked surprised that she had responded. Panic overcame her features, and she tensed to run. A glance around at how much she was outnumbered put an end to the idea.

'I'll trade you a name for a name. I am called Maddoc.' Maybe it would settle her down, and she'd have little claim over him. Better that way than one of the others.

It worked. Outwardly, she relaxed. Her shoulders dropped, and her old hands uncurled slightly as she let her eyes rest on him.

'Thank you. I still don't want no bargains or trades, no obligations at the end of this.'

'Agreed. Now, we have a long way to go and little time to get there. Shall we head down to your boat?'

The Lady reached out for Julia, touching her gently on the hand. 'May you fly freely on faraway winds. Should you return without my son, return here. One of my kind will visit here each sunset.' Then she turned and departed on the Path, leaving Maddoc on a hilltop with Julia and a very mixed crew.

'None of you have to introduce yourselves by name. That's my risk alone to take,' Maddoc said. 'Please show yourselves.'

The coblynau skipped a step towards her, his huge ears and crumpled face giving him a most unbecoming appearance. He looked up at Julia and grinned crookedly.

'I'm here to help in whatever ways I can. We don't know what we face, but my folk worked alongside humans for years. They aren't all bad. There are ways around them.'

Julia stared at him for a moment, walking round the small coblynau. 'You're a knocker? From the mines?'

'Aye, there's a lot of them round here as have been forgotten about. If we need to hide out, I've got you all safe. If you just need my help, I'm here.'

The twins walked towards her as one. 'We will help you sail and aid as we see fit.'

Maddoc wasn't at all surprised. No annwn did anything unless they wanted to or it amused them. The pair unsettled him even more than his mother sometimes. Two changelings tumbled out the bushes in human child form, and Julia gasped.

'You'll be no good on a boat!'

'No, but we may be unseen eyes and ears on the islands when we get close. People ignore children,' the redheaded one said before wrestling the dark-haired one to the ground and sitting astride him triumphantly. 'I win!'

'Is this everyone?' Julia asked.

'Not quite.' Maddoc looked over to where the mist still hung. 'Julia, we also bring a gwyllion with us.'

'A mountain hag?' she hissed. 'One of those *creatures* took my brother.'

'It was not me,' the gwyllion replied. 'And, as I know my presence will unnerve you, and I wish your trust—' She approached Julia and whispered something in her ear. Julia recoiled, and though Maddoc strained to hear it, he couldn't.

'So be it,' Julia said. 'Maddoc, show them all to the small cove below the cliffs where my boat is moored, then return to help me carry my nets out to her.'

As the sun rose for mid-morning, Maddoc rowed the small boat from the mooring down to the cove where the Tylwyth Teg waited. They loaded in, one at a time, the twins picking the changelings up and flinging them aboard on the first trip. As they entered the water, the hiss of departing magic shocked them, and they practically threw themselves into the small row boat on the second.

'Come back for us last,' the gwyllion muttered. 'Always the least special, always left out.'

The coblynau chuckled. 'We'll be on that liquid poison long enough …' The voice faded as Maddoc rowed further from shore, but he agreed with the sentiment entirely. He'd pushed the rowboat off the beach three times by the time everything had been stowed. One trip was just for all the food Julia wanted to take, and another for the sea-soaked net. He'd be lucky to recuperate any magic before they reached the islands.

Once they were all aboard, the changelings explored every space two small creatures could fit in. Maddoc raised the anchor, and they sailed out of the headlands, turning north for the island chain.

They reached the selkie island later that day, sitting squat in the high tide. A walrus soaked up the sun on a nearby beach.

They followed the southern coast of the island, weaving through smaller rocky formations as they sailed up the west coast. At the furthest point of the island, a small seal bobbed to the surface, with a few larger ones behind it. Maddoc felt the eyes on him as sharp as daggers.

'I have something for you,' the small voice called out, and the pup swam forward, dragging a section of fabric in the water.

'A flag?' Maddoc asked when he realised the pup was Gar. 'Why are you giving this to us?'

'Because you are braving the sea to find out what happened. Because you saved me, and I've seen another ship with this flag today. This one came from the ship Zora froze. My sister said it might help you get closer.'

Maddoc hauled the sopping wet sheet of fabric from the water. Julia grunted as he unfurled it on the deck.

'Huh, I've certainly seen that one passing through. First ones were about six months ago, but we've had a lot more in the last six weeks. There will be a golden tower on it if you open it right up, and a crown above it on some of them.'

Maddoc turned back to the rail, but there was no longer any sign of Gar. A group of seals watched them pass from their sunbathing spots on some ledges. He couldn't help feeling that the weak sun wouldn't do much to warm them.

As they left the selkie island behind and headed north, Maddoc retrieved the damp square of turf from his bag and placed it on the deck so he could step onto it.

Far ahead in the distance, he saw the bulge on the horizon that he'd noticed before. Maybe slightly to the west, though. He couldn't make out how many islands there were, but the turf was working.

'What are you doing?' Julia called.

'This is how we find the islands. Come look for yourself.'

Julia passed the helm to one of the twins. 'Keep it straight,' she instructed with a glower and strode to the herbal square.

'Stand on it.' Maddoc pointed, feeling rather foolish. If she didn't see for herself, then maybe she'd not trust his directions. She stepped forward, and he noticed that she'd tucked the knife from his mam into her belt loop.

'You aren't joking. There's islands over there. I've been by there a thousand times and never seen them before.' She stepped off the square and back on again in wonder. 'Today brings a multitude of wonders to my old eyes.'

She wandered back to the helm, shaking her head and muttering something low and incomprehensible. As soon as she was off the square, the changelings leapt on and off and on again, delighted by what they could see.

The twins remained impassive, but once the changelings were done, Maddoc had to hide a smile as one appeared to cross the deck in total nonchalance, only to accidentally step on the herbs. They were so determined to show that they were above all the other classes of Tylwyth Teg that they were unwilling to let their poise go, even for a second.

The waves in the narrow sea between the main isles of the territories was choppy and the water limestone-grey, much like the sky. Wavelets rippled low and fast like they were racing to the islands ahead. Maybe they were.

They'd sailed for hours with no other vessels passing them, and the islands didn't get any closer. Every once in a while, the changelings hopped back on the square, but the novelty had worn off, and Maddoc would hear a sigh of disappointment. Spray crashed past them as the wind picked up, and saltwater drifted over the deck in tiny droplets.

The coblynau ran from rope to rope, doing whatever Julia asked, and the gwyllion just drifted around. Even magical islands could not hide forever, though, and eventually, a squeal of joy from the smaller changeling alerted them to their closeness.

'Run that flag up the mast,' Julia said. 'Let's be properly dressed before we get in sight. Can you two do something about your appearance?' she asked the twins. 'You stand out too much. He's okay,'—she gestured at Maddoc—'and the small ones as kids are fine, though they may be better below deck. What about you?' she asked the gwyllion. 'We need to blend in.'

The gwyllion emerged from her cloud of mist. She sent a gently bobbing globe of light to rest atop the mast that the coblynau was halfway up as the three smaller crew hoisted the flag.

She shifted her shape slightly to look more muscular and much younger. 'I'm ready for instructions,' she sang out. 'But I'll not promise I won't lead any of these strangers to their doom. Especially those who need to leave this plane.' She strolled over to the patch of herbs and stared forwards. 'No! That can't be right.'

Her arm shot out, and she dragged Maddoc close to her, so they both squeezed onto the herbs.

The island chain spread out in front of them – there must have been dozens of vessels around each island. More than he had seen in one spot for a long time, but it was the taller central island that caught his attention. The roofs glimmered gold in the sunlight. Even from a distance, it was impressive, but above the glory stood a tower, its top wreathed in a cloud of writhing darkness.

'What is it?' Maddoc breathed. He was sure he knew what he was looking at and who was creating it, from the stories he'd been told of the attack on *Black Hind*. The creature, Diana, must be based here, and unless they had earplugs, there was no way they were taking that town from the pretender queen.

'You wanted some lost souls. Will that be enough?'

A deep, throaty chuckle emerged from the gwyllion. 'It's definitely not my way, and I'm actually worried where that many have come from to be trapped on the isle. I'm not sure I could do anything with those.'

'Rialta took them into herself,' Maddoc muttered, remembering her exhaustion.

'Who's Rialta? I can't. But maybe I can release them in some other way.' The gwyllion tapped her foot and huffed. 'I'll need to think on this.'

'I don't really know what Rialta is,' Maddoc replied. 'She called herself spirit-taker, but she was able to use the gods hole to open the hidden library. I just thought as you both took in spirits …'

'A spirit-taker, a god?' The gwyllion rolled the words around her mouth. 'Then this Rialta can make both your life and spirit vanish, leaving nothing but a physical shell. Though we both burn with the strength of stolen life force, not all spirits can be taken by my kind, especially once long dead. I can't kill with my touch. That's what my light's for – to lead the unwary to their own demise.' She shrugged as she said it, so Maddoc tried to look reassuring.

He was glad he could just eat food for his sustenance. The gwyllion carried on. 'What you see around that tower are ensnared spirits. Someone's siphoned their life force but retained their tormented spirits here, unmoored, unable to pass to the Otherland. It is both foul and cruel.'

They closed the gap between the islands and Julia's boat until there came a point where one of the twins, who stood immobile and silent on the deck, pointed to the islands. 'I can see them now.'

Inside whatever magical perimeter had been set, the islands were visible. Julia sniffed. 'Well, maybe the lobsters will be magically tasty here too. At least I can fish while I wait.'

'Yes,' Maddoc said, 'it might actually be good to do that as we watch. While Y Plant might realise we shouldn't be here accidentally, maybe we can elude human notice for a little longer.'

'We're flying their flag.' The coblynau chuckled. 'I don't think we need to hide the boat – just ourselves.'

'Onward then,' Julia said.

Maddoc tried to count the boats in the harbours around the main islands – there must have been easily twenty. Why were Y Plant Rhys Ddwfn letting so many humans overrun their islands? He opened himself to signs of magic but felt nothing but that of those around him, his senses overwhelmed by their power.

'Can you all dim yourselves a bit?' he asked. The twins frowned, but he felt them dim.

The gwyllion shook her head. She gestured up at the mast light. 'Not if I'm keeping the mast light lit as we head into darkness. Can you taste Y Plant?'

Maddoc shook his head. 'That's the thing. I can't feel anything outside this boat. If any of them have my capabilities, we'll be lit like a beacon.'

He took a deep breath and closed his eyes, opening himself again. Pushing past the limits of the boat, he could feel – no, the gwyllion was right – it was almost a taste. Dark and sooty, mixed with decay. It felt very, very wrong. He opened his eyes again and looked in the direction it was coming from, unsurprised to find it was the central island. Surely, there must be some Y Plant still there, or the islands would vanish beneath the waves.

'I can't feel any,' he said.

'Try again,' the old gwyllion murmured. 'There must be some. Maybe they need us as much as we need this to stop.'

Maddoc sat on the herbs and opened his mind, feeling the power on the boat dim to the smallest that his companions could dim themselves to. Far to the west was a small prick of clean light, like a drop of clear oceanic water in a muddy estuary swirling with the churning mud. And as he hunted through the sooty rot, he found a small cluster of points in the darkness.

'We need to go that way,' he said as he opened his eyes, trying to hang on to the awareness of the single point moving freely. It was out to the west of the islands. Julia changed course immediately, sending Tylwyth Teg running around and following her instructions. Loosening one rope, tightening that one, changing sides as the boat heeled in response to the wind.

Boats sailed between the islands as they passed. Some were small and utterly unsuited for a voyage of any distance on the open ocean. The faux queen would find half her fleet sunk before she reached the Terranian Sea. Some of the vessels were larger, though. Near the main island, a huge multi-masted vessel was anchored up, with a fleet of well-maintained smaller boats nearby. Some showed singe marks. Sailors appeared to be working on the vessels, painting and repairing them.

Foreign accents drifted on the wind, and strange scents accompanied them. Wherever the queen had gathered her force from, a proportion had travelled a long way. Some vessels also flew the old flags of Engad; he even spotted one from Isle of Wolves. They were clearly recruiting from those communities scraping a living in the south. Those who believed that there was greener grass to be had elsewhere made easy targets.

They passed the boats and headed out to sea, still aiming for the bright spark of magic. Maddoc hung onto its tenuous flicker as tightly as he could as they left the islands behind. The only thing in sight was a small reef of rocks protruding through the water, spray breaking over them as waves collided with their western flank.

Maddoc waved at Julia to slow the boat. They set the sails

loose and let themselves drift briefly as Maddoc tried to work out where the magic was coming from.

'I see you,' he called out, remembering what the selkies had said at the island.

'No, you don't.'

'I hear you.' Maddoc held back a smile. At least he was getting a response.

A wave of mist rolled over the rocks, and a shadow darkened within it. 'You fly her flag. Why should I talk to you?'

'Where are the rest of your kind? Why do you welcome her if you trust her flag so little?'

'Are you a traitor? Is that what you ask me?' the voice hissed.

'No!'

'Then why rub fresh water in my wounds? Why torture me? If you fly her flag, you know that she holds all those that remain to keep our home above water. She harvests our land to allow her ships to find their way, and her death-stealer creates clouds of undead from our lost, sending them out in torment instead of resting. Even you.' A finger pointed at the twins. 'Even the annwn who rejoice in death are not so cruel. To lose our home and riches to the warming was bad enough. To lose it to a human and her companions, all of whom break the Pact at every turn …'

Maddoc sat heavily on the deck. 'We stole the flag. The Pact is what brought us – the failing Pact. Lord Flame wakes, and his egg is stolen. We need to get ashore to find out what we can. This army musters to head south.'

'Then let them travel!'

'Have you seen the egg? Do you want your islands razed to the seabed as Lord Flame searches for it? Do you think they will free your fellow Y Plant before they leave?'

The head dropped, defeated. 'No.'

'Then help us help you. We need to get ashore,' Maddoc replied. Mist rolled over the water, coalescing on the deck. An individual walked out of it.

'That's a great trick,' the coblynau muttered. 'Think you could teach us all to do it?'

'No. Who's in charge here?'

'I am.' Julia said to Maddoc's surprise. 'This is my boat, and you are welcome aboard! It's been too long since you visited, old friend. I thought you'd given up on our trade and lost faith in the bargain we made.' She held her arms out, and the pair embraced.

'Lewis, this is your rescue party. Cleverly put together by young Maddoc.'

Maddoc watched with amazement at the reunion. If Julia had known about Y Plant the whole time, she could have saved them all a lot of time!

'Julia? I think you have some explaining to do,' he said.

She loosened her embrace. 'My private business is my own. I knew Lewis many years ago. I haven't seen him for a long time.' She glanced at Lewis sideways. 'I suppose I have as many questions for him. Much water has passed my keel, and many things are changed. I'm not entirely surprised to find him here. That's as much as you need or are getting from me on the matter.' She nodded her emphasis, and Maddoc knew he'd get no more from her.

'If the pair of you mist-creators can get us quietly ashore somehow without our boat being seen, I'd be thankful.'

'I'll help create mist to cloak the boat, but I'll not join you ashore,' Lewis said. 'I'll stay with Julia and keep your escape clear. That way, we can leave the island's magical embrace, but I'll always be able to find my way back. Find those Y Plant they still hold. I'd rather lose the island than be the last of my kind.'

26

SPIRITED RETURN

TELLIN

We passed through the Narrows with the sun warming our faces the next morning. Shadows filled the curves of the mountains to the north, too shaded to see whether the presence of two hinds had resulted in noticeable change yet. Would their joint presence have once again enticed some of the other lost spirits home?

Below the tree line, a sliver of golden sand teased the waves. Theo had moved above deck once the waves had lessened, and Zora was helming. Ria moved to stand alongside me, and we sailed past Cor's cairn on the clifftop in silence.

Ria reached for my shoulder and squeezed it gently. 'I know they can never be replaced, but you need to start thinking about it, Tellin.'

'I know. I'll let fate decide who and when,' I murmured. I couldn't replace Eden consciously, but over time, we'd fill the crew – it had worked for us with Ria. I considered Ash for a moment. Her technical knowledge was certainly high, and she could fix things. Of that, I had no doubt. But she was no climber. Maybe that was the problem – we couldn't replace Eden. I needed to recognise the skills we lacked and fill the gaps myself. After all, for much of our time, I had brought little, bar my willingness to kill and my focus on the tasks. I decided to try and learn as much as I could that morning. I aimed the promise on the wind to Cor's cairn before turning my focus back toward the Narrows and the potential for piracy.

No boats barricaded the channel. We'd seen most of them sunk, but still, I'd assumed that once Anard returned to his palace, they would sneak back to the water, that others would fill the void. It was a relief that his peace was holding.

'Shall we overnight in Orange?' I asked.

'We don't have time,' Theo replied. 'We could stock up with some fresh food if you want to, but just a couple of hours – no longer.'

He stared to the horizon ahead, his normally ruddy complexion pale and washed out. The light caught the purple eye patch, glinting off the embroidery and reminding me for the hundredth time how lucky we were to still have him.

'You wouldn't get away with dressing as my fancy, rich husband with that,' I teased him.

Theo huffed out a single laugh. I wished I could heal him, could ease some of the pain he felt. 'I'll not come ashore with you,' he said, his shoulders dropping almost imperceptibly.

'I'll bring you back one of Fish's specials.' It was a small thing, but maybe a drop of that delicious, sunny drink would make him smile again. Even for a moment.

'Best not. It has alcohol in it, which is no good for my healing,' Theo replied. Oceans take those who'd stolen his happiness. Theo rested his splinted hand on his lap. 'Go grab some food, restock. I'll be fine here while you do.'

My gaze met Zora's over his shoulder, and she shook her head. 'I'll stay with Theo,' she replied. 'I'm sure Ash could use some time ashore, as could Alex. We're in range of Safe Harbour now. Take this.' She fished in her pocket and pulled out one of the alerters that Sal favoured. I stowed it in my own clothes and went below deck to find the others.

About an hour later, we pulled alongside the pontoons, and I leapt ashore, holding *Black Hind* steady as the others disembarked. Zora took her gently back out to sea under the motor once we were all off.

A flash of green caught my eye. An old man rowed his small fishing boat to the other side of the jetty; he looked tired and slightly shaky. We rushed to hold his small boat steady.

'Did you see that too? Or, has my sanity finally sunk beneath the waves?' He glanced up at me, then buried his face in his hands.

'See what?' Ria asked. He raised a shaky hand to point at a small, green creature flying back out over the waves.

'That.'

Ria's face lit up. 'Te— Georgie, it worked. Look!'

'What is it?' I asked

'A ventoline! I haven't seen one in more years than I can recall. The other spirits must be returning!'

A warm current flowed through me. Amidst all the worry of the egg and the preservation of a land not my own, we'd be able to let Sal know that returning the hind had been worth it all. Our adopted homeland was recovering.

'I'm not losing my mind,' the man muttered as he hauled his catch from the boat. I offered to carry it, and he accepted gratefully.

'Would you sell us some of your fish?' I held out a handful of coins, and a small smile grew.

'If we have spare, I'll gladly sell it. Help me home, and I'll see what we can do.'

We wound through the shoreline's white buildings, past the noise and excitement of Orange that bubbled out from the flat roof terraces above us. The guards at the safe-keep waved us past with a grin. The whole town felt lighter and happier ... until we reached the pleasure district. There, the big buildings of the electric side of the road remained gaily illuminated, their patrons scavenging for status like hungry gulls. The living side, as I liked to think of it, was budding into spring life. Fresh colours carpeted the ground around Fish's Bar, and flowers ready to burst open covered every surface.

The fisherman followed a small track behind the bar to a small, rounded home with walls woven from living plants. The water pipes wound in an intricate pattern around its grassy roof. I waited patiently to buy some of his fish. We probably could have got some from the docks, but it felt important to take time to help the man. I'd stop by Fish's on the way back and collect some fresh drinks. And maybe a tub of mussels.

I was so lost in thought, staring at the homes around me, that I lost track of Ria's conversation with him.

'I'm sure we can afford that. Maybe Alex could have a look at your grandchild's wound if we're quick.' Her suggestion of a longer stop for someone else's medical needs drew me back to the moment.

'Can we afford the time?' I whispered.

'Can you afford not to look after them?' she replied. 'Besides, I want to talk to them a little longer. If one spirit is back, there may be rumours of others that I'll pick up. Wouldn't that be worth it? Imagine Terrania as alive as

Mynyw, as filled with its spirits and power. What if we truly have restarted that?' She sighed, and I could smell the happiness radiating from her.

'I'll go get Alex,' I said, following the winding path back to Fish's.

Alex sat mournfully, staring at someone's glass of the orange-coloured drink.

'Did you want one?' I asked him.

'I can't, can I? I need to keep Timothee in one piece. I can't lose focus. What if I miss something and he loses more than a finger? What if I mess up?'

I couldn't blame him for the outburst. It was the first time since he'd been forced on us by Aline that Theo had been out of hearing range.

Ash put a hand on his shoulder, patting him as I'd pat a young pup – reassuring but firm. 'You have it under control. I trust you. We'll buy a bottle or two to take back aboard. Then, you know it's waiting for you.'

'I'll buy you a few of them if it helps, but now I need you to go to that hut' – I indicated where Ria stood – 'and see what's wrong with the grandchild. We represent Sal here, so we'll care for the people.'

Alex groaned as he pushed himself off the stool. 'I know it's the right thing to do. Kindness brings trust, and these people have been through a lot. If you want them as part of Terrania, which is what Aline says, then I'll show them that we aren't like those who used to run this town. If the Narrows remains open, more of our kind can sail freely, and the sea-folk can reclaim the open waters.'

It was all rather idealistic, but I nodded enthusiastically, and he headed off to the hut. Fish leant over the bar. 'That's a high and mighty speech for a lad so young. He's better off letting people make their own minds up around here. We've dealt with pirates and princes long enough. No one wants to be owned or run by anyone but ourselves these days.'

I hid a grin at his ever unsolicited and ever practical advice. 'What's on the menu?'

He gestured at a bowl of seafood someone else was enjoying.

'That'll do, thanks. And a few bottles of your orange drink too.'

Fish looked puzzled, but Ash jumped in quickly. 'The spiced local fruit rum.' She gestured at a dark bottle on his shelf. 'We'd like a whole bottle.'

'Sure.' Fish pulled a bottle from under the counter. The cork was broken on the outside, and tiny handles on the sides were more for ornamentation than any practical reason.

We sat quietly waiting for our food, Ash studying the bottom of her glass and myself wishing I knew what the big banner of writing said across the front of Gilded Heaven. Maybe if I stared at it long enough, Fish would offer an opinion on it and clear the matter up, but he was already busy with customers elsewhere. We'd sat for quite a while – almost polishing off the bowl of shellfish – when Ria and Alex rejoined us.

'Kid will be fine. Fell over some stuff trying to escape from a duende.' Alex chuckled. 'I haven't heard people talking about those for a long time.'

'Did they allow us to buy the fish?' I asked.

'Yes, no problem. I suggested they leave some milk out overnight, reminding them that all spirits appreciate kindness, and it's a good thing they're back. I think they understood.' Ria reached into my bowl, finding a mussel that I had missed, and stuffed it in her mouth before I could reclaim it, continuing on through her mouthful. 'We'd better head down to the harbour before the sun fades and the stalls are packed away. We still have a good day or two of travel ahead.'

The sun was indeed past its height as we left Orange. Zora and Theo were subdued when we re-boarded. Theo vanished below deck as soon as we were all there, and Zora offered the helm to Ash before coming to stand alongside me.

'I bought you and Theo some of Fish's special drink.' She beamed at me. A rare glimpse of the Zora I knew, breaking through the strain of recent months.

'Thank you. Maybe you'll join me for a glass later?'

'I do love it, and I suppose there will be little call for me to use any full glamours over the next few days.'

Zora smiled. 'If there is, we've got bigger problems than you being a little drunk.'

'It's not about being drunk. It messes with my magic,' I muttered.

'Theo won't tell me where the flotilla is.' She sighed. 'I just wanted him to rest and take the strain off, so I could helm if necessary. But apparently, we must all be below deck from tomorrow midday, aside from you and Ash. As if I can't work it out from the angles and the wind and—'

'He's lost a lot, Zora. Give him this. It matters to him.'

'It mattered that I took you to meet my father. It matters that I revealed the home of my people and took you to the lake.'

'We're all tired. His mother's life is at stake right now. Please, Zora, humour him.'

She sighed again. 'Fine. You're right, of course. Where's that drink?'

Ash and Ria watched us as we went down to the cabin.

Alex sat in the bow, more relaxed than I had seen him yet. Something about our trip ashore had brought him out of himself.

We sailed all night through the warmer waters of the Terranian sea. The green fringes of the land with their clusters of houses receded from view as we headed into more central waters – towards Theo's mother and his flotilla.

Ash took the helm as the sun went down the next night, and Theo gestured for me to sit alongside him.

'My hand is throbbing,' he said quietly. 'I think I'm going to lose at least one finger. My eye still hasn't settled, and I may never see from it again. I don't know anything but the ocean, and those sailors with rotten crab guts for spines and venom in their hearts have stolen it from me.'

'You always have a place with us,' I reassured him.

'Aye, a place to steer the boat in calm seas. To only work the winches one-handed. I'm no idiot, Tellin. I know what this means for me, I can't sail Black Hind solo. Please, don't let my mother know. Let her keep her dreams.'

I snorted. I really didn't mean to, but the idea of hiding the damage to Theo's hand and eye was ludicrous. 'I think she'll notice,' I said as gently as I could.

'She will, but I need you to distract her. Carry the egg, because I can't. Once we're back aboard *Barge* and my hand's healed up, maybe I can be of use to Aline. An extra medic is always useful.' He leaned in close, whispering in my ear. 'Ash is better than she thinks. She's always had an instinct for the waves. Offer her my spot on *Black Hind* – just, maybe, let me come along, too, on occasions.'

'Will she be able to solo sail her?' I asked. It had always been Theo's biggest contribution to the crew. A boat hidden off-shore, ready to swoop back in at a moment's notice.

'By the time we return to Terrania next, yes, she will.'

We sat together for a while. I stared up at the stars, trying to work out which way we were headed in the darkness.

'Go rest,' Theo said. 'Send Alex up before you do.'

I climbed down, aware of the real change in my friend. His brash laughter when we'd first sailed together, his confidence and optimism ... all crushed under the weight of injuries. I shook Alex awake. 'Theo wants you,' I whispered. Ria would probably not be asleep yet, but there was no point in disturbing her.

As he left and I turned towards my own bed, Ria coughed gently. 'Theo's spirit is tired. I brushed up against him on purpose earlier. He can't keep fighting that pain indefinitely.'

'Don't talk like that in front of Zora,' I hushed her quickly. 'She'll get all prickly again, and I need her to be calm as a sea cucumber.'

'Of course. I was just letting you know. If he lets it carry on, he may not have enough energy left to fight it.'

Carrying that burden of knowledge, I pulled the heavy curtain aside and clambered into the top bunk. Hopefully, Alex's newfound confidence would lead to some action on his part, and Theo's acceptance of the situation would make it less of a battle.

As the night ended on the seventh day of our voyage, so did my optimism. I'd hoped to have the egg by then. So far from Lord Flame and his consequences – which I still didn't fully understand, despite Ria's best attempt to explain them – other things were more important to me. I wanted to make Theo feel strong again. He looked even paler than the day before.

'I promise that as soon as we have the egg, I'll let Alex operate,' he said in response to my worried gaze.

'See that you do.' Zora was helming, her eyes fixed on the horizon, trying to avoid meeting mine. I knew she was every bit as frustrated as I was.

'We'll need to anchor up for the surgery,' Theo said, seeing my fixed face. 'No need to glamour that smile for me, selkie! We'll be heading to the flotilla this afternoon if the wind remains our ally and the ocean is willing.'

As the sun began her dive into the oceanic horizon, Theo strolled as casually as he could to the helm.

Zora avoided his gaze and quietly slipped below deck, followed by Ria and Alex, who shot Theo a concerned look before following the others. Once they were out of sight, Ash stepped away from the helm and moved closer to me. She alternated between scanning the horizon and checking Theo didn't need anything. It was subtle, I suppose. A quick glance or a hand resting on a winch for a moment more than in passing. His replies were almost as subtle; a twitch of the lips, a tilt of the head. They worked together as though they could read each other's minds. I suppose that knowing each other as long as they had, it shouldn't be surprising.

'We can't get the egg into the hold without passing the others.' I was stating the obvious, but if we were rushing to get Theo away so that he would allow us to act, I didn't want to be anchored up for hours.

'It'll be fine,' Theo replied.

Some signal too subtle for me passed between them, and Ash rushed to loosen a winch so that we could tack.

'We'll be there before sundown,' Ash puffed as she wound the other winch. Seeing the flotilla in daylight was an experience I looked forward to. Our last visit had hidden much, and I was certain it would be a whirlpool of colour and life. The horizon blurred, giving away the presence of land. I called it, and Theo smiled.

'We'll be there soon. When did you last go home, Ash?' he asked, adjusting our course ever so slightly.

'It's been a while,' she replied, searching the horizon.

'There,' Ash called, pointing at a shadow on the growing cliff face. 'It'll be nice to see home again, even fleetingly.

27
ERUPTION

MADDOC

They closed in under cover of darkness. First, the gwyllion hung a light off to the landward side to distract any watchers from their actual location, then Lewis created a carpet of mist that coated them as they closed. He'd told them to head to a small cove on the northern side of the isle, warning them that they'd either have to swim and lose their power for days or trust him to get them ashore.

As they neared the shore, Lewis sent mist rolling toward the beach and travelled with it, to appear on the shore.

No voices called out to challenge him, and before long, the splashing of oars carried over the water and he reappeared with a small rowing boat.

The changelings were unusually still and quiet as they crossed with Maddoc, their exuberance and playful nature dimmed by the reality of their precarious position. Lewis returned to bring the others to shore.

Once they were all across, Lewis rowed the small boat into

the bay before sinking it to the bottom. 'You'll not need it to swim to us, and if you need it, you'll find a way to raise it,' he said as he misted past Maddoc. 'Good luck. Follow the path to the top, and you'll find the queen presiding over all. The islands are supported on the lives of my kin. Find them, free them.'

'As soon as I can,' Maddoc replied, but Lewis was gone. The night was too dark to see them sail away. Maddoc and the other Tylwyth Teg were alone.

'We'll find some children,' a changeling said. 'We'll play and see what they say, talk and dance the night away.'

'I'll be searching for another way in,' the coblynau muttered. 'There's always tunnels in places, and us coblynau are natural tunnellers. I'm really good at tunnels.' He slipped into the night before Maddoc could arrange to meet back up. The problem with Tylwyth Teg was that they were all such *individuals*.

'Where will you go now?' one of the twins asked.

Maddoc sat on the sand. 'Honestly, I don't know where to start. I can't go running anywhere or away from any trouble with this injury.' A hand pressed onto his leg, and a strange warmth ran through it.

'Maybe it is better than you think it is,' one of them said.

Maddoc tried to stand, finding that although it was by no means normal, he could weight-bear without discomfort.

'We are not here to look pretty,' the other twin added. 'Now we are away from the human, let us talk. The changelings will find gossip. They will find things that either make this easy or make no difference. Children tell stories. They may find tales bigger than their dreams. We must work with reality. What can you feel, and where?'

Maddoc closed his eyes, shutting out the sound of the waves as well as he could. He searched first for the dark, hot taste. He was closer than before, so the scents were more distinct and came from different directions. Maddoc drew lines in the sand, pointing towards each pull, then reached his awareness out once more, searching for bright, clear magic like that of Lewis. Catching the smallest thread, he reached further, but it felt dimmed – muted or masked in some way. When he moved to mark it on the sand, his finger found the groove of a previous mark.

'Y Plant are in one direction, with something dark, hot, and smoky.' It sounded odd to say aloud.

'What about the other creature?'

'That's in the opposite direction, maybe even at the top of the island.'

'With the queen? That makes sense. We should try to free Y Plant first. That way, they will be away or aiding us before we deal with the Irrlicht and her pet human. Let us get underway before people start waking.'

Maddoc felt for the tenuous thread of brightness and gripped it with his awareness. 'You might have to help me,' he muttered through gritted teeth. 'It's going to take most of my concentration to keep hold of them.'

He didn't like relying on the twins, but they'd volunteered, and while they might be there for their own personal amusement, they were at least willing to help Y Plant, even if it was just to save the Pact. Maddoc decided – that in a sort of exchange – he could manage to offer a temporary trust to them. They strolled from the beach into streets of ornate houses. Gentle lighting from occasionally un-shuttered windows warned him of the island's imminent awakening, and revealed intricate spirals and woven knot-work on the walls themselves. A moving light from above skimmed the street. He froze, pressing himself to the nearest wall. No one came, and as he moved back out accompanied by the twins, he realised it was simply reflected light from the gilded rooftops.

'It is every bit as decorated as the old tales,' murmured the twin to his right. He considered asking their names, but he didn't think he could tell them apart even if they did tell him. Names were power; names were a sign of trust. They knew Maddoc's name because all the Tylwyth Teg did, yet he knew so few of theirs. His toe caught on a loose tile, and the twin on his left grabbed his arm, steadying him.

'That would not have happened in the past,' they said. 'Nothing should be out of place. Everything is supposed to be perfect.' Left Twin chuckled, low and deadly, like his mam before she killed someone.

'We will run its gilded streets red if we have to. No doubt Y Plant can fix it all later.'

Maddoc quelled a shudder. He'd signed up for a search and information-gathering mission, not a slaughter. They were so outnumbered he had no doubt that it would be their blood, whatever additional powers the twins possessed.

The pull grew stronger, but off to one side – they must have changed course as they climbed. Putting the stench of death firmly behind him, he focused on following the most direct route. More lights came on, and more curtains opened. No one questioned their presence. In a place with so many strangers, what were a couple more new arrivals? Nothing to be bothered by, he hoped.

The island was small, unlike the lands beneath the lakes, which were larger than even imagination could perceive them to be. The islands of Y Plant Rhys Ddwfn were exactly as they appeared, both in size and texture; the true magic was in hiding something so real, so solid and true. Much like Y Plant themselves, a mysterious fog of magic that concealed their real treasure.

They passed out of the houses and into a field of fragrance, and Maddoc fought a grin as the familiar scent filled his nose. More buildings rose on the far side of the open area. As they went to cross it, a shrill voice called out from behind.

'Where are you going? You aren't supposed to be on there. Even I know that, and I'm five! I'm getting my Da!'

One of the twins turned, fast as a snake on a hot morning. They struck out to the houses at a sprint, but whoever had spoken was gone, vanished into the twisting pathways.

'By the Tree, that was not what we needed,' the other said. 'I hope they do not catch the kid. Even if it saw us, I do not want a child's death on our hands. That makes us a target. Keep moving. They will rejoin us.'

They ran across the clearing, ducking into the shade of the nearest building. On the far side, a small child appeared, leading an adult and pointing across the field towards them. The adult crouched next to the child for a moment, then led them away. Three steps later, the adult turned and stared directly at their hiding spot. Maddoc hoped that the light was dim enough to blend them into the shadows.

'I do not think the kid's Da believed them,' the twin muttered. 'Let us go.'

Maddoc stopped studying the wall of the house and glanced to his side, only to see the twin he'd run with splitting into two individuals. He tried to look away, but the separation was slow, and the bodies pulled apart a moment later. Maddoc found himself staring at the almost liquid separation of their bodies.

'I don't—'

One of the twins put their hand up. 'It is not limitless, and it hurts, but it can be useful. It is more appropriate to merge ourselves and re-separate than it is to walk exposed across a field. And no, most folk do not know. We would appreciate it staying that way. Everyone under the lake has their secrets.'

Maddoc shrugged. 'Your magic is yours to use as you choose. I was just going to say that I don't think this building was made by Y Plant. It's really plain and rough.'

They peered around the side. It was oddly quiet. The scent of the hot magic grew more intense and the glow of Y Plant more distinct. Maddoc was certain he'd be able to identify individuals quite soon.

'It's in the middle of this area.' He gestured ahead, and as the sun crested the eastern horizon, bathing the sea in morning's caress, it illuminated them clearly. A woman wearing a mish-mash of knives stepped from a doorway to block their route. Her hands rested on the hilts of her weapons, and she stared at them, immobile.

'Where the fuck are you going? This area is off limits. Everyone knows that.'

Maddoc raised his arms in mock confusion. 'We arrived overnight, sorry. Won't do it again.' He felt around him for the scents. The hot one was in the part of the house directly behind the woman, and the clean one was strongest from the door she'd stepped out from. Interesting that they weren't in the same spot.

Maddoc kept a close eye on the knives as he tried to work out his next move. The hot anger didn't directly imprison Y Plant. If they could get in and out without alerting the other magic user, they might have a chance. Get them off the island and then see if they were willing to help deliver revenge.

'We clearly should have gone *left* at the pathway,' Maddoc said very loudly.

The twins looked at him; one glanced to the left and nodded. Then, to Maddoc's surprise, they stepped forward to within an arm's reach of the woman, and much as his mam did, created a knife of pure energy from their own bodies, stabbing her before she could pull a dagger from its sheath. Maddoc swallowed hard to hide his surprise. Either the Pact was more damaged than he'd realised, or the woman had been from outside Mynyw. Either way, the twin had been certain enough to expend magic on creating the knife.

'I hope whatever is in the house is worth it,' a twin said, looking at the sturdy door.

'How do we get in?' Maddoc asked. 'If we kick it down, we'll attract attention, but if we magic it apart, then the creature in there ...' He gestured past the woman as her blooming blood graced the soil.

A twin strode past the body and gently tested the door. The handle hissed as the metal made contact with the twin's hand, and they recoiled in pain.

'Definitely not made by Y Plant,' they said through gritted teeth, clasping the hand to their chest. Great, iron door handles. Maddoc hoped it was coincidence. Pulling a hand far inside his sleeve, he tried the door. The handle moved smoothly. He gestured for the other twin to join them.

Inside, the room was entirely dark. The bitter tang of iron filled the air, stronger than the clear taste of magic – no wonder it was hard to detect. Maddoc crept forward, hearing the twins enter behind him. Why would the woman be sitting in a dark room? Unless it was coincidence that she had stepped out?

'We could use some light. I don't suppose that's another one of your tricks?' he whispered.

'Sorry, no,' came the reply. Dim light trickled into the room as one of the twins found a curtain. He successfully managed to work his way past the small bed and a chair, but stubbed his toe on something low down. He crouched to try and work out what was there, finding a lump of deformed, melted metal next to a table. He became far more conscious of the hot pull of magic from further in the house. Could it be the creature that had melted its footprints into Lord Flame's library floor?

Maddoc stood and carefully moved around it to the next door, then placed his ear against it, hoping to hear something from the far side.

It was silent. Too silent.

'One of you needs to stay here,' he whispered. 'That way, you can do your trick if you need to. I don't like the feel of this. I can sense Y Plant close by, but I almost don't believe it as there's so much tang in the air.'

'Need to be in sight to do that. I will wait here, especially with this much iron around. Whoever is in charge knows what they are doing. Must have expected Tylwyth Teg intervention at some point.'

Maddoc paused. Did that mean they knew Lewis was out there? That he'd led them into a trap? It was too late to go back – he was too close.

Maddoc swallowed hard and pushed on the wooden door. It didn't open at a touch; the handle didn't flex when he tried it. They should have searched the body outside. He checked the door frame, and near the top, his fingers met a drop bolt. 'Can you lift this?' he huffed after trying himself and finding he didn't have the height to raise it far enough. One twin lifted it, and Maddoc eased the door open.

The room beyond reeked of blood and urine. The acrid stench of unclean bodies and their waste rolled over them like a bank of fog engulfing their senses. Maddoc couldn't hold his stomach and doubled over, vomiting in response. His eyes streamed as he looked around, trying to take in the horror of Y Plant's captivity.

They were huddled in small groups, maybe ten in each of two cages. Rather than bars, there was a fine laced mesh of thick wires, a net of impenetrable iron to stop them passing. No wonder their light was dimmed – no wonder they only needed one guard. He searched for a door, a gate to allow access. They had to have been put in there somehow. A stripe of melted wires in a rectangle gave him an answer he didn't like – they'd been sealed in. His heart sank. There was no easy way out of there. Some form of cutters and time to get them out was the best chance they had.

One of Y Plant looked up at him, their hollow eyes empty of feeling, dead to emotion. 'Nothing you do to us will make this any worse. If you kill one more, the islands will vanish,' he sneered.

Maddoc held out his hand. 'I'm here from The Lady. We're here searching for Lord Flame's stolen egg.'

'Like we care about that. We've been imprisoned here for years, and you only turn up when the egg goes missing?'

'That's annwn for you,' another Y Plant muttered. 'Always has been, always will be.'

'The Pact is fading,' Maddoc replied. 'We are here to help you.'

'Of course, the Pact's fading! There are creatures that don't belong in Mynyw using magic against those from here and inside the boundaries. Can you get us out or not? Because if all you can do is stare at us, I'd rather you pissed off and dealt with the real problems here while we just try to keep our islands afloat.'

'Why not let them sink?' One twin had moved up next to Maddoc.

'We'd lose everything. These fools want to go and wage war elsewhere in the world. When they leave, we can have our home back.'

'Fat lot of good that will do you stuck in a cage,' Maddoc muttered.

'Others are out there. Others will find a way.' Desperation threaded through the voice.

'I could only feel one. He delivered us to you, so we are your way out, whether you like it or not.' Maddoc moved closer to the cage, searching along the walls for a weak spot – for a way to free them.

'Do you not think, annwn, that we have searched every thread of this fence? Every join and every melted seal? Even were we to get out, our magic is limited. The islands float only because we do.' He raised his hand, and iron cuffs glinted. 'You see, we are truly as useless as the plague of humans who have overrun our home.'

Shouts outside caught Maddoc's attention. 'Is there another way out of this place?'

'Three mighty annwn, trapped by puny humans?' Y Plant responded. 'There's another door on the far wall, but—'

Maddoc didn't wait for the rest of the sentence. He knew where they were and could find a way back to free them. If he got caught, it was over. He dived into the darkness on the far side of the room, his hands searching frantically for a handle. Steps followed. A door closed from behind. The twin or twins – he didn't know anymore – was alongside him,

'What have we here?' a deep voice in an unfamiliar accent called, accompanied by the hiss of metal as a knife or sword slid from its sheath. He found the handle, and pushed through the door, pursued by the sound of deep laughter.

Who laughs when their quarry escapes? Maddoc didn't stop to consider the man's reaction until he'd run into the next room.

It was windowless and dark.

It smelt hot and wrong.

It smelt like the magic had tasted.

The door closed. In the darkness, Maddoc was unsure if

the twins had made it through or if the breathing near his right side was the source of the scent. Footsteps to his right. Two-beat, like his own. Padded footsteps came from ahead, claws tapping on the tiled floor.

Waves of heat rolled towards him. He could feel them with his mind and his taste, but as yet, no heat seared his face or warmed his shivering hands. From the darkness, a pair of glowing, red eyes stared at him.

A rumbling growl filled the room. The glowing eyes blinked, then the creature leapt towards him. Maddoc jumped to the side. The air crackled with simmering fury. It turned, and the stench of ash from the creature's breath filled his lungs. Maddoc tried not to cough, but in desperation for fresh air, he failed to hold it in – doubling over with a hacking cough. Given an easy target, the creature landed fully on his back, sending him sprawling to the floor. Again, it rumbled.

The weight of the red-eyed creature pinned him to the floor, his face pressed against smooth tiles. A fur-covered creature, out of place and far from its home. What was the beast? The breath against his neck was so hot that he could smell his own hair burning. A drop of drool fell on his neck; a hiss and spit of his burning flesh as the drop made contact. Maddoc bit back a cry of pain, unwilling to initiate any instincts further. Were the twins in there with him? Was there any help coming? Maddoc was no fighter – he cared for a tree, and he liked cheese sandwiches and peaceful contemplations. His magic was utterly useless in a fight. He willed a spike from his hand in desperation, but his magic didn't respond to his will.

More heat accompanied a voice, speaking a language he did not understand, deep and rumbling like a volcano ready to erupt.

Claws ripped into his flesh, slicing through his clothes like butter, and the scent of burning grew even more intense.

A scream filled the room. It took Maddoc a moment to realise it was his own. He tried to kick upwards; his foot collided weakly with the creature, the heat of its breath receded, and again he tried to kick. If he moved his body any further, those claws would rip him open. Fear coursed through him. He reached deep inside and tried once again to create a knife – any sort of blade – from his body. Nothing happened. Then, the weight lifted, and the creature howled. Maddoc scrambled to the nearest wall, pushing his oozing back against it and searching for the eyes of the creature in the dark.

'Find light!' one of the twins shrieked. That was easier said than done. Maddoc crawled around the periphery of the room, hunting for anything that might open. There must be another way out. It had been ahead of them out in the street, so there must be another room beyond, a different way in. He whimpered in pain as he tested the wall, feeling for the give-away crack of a door frame. Fine leader of a rescue mission he was. Hot, wet blood trickled around his neck. He supposed that was positive since it wasn't pouring out.

Every time he heard the growl, he braced for the next impact, the next attack. Aware that it could be the last. Those teeth ... the sulphur stench of its breath ... Keep crawling, stay low, stay at the edge. Finally, he found the edge of a door. He needed to stand up. One of the twins cried out in pain, and Maddoc pulled himself upright, searching for the handle. His fingers closed on it as the creature landed on him.

It flung him across the room, smashing his body against the wall and breaking everything in his bag, then padding across to breathe in his face again. It opened its mouth. He felt rather than saw the increase in heat. Maddoc raised his hand, smacking it under the jaw as one of the twins attacked from behind.

More liquid on his back, but from his drink container bursting. He imagined the swirling of blood in milk; the red and white mingling around his body. The creature swung its head away, the blazing eyes turning away from his own in response to an attack from behind. The twins attacked the creature from both sides. Frustrated howls rose from its mouth as they attacked; he suspected that given its magical nature, their blades were doing very little damage. Had they attacked the head end, he thought they might have melted.

It bought him a few moments to breathe before the beast came back for him.

'There's a door. I'm going to try to reach it,' Maddoc called. There was little point in stealth anymore. He slipped his arm out of the useless bag and headed back to where he thought he'd been thrown from.

His head felt unstable, his balance uneven as he stood, and his legs shook. Maddoc's clothes were soaking wet – he had no idea what was blood and what wasn't. For the second time, he reached the handle. Anticipating the attack, he grabbed it and flung the door open.

No light came in. It was as dark in the next room as the one he'd left, but at least a crack of light shone, a sliver of hope on the wall. He pulled open the curtains and flooded the room with light, illuminating a child's bedroom. It was the pinkest room he'd ever seen. The wall had marks and numbers on it, just like the way families he knew in the village measured their children's heights. A picture of a tall, slender woman with hard, grey eyes hung on the wall. She stood in front of a castle in a land filled with plants he didn't recognise. He pulled the curtain back further as a growl drew his attention back to the beast.

It was enough for one of the twins to find a way of lighting the other room.

Maddoc limped back in to find them staring at the creature. Its glowing red eyes dimmed as it visibly shrunk in front of them. Giving out a small whimper, it walked over to his bag and began to lap up the blood-enriched milk. It continued to shrink until it was merely the size of a very large dog; the heat of its magic reduced, and it was entirely bearable to approach it.

'What is it?' Maddoc asked.

One of the twins huffed. 'A tibicena, a long way from home. Given its strength, not too long removed, and given its hunger, not recently appeased either.'

'What happens when it gets dark again?' Maddoc asked.

'Then it returns to the hunt. It should not be here.'

'Can we appease it further to keep it calm?' The huge beast still drank the milk, although it was almost done. If hunger was its driving force, Maddoc was keen to either restrain it or get away.

'How much milk do you have?' the other twin laughed. 'Truly, I do not understand the fascination, but the changelings and many smaller Tylwyth Teg are obsessed with the stuff.'

As the panic from the fight receded, Maddoc was aware of all the other bites, the burning claw marks in his back. At least with them being so hot, they should have burnt his skin. It might not get infected. Pain pushed through his awareness, and the intensity rose until it became unbearable.

'I need to get out of here,' he said as one of the twins rushed to support him.

'We agree. We know a way in to rescue Y Plant now. All we need are lights and milk. Let us make a plan once we see what the others have discovered.'

They walked as quietly as they could through the door, closing the tibicena back into its room. The pink bedroom had yet another single exit. By the light of the open curtain, Maddoc could just make out someone's boots, a basket, and several chairs arranged around a table that didn't fit with the rest of the decoration. On the far side was a small fireplace. It fitted with his certainty that the structure wasn't built by Y Plant. It felt much too human.

Just before they reached the far door, it burst open. A large man stood across the threshold.

'You aren't leaving here alive,' he growled and lunged for the nearest twin. The other rushed past, and then they re-merged on the far side. The man turned to Maddoc in frustration and swung the long pole in his hand at Maddoc's head.

He crumpled to the floor as darkness claimed him.

28
A STORY BEGINS

TELLIN

We sailed in with no running lights and our masthead unlit. As unnoticed as we'd left the flotilla the last time – like a predator slipping between the rocks – so we entered it that day. I'll admit I was disappointed that once again, we began our passage between the boats as night fell, any hoped-for view of all the vessels stolen by the descending sun. Theo knew those waters as well as I knew the tides, rocks, crevices, and swirling currents around my pack's territories. He'd timed our entrance.

At least Theo allowed me to remain on deck and help him again. Downstairs, Zora was restless with frustration. To keep themselves occupied, she and Ria were devising a safe and stable space in the hold for the egg to be transported in – as much as they could with what we had aboard, anyway.

Bobbing lights came into sharp focus as we drew closer. Theo wove us expertly between glimmering lights of floating gardens and welcoming cabins. The purple mast light of our target caught my eye, and I pointed it out to Ash.

'She's always been on the edge,' she said. 'I guess it helps her feel as though she could sail away at any moment.' She tipped her head towards the big man at the helm. 'Like mother, like son. There's no way he'll cope with living aboard *Barge*. I'd bet a bottle of Fish's rum that he'll be back here or somewhere else free and open if he can't sail. *Barge* would suffocate him.'

Ash was probably right, but I wasn't ready to let go of Theo just yet, no matter what either of them said.

We slipped through the flotilla and gently came alongside Seaspray's boat. There was another vessel tied to it as well. Ash raised an eyebrow at me, clearly visible in the gentle light washing over us from Seaspray's boat.

'Tie us off,' Theo called. Ash and I dropped the fenders and secured us carefully. He cut the engine and leapt across the deck. 'Come on, Tellin,' he called as he vaulted the rail with his good arm. It would be a short-lived act if he kept that level of energy up.

I buried my concern, plastered a glamour over my face, and followed. Theo had stopped at the entrance to the cabin, where a gentle glow lit two figures and – to my great relief – the egg.

'It's not exactly hidden from her guests,' I said.

Theo's lips pulled back into a tight smile. 'I'll worry about that after we get it away from her.' He slid the door open. 'Hi, I'm ho-ome!' he sang, strolling in and sitting next to Seaspray. He embraced her with his good arm. I stood in the doorway watching, reluctant to intrude.

'Part of you is.' She reached for his eyepatch. 'In all the years, you've never had an issue that has remained a problem.' She lifted it, and Theo let her.

'Oceans and Gods of Below! Who did that to you?' Seaspray rose to her feet, ready to fight the world, and I had a glimpse of a younger woman, one filled with fire and fight.

'It's okay. I'll be fine,' Theo murmured just before she spotted the splinted hand.

'Oh, Theo. How bad is it?'

'All my fingers.'

Tears rolled down her cheeks.

'I know. Please, don't say it.' He hugged her again, and she drew a deep breath, sadness pooling in her eyes as she studied me over his shoulder.

'Is this your doing? What did you drag him into?'

I opened my mouth to respond, but Theo held out a hand to stop me. 'Nothing I would not have done willingly. The pirates of the Narrows are now massing in the north to try and return with a new queen to replace Anard of Terrania.' Theo sat back.

'And?' she replied. 'We're sea-folk. Their battles don't concern us.'

'Normally, I'd agree. But they are massing in Mynyw. They are ruining the balance there, just as it was ruined here. And this' – he gestured at the egg – 'is one of many things they took without permission.'

'Mynyw?' She stared at the huge egg in amazement. 'The northern dragons have been gone for hundreds, if not a thousand, years. This cannot be a northern dragon egg.'

Theo laid his hand gently on the egg. 'It could be. One of our crew has met its father. Mum, there is at least one northern dragon left. This could be the last egg.'

Seaspray's companion sat silently throughout the whole exchange, but at those words, his head lifted, setting the shell beads in his sandy hair rattling. He stared intently at Theo. I wasn't good at ageing humans, but it was apparent that he was probably older than Zora, but not as old as Theo. The weathering of ocean life lined his features and his blue eyes were the colour of the Terranian sea on a sunny day.

'If what you say is true, I ask to accompany you. The egg has already started to crack, and I would see the story unfold to tell it to future generations.' His voice had a deep and melodious tone.

'You're the Storyteller ... that's why you're here. Theo sighed. 'We must make speed, and any extra weight is deadweight, Ventios. You can come aboard only if you do whatever the crew tells you.'

The Storyteller cocked his head at Theo. 'You'll have me aboard your vessel? I'm not sure about that. I'd rather follow in my own. You say there will be a battle – will you not need more boats? More people?'

Theo glanced up at me. He'd just added to our crew without checking. I held back a sigh, trying not to show my frustration. We had no time for gathering extra boats and leading others to Mynyw.

'Well ...' I was reluctant to decline an offer of help, but conscious that we still didn't know what we faced and these boats might not be as fast as *Black Hind*. I shifted from foot to foot, reluctant to say no. We might need them.

Theo picked up my hesitance. 'You can come with us – alone. Mother, once I take this egg, I charge you with explaining the situation to the fleet leaders. As you say, this is not our fight. What I do know is that since we returned the hind to the lands west of Orange, the spirits are returning. I also know that there were guardian creatures stolen from coastal communities of the southlands by the same crews. Should you wish to help protect them from further incursions, I suspect you would be welcomed with open arms. For those who seek to fight, there will be a welcome in Safe

Harbour. No one will judge a decision to remain hidden. It's kept us alive for many years.'

'Let me get my things,' Ventios said. 'Seaspray, pass the care of the boat to my apprentice, Foamcrest's girl. Just in case …' He left the cabin, and I slid into his place, reaching forward to touch the golden egg. I was sure it had grown slightly since we last saw it, and the tiniest of cracks in the leathery case was indeed beginning to appear. We needed to be fast, or we'd be food.

'I would travel with you,' Seaspray said. Theo's jaw tightened.

'No. I'll remove the egg from your care, and you will be safe.'

'What aren't you telling me?' she pushed. But Theo embraced her again. 'Thank you for always being strong. I should never have asked this of you.' He whispered so quietly that a human would likely have missed it. I pretended I had too.

'We need to get going.' I wrapped my arms around the egg to lift it, and it flexed as the creature inside shifted.

Theo reached for the egg quickly. He caught the opposite side as I struggled with my balance. 'Steady now,' he murmured, and to my shock, the creature did just that. It sat still. He wasn't holding the egg, could not have felt what I did. I took advantage of the moment.

'Great to meet you again, Seaspray,' I called as I struggled out of the cabin with the huge egg.

'I'll be back in a moment.' Theo turned from his mother to aid me over the rail. 'Go get it stowed, and then we'll get underway as soon as Ventios boards. I just want to say … goodbye. You know, just in case.'

I did.

Zora waited below the hatch with Ria. They'd rigged up a sling to stop the egg from rolling around; we carefully slid it in and fastened it to a hook above us.

'The hold is fireproof now, right?' Zora asked as we padded around the egg carefully.

'It might be, but I wouldn't count on it. Ria, can you feel the dragon?'

'It's practically bursting from the shell with life.' Ria grimaced. I could see worry in her expression and a slight shake of her hands as she tied the last knots in place.

I was about to add that it was practically bursting from its shell too, but they looked so concerned that maybe it wasn't the time. Whatever happened next, it would be up to us to deal with, not the flotilla in their unknowing innocence. 'We have an additional passenger for the journey back,' I said instead.

'Why? More weight will slow us. We don't have time for that.'

'I know, but Theo's agreed to it. Someone he calls Storyteller.'

'Oh, today just gets better and better. Now we're carrying a living human recording device,' Zora huffed. I reached out and squeezed her hand. It felt like a good thing to do, but she looked at me in confusion before smiling. 'It's okay, Tellin, I'll cope. We just have to make sure he earns his keep. Hopefully, he can cook or something useful.'

'I cook just fine,' Ria muttered.

The tension of having the egg so close, along with the pressure we were under, was causing cracks to reflect in the crew. It was going to be a long seven-day return to Mynyw.

'I need to get ready to cast off,' I said. 'All will be okay.'

As I placed my foot on the bottom step, I felt *Black Hind*

move. Theo hadn't waited for me – we were leaving the flotilla.

I emerged into the darkness to find the three sea-folk working together like a single body.

Ash may have preferred life on *Barge*, but she was so fluid – so capable – on *Black Hind* that it was hard to remember she wasn't our crew. She was Driftwood, and for the first time, the name made sense. They were all sea-folk washed up by the tides of circumstance on *Barge*, carrying their stories of the sea with them. They slipped in and out of *Barge* on the tides, and the silent language they spoke – that of gestures and expressions – could be used through the loudest of winds.

'You can rest. We have the deck under control.' Theo made me jump, he was so close, and his silent feet belied his size. 'The egg will get back faster if we don't have to rest at all. With Ventios aboard, Alex can operate on me, and you still have enough hands on deck for rough weather. Is the egg secure for some speed?'

'Yes,' I replied. 'Are you sure you have enough help?' I felt the weight of his splinted hand on my shoulder. 'Trust me. We have it. We'll take shifts now, no stops. You heard Ventios – there's a crack.'

'And the egg heard you,' I said, the words slipping out unintended. It had already been too long that I had not played at diplomacy. Sal would not have been impressed.

'What on the water are you talking about?' Theo chuckled. 'Seriously, get some rest.'

Down at the table, Alex sat rubbing his eyes while Zora and Ria kept glancing at the hold door as we started to heel with the wind.

'You did a great job,' I assured them. 'Let's do as Theo suggests. Get some rest, and then we can take shifts. Alex, if he needs it done now, do it. We can sail back without him. Just keep him alive.'

He nodded at me. 'I can't do it on angles like this.' He gestured at the slope of the table.

'We'll keep her flat as long as you need,' Ria said. 'Let's rest.' And, with a last glance at the hold door, she walked to their room with Alex following.

Zora and I were left alone. 'I don't like this, Tellin. There are too many people on our boat, and they listen to Theo, not me.'

'He trusts them. You never trust anyone.'

A small smile crept across her face. 'It's kept me alive.'

'I'm glad it has,' I replied. 'Come to bed. We'll deal with the rest in the morning.'

Zora sighed as she pushed upwards. 'Fine. After all, it's your boat. I'm just the captain.'

'You are much more than that.'

She pulled the curtain aside and dropped onto her bunk. As I clambered to the one above Zora, I heard her arranging her blanket and securing herself for sleep.

'You're right. I'm a Sea Witch, and if they annoy me or damage my boat, that Storyteller will go overboard.'

Sometimes humans, even half-humans, were so difficult.

Theo screamed. The medicines and the pain relievers weren't helping. His pain was shouted through the open hatch and flew over the waves. The power in his cry was almost as intense as if he spoke in Ocean. If that egg had truly responded to him before, I didn't dare think what this noise was doing to it.

'Is there no way at all you could have done that away from the egg?' I called down.

'Fucking urchin's arse of a bastard, just cut it,' Theo shouted.

The egg swayed in its hammock, fluid leaking from the crack in the shell. I touched it, finding the stringy mucus tingled. I reached past, stroking the crack and the shell.

'It's okay,' I murmured, knowing my voice would have little impact.

'It's bloody not,' Theo cried. The big man had tears streaming down his cheeks, and his exposed hand showed the cause of the pain and trauma. The finger that had previously been thin and unhealthy had turned black, and the darkness spread down his remaining stump and onto his palm. He'd lose them all if it didn't come off, yet, Alex hesitated.

'I'll hold it still,' I offered. 'You cut.' I reached for Theo's hand and gripped him at the wrist against the temporary operating table. I wished for Ria's strength at that moment, but if she wasn't keeping us level, we'd never be steady enough for the operation. The dragon mucus made my hand feel hot. A string of it landed across Theo's finger, and Alex gasped in horror.

'Clean your hands first!'

Theo stopped swearing for a moment. 'That's odd. Touch that stuff on it again.'

'No, it's an infection risk.' Alex's pitch was rising.

'Why, Theo? He's right.' I understood little of human medicine, but I knew enough about cuts and damage to believe Alex. I mentally flipped myself for my carelessness.

'I think it hurts less.'

Foul siren fluid. The stench of it invaded my memories as I stared at my hand, with threads of dragon egg fluid hanging from it. I lifted my hand away, and I would swear that the fluid *reached* for Theo. The stuff was beyond my experiences.

'Look, it's getting cut off either way. Why deny me a chance at less pain?'

'Or more infection,' Alex grunted.

'We'll clean it right away.' Theo stared at the finger. 'Honestly, I think it makes a difference.' He looked up at me. 'Do it.'

I wanted to back Alex, unsure how mentally aware Theo truly was, given the combination of medicines he had taken in preparation for the operation. But he was my friend, and I trusted his judgment – on more than one occasion, with my life. I nodded and gently wiped the liquid from the egg around his palm and over the deformed finger. The others looked strange, clunky, but they were not blackened. I added a little to them, hoping that maybe it had similar powers to siren fluid.

Alex stood alongside me, his palms open to the sky outside the hatch. 'How am I supposed to keep you clean like this?' he muttered. But his respect for Theo won out, and he stood by to let it happen. He never took his eyes off the hand – despite his evident frustrations with us.

I didn't expect anything much to happen. My own magic just did its thing quietly, and I couldn't help but think that if the fluid did anything, then it was more than a simple fluid. Draconic magic must be involved in some way.

Theo turned his hand over, staring at it wide-eyed. He poked it. 'Urchin guts, it worked!' He laughed and peered at his palm. 'The darkness is clearing. I wonder if this is one of the reasons we hunted them? Why they're so rare?'

'Nah, but I reckon it's one of the reasons people would steal an egg, regardless of its age or owner,' I replied.

'It's remarkable,' Theo agreed. 'It's not going to heal the damaged finger – nothing could resurrect that – but the rest of my hand will be saved. While it doesn't hurt, let's get this done, Alex.'

He stood taller, prouder. Theo held his own hand flat on the table, giving a sharp nod to Alex.

'We've got this now.' Alex picked up the small serrated tool and began to cut through the withered finger. The sound of it cutting bone made me feel slightly hungry. I could really do with some fresh fish to crunch.

I glanced back at them as I closed the door, giving them the semblance of privacy – though the hatch to the deck remained open for light – and went to search for food. Theo would be fine. I was sure of it. He might not sail solo, but he might keep the rest of his hand. The silly human should have let us do it sooner.

With the amputation done and Theo sleeping, we pushed ourselves onward towards the Territories and *Barge* as the crack in the egg widened, and the dragon grew ever closer to hatching.

29

SING ME A SONG, SAILOR

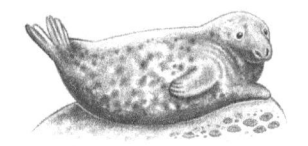

TELLIN

Three huge vessels broke the horizon, their bulk silhouetted against the setting sun. The royal standard flew from the largest, whilst the two companion ships escorted it closely.

We didn't really have time to stop, but if we could get Anard's attention and pass on what we knew, it might be worth a short delay to try to persuade him that he needed to send some of his fleet north with us. He didn't want to get involved in a war outside his borders or risk being accused of overreaching. Not that many would question him, aside from the heads of other nations, and Mynyw had no leader, so it could be seen as a true act of aggression.

It would do Anard no good to join us there. But, with what we'd learned, the risk posed by the queen was to more than Terrania. Mynyw was valuable as a source of magic, a home to Old Ones, and a haven to humankind. It was an example of how things could work. If Terrania continued to be repopulated, humans there would need to learn to live with Old Ones once more.

We raced towards King Anard's ship as I outlined my thoughts to Zora. She was in favour of a quick stop.

'Extra fire-power might be useful.' She looked at the ships. 'Are you sure he'll be aboard?'

'No, but a ten-minute chat won't flood a rockpool.' She nodded, and I looked to Ria for her reaction. She glanced at the hatch to the hold before she spoke, took a deep breath, and opened her mouth to speak … then simply exhaled. It was unusual to see her so unsettled.

'I'm not certain that the egg has long until it hatches,' she whispered, low enough that it was only within our hearing. 'The crack gets wider by the day, and the dragon's spirit grows stronger. It's so huge, it would fill me to bursting.'

'No one's asking you to do anything with it,' I reassured her. But she winced and looked back at the ships growing ever closer.

'Just maybe don't tell Anard that the egg is aboard *Black Hind*, and get it back as soon as we can,' she suggested.

I nodded and left them stood together at the bow to return to Ash, who was helming. I ran my hands along *Black Hind*'s rail as I walked her length, feeling the smoothness of the wood and the delicate spray of the parting waves caress my fingers. As ever, the Ocean called me home.

Soon. I cast the thought out to land in the waves, then focused myself on what had to be done.

Anard slipped aboard with no fanfare, his small boat humming alongside until we pointed head-to-wind to let him board.

'Why are you here?' he asked – blunt and typically Anard.

'Because we had to collect something important to help calm the situation.'

His eyes flickered towards the hatch, and I knew he had suspicions, so I pushed on, drawing the rivulet of his wandering attention back to the main flow I was directing.

'You were right about all of it. Someone gathers an army, claiming to be the rightful child of your father. They collect rogues and mercenaries. We heard southern accents amongst those travelling west. There's a high probability that any of Jake's crews who escaped have joined her for revenge – along with anyone gullible or hungry enough to believe that Terrania holds riches or loot.'

His eyebrow raised at that. 'To me, Terrania is filled with treasures.'

'Yes, yes, I know. Your royal self has always seen the beauty in things.' I said, thinking back to Sirena's artwork. 'But you need to be aware that there's magic involved. Old Ones we have yet to definitely identify pull strings and manipulate the humans. In a seashell, your sister's actions have led to the breaking of an ancient Pact, and the Tylwyth Teg of Mynyw, the selkies, and others are all now involved.'

We were chatting in the cabin for a semblance of privacy, and his fingers ran absently over the buttons as he formulated a reply. I resisted the urge to pull his hand away or point out that he probably shouldn't touch anything. Instead, I waited until his hand settled before I continued.

'They kidnapped Theo, tortured him. The self-proclaimed queen has some dark and terrible power working alongside her. Something not from Mynyw, if it's chosen to break the Pact.'

'Why you? Surely you could have sent another of Sal's

boats south for me.' He was looking back toward the hold again.

'Do you trust me?' I asked. The entire conversation would have been smoother had I been glamoured as Lady Gina.

'Yes, I trust Sal, and you have not led me false yet.'

'Then trust me now. Send some ships to Mynyw. *Barge* cannot fight, and we are too small to take on a fleet – and entirely unarmed.'

'A fleet would draw too much attention. It would legitimise her claim if I were seen moving against her. It would set me up as a reflection of my father or brother – desperate to hold onto power with force. No, I will not do that. I trust you to get the job done. I don't need her killed, but I do need her claim quashed and her forces dispersed.'

'An entire fleet? You want one boat to take on an entire fleet?'

'You just said you have the Tylwyth Teg and selkies as allies. I suspect my human-crewed vessels would merely get in the way. What are humans against charms and magic?'

I truly wasn't sure that the selkies would do much, aside from condemning the aggressors from the safety of their islands. I'd have to get them to see that their own territories were at risk, that trawling and fishing were not their biggest enemies. If Anard gave us both his trust and the entire weight of duty, we were going to need a lot of help. Then again, those fighting for the integrity of their Pact and the long-term security of Mynyw would probably fight harder than crews far from home.

I thought about how connected I felt to my own pack's home territory. How its waves flooded my spirit and my life revolved around the moods, ebbs, and flows of home's watery currents. How it was both restricting and freeing to follow those rules, to play when the water was deep enough and time the hunt for shallow water.

The slow rhythm of the waves was the beat of my heart; the coast, the anchor that held me fast and drew me home. Maybe he was right. I'd wanted a crew of Old Ones for *Black Hind*, so raising an army of them would do instead. I'd have to be really nice to Maddoc and hope that Ria and the egg could get us the help we needed under the guise of helping them.

'Promise me that if we don't succeed, you'll be ready to fight here?'

Anard nodded. 'A promise easily met. I have no intention of letting anyone – human or spirit – undo what we've begun to fix. I told you it was my calling, and I meant it.'

'King Anard, if you want to see change happening, watch old men row a boat out from Orange. You'd better get back to your ship. We have to return urgently, else the entire situation could get far worse.'

'If *Black Hind* is involved, the end result will be quite the opposite, I'm sure.' He clapped me on the shoulder. 'I'll take your advice. Good luck, Georgie. Send my regards to Gina, won't you?'

He exited the cabin and climbed back down to his boat before it hummed quietly off into the falling darkness.

We sailed for days. Theo was in gradually less pain and followed all of Alex's instructions. We'd have no real idea about the mobility of his hand for a while yet, apparently. His swollen eye had reduced in size, but he complained of double vision, blurring, and headaches when he took the eye patch off, so it remained in place.

I suggested he put more dragon egg goop on it, but he

declined. 'The hatchling needs it far more than I do. I'll try if it hatches early.' He'd taken to sitting in the hold with it, and I caught him with his hand resting on the shell one morning as Zora and I headed down to rest.

'It's not moving as much today,' he said as I entered the hold.

'Shall I get Ria?' I asked.

Theo nodded.

Ria placed her hands on the egg, and I saw the quick shuffling of weight. Her voice did not tell the same story as her body, though, and she turned to Theo with a bright smile. 'I'm sure it will be fine. Why don't you try singing to it?'

Theo blinked. 'Singing? Me?'

'Yes, something lively. Put your good hand on the egg – just like that – and sing ... something from the flotilla maybe? A legend of dragons and sirens.'

'I think you got me mixed up with the Storyteller,' Theo grumbled.

Ria gestured for me to feel the side of the egg as Theo shuffled closer, his fingers moving as though he was flicking through pages in a book. Ria hummed a song that sounded a little like the tune Zora played at Cor's Cairn, and Theo looked up. 'No, that's too sad,' he said. He placed his hands on the egg and began to sing a lively song.

I felt the pulse of magic grow, and the presence of the hatchling fill me. When he stopped for a break, Ria picked up her tune, and though the hatchling remained bright, its power grew no brighter, and it stilled. I removed my hand, and she nodded as though having shared some conspiracy.

That was the second time I'd noticed the hatchling respond directly to Theo. Why him?

Ria was right. Theo somehow needed to keep the hatchling's energy and life topped up. How under all the oceans was I going to explain that and have him believe me?

Ria followed me out of the room, and we closed the door to keep Theo's singing quieter for those about to sleep.

'What's going on?' I asked her.

'I don't know. It's responding to him, and only him.'

'Has it bonded with the voice of his mother? He is her blood?'

Ventios dropped down the steps with ease, swinging into our space as though he already knew every nook and cranny of *Black Hind*. I looked at Ria, and she shrugged. It was worth a try.

'Any ideas about dragon hatchlings in your stories?' I asked in hope.

He laughed. 'Loads, if you want to hear how brave someone was just before they were eaten by the hatchling.'

'Did you tell that to Seaspray?' I asked in horror. Had she known about the hatchling from the start? Realised the risk we were taking with her life, even as we didn't?

'No. Some tales are best untold until the time is right.'

I took the deep breath I needed and blew it out slowly. Underwater, I liked to watch the bubbles rise from a slow breath – keeping them even and straight helped me focus. On land or in the boat, it wasn't so useful.

'What's he doing in there?' Ventios asked, staring at the door through which Theo could be heard singing a bawdy song.

'I told him to sing to the dragon.' Ria beamed. 'It was sad, and its spark was going out. I hadn't felt it move for days, but it seems to like Theo's voice.'

Ventios turned away, rolled his shoulders, and straightened his posture. 'Does it now?' He smiled. 'I suspect there is a story about his own family that Timothee Maritim needs to know, and now seems as good a time as any.' Without another word, he marched through into the hold, closing the door behind him.

'Well, that's not what I expected him to say. What's all this about, Ria?'

She sighed. 'It's fading. That bit is true, but somehow Theo brings more out of it. The hatchling responds to him in a way it doesn't to anyone else. I don't understand why, but I'll use their connection if I have to. We must get that egg home to its father before his wrath is unleashed.'

Theo's singing stopped. I strained but couldn't hear the conversation through the door. We were evidently not invited, so I gestured to our room. 'I need rest, Ria. I'll see you in a bit.'

Rest and time to think. Zora was still awake as I entered

'Everything okay?' She yawned mid-sentence, and I decided against repeating Ria's concerns.

'It's all fine,' I replied and clambered up the ladder to the top bunk to try to sleep.

30
MADDOC IMPRISONED

MADDOC

Day turned to night and back to day; the sliver of light around the door frame Maddoc's only indication of the changing hours. He slumped at the back of the cell. Unlike Y Plant, with whom he shared the space, he was able to touch the mesh wires of their prison, even if he couldn't grip them.

He didn't understand why, when he'd been added to their number, they hadn't made a break for freedom, or at least one of them tried to get out. When he asked, they simply shuffled their feet and looked away from him.

Maddoc was left with little to do but plan. He was confident in his belief that someone would rescue him rather than face his mother's wrath. He reached out to feel the tibicena, but the strong tang of the iron grid around him hindered all attempts. That and being enclosed with a host of Y Plant. Even shackled, they were brilliant with magic. If he could find a way to break any of their wrist bands, maybe they would work with him to resist their situation.

It was too dark to achieve anything right then, so he decided to sleep and save what energy he could for daylight. He rested his back against the cold wall, dreaming of his cottage and the ancient yew; of nights spent sat in the safe embrace of its trunk with a cider and a cheese sandwich. For a moment, Maddoc let himself wonder if anyone in the village had noticed his absence. When he got back, he was going to head straight for the bakery. He imagined the smell of the fresh bread, and with the images of home filling his mind, he rested better that night than he had for days.

The ball of light hovering outside the bars hurt his eyes as he tried to see past it. Was it the Irrlicht? Or the gwyllion?

In truth, they were sister *Sidhe* of different origins, both focused on leading humankind to their deaths. He just had to hope that the ties of the Pact were still stronger than the old hag's instincts.

'Maddoc, wake up.' It was the gwyllion. A body lay on the floor of the room, illuminated by her glowing light.

'They'll find that.' He gestured, and she laughed. It was so high-pitched and eerie that it made his skin want to crawl from his flesh and hide back in the darkness. Despite being mostly sure she was on his side, he was petrified. The human instincts of his father quaked inside him as he tried to maintain a semblance of control. 'Can you get me out?' he asked.

She shook her head.

'No, but we will get you out soon. Listen for the coblynau's knocks.' She turned and stared at the door for a moment before drawing a cloud of darkness around her and extinguishing her light. 'I need to go.'

The door closed behind her, leaving Maddoc with Y Plant.

'The knocks?' their spokesman said. 'Who the heck are you to have a rescue party when no one came for us? And if I heard that right, you've got coblynau tunnelling us out.'

'I'm just here to help,' Maddoc replied. 'We do have one, yes.'

'One? That won't be quick. But at this point, we are good at waiting. I'm Gwyn. We may as well get acquainted now you're stuck with us.'

'Maddoc, Guardian of the Pact. I know patience might have worked for you until now, but by my guess, we have less than a week before Lord Flame attacks.'

'If he can find us. We need these bands off to help hide us. Not that we can blame him for being fired up over the loss of his child. Fired up …' He grinned at his own joke. 'Never mind. We have an exit strategy, and now we need to get these bands off somehow. Is there anything in your repertoire that can help us, annwn?'

Maddoc was loathe to reveal any of his weaknesses. 'No. We need them cut or melted off.'

'Then you'd better start trying to work out how to tame that beast.' Gwyn nodded his head at the door.

31
OTHERWORLD

TELLIN

As the moon rose, my heart sank. We were close, but we hadn't made it back to Mynyw in time. We'd reach the south of the Territories inside Lord Flame's time scale, but still at least a day from where we needed to be. The egg was cracked to the point where I expected to walk into the hold and find Theo eaten every time we changed shift, and Theo himself had grown even quieter, spending more time with the egg than the human members of our crew. I'd expected him to want to see it hatch, to finally meet a dragon, but not at the expense of his own life.

'There must be somewhere we can get word and the egg to The Lady of the Lake faster than sailing,' I muttered as Ria and I stared out at the imposing cliffs of the coast ahead.

'I agree, but I don't know the way, and I don't know if I can use the Path alone, let alone carrying an egg with its own type of magic.'

'Can you feel the Paths, or whatever they're called?'

'I'm sorry, I don't think I can. Maddoc said they'll be waiting for me as soon as we arrive. I'm certain that help will be there. Having used the Path, it could be within moments.'

'We'd better push on then.'

We had let them down. Would we have made it without our pause in Orange? Or the quick stop to connect with Anard? I wasn't sure that cutting either out would have made enough difference. My knuckles were white as I gripped the rail and stared over the choppy waves, trying to hide my worry from the others.

'I'll flatten the waves. We've got a perfect breeze today, so let's see just how fast we can get *Black Hind* to fly.' Zora's action would do more than my worrying. I uncurled my hands; we needed speed, not worry. Maybe Lord Flame would sleep through the day or wait an extra night.

'We could put the dragon-wing rig up?' Theo appeared from below. The fold of skin under his visible eye was as deep as a sea squirt, and his skin was almost as pallid.

'It will advertise our presence to anyone who knows us.'

'It might. But this egg is so precarious, so close to hatching, that at this point, I'm willing to risk it. The hatchling is asking me for fire. Tellin, it's talking to me! I can't give it fire. All I can give it is songs and myself while I persuade it not to hatch. It's getting harder day by day.'

Ash gestured to the helm. 'Do you want to take a turn?'

Theo nodded gratefully. 'Thank you. The others will need help changing the sails. You'll really feel us fly then. No sleep until we arrive.'

'No sleep,' I echoed, knowing that the humans on the crew would find that more difficult than Zora, Ria, and myself.

Alex grumbled inaudibly at the sight of Theo on the helm; his eyes narrowed and his frown thunderous.

'I won't use the bad one, Alex. Your hard work is safe. Come on. Let's get rigged up.'

We dragged the spars and red sails onto the deck. I'd checked on the egg as we retrieved them, brushing my hand over it. The force of power the egg held was immense. If that was the power of an unhatched dragon, we desperately needed to avoid his father out on the hunt.

I climbed the rigging to spar height and found Ventios an arm's length below me.

'Two sets of hands are better than one,' he called up. Sure enough, as I began to attach my spar, he moved to the other side of the mast and hooked his in, threading the leader rope with ease and setting the sail on his side faster than I could, though he started after me.

We finished quickly, and I let him descend first while I tweaked the rig. Theo conferred with the other sea-folk, and once I'd finished their list of demands, I dropped to the deck so we could pull the wings open on their pulleys. Wind filled our sails, and we flew for Haven.

We were escorted into Haven by stout, rainbow-beaked puffins. Silvery eels hung from their beaks, and their orange feet were tucked in tightly as they flew past us, headed for the red-folded rocks of Sal's home. The cliffs felt ominous, portents of the potential for spilled blood – or would they both be more akin to the possibility of Lord Flame's fire scorching the land in search of his child? That very same hatchling we carried aboard *Black Hind*.

Zora was on her knees with exhaustion now, and I was as ever in awe of her power and focus. Our passage had been smooth, thanks to her. Her head drooped with tiredness as she struggled to remain awake. It wouldn't be long before she passed out and we'd have to battle the waves once more. At least it wouldn't be for long.

As though manifested by my thoughts, her hands fell to her sides, and she slumped to the deck. I ran to her, gently cradling her exhausted form as I tried to gauge how long the last part of our race home would take; less than an hour, I decided.

As the waves rose, we were joined by an escort of porpoises leaping to either side of our bow wave.

'Reef the wings,' Ash called. Ventios leapt to action. Ria poked her head out from the cabin.

'The egg's crack is almost full height,' she said. 'Theo, you need to try and persuade it to stay in there a little longer.' She glanced at Zora and clambered out to help me.

'Let's take her below deck. It's too choppy to leave her out here,' I said, and we carried her down to our room with Theo following as he headed for the hold.

'Zora did amazingly,' Ria murmured. 'That's the longest I've seen her hold the waters calm.'

'She did, but we'll need her in the coming days. She needs to rest.' I brushed a stray curl off Zora's cheek before going back on deck.

We surfed through the swell of the headlands about an hour or so later to be met by *Petrel*. Sal's braid flew behind him as *Petrel* skipped across the waves. Môr was with him, whooping in delight each time they flew off a wave. The novelty of life away from the pack was still clearly in play.

As they drew near, I called across. 'We have it, but the situation is precarious. Ria needs to reach the Tylwyth Teg Path as quickly as possible.'

Sal drew alongside us. 'Jump,' he said. Ria didn't need asking twice.

I worried that she might cause a hole in the boat as she landed, but she did so with grace and calm. 'You too,' Sal called up. I swallowed hard before taking a running leap off the side of *Black Hind*.

'Don't moor up,' I called back to the crew. 'Keep moving, and keep Theo in the hold.'

Sal frowned. 'Why?'

'I'll tell you later.' We pulled away from *Black Hind* and shot across the bay, following Ria's directions.

Wind tried to steal my words as I worked to persuade Môr to help us. 'Can you prepare the selkies to aid us? Will they help preserve their own peace?'

'I'm going to try,' Môr replied. 'If the whole pack won't aid us, the bachelor pack will for certain. I'll try to persuade some of the females to help too – their charms could be effective distractions. Sal has explained how you work. We need to get you close to this queen without her realising.' He winked. 'I'm sure we can distract a lot of gathered forces very effectively.'

'Don't get captured in the process!' I replied. 'Ocean knows it's not easy to reclaim a lost skin.'

He laughed. 'We'll leave ours under lock and key on *Barge*. No one will hold us hostage.'

Petrel bumped onto the sand, and Ria and I leapt out.

'Follow me!' she called, and I ran after her as she wove through sharp, leg-scraping bushes. Thorns gouged slices from our legs, but she ignored it and kept running onward to the summit of the hill.

A small child sat in the sunshine, playing with a ball as we approached. 'Rialta?' they called out.

'Yes, get The Lady,' Ria gasped as she stumbled to a halt. The child stood and vanished.

A matter of minutes later, a tall woman appeared in the same spot. She moved with such grace and poise that she appeared to float towards us.

'Where is it?'

'The shell is cracked beyond the ability to carry it. One of our crew keeps it in the shell,' Ria replied.

'How?' The Lady frowned. 'Dragons are immune to flattery and persuasion. All know this.'

I didn't, but I nodded all the same. 'It responds to him.' I shrugged. 'It always has.'

'Then he is no true human,' The Lady of the Lake said. 'He has dragon or siren blood. They are the same thing.'

'He was entirely susceptible to a siren's charms, and she never said anything.' Theo was just Theo. It was a rare hatchling, that was all. It had to be.

'Would you expose one of your own?' The Lady asked. 'You cannot bring it through the Pathways if it's damaged. The transit would cause further damage, and I am not risking that happening. There is a chance it could die. Lord Flame has never used our Path for good reason. The magics are not compatible. You will have to carry the egg over land to him.'

'It won't make it.' Ria stood, facing up to the woman, who, to my astonishment, backed away a pace, noticeably uneasy in Ria's presence.

'Then find another way. Carry the spirit inside yourself. Reunite them when you're close.'

It was Ria's turn to recoil. 'I can't do that! For one thing, I carry thousands of spirits inside me. Huge as this is, it would still merge with the others. There's no guarantee that I could return the right one to the dragon. I've never attempted to do such a thing. It's wrong – on all levels. I take the spirits, but I can't return just one. What if I returned one such as Mona?' She turned to me, desperation in her usually calm tone. 'I can't do that.'

'Then empty yourself,' The Lady replied. 'One spirit, no chance of a mistake.'

'I do not know how.' Ria folded a little. I knew she'd be fighting her own battles, and my heart ached for her.

'Can't you simply tell Lord Flame to come and get their hatchling?' I asked. It appeared the most sensible option. So, some humans saw a dragon. If he flew at night, then he could make it in time.

'No. He left the library this morning. You will need to take it to him in the hidden isles of Y Plant Rhys Ddwfn.'

Urchin's arse, we were too late. 'What if they capture him?' I asked.

She laughed. 'Then there will be death and destruction, damage and loss. Many lives will be lost in the attempt, and the entire country destabilised. Our Pact in tatters, our magic weakened. He is the last northern dragon. It would be the end of his kind, for without the fire of life, then the hatchling will not survive long.'

'You said that the sirens and dragons are the same? If sirens exist, surely that means there can be more eggs, more dragons?'

'Without the dragon, the siren beget only siren. Have you ever seen a male?' She was right. I searched all my memories and all the legends, but I could not recall a single male.

Ria pushed her shoulders back and looked up at The Lady. 'If I can empty myself, I will do it.'

'The Lady nodded. I will take you to the Otherworld gate that the gwyllion use. I don't know how they use it, only that they do and have done so as long as they have existed in this land.'

'I'm coming too.' I stood alongside Ria, wishing I could do more than support her.

She flashed me a grateful smile. 'I'm not sure if you can use the Pathway.'

The Lady looked at me. 'Selkie, I will grant you safe passage.' She reached towards me, and from her hand formed a glowing circle of magic that solidified into a glass-like ring. 'Look through it, and you will see the Path. Hold it tightly, and do not let go. Should you release it, you will fall. Our Path travels far above the land, and you will probably die.' She laughed at the thought. Her joy over death was foul and unsettling, I wasn't sure that I liked or trusted her, but that was all the more reason to accompany Ria.

At the place where the child had vanished and The Lady appeared, I held up the lens. Through it, I saw rippling threads of magic so thin and delicate that walking along it would be like balancing on a rigging line from one boat to another. Ria closed her eyes and stepped onto the line, moving as easily as if she walked on ground.

I swallowed hard, took a deep breath, and followed. Looking down as we crossed the land was one of the worst sensations I'd ever experienced. I had no fear of heights, but that was something entirely *other*.

We took ten steps. Just ten. The Lady stepped off the line, and Ria and I followed. We stood in a valley surrounded by steep-sided green hills. A breeze rustling spring leaves just beginning to uncurl from the branches of trees, water burbling over pebbles in a small stream, and trilling birdsong were the only sounds that broke the silence. Far in the distance, a deer barked.

Ria pointed at an ancient tree. 'The entrance to the library is that stone standing near the yew.' An inconspicuous upright stone protruded from the overgrown grass, off to one side of the worn markers of a human graveyard.

'This is a place of ancient and old magic so powerful that humankind chose it to build their own sites of worship on.' The Lady gestured to the only remaining stone structure not enveloped by the vegetation. 'They built it on the site of the gate to our Otherworld.'

'Is there not a risk that they would pass through?' I shook my head. It seemed a ridiculous idea, even for humans.

'That's what they counted on. Many princes of Mynyw were buried here in the days when a monarchy ruled these lands, long before they learned to work together without needing one leader. Here, humankind have lived according to kindness and fairness for centuries. It works as long as they take it in turns to coordinate things. No princes are buried here any longer.'

The gate was a huge stone structure. An arch inside an arch, which was inside another arch. Layers of stone formed the gateway, bound by what appeared to be strands of stone carved across them and anchored with complex carved knots. I lifted the lens to look at it. The bindings glowed with the same light as the Pathway, holding the arch open. I wondered what would happen if someone were to cut the magic. Would the binding fail and the stacked arches collapse, sealing the way?

Ria walked up to it, running her hand over the arches as she walked past. 'I can definitely return?' she asked.

The Lady nodded. 'You of all of us ask this?'

Ria smiled gently. 'What I am and who I am are different

things, Lady.' She turned to me. 'If I don't return, try not to get eaten. I've loved knowing you. Thank you for freeing me.'

Then she turned and walked through the archway. Darkness filled the arch; swirling smoke-like tendrils reached in and gathered around her until they filled the entire inner space. Ria stretched out her hand towards them, glanced back one more time, then vanished into darkness. The arch cleared, leaving me to stare up at the mountains beyond and pray to the old gods that she would return.

32
RETURN FROM THE FLAMES

TELLIN

I walked closer to the arch, pausing at the threshold to reach my fingertips towards a spot the dark coils had seeped from.

'It will not open for you,' The Lady said quietly. 'It has never opened for me either. We are creatures of many forms, yet our spirits flow with life-giving water. Your friend, Rialta, is a minor god of death. It calls to her as she to it.'

The revelation didn't surprise me. With all I'd seen Ria do, it felt right. 'Will she be back?' I asked.

'They usually are. Assuming she makes the journey complete, I should warn you that she will be changed. Her long life is lived on borrowed time from untimely deaths. Rialta may not feast on it as a gwyllion or delight in it as many of their ilk are known to, but still, it changes her.'

It made sense to me; magic has a cost. Magic has rules, even if I do not truly understand how it works. Mine is innate – as much part of me as the energy I wake with each day. I use it, and when I get tired, it fails. It recovers as I rest. Ria's could exist in a similar way. I tried to think if I'd ever seen her exhausted and could only recall the occasion when she had taken in all the lost souls off the south coast of the Territories.

By emptying herself, would all the souls she had taken in finally find a final rest? A blackbird alighted near me, its plumage dark as the night sky and its beak as brilliant as the sun that follows. He cocked his head to one side, staring at me with his gold-rimmed eye.

'Bring her back,' I murmured, looking back to the arch.

The blackbird began to sing, dipped his head, and spread his tail. He hopped a little closer and tilted his head the other way as though studying me. Then, he pecked at my hand, drawing a droplet of scarlet blood, which he drank. He glided towards The Lady, landing at her feet. He bobbed his head and turned away from her, spread his wings, and took off toward the gate, his trilling song cut off as he vanished into a small pool of darkness.

I glanced at The Lady. She smiled, but it held a trace of sadness; her eyes did not smile as her mouth did. 'You know not what you just asked. He will bring her back if her spirit goes too far. I'm sure she won't be long now.'

She was wrong. The sun crested the mountain and was descending past the horizon by the time the archway came back to life. Tendrils of grey smoke curled once more. Reflecting the fire-filled sunset, they licked at each other as tongues of flame rather than smoke, flickering with life and dancing in reds and golds.

My breath caught. I'd seen that before but thought it was fire. I rose to my feet, knowing in my heart that it had been the right thing to do. It was what the hind had shown me. A silhouette appeared through the flames of smoke, growing more compact, more focused, as Ria closed on the archway from the other side.

Her final step revealed the truth of The Lady's words. The hind's image was not a truth I could see. Ria carried the blackbird in her open palm, as step after faltering step, she crossed back into our world. She was hunched, her skin wrinkled and thin, her knuckles swollen with age, and her fingers fixed with pain. She stumbled. I ran to catch her. She raised her head to look up at me, and I swallowed back a gasp.

Her eyes were white with cataracts. I'd seen old seals with them before, entirely blind bar their whiskers. Ria had none of those. She reached up with her other hand and touched my face, feeling my true mouth through the glamour.

I let her.

As she touched my sharp teeth, she smiled. 'I made it back then, Tellin.'

I swallowed hard and embraced her tightly. 'You did.' It was all I could trust my voice to say.

'I understand how to push the spirits out now. I don't know how hard it will be here, but I do know how to. Lady, are you here still?'

The Lady's eyes sparkled. She appeared to be taking joy from Ria's condition, and fickle as I knew Tylwyth Teg were, it still upset me – I'd definitely been too long amongst humans.

'If Ria cannot see it, how will she navigate the Path?' I asked.

'I will carry her. Her sacrifice is noted and honoured.' With that, The Lady swooped Ria up in her arms. 'Come. We have no time to waste.'

The blackbird sang one last song and flew back to the bushes from whence it came. I followed The Lady back to the Path. As we walked above Mynyw, I searched the waters below, hoping Sal wasn't far off the shore. We'd need him or one of *Barge's* boats to get Ria back to the hatchling.

We emerged back on the headland, and The Lady gently placed Ria on the ground.

'The damage may reverse when you take the dragon's spirit. But the effects will not be permanent, and you'll be left aged and crippled once more. Tellin, keep the lens in case you need it. Do not let it not fall into any other's hands. I return to prepare my people. If our barriers fall and our world becomes visible to humankind, then we must be ready for whatever consequences that entails. Head north, and pass the isles, staying close to the coast. Past the selkie isles and keep heading north. You'll pass one spot where the water invades Mynyw, flowing deep into our heart.

'Beyond that, there is a point where two hills stand proud at the meeting of three waterways. Dependent on the tide, they may be islands rather than headlands. Take the most southerly and travel along the south of the river until it turns north. There, one of us will meet you to take you the rest of the way. From there, you have one day of hard travel to reach the sky lakes. Hopefully, my son will be back soon, and he can lead you there. Lord Flame should arrive as daylight does.'

'Maddoc is not returned?' Ria turned her blind eyes toward The Lady. 'He should be back by now.'

'None of the party I sent to search the isles of Y Plant have returned,' she admitted. 'Now go. I will deal with my folk – you have a bigger issue to handle.'

Petrel was nowhere obvious as I looked out to sea. I'd coaxed and guided Ria through the vicious thorns and led her through the village houses to the sea wall.

'Do you think you could swim?' I asked as I studied a selection of small boats on the moorings.

Ria chuckled. It sounded dry as a desert and crackly like dead twigs. I winced, glad that she couldn't see my reaction. It hurt seeing her like that, even if it was her more true form.

'I doubt it. I could certainly breathe – or not breathe – well enough, I suspect, but I am so frail, you'd have to drag me through the water. In your skin, it might be possible. In your belegged form, it's never going to happen.'

How far would my Ocean voice carry? I wondered, filled with visions of Ria riding a walrus back to *Barge*.

'Stay there,' I said.

'I'm not walking anywhere until you move me. Don't worry,' Ria replied, clasping her gnarled hands in her lap.

I strode into the water. Once I reached waist-deep, I ducked my head under and called for aid.

A reply reached me moments later, not from the walrus, but Sal himself. I sighed with relief and waded back to wait with Ria.

The hum of *Petrel's* engine followed Sal's call by moments. Môr appeared from the darkness soon after.

'Carry her,' I said, gesturing to Ria.

'Really?'

'Yes.'

He stooped over – his silhouette in the dim light from the village just about visible – and scooped her up. As we moved through the water, he murmured in Ocean. 'She feels much smaller than I expected, and bonier.'

'She made a sacrifice for the dragon and your Pact,' I responded, filling my words with emotion and conveying the truth of the sacrifice to him.

'Then I carry her with honour.'

'I can't understand you, but I'm certain you're talking about me,' Ria rasped.

'With much pride, Ria,' I said as Môr gently lifted her over the side and into *Petrel*. We clambered in after her, and Sal turned us out into the waves, speeding through Haven to reunite us with *Black Hind*.

Black Hind was tucked in *Barge's* shadow, close enough for help should they need it but far enough to keep the egg from prying eyes.

Petrel slipped between the vessels as Zora leapt to catch a rope from Môr. 'What news?' she called. I was glad to see her up again. The Lady's plan had a major flaw, and I needed Zora to fix it.

I helped Ria to her feet, supporting her unsteady steps as she prepared to climb into *Black Hind*.

'Ria?' Zora stared at her as she reached for the ladder.

'I don't know if I can climb it.' Ria grasped it with one stiff hand, and I gently supported her weight as she began to climb. Môr moved to help me, but from the corner of my eye, I saw Sal shake his head.

'We all have limits, Môr. You can do it, Rialta.'

She fixed a tight smile across her thin lips and took hold of the next rung. As slow as a grazing limpet, Ria climbed. She reached the top, and Zora leaned down to her.

'You don't have to prove anything. Take my hand, and let me help you aboard. We are family, and families support each other.'

'Thank you.' Ria reached up, and Zora's strong arms helped her over the rail. I relaxed and took my eyes from her frail form.

'Sal, we have to do this alone. No Anard, no guarantee of help from the Tylwyth Teg – though they are preparing for war should it reach the mainland. They stick to the principles of the Pact and will not raise weapons outside their lands. It's down to us.'

He rested a hand on my shoulder. 'We've taken down a king and rescued the hind. We have the powers of Old Ones with us. A subtle hand will work in ways that an army cannot. As much as I hate to send you all into the whirlpool, you can do this. Do what needs to be done this night, then meet me once the hatchling is safe. We'll make a plan. I know an emptied spirit-taker when I see one.'

'I'll be back once everything is secured.' I climbed up the ladder and rejoined the crew.

'They've gone down already.' Ash gestured below deck.

'Where's Ventios?' I asked. Ash chuckled.

'Where do you think he is? He thinks this story will make him famous. Crazy man. He should worry about remembering the details, not audiences in the future.'

Ash's dry humour and ready smile took the edge off my nerves. Down in the hold, Theo, Zora, and Ria were all arrayed around the egg. Ventios was there too, making himself as small as he could in the corner.

The egg was still in its hammock, and Theo was sat with his arms around it. He appeared to be holding the shell together with sheer willpower.

Ria moved alongside him and reached for the egg. Her breathy intake was a wheeze of dismay. 'I'm almost too late,' she cried.

'I've got him,' Theo said. 'But I can't hold him long. What's the plan?' He appeared entirely oblivious to the change in Ria.

'Zora, this needs you as well.' I said, feeling – as I often did – that I simply coordinated the amazing talents of my friends.

Watching on from the sidelines, useless unless someone needed killing. 'Theo, you need to tell it to trust Ria. That it will die without fire.'

'It knows that, and I know that.' Theo grumbled. 'It's the only reason he's remained in the shell.'

'Ria is *empty*.'

He looked up at me then, and more carefully at Ria. 'Oceans, Ria, I thought *I* looked like a crushed barnacle – you look worse.' Zora frowned at him and opened her mouth to say something, but Ria sighed.

'I'll return to myself eventually. This is more important right now. Theo, I need to take care of the dragon's spirit – carry it whole to its father. From what you say, he doesn't have long after hatching, so I need him to come to me willingly and soon. Once he's transferred, the split second ... I need you to freeze his body, Zora. Preserve him, protect him in an egg of ice. If we can transport him in two parts, with his spirit entire and his body safe, then we can save these lands and preserve the Pact for all Old Ones to have a haven here. As important, we preserve the northern dragons for one more generation.

'I can do that.' Zora flexed her fingers.

'Theo?'

'I don't like it, but I can't see another way unless you can get its father here in time?'

I shook my head. 'He's gone, Theo. We need to take the hatchling to him.'

'Let me get this right before I agree to this. We're killing him, then carrying his body to his grieving, fire-breathing parent?'

'No,' Ria croaked. 'I'll return his spirit to his body. As long as Lord Flame is there, it will work.' Her shoulders dropped slightly. 'It must work.'

'Give me a moment.' Theo placed his face flat against the

side of the egg, his arms still embracing it across the almost entirely separate halves. His lips moved, but I heard no sound. Then the egg began to flex; it pushed apart, flinging Theo away from it. The halves fell open, and the hatchling raised its snout upwards and roared.

I say roared, but it was a fairly small, croaky noise, given it probably still had stuff in its mouth. It flexed its wings, the dim light exposing the still-wrinkled tissues, not dry or extended enough for flight yet. It stood over Theo, head tilted to one side, then touched its snout to his head before flapping frantically towards the hatch above.

'He's so weak,' Ria said, her dry skin streaked with tears. 'I never thought I'd have to take a dragon's life.'

'You can do it, Ria,' I urged.

Theo sat up, watching his charge. 'Please, Ria. You and I know that he won't even survive as far as the mainland should he try to reach his father. I trust you.'

'So do I.' Zora stood slightly to the side of us, her hands following the path of the panicked hatchling. 'If you don't do something soon, one of us will become food.'

Ria reached for him and made the briefest of contacts, a brush as light as a butterfly's passing wing on one's cheek. The hatchling fell to the floor. I was reminded of the time when she did the same in Lady Rene's lands when we ran for our lives. But with the dragon, she took his life to protect it, rather than protect Gar.

I leapt forward to try and protect the hatchling from hurting itself, but Theo was already there, cradling the body in his arms.

'We need to make him compact – transportable. The Lady implied that it would take a day of tough walking through the mountains.'

'You need to make it fast,' Ria said, her voice strong and

rich. She almost glowed with power. I was convinced that when she turned around, she would look her normal self. 'This is going to be a wild few days. I can hear him. He clamours to get back to his body. Were I to touch it, he would flow straight back in.'

We tucked his wings carefully back and stepped away, except for Theo. 'I'll not let this head go until you've encased the rest. He trusts me, and I will take as much care of this hatchling as I would any one of you.'

Zora started at the chest, reaching around and encasing it in a coating of purest ice. She froze his tissues with tender care, her hands moving in a caressing fashion rather than the dramatic gestures I associated with her ice work.

'It's done,' she whispered, then crumpled to her knees.

33
SIZZLE AND BURN

MADDOC

Night fell, and with it, the screams rose. Night after night, the screams of the undead spirits trapped around the pinnacle carried on the air. Their despair crawled over his skin like swimming in a pit of insects, each noise small and inconsequential alone, but after so many nights and with so many voices, they were a constant drain on his awareness – a discomfort he needed to itch. His discomfort was nothing compared to that of the tormented dead.

That night, the screams were different – louder, shriller. The visceral cries of pain filled his ears; something out there had changed. Were the Tylwyth Teg attacking? Were the twins cutting a swathe of confusion through the population? Or maybe his mother had come to rescue him. All he could hear was the screams and his heartbeat, a pounding fear so forceful that he felt certain it could burst from his chest. He risked the pain of the dark magic and pushed as hard as he could to feel what was out there.

As his own fear collided with the sheer power above him, he realised two things. He had been captured for longer than he realised, and if Lord Flame attacked any one of Y Plant, the remaining threads of the Pact were shattered. Their confinement in the cage was, for the first time, a good thing. He turned from the iron mesh. His face had been pushed so close to it that he was lucky not to have burn marks.

Y Plant were as far from the door as they could get, their backs pressed to the solid stone wall behind. Without exception, they stared upward.

If only the coblynau had found them already. Wherever the rescue party had got to, they were quickly running out of time.

Maddoc sat and watched as the thin cracks of light from the next room flashed brightly time and again. Lord Flame was burning something out there. Maddoc hoped it wasn't the boats. Wherever the people were supposed to have gone, they'd be trapped on the fringes of Mynyw. The screams went on all night. Maddoc dreaded the sight of the islands – beautiful houses and landscaping might be charred beyond recognition. Some of Y Plant cried freely now.

'Our home,' one sniffled. 'Why does he burn our home?'

'Because someone stole his egg. Because he believes it might be here, and he hopes to frighten them into revealing it.'

'But we don't have it.'

'You don't have much of anything right now.' Maddoc sighed and returned to his spot. It would have been a small mercy to have the building burnt. Maybe that way, he could have got out.

He was woken by the chill air hours later. The screams of the living had stopped, and a cloud of darkness rolled into the room.

'Gwyllion?' he whispered.

'While the humans are distracted by the mess, I've brought help,' the old hag replied. The door closed, and darkness dissipated to reveal three figures.

'She brought us, and we brought milk,' one of the twins said.

'And honey,' the other added. 'Coblynau is finding it slower going than expected, and with tonight's turn of events, we haven't time for the safe option anymore.'

Maddoc rubbed his eyes. 'Milk and honey ... it's worth a try. If it's our weakness, maybe ... Who doesn't like honey?'

The rustle of clothes and a muffled yawn gave away Gwyn's shuffled approach. 'Show me any Old One who doesn't like honey, and you're a liar. I agree – it's worth a go. Be warned, you may subdue the creature for a while, but eventually, it will return to its ways. Whatever we do needs to be well-planned.'

'I agree, but killing it would be as bad as killing each other. Every creature has its place. I can make exception for killing of warped Old Ones, of those bent on gain or destruction. But the tibicena is doing no more than its instincts tell it to. Balance is needed, and it should be taken back to the Respites.' Maddoc didn't like it either, but balance was needed across the world, and the hound was part of the balance. Besides, if all the creatures that should be back in the Respites were returned, maybe the Everstorm would calm.

'I don't want to agree because it makes our job harder, but I do. How do you propose that we do that?' Gwyn mumbled.

'I propose that we don't. I'm confident that I know some who would return the tibicena – if we can get it to them.' Tellin and her crew – Maddoc was certain Sal would get on board with the idea. 'How bad is it out there? How long have we got?'

'A few hours at the most while they dampen the fires. We have until morning,' a twin replied.

'I have an idea.' Maddoc gathered them close to outline his plan.

Shortly afterwards, the twins opened the door a crack and pushed a bowl of honeyed milk through to the tibicena. Silence stretched on, and the screams remained absent, the undead as quiet as the living.

'Open the shutters,' Maddoc said as a crack of light lanced across the floor from the first room. 'Get to the main door, Be ready to run.'

One twin strode to the door, opening the shutters on the way. The gwyllion drew a cloak of shadow around herself and grasped the remaining bowl of honeyed milk close.

'Are we all ready?' Maddoc scanned the room. Every one of Y Plant huddled together, ready to break for freedom if the plan worked.

'Remember, stay quiet!'

The twin edged the door open, letting light enter the room beyond, and a canine head poked through. Red eyes glowed, its dark fur absorbing the light. It padded forward, sniffing as it tried to scent out the milk and honey; sizzling hisses accompanied it as drool fell to the floor. So far, no growl or rumble of the anger that Maddoc experienced while pinned down. Still, his heart raced.

The gwyllion dribbled a little of the honey, and the tibicena turned immediately, dropping its snout to the floor. It might work. Maddoc allowed himself the tiniest bit of hope, remembering the lump of melted metal. The twins stood, one by the door and one watching out the window. Everything hinged on honey, milk, and time.

A drop of honey on the bottom of the cage.

A tongue licking at it, sizzling metal, then the tongue moved on to the next and the next ... Maddoc crept across, a hand-span separating himself from the tibicena, the heat of its breath, the scent of its magic.

He reached to touch the cage, unable to hold back the smile fighting to beam from his face. The melted stump of the wires ended just where the tibicena had licked it.

A tongue so hot that it melted metal, but somehow the entire building remained standing. He shuddered to think what might have happened had anything flammable been in there.

'Higher,' he whispered, and the gwyllion spread honey above it. Again, the hiss of metal, and the section of cage fell out.

He poked his hand through.

'Try it,' he rasped, nerves ringing and his legs quaking. She daubed a drop of honey on each of the iron bracelets. Maddoc moved his arms close to the tibicena's searching muzzle.

'Gentle now,' he murmured, trying to expose as little flesh as he could by holding them above the tibicena so that they had to lick the drips of honey from below, and any slobber would fall away from him. Heat shot through his wrist, and he realised he'd made a hideous mistake. The smell of burning flesh filled his nose as the metal did indeed melt, and fused tighter to his skin. He quickly pulled the other hand back.

'We'll get out first. The iron cuffs we'll deal with once we're out of here,' he said through gritted teeth. Gods, but he wanted to scream. The pain was agony, the searing, skin-peeling pain. Were his arms blistering? They were. He whimpered and sat back from the cage as the gwyllion teased them out with milk and honey.

'Still want to take it with us?' Gwyn placed a hand on his arm. 'That was brave. Thank you for testing the theory. We'll do what we can for you, I promise.'

'Stuff me, just get out of here and make the malignant warts on the face of Mynyw who are wrecking our home be dead. The Pact is worth more than one person, more than any of us.'

Gods, it hurt. Maddoc struggled to remain fully conscious as the pain increased. Still, the blistering developed. The burn from the tibicena's saliva on his neck had been painful, but his whole hands? The world went black as darkness closed in his vision, then eased again.

He opened his eyes to find Gwyn staring closely at him. 'You still with us, Guardian? The hole is big enough to get out. Those annwn might be able to heal you up a bit if you can get out.'

Maddoc scrambled through the gap in the bars after Gwyn, ensuring all Y Plant were out. 'We'll have to leave it here and come back later?' he asked, gesturing at the tibicena.

The gwyllion shook her head. 'We'll not let them use it as a weapon. Much as Lord Flame, there are some powers that must be checked, even if their balance is essential. As air is to soil and water is to fire, it is needed. In the Respites, it would live in the deepest of caves. We have a use for the coblynau's work, after all. At least until you can recover it?' Y Plant gathered together, whispering amongst themselves.

Gwyn relayed their decision. 'We agree to hide it until someone can return it. Milk and honey are low and easy prices to pay for our freedom. How will you get it there?'

The gwyllion lifted her bowl. 'I'll lead it.'

Maddoc looked at the bowl, struggling to focus through the pain in his arm. 'Won't it melt?' he managed eventually.

'No, it's annwn made.' She held it towards the tibicena, and it nosed the bowl as she stepped away, letting it have a single lick.

'She's going to get pounced on,' Maddoc muttered. *Fool hag.*

'Do not let her hear you say that,' one of the twins murmured as they grabbed his arm. 'Let us see what I can do …' They started to funnel the warmth Maddoc had felt before into his arm.

It got hotter and hotter until he pulled his arm back, gasping for breath. 'It's not working.'

His arm looked worse, if anything. The metal stopped the healing. The iron embedded in his flesh, somewhere under the swollen tissue filled him with throbbing pain. He stared at his arm, unnoticing of Y Plant leaving until their absence was more notable than the noise of their presence.

'Come on, Maddoc.' The twin hadn't left his side.

They tried to support him to his feet. His bloody legs should work, after all – it wasn't them that got burned. How stupid had he been? He was not only injured, but he was going to slow their escape and risk letting them all down.

He hobbled out, the ache from Lord Flame's injury to his leg adding to the meal of pain his body was serving. Maddoc let the twin lead him away from the building into the charred and smoking field beyond.

34
THE TRUE PRICE OF A DRAGON

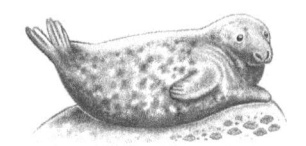

TELLIN

Ash vanished into the depths of *Barge*, and Alex scurried away to see Aline, dragging a reluctant Theo with him.

'The dragon is safe. Get checked, and then you know you can do what needs to be done for the next few weeks without worrying,' Alex cajoled him, and reluctantly, Theo had followed.

He returned to *Black Hind* as I did from my conversation with Sal. Our plans were finalised and we had prepared back up plans.

It would take *Barge* at least a week to return to Terrania, and Sal would be ready to leave on our return, no matter the outcome of our journey. He would head home riding a breaking wave of good news or rushing ahead of the crashing surf of Anard's sister. If it was the latter, we would go with him, my skin remaining out of reach for a while longer.

Daylight revealed the boat we'd claimed on our rescue of Theo was tied alongside *Barge*, patched up and ready to sail.

Môr glided around the deck, as lost as I had been on my first days under Zora's tutelage. Behind us came the gentle noise of waves lapping hulls as small vessels arrived, carrying supplies we needed.

Seren raided our supplies, and I raided my closet. Many of our courtesan's most revealing dresses were being loaded onto Môr's boat, along with an assortment of men's clothes. Ash returned to the water-deck with a selection of winches and some assistants, all of whom looked as though Ash had dragged them from their beds.

There was a serious amount of grumbling and swearing as they clambered aboard the other boat, and Ash started to direct them to change its winch layout. Ash clearly intended to sail the other vessel with minimal help from the selkies Môr hoped to gather.

Môr and Ash gestured broadly at each other as they discussed the layout, and I gave in to a growing smile. Sal liked gifting boats, it appeared.

There was no time to fit this one out properly, but maybe in the future, there would be a second vessel crewed by Old Ones.

Zora woke, and so did my sun. She smiled broadly as she stretched in the morning sunlight, and it lit me up too. Her happiness meant so much to me, and it was easy to get lost in Zora's attentions if one wasn't careful. Theo appeared over on another water-level deck of *Barge*, and a small vessel whipped him over to us, with Ivy at the helm.

'It's good to get out of there. Sal says we're to join you, hold the ships off-shore should you need us to, so you and the selkies can do your thing,' she said.

'We don't plan on violence,' I replied.

'No, not unless you see this queen. I appreciate the elegance of Sal's solution, as the Pact of Mynyw is precious.

War between her races is too risky. Which boat do you want me on?'

I looked across at the other boat with Ash standing square at the helm, facing off against Môr. 'That one,' I chuckled. 'Stop them killing each other if you have to, and stop them revealing themselves while Ash is helming if you can. Will you cope with being close to Môr?'

Ivy shrugged. 'Yeah. He's attractive but not my type. I like my mates human.'

Theo scrambled aboard. 'You aren't going anywhere without me. Aline says what's left of my hand is doing well. It'll never be the same, but I'm set to join you.' He brandished a bag of dressings. 'You or Zora can re-bind my hand every few days, so we're good to go.'

'As though you'd leave our cargo behind. Come on.'

Theo leapt over the rail using his good hand for support and whistled as he went below deck.

We needed to get under way soon. Every minute Zora had to maintain the ice cocoon would tax her, and if things went wrong with Y Plant, or Lord Flame got more upset than he already was, we needed her.

With Zora, Ria, Theo, and Ventios, I would follow The Lady of the Lake's directions and hope that Maddoc would meet us there. If not, I had to hope we could attract Lord Flame's attention before he went too far. If Y Plant Rhys Ddwfn had truly sided with the queen, I didn't mind him singeing a few of them before we removed the threat.

If we left right away, we might not be far behind Môr. It would take them hours to prepare the other boat, plus a further delay while Môr tried to recruit the selkies. I hoped that his bachelor pack were every bit as keen and loyal as they'd appeared.

We sailed up the coast, skirting the selkie islands and hugging the cliffs as we headed toward the convergence of rivers that The Lady had described, and the sibling hills between them. Zora cloaked us in a fine mist to avoid notice.

We sailed all day, passing small coastal towns with gentle ascents behind them, searching for features we had been told we'd see. As evening fell, we reached the first large inlet The Lady had mentioned. We continued on to the point where waters poured out of Mynyw, where we found the two hills – one taller and one lower – separated by a wide harbour.

The route took us south of the smaller hill, avoiding the harbour and, we hoped, prying eyes. We dropped our sails as we entered the valley, taking *Black Hind* up the narrow channel under motor until the mist around us was more obvious than the boat alone.

There were few buildings there. Scattered ruins graced the slopes to either side. The river turned south in a sweeping curve, narrowing suddenly after to an unnavigable strip of water. We stopped and were hauling *Black Hind* against the southern bank when a huge dragon-shaped shadow passed out to sea.

I screamed and waved my arms. It was a vain hope that he might hear us, might turn around, but I suppose screaming from the ground is a fairly normal response to a dragon, and his wingbeats didn't pause. I had no idea what we might do if he'd turned, as the hatchling was still in the hold, frozen.

'What if someone steals her?' I asked. Theo and Ventios stowed the ropes, and Zora locked the cabin and deck doors. If we lost *Black Hind* – again – we would have no rescue party.

'They won't,' Zora replied. As soon as the last of us was on the shore and the hatchling's body gently cradled in Theo's arms, she gestured along the river. A wave of water rose, spilling over the channel as it carried *Black Hind* and deposited our boat in a small, sparse woodland. With tiny leaves starting to uncurl, it wouldn't give much shelter, but I suppose it broke the mast's outline by hiding it amongst trees.

'Very nice, but I'm sure we could just have asked Ventios to stay aboard and hold her ready to leave.' I knew I was scowling but couldn't hold it back – that paintwork was definitely going to need redoing. Zora was endlessly inventive with her magic, and despite my misgivings, I was secretly impressed. She winked at me.

We followed the river towards the east, heading along the valley and hoping our guide would arrive soon. Theo cradled the ice-bound body of the small dragon as though it weighed nothing. He refused our help, and I was pretty certain that his legs would have to give way before he relinquished the hold on his charge.

Green hills rose to either side, tree-covered and whispering with the slim spring growth as the miniature flags caught the wind. Red-chested birds shouted at us from low branches. The terrain wasn't hard to walk across as we followed the river, keeping the water ever in our sights while taking the easiest route we could.

After a while, the hills began to crowd in on us, and we were guided between their high sides and rocky escarpments back towards the north.

'We're heading the wrong way,' Ria muttered. 'We need a way to the east. Stop here.'

We did as she asked, and she stopped for a moment, scanning the hills. 'There must be one somewhere. Tellin, have you got the glass The Lady gave you?'

I rummaged in my bag and passed it to her. Ventios's eyes widened.

'What's that?' he asked.

'A magical Tylwyth Teg thing that let me see their Path.'

He grinned in excitement. 'This story is going to be amazing.'

'If we survive it.' Zora's mouth twitched, and I could see her holding back amusement at his eternal optimism.

'Got one!' Ria called excitedly. 'There's one on the top of that hill. Let me see if I can get us a guide. I'll be right back!' She ran up the hill with more speed than I'd ever seen. When she was out of hearing, Theo placed the hatchling carefully on the ground as Zora fussed over it, ensuring that all the edges of her magic remained intact.

'What happens when she gives the dragon back to his body?' Theo asked.

'I presume she returns to being aged, in pain and discomfort.' I shrugged. 'This was her choice. No one pushed her into it. I'm expecting that it will take us far longer to get back.'

'Will she cope with the voyage to the islands and a battle?'

Was he kidding? Theo, the one-eyed and one-handed, was worried about someone else's ability to sail or fight! I bit back a retort. He was just being himself, kind and thoughtful.

'I don't know.'

If we're set upon by Diana's swarms of spirits, would Ria recover as she took them in? Or would it make her weaker? I was certain that she wouldn't kill to ease her pain, but I would to get to the queen. I just needed to make sure Ria was near me at the time.

I noticed a herd of sheep roaming across the hills. She'd taken in Cor's spirit. Would sheep help too? Or was Cor only possible because of how entwined he was with Eden? Ria had reached the top of the slope, and light glinted from the glass as she held it up before vanishing into the air. Help would not be long.

'Take a rest,' I suggested. 'We aren't going anywhere without Ria. She's the only one who's met Lord Flame.' I pulled out a bag of shellfish, detaching the next sticky foot from the side of the bag as I crunched the previous one.

Zora grimaced and followed my lead. Her food looked rather unappetising– strips of cooked, dried meat and some fibrous chewy fruit. It stank of sweetness and sugar. I tried to focus on the crunch squish of my food; we needed to eat while we could. It would be a long night ahead, and we needed to be at the library by dawn. Nothing we did could stop the damage that Lord Flame would do overnight or had already done. The rest was down to Ria and Theo.

It was fully dark by the time we heard running feet approach.

'You'd better still be where I left you,' Ria called.

'No, we moved on without you,' I replied, and Ria was upon us in moments.

'I brought help,' she panted. It sounded as though she collapsed to the ground.

'It would take us about four hours in daylight, apparently. But it might be slower as we can't see our way.'

'I can deal with that,' a musical voice said from the darkness. A glowing ball of light appeared in an outstretched hand. I took it and recoiled.

'It stings. I can't hold that.'

Zora might have similar issues to me. Her magic had never caused me pain, but we were both of the ocean. Ria could probably use it, or one of the humans.

'Ventios, you try,' I said.

There was delight in his voice as he took it from the Tylwyth Teg. 'Wow.'

He waved it around, illuminating our group, and his smile was as bright in its illumination as the ball of light itself. The Tylwyth Teg produced another and gestured off to one side.

'If we follow the old road, it will take us most of the way.'

I prepared myself for a road like that in The Barren, where dead ground was decorated by occasional scattered plants, but it was nothing like that. We walked on uneven surfaces where tree roots had forced the ground into lumps and bumps and where bushes grew through cracks, their violent caresses ripping my clothes. Four hours for a Tylwyth Teg, maybe – it was going to take us all night.

Scratched and exhausted, Theo finally conceded that he needed help, and I took my turn in carrying the hatchling's body, surprised at how light it was. But then, dragons did have to fly. I held the icy cocoon across both arms and followed closely behind the unnamed Tylwyth Teg. Ventios had tried to get their name, suggesting that he could tell tales of their greatness in his stories, but the laugh he was met with silenced any further asking.

As the sun's light seeped over the mountain, golden-crested hills in the distance beckoned us forward.

'Not far now,' the Tylwyth Teg said and gestured along a branch of the uneven road. In the distance, I could see the archway.

Ria rested her hand against my arm, drawing a sharp breath. 'The stone is near a twisted yew,' she said. 'We can take it from here, thank you. Please, let The Lady know we are almost there.' The Tylwyth Teg ran off.

Theo reached for the hatchling's body. 'I would carry it home,' he said.

I released it into his care.

The burning disk of sun rose from behind the distant sky-lakes as we reached the archway, and I couldn't help but be reminded of our last visit there only a few days ago. But instead of the arch, Ria led us to a nondescript stone about knee height. There were five holes in it, each arranged around an engraved shape that resembled a very weathered sword.

Ria paused in front of it. 'Tellin, you need to put a finger there. Zora, try that one, and Theo this one.'

We did as she told us, Theo carefully placing the body at his feet. Zora looked as tired as he did, and I was certain that maintaining the ice cocoon was taking more out of her than she would admit.

As we crouched around each other, Ria placed her finger in the central hole, and a crunching noise sounded from the yew tree.

'Come on,' she urged, running toward it and climbing between the branches.

Theo stopped at the periphery, trying to find a way to get the dragon's body past the interwoven branches and failing. 'We did not come this far ...' he muttered, and before I could stop him, he broke a branch off the ancient yew. My breath caught, and I listened for any changes, any grinding of rocks.

A blackbird flew from the branches above, alighting on the wall alongside us, but nothing more happened. I climbed into the centre of the tree and helped Theo wriggle the hatchling through the gap. Ventios waited for us. From the corner of my eye, I saw him tuck something in his shirt, then he rose and slipped between the branches. He didn't meet my eyes as he disappeared down the stairwell. Probably a bit of ancient yew for an instrument or a memento to help him tell the tale, I decided.

Once everyone was in, I followed. Just before I closed the door, a huge shadow glided over the land. Morning sun glinted off red scales, and an arrow-shaped tail swished from side to side to control his landing. There was no doubting who it was, and there was no way he was fitting in the same entrance as we had. I rushed after the rest of the crew.

Our globe lit the room with a gentle blue glow, illuminating shelf after shelf of books and scrolls. All those words ... who had time to read them? Ria headed straight into a tunnel on the far side and gestured for us to follow. We scurried across the dusty floor, clouds of smoky ash stirred up from our feet as we pursued her into the dark passageway.

'Shhh,' she whispered as we closed in. She'd stopped at the entrance to the room.

Beyond her, a huge dragon circled, smoke pouring from his nostrils as he dragged his claws across the floor, frustration and anger evident in his bunched muscles. I'd never seen a dragon before and was not prepared for the sheer size of Lord Flame. Seeing him overhead was one thing, but realising I barely reached his knees was quite another. We shrunk slightly back into the shadows.

'What do we do now?' I whispered.

Lord Flame's head whipped in my direction. 'You enter my chamber, creature of the sea.' His snout lifted, and smoke spiralled back downward as he inhaled.

'Urchins arse,' Ria muttered. 'Let me do the talking.' But Theo had already pushed past her.

He strode into full view of Lord Flame, carrying the body of the hatchling. He bowed deeply and placed it in his sight. 'I return your child.'

'Dead? How dare you torture me so? If you return, does that mean you also took?' Lord Flame approached Theo, smoke belching from his nostrils and fire licking his maw. Theo stood between the hatchling and the dragon.

'The hatchling lives yet, in two parts.' In the face of almost certain immolation, Theo held his ground. 'It hatched two days ago.'

'Then it is dead, as are you. I will burn my child as should be done. From fire to fire, from life to ashes.' He opened his mouth, and the heat of Lord Flame's breath washed over us all.

'No!' Theo roared. It was filled with as much emotion, as much power, as I had ever heard in Ocean.

Lord flame stopped, swinging his head sideways to stare at Theo. 'Who are you? What are you?' In that moment of his distraction, Ria and Zora acted as one.

'Now!' Ria dived to the hatchling. She laid her hand on the ice, and Zora released the spell. As soon as Ria's hand hit the scales, her body shrivelled and curled up.

Theo stepped aside.

The hatchling gasped for air, opening its mouth much as a chick begs for food.

Lord Flame's eyes spun frenetically. He reached his great head forward and made a strange choking sound, then vomited a small lump of blackness, glowing with tiny flames, into the hatchling's mouth. The hatchling belched a small burst of fire and flapped its wings with renewed vigour.

'We did it.' Theo folded to the floor as the hatchling took a short, hopping flight towards Lord Flame.

'You all did it,' I said. Theo, Zora, and Ria were amazing. I burst with pride to be part of such a crew, and currents of turbulent emotion poured over me as I crouched by Ria's fallen body. 'You did it.' I reached to hug her. She was unresponsive.

'No!' Zora fell to her knees next to me as I searched for breath or a pulse – anything to show that Ria was alive.

35
A BLACKBIRD'S LAST KISS

TELLIN

Ventios reached Ria at almost the same time as I did. He studied her, and his shoulders dropped. 'Is she …'

'I don't know. If she lives, it's barely.'

He bent over her body, his cheek alongside her face, and I swear he whispered something in her ear. Then, he reached inside his top and removed a blackbird. It stared at me and bobbed its head before hopping a few steps closer to Ria and placing its beak close to her ear. It opened his beak and sang – probably the most beautifully I had ever heard from a bird – then it touched her face with its own and fell over, its life extinguished, and its last song heard by two sea-folk, a selkie, a Sea Witch and a pair of dragons. I felt lightheaded – momentarily weakened – as a thin river of pain ran up my arm from my finger.

Ria gasped a thin breath.

'It worked!' Ventios said, reaching round to try and sit her upright. 'I did what you told me to, Ria. It worked.'

Her eyelids fluttered, exposing eyes as white as they were before she took the hatchling's spirit. 'Then I have a little time. Lord Flame, I implore you that as I sacrificed myself for your son, you would allow me to aide others one last time. Carry me to the isles of Y Plant Rhys Ddwfn. Let me release what spirits I suspect the Irrlicht Diana has ensnared there – let me take them to their rest.'

'I have seen the spirit smoke that I could not burn. You have but moments, the last breath of an old blackbird's time,' Lord Flame said. His voice was calmer, his demeanour tempered by the hatchling crawling across his scales. He glanced back at the small dragon, and his eyes span faster.

'I know. Let me make them count.' Ria turned toward me and smiled as she pushed herself to her feet. I reached to support her, but to my surprise, the huge head of Lord Flame was already there.

'I'll save you all a slow return trip,' she said. 'I hope to see you again one day, Tellin. Thank you for your friendship.' The old, gnarled hand that held my own was not the hand that I knew, but the heart of Ria was ever unchanged. She claimed not to judge, but she was using her last moments to ease the pain of those spirits.

Lord Flame bowed his head. 'I will take you.' He swung his huge head to stare at Theo. 'Stay until I get back, Dragon-child.' Lord Flame helped Ria climb onto his neck by lying flat, and a throaty chuckle rolled around the room. 'Last time, spirit-taker, you held the power. Let us go. I must be back before my son is hungry. Then he eats sheep, not your companions.'

With that, he moved away from us, and they were suddenly gone. I walked to where he vanished, staring through my glass circle at the shimmering door ahead of me. But my hand would not make contact or pass through it. It was solid as any wall.

The hatchling fluttered from shelf to shelf around the main chamber as papers fell around him like flakes of snow drifting into heaps.

Theo strode across to his perch and attempted to persuade him to have a sleep. Zora stood with her hands on her hips in a pose that I knew spelt trouble as she stared at Ventios.

'I have so many questions I don't even know where to start.'

Ventios nodded. 'I can see why that might be the case. Shall I tell you a story?'

'Just tell me why you had a blackbird in your shirt and how you knew to use it.'

Ventios deflated slightly. 'But that *is* a great story. Half of it I had directly from Rialta herself. It relates to her journey through the archway to the Otherland—'

'Just the facts.' Zora's hands slid to her weapons as they did when she was edgy.

'Ria told me she thought she might come very close to her limits as the hatchling was so strong, and that Tellin had already sealed a deal with a blackbird – a guardian of the Otherworld gates – to bring her back, to sacrifice the blackbird's life to supplement her own. It would be waiting at the gate, and I just needed to bring it with me.' He shuffled his feet. 'She made me promise that if it didn't go to her willingly, I would not kill it to save her.'

'Why did she tell you this and not me?' I asked, feeling the hurt of not being the one she trusted to do her bidding, not the one entrusted with helping save her life. Then, I realised that I had saved her. That moment of discomfort which came over me as Ria was revived by the blackbird's gift – the blood droplet –I had sealed the deal in blood. The Lady's words came back to me, and they now made sense. But I still couldn't understand why Ria had trusted Ventios over us.

'She told me it was because she wasn't sure that if you knew the risks, you would let her go through with it. Rialta said the dragon and Pact were more important than her, and she didn't want your friendship to change her decisions. She told me because I am a Storyteller. It's what I do – I listen, and I recall. Sometimes for an audience of one, like Theo, and sometimes for many. She simply didn't want to worry you.'

'And almost dying in front of our eyes was supposed to be less traumatic? We've lost one friend in the last few months. Another so soon ...'

'You have only lost her for now. When she passes through the gate next time, she will not return for a long period – Rialta indicated she'll need time to recover.'

Her farewell words suddenly made sense, but her sacrifice for those lost spirits sat heavily on my shoulders. I was losing another friend. As long as selkie lives are, I hoped she was right and that we'd meet again one day.

'So, that was goodbye?' Zora paced around me, throwing her hands in the air. 'Don't you think we deserved more than that? We saved her, we looked after her ...'

'And she paid us back many times,' I said quietly.

Zora exhaled, and a cloud of steam came with it, her own powers flaring in response. I knew they hadn't been close, but a part of me was glad to see that Zora cared enough to get upset.

'There are many tales of gods retreating for a short while,' Ventios offered up. 'I can tell you one if you like?'

'Maybe another time.' I held back traitorously human tears from my eyes. Ria had been more than a friend; I relied on her in so many ways. I tried to cast a smile in Ventios's direction. 'It's nothing personal. I think we're just tired and emotional right now.' If I was feeling the pain, the humans would be doubly so.'

Theo sat heavily on the floor, his one eye watching the hatchling. 'I'll miss her shadowy, soul-stealing self, and sailing *Black Hind* without her is going to be hard work in high seas, but we're a team. We can do this. Ria is part of our family, and when she is ready, she'll be back. I'm certain of it. So, stem your salty tears, selkie.'

He reached over and gave me a hug. It surprised me, and for a moment, I recoiled, but it felt comforting, warm. Eventually, I leant into it.

Theo chuckled. 'Even selkies accept my hugs in the end. I touched you and still don't need to own you. Did you hear what Lord Flame called me? Dragon-child!' A little extra spark glinted from Theo's remaining eye. 'Maybe there's something to your story, after all, Ventios.' He removed his arm from me and gestured to the hatchling. 'Ria would not want us moping. She would want action, readiness, and for us to follow her sacrifice through to its end. We need to plan – as soon as this one settles down. Do you think he'll be like a child? Manic energy and then sleep?'

He was right. If Ria was removing hordes of spirits Diana had undoubtedly amassed, then we needed to be ready to attack as soon as we could after Lord Flame's return. An overnight trip wasn't going to be quick enough.

'Does anyone else feel as though we should maybe move these books back into the other room while we wait?' Ventios asked, reaching for a few displaced books and starting back down the corridor.

'Fine, we'll move books away from the flame-spewing baby, then sleep. It will let us travel faster.' Zora grabbed a pile as well, and we carried them back to the entrance, leaving

Theo to watch the hatchling. We moved as many as we could before the hatchling fell asleep.

Theo waved us away. 'Rest. It's a long walk back. I'll wake if he does.'

We took his advice and settled down in the far room, well away from the potential to become a first meal.

36
DARK TOWER

MADDOC

The tibicena loped into the long cave with evident delight.

'Should we seal it in?' The coblynau's eyes boggled at the huge canine strolling through his cave.

'We do need to hide the entrance.' Maddoc didn't like the idea of it being loose and what might happen if it roamed freely. Balance was well and good, but they needed to reach the tower and take down an Irrlicht, not have to worry about the tibicena too. With just the five of them, it wasn't going to be easy.

He glanced out at the other islands, as he had several times since they'd reached the beach. Would his mother notice he was missing? How long would it be before she had no choice but to intervene since Lord Flame himself broke the Pact? Smoke still coiled into the sky from the field he'd targeted overnight, and the nearest buildings to its periphery smouldered, their once beautiful structures and golden roofs a twisted mass of metal-clad stone. While the Pact held, the races of Mynyw were shielded from harm, but any foreign sailors in those homes were little more than charred remains. How long would the magic remain intact – the bonds that tied every individual born in the land. It might be mere days? Hours?

He sighed. If he could see the old yew and the arrow, he'd have a timer. But as he couldn't, he decided to assume it was as close to over as possible. If he could hurt a selkie or the selkies hurt a Mynyw human, it was over; the intervention of outsiders in their affairs, had opened a weakness that they hadn't foreseen. If they could just evict the foreigners from their lands … Maddoc needed to get up there. He shook himself from his spinning thoughts, focusing on that which he could control.

'Can you loosen the stones above the roof of the cave entrance? Stay close, and let them fall if it tries to escape? Otherwise, just leave him rest in safety.'

The coblynau nodded. 'It means I have to stay here.' He cast a glance up at the towers, wringing his small hands together. 'It would mean I can't help you with that.' His twitch of the head towards the tower still meant he didn't stare at it fully. Coblynau were natural helpers and tunnellers. Killing wasn't in their nature.

It wasn't in Maddoc's either, if he was honest, and he had no idea what they would do once they reached the Irrlicht. But he sympathised with the small Tylwyth Teg.

'This is your job. It's vital. If the tibicena gets out or anyone gets in, there will be more fires and more death. I charge you in my mother's name to guard this cave.'

The coblynau stood a little taller, the set of his chin raised and his expression noticeably more determined. He gave a sharp nod.

'Guardian, I accept the charge.' He moved to stand under the cave entrance and studied the section above him. 'If I loosen that seam, and that rock, yes ... I have this.' He turned to them. 'You play your parts. I promise the tibicena won't leave this cave. I'll see you back here later.'

The twins turned from the coblynau without a word and stalked off; the gwyllion rolled her eyes and tipped her head in the direction of the town.

'Come on then, Guardian,' she said, and they walked towards the end of the beach, following the twins.

Above the tower, the dark cloud of spirits circled, maybe even more than there had been the day before. He repressed a shudder. What had the Irrlicht done with all those killed the previous night? The Pact had ensured peace for so long, but it had been shattered, at least out there. He hoped that maybe the breach could be confined to the islands. It was a vain hope, and one that faded from his mind as a dark cloud dissipated, and the huge, red form of Lord Flame reappeared in the sky.

'In daylight?' one of the twins hissed. 'He has truly lost it!'

'We need to stop this. There is no chance he flew over the land unseen,' the other added.

Maddoc squinted up at the circling dragon, seeing a silhouette sat atop his neck.

'There's every chance,' he said, hope soaring as long dark hair fluttered in the breeze of Lord Flame's descent. He circled over the islands as though searching for a landing spot.

'Can anyone bring them to us?' he asked. 'Catch Lord Flame's attention or that of the god who rides with him.'

The gwyllion sent her ball of light upwards, then out to sea. Lord Flame's head turned, and he changed course, heading directly for their beach. He vanished into a cloud of darkness once again as he descended. Maddoc sighed. It was such a big cloud that it was unlikely to be ignored. The darkness alighted on the sand, and Maddoc rushed to meet it.

'Rialta?' he called, stopping at the periphery of the shadow.

A deep rumble responded, and Lord Flame replied. 'She is not as you remember. She gave her lives for my child. Take her to the tower. She will take the lost spirits home.'

The gwyllion gasped. 'That will be too much. There's no life force left in them – even I know that. One or two, maybe. But to take them all …'

A thin, quavering voice, both familiar yet not, preceded the appearance of an aged, wizened woman as Rialta stepped from the shadow she'd created. 'I know this. I have but a short moment of life this side of the gate before I must rest. I already took in many of Diana's swarm. Their pain overwhelmed me. I cannot leave them as they are.'

'I will guide you.' The gwyllion bowed to Rialta. 'Few can do what you have done once, let alone twice.'

Rialta smiled, her papery skin wrinkling at the motion. Her white eyes crinkled at the corners in the direction of the gwyllion's voice. 'Then let us go. I have but a blackbird's breath of time to do this, and then Lord Flame will return me to the arch. He has his son safely returned and will do no more harm here. It is for the rest of you to return the peace.'

Maddoc faced Lord Flame, bravery filling him a little at the sight of Rialta and her words of sacrifice. 'Lord Flame.' He bowed so deeply his hair grazed the sand. 'Could you see a way to removing the iron bands placed by the foreigners around the arms of Y Plant Rhys Ddwfn? And maybe see a way to remove mine too?'

He gestured Gwyn forward, who held out his arms with a little encouragement. Lord Flame rumbled once again.

'I will free you from this heinous imprisonment. Come closer.' Gwyn shuffled towards Lord Flame. Light glinted off a huge eye as a red snout appeared from the darkness and snapped the band in its teeth, pinching it gently before severing it with ease.

'Let me fix the Guardian. I can break others while I await Rialta.'

Maddoc reached his swollen arm forward, wincing as the hot breath singed the blistering mass that remained despite the twins' ministrations.

'Turn it over.'

Maddoc turned his arm.

'Come closer, Guardian.' Maddoc's heart pounded, and his leg throbbed with the reminder of pain caused not so long ago by the very same creature he just begged to heal him, or at least free his magic. If they were to reach the top, to get close without catching the wrong attention, he needed it.

'I am no siren,' Lord Flame rumbled quietly. 'I cannot heal you. Flame dries the fluids that my body produces. I can cut that off, but you will need help after.'

'We are ready,' the twins chorused from behind him.

'Let's do this then.' Maddoc reached his arm forward. As Lord Flame's teeth closed around the melted iron, they pierced the blisters, and Maddoc felt the world close in as blackness took over.

He awoke to gentle shaking by the twins and Rialta's voice. 'He's still with us. Don't worry. He's stronger than he looks.'

'Thanks, I think.' Maddoc sat up. 'Where's Lord Flame?' he

asked as he looked around, trying to work out how long he'd been unconscious.

'Not far away. With Y Plant freed, their misting ability is returned. Lord Flame says no one's on the far island, so they have hidden it for him while he awaits our return.'

Maddoc lifted his hands to inspect the damage. There was angry, red scarring on both wrists. It was worse on the one the tibicena had burned, but the iron band was gone.

He closed his eyes and reached out to feel the magic sources in his range. Lord Flame pulled at him from the distant isle, and he recognised Rialta's traces, although faint compared to what she had exhibited at their first meeting. A thread of power ran through her like a core of strength.

Further up the hill, he could feel the soft warmth of the coblynau, and if he pushed beyond that … Yes, there she was. It was like Rialta, once they were near each other, and like the gwyllion, too, yet different. It was darker and almost oily. Slippery and difficult to pin down. She's up there.' He pointed towards the soaring tower surrounded by the black cloud.

Rialta laughed. 'No point in you pointing, waving, or gesturing. Unless we find an accidentally-killed person, I'm not seeing anything again of this world. It's all okay, though. We each have jobs to do. As my friend King Anard would say, I now realise what my fate is, what task I was always destined to carry out.'

'But you are a god? Aren't you beyond destiny?' Maddoc winced as the words left his mouth. Who was he to question her?

'Fate, destiny … my entire function of being is to capture loose spirits. I never fully understood why, and those early deaths, yes, they weighed me down, but I used their life force to prolong my own. It feels good to have released them on the other side.' Rialta gave a shaky smile. 'These spirits deserve that chance too. Others like the gwyllion can do parts of my role, but not everyone can cross multiple times. I know that now. Take me to them, so I can ease their pain. I'll leave fixing the rest of the Pact to you, and the queen to my crew mates.' Her voice crackled like autumn leaves underfoot. 'I feel sure you won't be alone for much longer. The selkies are coming, and the crew of *Black Hind* will be with you too. Trust Tellin. She'll do what's needed.'

The gwyllion took Rialta gently by the elbow. 'I will lead you to them.'

Together, they edged their way up the slope towards the town. Gwyn shrugged and gestured after them. 'How much harm can two Old Ones do alone? Come, Guardian. Keep our route clear of trouble. Your godkin appears certain help is coming. Some of us will watch for the selkies and ease their passage ashore. I have no doubt that once here, they will unleash quite enough of their own special distractions.'

'Do nothing to break the Pact., Maddoc insisted as he scanned the faces of Y Plant. 'Kill no one.' Then, he, Gwyn, and the twins strode as fast as they could to catch up to the gwyllion and Rialta.

His leg ached, but he could ignore it a while longer. He reached out again, trying to get a grasp of where all the magic was on the island. Maddoc reached as far as he could, identifying the Irrlicht, Y Plant, the tibicena, and the coblynau, so close they were almost intertwined from that angle. Out and out he reached until he felt it. Far in the distance was the tang of the selkies. He didn't hold back the smile.

'Rialta, they come.'

'I knew they would,' she replied. Her pace didn't slow – if anything, she sped up, the gwyllion trotting to keep pace.

Maddoc drew his awareness back in and focused on the Irrlicht by trying to penetrate the darkness, the wrongness of the cloud of spirits. People moved around the town, and their odd group was beginning to attract attention. Pointing and whispers, the inevitable questions would lead to altercations. It was one thing to kill a foreigner not bound to the Pact, but there might be humans from Mynyw there too. He was bound to leave them safe, whether their short human lives recognised it or not. Maddoc really hoped they didn't. Maybe the threat of violence would be sufficient? He eyed the twins, walking in a single form as one individual, and was glad. Their unearthly beauty was noticeable enough, let alone if there were two of them.

'She's moving.' The Irrlicht had moved away from the tower, her darkness growing distinct. The closer they drew, the more Maddoc realised it was not a power he could fight – as if he could fight any. They needed to do what they planned to, and then follow her to get information on her patterns or her routine. He should try to see what she looked like and then hand it all over to the crew of *Black Hind*. With Lord Flame and Y Plant on side, he just had to persuade his mother and the selkies to refresh the Pact. He paused in his meandering thoughts as they were stopped by a barricade of armed men.

'Who the fuck are you?' A small man stepped forward. His skin was sun-browned, aside from silvered scars that ran across his face like the talon marks of some huge beast. He looked up at the twins, who smiled charmingly back.

'A pleasure to meet you too,' they responded, their single mouth producing the harmony of their voices. A hand clenched behind their back, and Maddoc had to restrain himself from reaching out to stop them. He could feel the swelling of their power from there, and given that was no Mynyw accent, the man would find himself on the end of an annwn dagger shortly.

He tugged his sleeves down to cover his injured wrists as well as he could and stepped between Rialta and the group.

'We heard that there was a famously beautiful queen on these isles and wished to pay our tributes. This man' – he gestured to the twins – 'is a prince in search of someone powerful to join him in reclaiming his birthright in the lands across the sea.'

'Then why have you brought two old women? Where is his honour guard?'

'I do not need one.' The twins stepped forward, reaching their full height and towering over the short man. 'Take me to meet her.'

Maddoc tried to stand calmly next to the twins, swallowing down his fear. That wasn't the plan. Find the spirits, take them, and return to Lord Flame, maybe a little spying on the Irrlicht – that was all! He plastered a fixed smile on his face and strode forward, hopefully looking far more confident than he felt, to stand at the twin's shoulder.

The gwyllion slipped in behind him, gently tugging Ria with her. 'We've got this,' she whispered. 'Do what you can.'

Silver Scar looked the twins up and down, then shrugged. 'Is there much loot to be had in retaking your land?'

The twins laughed. 'Oh yes. More kinds of treasure than you can possibly imagine.'

One of the others had been frowning throughout; he shuffled up and whispered something in Silver Scar's ear. He swatted him away like an annoying fly, but a cloud of confusion floated past his face for a moment. 'How did you find us?' he asked more slowly, his hand dropping to rest on the gun at his side.

'How else? We were invited.' Rialta's voice held power, even as she slipped from the thoughts and mind shortly afterwards, fading into shadow. After a momentary pause, he turned and gestured up the main pathway.

'We'll escort you there, Your Highness,' said Silver Scar.

The twins didn't wait and walked confidently onwards. Maddoc followed closely, and Gwyn filed alongside him. Rialta and the gwyllion trailed behind, stumbling and resting on each other. The gap they opened up left the rabble of sailors no choice but to move past the older women and stick doggedly to the front group's heels instead. That left a couple of younger men to walk with the two women, disregarding the most dangerous of their number for the sheer physical threat and presence of the twins' small group. It was better than Maddoc could have hoped – from their perspective, at least. The less anyone looked closely at the two women, the better.

He reached out gently with his mind. The Irrlicht was very much ahead of them in the direction they walked, and he couldn't see a way around coming into contact with her.

Darkness built over their heads, and unease bled from their escort's bodies. The closer they drew to the tower, the more edgy they became. Stroking of weapon hilts, and glances over their shoulders; little nervous tics that gave away their discomfort to a stranger. The leader spent more time looking backward than forward by the time they reached the open lawn in front of the tower.

'What a nice place to have a rest,' the gwyllion called as they entered. 'I think we should pause here. We'll catch you youngsters up shortly.'

There was enough of a hedge to shield what they did if Maddoc could remove the rest of the escort – or take them inside – and buy Rialta time to work. It would have been so much easier if someone just killed one and gave Rialta what she needed to escape quickly. It wasn't as though they were from the area, so how much more would it really impact things? After all, they had killed at least three of the guards where they'd been imprisoned. Someone would soon realise they were gone. But Maddoc's guts roiled at the thought of deliberately killing someone else, and he knew that there was no way he could be the one to do it.

In daylight, the screaming was lessened, but it remained a constant presence in his ears. Nothing like the noise at night, but darkness filled the grounds as light struggled to penetrate the swirling cloud. Their escorts took smaller steps, hanging back as they reached an ornate doorway.

'At least they haven't ruined this,' Gwyn muttered. 'I have hope that the rest of the island can be salvaged too, if we can get them off.'

Maddoc didn't wish to point out how few of them remained or how many homes they would have to salvage. Rebuilding the islands even by Y Plant would take hundreds of years, if not more.

They were led around the tower to a newly cut door in the stonework.

'I spoke too soon,' Gwyn muttered. 'They couldn't open the main door.'

'Shh.' The twins turned to shoot them both a warning glance before drawing themselves up to their full height. 'I will find my future bride in here?' They gestured at the door, and Silver Scar nodded.

The others edged away and looked as though they would race back to the town at the first sign of danger. Maddoc reached for the Irrlicht again, reeling as he realised that her power was intensely close. What if she made contact with him? What if any of them were exposed before Rialta could remove the spirits and get away?

The door flung open, and a boy ran out, pursued by a

woman in flowing clothes, sheer and entirely too minimal for the weather. Long blond hair flew behind her as she pursued the boy, her strides easily eating up the ground.

'Did you see her eyes?' The twins stared after her, almost leaning in her direction. The wave of power as she passed was intense, and Maddoc leaned against the wall as casually as he could.

'Who was that?' Maddoc asked, already certain he knew the answer.

'Diana, Queen Maria's closest advisor,' Silver Scar said, and his gaze flickered to the cloud above. Maddoc wondered if they saw what he did, doubting it as soon as the thought appeared. Most of humankind didn't believe in magic. Even if they saw the spirits, they'd dismiss it as their own imagination.

Diana passed Rialta and the gwyllion without a glance. They continued hobbling forward, closer to the tower. Rialta held a hand out, and a small fraction of darkness dropped from the cloud above them into her palm, like a leaf falling in autumn. It was so tiny. How many spirits made up that cloud? Where had Diana taken them from?

Rialta swayed on her feet, and the gwyllion steadied her. Another spirit fell, then another, the stream of darkness growing in speed and intensity. The gwyllion moved Rialta slowly around the back of the tower until she was lost from his sight.

They needed to keep the queen busy and interested in the twins for as long as possible. The spirits were in Rialta's hands, literally. Two small figures slipped through to the lawn and danced toward the old women. Good – with the changelings' support, they should make it back to the beach and Lord Flame.

The twins entered the tower. Maddoc and Gwyn followed

them into the entrance hall, where a gilded handrail coiled upwards, framing the stairs. Their escort remained outside.

'Follow me.' Gwyn set off up the stairs. 'There's only one place anyone would choose to hold court in here.'

They passed a window as they climbed, and Maddoc paused for a moment. Their escort had left the lawn, and two children played chase in a growing patch of sunlight as a stream of spirits poured into a dark area nearby. He took one last look at the darkness hiding the only godkin he'd ever met.

'Thank you,' he murmured, then turned to follow the others up the stairs.

The room that Queen Maria had taken as her throne room was gilded from floor to ceiling. The ceiling itself was studded with gems, and the pile on the carpet was stiff and not quite as soft as it appeared. It glinted as the twins' feet moved through it. Queen Maria bestowed a smile on the twins, and she slowly blinked, a crease crinkling the sides of her young face. Sea-grey eyes stared at Maddoc with a hard intensity, although they softened again when she looked back to the twins. The ease with which she accepted the Tylwyth Teg unsettled Maddoc. How could one so easily trusting of beauty and fine clothes possibly lead a fleet to war?

'Your Majesty,' the twins murmured, reaching forward to kiss her outstretched hand. Sat up on the seat, she looked young and vulnerable. No more than eighteen if he had to guess. She stood, and he saw that she was only as tall as Gwyn, young and not physically imposing; she looked as though she could barely scare a kitten. Was she really the driving force behind the failing Pact? A small petal of relief floated through his soul. Maybe she could be reasoned with and not need killing – less bloodshed was always best. The power of Mynyw relied on peace to protect it, and blood on any of their lands was not something he wished for.

'Would you all like some refreshments?' Queen Maria asked. She gestured into the corner. 'It must have been a long journey.'

The twins took the glasses from the tray, and Maddoc tried to hide the grimace he felt creeping onto his face. He or Gwyn should have done that, not a supposed prince. Maddoc took the drink politely; it smelt fresh and quite delicious.

'Fruit juices from Terrania.' The queen drank deeply from her glass, separately delivered by her assistant, and smiled. 'My mother used to send it to me so that I would know the tastes of my home when I returned to claim it. I'm sick of this dreary island.' She flashed a smile at the twins as they drew a long sip from their ornate glass. 'I grew up here, you know. In the stupid houses on the far side of the island. Diana was always too scared to take up residence in this tower while the fairies were here.'

Her tone dripped with scorn. 'Mother's blessing they called them over on that wet land. No blessing to me. Mist and fog and cold weather. What is the point in having such beautiful houses if they never get to shine? Just like my mother.' Her voice lowered. Gwyn had been sipping his drink with a glass held so tightly that his knuckles were white, and Maddoc could barely believe the glass had not smashed.

He was a little tired after such a long day, he realised. The escape and the planning, all the potential things that could have gone wrong. Maddoc stifled a yawn.

Gwyn's eyes were drooping too. His knees were a little wobbly. But the twins stood tall, their calm expression as unreadable as Maddoc had always known it. He hid another yawn in his drink, hoping that Rialta was finished. The risk of her getting caught was still high, and in her condition, he didn't think she'd get far. He stumbled closer to the window. He wasn't that tired, surely.

The sky was bright, and the clouds over the tower gone. Maddoc gripped the sill as his legs gave way, dropping the glass.

Maddoc looked down at it in confusion, then raised his head to see the twins were stood with their arm around the young queen's waist.

'Sleep well, Guardian. We have brought you to the end of your watch. As of today, there will be a new kind of Pact to sign.'

They smirked before leaving the room together, the queen leading them by the hand up a small stairway.

37
GOING POTTY

TELLIN

Lord Flame's head pushed through nothingness at the end of the chamber, followed swiftly afterwards by the rest of his shimmering body. I waited, my breath held in hope and every muscle tensed, but Ria didn't follow him.

'She has gone for now,' he rumbled.

My shoulders dropped, and I felt a little less. A part of my crew, someone who had been my shadow in all ways since we'd met, was gone. One day, she would be back, and I was certain that she would seek us out. Oceans, but I hoped that the world was a kinder place then, that we had restored more of it.

I wanted Ria to return to a world safe for our kind. I filled my core with rocks and used them to support me. We'd returned the dragon hatchling, so the next step was to remove the pretender from Diana's influence. After Lord Flame confirmed her presence there, I was as scared as I was determined. The safety of Terrania had to remain in Anard's hands, and we would leave Mynyw untarnished by her presence.

Theo stood tall too. Whatever resolve ran through his head showed in his bearing. 'Lord Flame, would you do us the honour of a flight back to our vessel? Your son sleeps, and I would like to capitalise on Ria's advantage.'

Lord Flame lowered his head so that his eye stared directly into Theo's. 'You ask much, Dragon-child.'

Theo didn't back down. 'I do. I have lost much – but so had you until recently.' He pointed at his eye and hand, then looked pointedly at the sleeping dragon.

Lord Flame rumbled so deeply that the floor shook. I tried to hold back an involuntary flinch; he'd snap us in two within moments. The rumble grew louder, then small smoke rings began to pop from his nostrils, and I realised he was laughing. 'You are as bold as a dragon. The blood runs strong. I will fly you to your boat. Gold, not red, runs in your veins, but I give you this. Be proud of your blood, Dragon-child.'

He shook, and a single dragon scale fell to the floor. 'Step forward.' Theo did as he asked, and Lord Flame ripped the patch from his head. Then, he picked up the scale in one taloned foot and held it against Theo's face.

From where I stood, I could see Theo's brief flinch. Zora sat facing Theo and watched, her eyes widening as she clasped a hand to her mouth, laughing with delight. 'Theo, you really are part dragon now!'

He turned toward me, a wide grin on his face, the scale had fused directly into the skin above his eye.

Lord Flame glanced at his hatchling.

'I carry you quickly before he wakes. It is the turning of few pages to the coast.' He looked us over. 'I may have to fly twice.'

'I can use the Pathways once we're out,' I offered. 'If carrying only three makes it possible in one trip?'

He tilted his head as smoke curled from his snout.

'I can do it,' he replied. 'Use the far steps. You will appear next to a Pathway. Others, climb on.'

'We'll race you!' called Zora as she scrambled onto Lord Flame's back. I smiled and waved, trying to look more confident than I felt.

I slowly climbed the stairs Lord Flame indicated. It was a foolish idea. I'd not done it without Ria or The Lady. What if I couldn't use it? Would the others wait, or would Lord Flame return to find me? I stepped from the top step to be greeted by the most profound silence I'd ever heard. There were no birds, no voices, no lapping of waves. The island I stood on reflected perfectly in the still water around me.

There was no obvious way off the island. I pulled out the glass and held it to my eye as I slowly span around, searching for a flicker of the Path. I'd had a guide along it last time – my magic might not even work without one. But maybe if I could disturb it in some way, I could get help from the annwn.

I walked from one end of the island to the other, searching around me, then finally, as I returned to my starting point, I saw a thin, quivering line. I had no idea where I was and doubted that I'd ever been further from the ocean, but I felt its call in every part of my being. I would follow the pull. Once on the Path, I might even be able to see it. I quelled the rising tide of panic – selkies were not meant to fly – and stepped onto it.

Immediately, I rose upward, so high that far below, I spotted Lord Flame. From such height, I could see the thin threads of the Path crisscrossing the countryside. I chose a Path that led in the same direction the others were headed and took a bold step forward, momentarily forgetting how far it would carry me. Unfamiliar hills rose below me, and in the distance, the green of the land faded into the grey of the sea, and clouds rolled over the horizon. I searched the land for anything I recognised, but there was nothing. If I'd crossed it at night, aside from the mouth of the river, I'd be hopelessly lost. How close would the Pathways get to the sea? Could I navigate the same way as I had sailed?

It was like looking at one of Sal's maps or the ocean floor, I decided. As long as I kept the lens to my eye and looked through the line at the world below, I could almost imagine how it looked.

The Path had crossed the top of the hill near a big loop in the river, not far from *Black Hind*. So, all I had to do was find that river.

It proved easier thought than done. As many rivers ran from the lakes as rivulets from tide pools on a beach.

Several false starts later, and having retraced my steps more times than I'd admit to, I was starting to feel the frustration. My legs grew tired. Balancing on a tiny thread was taking its toll on my mind, and I was convinced I was no closer to the others. At one point, I thought I'd found the entrance to the river we'd sailed up, then realised the landmarks were wrong. There were too many ruins. Back up the coast I went again.

As I was about to start again, a voice whispered from behind me.

'Why is a selkie on my Path?' It was soft and musical, but there was no mistaking the threat implicit in the tone.

'The Lady gave me this,' I said, waving the lens briefly, trying to hold my position as well as I could without being able to steady myself through it.

'And what would happen if I were to take it from you? Why are you on our Path?' The voice was closer.

'You'd have gambled and lost.' I waited for the response.

'I could knock you off right now.'

'And with one move, I could kill you too,' I responded to a hiss of laughter.

'All you selkie are good for is curses and sex.'

'Some of us diversified. If you want me off your Path, I'd be happy to, but only once I reach my destination.' My fingers quietly readied my needles. I had no intention of attacking unprovoked, but nor would I accept the stranger's threat.

'You've been roaming the Path in circles. How do you know where you are headed? Or, are you lost? No one would even notice a lone selkie missing. The Pact is fading, you know, and some of us are delighted. It's been far too long since we could hunt outside its confines.'

'Both Lord Flame and The Lady would know I was missing.' I held my voice steady as I scanned the area below me, trying to get my bearing one more time from the sea. If the last town had a river leaking from it, then I'd gone too far south. It could be that first river we'd sailed past.

I heard the intake of breath, felt the disturbance of air as they drew close. I didn't wait to hear what they would say next. I was running for my safety on Paths they knew and needed to move fast. I jumped to a northern thread, keeping the sea to my left, then jumped again as laughter faded behind me. The Tylwyth Teg was enjoying the chase. Two hills rose in the distance, but my thread didn't lead there. I squinted through the lens. An adjacent one did – I could do this. I lined up the lens and leapt for the thread I needed. I wobbled, almost losing my balance. Deep breaths, calm like a tide pool in a cave …

'I can catch you, selkie.'

My heart pounded, and my hands grew sweaty. Oceans, not now! If I lost the lens … I gripped it as tightly as I could.

Not far now, surely – there was the river. I stepped again. The river was narrowing below me, a copse of trees alongside it. *Black Hind* would be just around the bend, and it was safer on the ground where my own powers were accessible. I took a final step off the Path, my stomach lurching as I dropped to the floor. Quickly, I gathered a cloud of darkness around me and slipped into the woods. It was too bright to work properly, but I'd be far less visible from above.

An unnatural rushing of water came from the river. Only one person could do that! I pushed through the woods, aware I was a seal on land, slow and cumbersome compared to my pursuer. If that wave was meant to dislodge *Black Hind*, I couldn't be too far away.

If I jumped in the water, would it be salty? The tidal volume Zora had dragged up might just be enough to save me. I edged towards it, hearing a twig snap not far behind and the sound of joyful laughter. Urchin's arse, I was left with no choice. I dived in. The water was barely brackish, but might be sufficient to keep my pursuer at a distance. I swam up the middle, stroke after stroke carrying me closer to the rest of the crew and *Black Hind*.

A hiss from the water's edge gave away my pursuer's presence. I turned to see what they looked like. Long, blonde hair vanished into the woods.

I swam and swam until I heard voices.

'I'm here!'

'Tellin?' Zora called back, her voice distant and thin but music to my ears. I pushed myself harder, and as I came around the bend of the river, I could see my beloved boat floating.

Ventios was halfway up the mast, untangling ropes, and Theo was tidying the deck. Zora held her hand towards me, palm upwards, and curled her fingers as though she crested a wave herself. A swell of water rose behind me, lifting me onto the deck. Zora embraced me, then stood back to pass her hands around my body. Droplets of water left my clothes and trickled overboard.

'Come on, crew. Let's get to sea. There's a boat filled with selkies on the way and an invisible island chain to find,' Theo said.

I decided against telling them of my pursuer. That could wait.

We raised the sails the moment we left the shelter of the coast. Desperate as I was to head to the islands, it would have to wait until we met up with Môr. I needed to know how many of the pack were with us.

As we headed south I searched for sails on the horizon. More than once, we passed another vessel, each flying the same flag that the mercenaries had. Clouds threatened us with rain, and the air grew thick and heavy with expectation. Finally, we spotted a vessel without a flag and rushed through the water towards them.

It wasn't Môr. An elderly woman relaxed on board with a slightly younger-looking man. They bobbed freely on the waves as they watched a fishing pot buoy alongside.

We slowed as we approached. She looked up at me, and her eyes narrowed as she saw Theo's eyepatch.

'Are you also the rescue party?' she asked.

'Rescuing who?' I swam carefully through my words.

'The fool guardian and his assortment of Tylwyth Teg who went ashore a few weeks ago. They're lucky I'm still out here if I'm honest. Only, I thought someone might come.' She frowned at Theo. 'Your talons weren't injured last night.'

'Huh?' Theo looked as confused as she did for a minute.

Ventios grinned. 'My lady, tales of dragons taking human form are legend and nothing more. Timothee Maritim is a legend in his own right, but no dragon.'

'I'm—' Zora dug her elbow into Theo, and he coughed instead of finishing the sentence.

'My lady, is it? Did you hear that, Lewis? Maybe you should call me that from now on.'

The man's eyes sparkled as he sketched a bow. 'You have always been *my lady*, to me.'

'You're soft, you know that?' she retorted. 'It's lucky I brought my traps. You lot took way too long. If that Maddoc is still alive, I'd be amazed. Lewis, give them the turf.'

He held aloft a rolled-up section of dried-out soil. 'It's not in great condition, but you'll need it to find your way in.'

We pulled alongside, and he held it out, Zora barely reaching him but close enough that the turf was passed to us.

'Won't you need it?' I asked.

'No, Lewis can take us home anytime he chooses to. You, on the other hand, need to rush. Something's happening there. The dark cloud over the tower has gone.'

Ria had done it.

'If you see another boat filled with selkies—'

'They went ahead of you. Hurry up, or they'll have all the fun.'

Lewis nudged the old woman and pointed at another buoy bobbing to the north. 'We've caught something.' Without another word, they returned to fishing, their boat headed off towards the buoy.

'Well, that was strange,' Zora muttered. 'What do we do with this turf, and where is Môr?' She held it in her arms as she scanned the horizon, then exclaimed in surprise. 'I see them. They're over there!' She pointed into an area with nothing but open sea.

'Show me.' Ventios practically danced down the deck. 'This is going to make such a great story!' He took the turf from Zora and squinted to where she'd been pointing. 'I see them. There's another boat headed that way too.'

'Then let's get after them,' Theo called. 'Full speed ahead, and to the gods with stealth. Zora, you can deal with that, right?'

'No,' I replied. 'We don't know who or what we face yet, aside from Diana – and without Ria.' I let the rest hang unsaid.

Theo nodded acceptance. He shouted his instructions, and we ran to tweak and adjust ropes, making the small adjustments to the rig he needed as Ventios kept a watchful eye on the other vessels.

We closed on Môr quickly. I guessed that Ivy or Ash had recognised us as they sat with their sails flapping and bow-to-wind as we approached.

Môr stood in the bow, waving enthusiastically, while Ventios did the same back.

'Given that they have both lived in or on the water for their entire lives, could those two appear any less salt-wet?' Zora laughed.

'It's hardly a surprise. Knowing the sea and knowing sailing ...' I paused, unwilling to sound like I was still inexperienced myself, but the words weren't there. I opted to smile in what I hoped was a knowing way and shrugged. 'Ventios may be sea-folk, but he's probably been moored in the flotilla for most of his life.'

'True.' She flicked a curl from her eyes. 'He's great at climbing – when we aren't moving.'

We sailed alongside each other for a while, closing in on a group of islands. They were close enough to the land that I should have seen them from the Path. Even knowing there was a magical component to their existence, it was still wondrous to see them simply appear.

A cloud of mist rolled from a cove north of the tower, enveloping both boats in its caress. As it did so, a figure emerged on each deck.

'Selkies? In our waters? Were you not content with taking our southern islands already? When the waters rose, we were homeless. We came to you, but you turned us away. We hid amongst the creatures of the Mynyw deep, and now that our islands rise once more, now they are already besieged, you appear?'

I let the ragged and untidy beings speak. They stank, and the sores on their wrists showed more than I suspected they wanted us to know. Y Plant were apparently creatures of riches – of gilded homes and famous for the beauty of their islands, according to Ria. These individuals were a shadow of that. I felt sympathy for them, fuelling a growing whirlpool of disgust for the way the humans had treated them.

Humans and Diana, I suspected. The beings were Old Ones. Their powers protected the seas as much as the presence of selkies. The combined strengths of the land of Mynyw was embedded in the Pact that the Old Ones held so dear.

I bowed – respect was a trait worth showing in their lands. 'My name is Tellin Dark. Those on the other vessel are companions of mine from the islands to the south. They are here to offer you their aid in reclaiming your islands. Both Lord Flame and The Lady wish the Pact preserved at all costs. I have been living for a time in a land where no such thing exists.' I shuddered at the memory of the lands around Orange before we returned the second hind. 'I wouldn't wish that on anyone.'

'Then we'll kill the foreigners and reclaim our home together.'

Zora held her hand out to interrupt him. 'It's not that simple. We need to remove the self-proclaimed queen and Diana. Any others who should not be here need to be returned home.'

'You're just going to let them go? How by all the dead gods do you plan to do that? There must be well over a hundred of them across the islands.'

I grinned. 'We have our ways if you can get us ashore. That's ten each, Môr. Think you can handle it?'

Môr looked thoughtfully out into the mist, his braid hanging much like Sal's. Aside from the colour the styling, even his pose, was similar. Maybe Môr had a little less charisma. 'Ten is a lot. It's not impossible, but that depends on the supplies we have. And what we plan to do with them afterwards.'

'We don't kill them.' Theo ran his hands through his beard. 'How long will it take you?'

Môr frowned. 'It depends where they all are, how many boats they have, and how we get them aboard.'

'We could use a few stray aria about now.' Theo held a hand up to show he was joking as Zora opened her mouth to speak.

'Are there any caves?' I asked.

'Well, there is one, which currently houses a tibicena.'

'Here? That needs to go home.'

'Maddoc said you'd say that,' the one on our boat replied.

'Where's Maddoc now? Is he on the island?'

Y Plant shrugged. 'He went up to the tower this morning with our leader Gwyn, the annwn who is both two and one, a gwyllion, and a goddess. The last two came back down a short while later. The goddess was frail and carried by two changelings. Lord Flame took her away. But Maddoc and the other two haven't come back. They went to try and kill the Irrlicht.'

'Irrlicht? Are you absolutely sure that's what she is?' I asked.

'Like the goddess, but darker. The goddess takes spirits with or without life, in a way she is an extension of the Otherworld. The Irrlicht takes the life but leaves the spirit on this side of the arch. It's so very wrong.'

'This is all very nice,' Zora interrupted, 'but I think we need to worry about the logistics of getting a hundred or so people off the island without killing them. Assume Maddoc is gone. We need to take out both a queen and Diana to leave them leaderless and dispersed.'

I considered it for a moment. 'If we can get all the sailors indisposed to movement, could you ferry them to the least inhabited island, ring it in mist, and keep them there?'

They looked at each other for a long time. I was beginning to think they had frozen themselves, when they finally broke away from each other's gaze. The one on *Black Hind* nodded. 'We can do that. Can't guarantee some won't swim off, though.'

'Leave that part to us,' I replied. I climbed down into the cabin and retrieved the two bottles Sal had given us before we left. 'We need to get ashore before dark for this to work well.' I glanced at the sun. We had some time. 'Ventios, you might want to cover your eyes.'

I dropped my glamour and faced the crew of the other boat. Môr had massed nine selkies. No wonder we'd caught them easily – the boat was not designed for such a large crew. Most of them were males, from his bachelor pack, I guessed, but a few females stood amongst their number.

'Dress yourselves in human finery, entice and seduce them. Cavort in the evening light. Bring them close to you. If you can, cover your teeth – it'll make the task easier. Once they're alone, put them to sleep.' I bent my wrist back, exposing the tips of my own needles. My left hand, as ever, would have a sleeping toxin on it – one I knew was effective and lasted long enough. My right had something far more deadly. In case news travelled fast, it wasn't blue-ringed octopus, but something with different symptoms and the same final outcome.

I alone would shoulder the responsibility for delivering the blow to the queen. I'd promised Anard that he would be in no way implicated, and I planned to keep it that way.

38

GLAMOROUS DISTRACTIONS

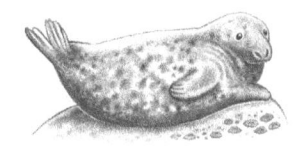

TELLIN

We dropped our sails while one of Y Plant misted their way back to shore to communicate the plan to others, then prepared ourselves for the approach. I donned my black suit under my clothes to better aid me as night fell, and Zora slipped into her own less colourful clothing. With the small amount of toxin I'd left myself, I prepared my needles as we waited for the signal to start moving.

Ventios joined us at the table, where Zora read her tattered old book, losing a few more corners as she read, and I slipped the needles into their sleeve sheaths.

'I want to come with you,' he said.

Zora looked up. 'Can you fight? Because if you can't bring anything to this, you are a liability. We don't have time for one of those. I'm sorry, Ventios.'

'Only with my words and stories.' His shoulders drooped. 'I really wanted to see the adventure to add to my stories!'

'We'll tell you all about it afterwards. What you need to do is be ready to get us out of here faster than a diving gannet.' I reached for him and patted his hand. He recoiled in panic, staring at my sleeves.

'I can do that.'

'It's an important job. It's the bit that doesn't get the glory in the stories, but the extraction teams are so important. Without a clean getaway, this all unravels, and you'll have no story to tell.'

'I'll help Theo start unfolding the dragon-wing rig and get it rigged while you are ashore. Good luck over there.'

'I think we'll need it,' I said under my breath. Zora heard and raised a single eyebrow.

'We have you, me, a bunch of beautiful selkies armed with sleep, and our own clouds of mist – that I haven't had to make. Once ashore, we have whoever Maddoc has brought along, if we can find him. Our biggest issue is doing this almost unnoticed.'

'No feast, no magicians, no cover,' I reminded her.

'Then you'd better get your best glamour head in place because you'll be shifting through them.' She was right. It would test me even more than holding Dottrine's guise. I had no idea what I would need to change to, or who. Oceans, I didn't even know for sure what we'd be facing.

In a cloud of mist, our boats hummed quietly ashore near an empty beach. One by one, we slipped into the water, striking out for shore. Zora dried us quickly, pulling our clothes free of water, and I checked each of the selkies' sleeves before we readied ourselves to cross the island to the town. Ivy wiped all her blades dry and tucked them back into her clothes before shooting me a grin. Having her on our side might be a game changer too. If Zora exerted herself too far, I knew I could count on Ivy to stick her knives where they were needed from any height.

'It's a busy cove for one so hidden.' A voice came from the shadows under the cliff. An old woman stepped out and walked towards us. 'Given that you arrived with the grace of the island's owners, am I to assume you're the rescue party, here to help?'

Zora strode forwards, reaching out her hand in a gesture of friendship. 'That's us. You are?'

'I'm a gwyllion.'

'No name for us?'

The old woman shook her head 'None that you'll get from me today. Names are power, and trust is earned.'

Zora shrugged. 'Power is as long as it survives. We take power back from those who shouldn't have it.'

I understood her sentiment, but Zora was essentially raised as a human, despite her powers. I didn't think she truly understood the power in a name. But I was an Old One, too, and I did.

I inclined my head in respect to the gwyllion. 'I will share my name, in trust. Tellin Dark at your service.'

'Pah, names for selkies cannot recall you or enslave you. It is little enough as a gesture.' She paused at that. 'Tell me you have not brought your skins in reach of these islands.'

I glanced at Môr. He shook his head. 'They're safely locked away, far from harm. None can reach them, even should they try.' Sal had them then. I rolled my shoulders, loosening the quietly building tension as a pair of children tumbled, laughing and running onto the beach.

'These will be your guides,' the gwyllion said. They have spent the last few weeks playing in the town. They know who everyone is and who to target first.

The girl spoke up first. 'We know who likes girls and who likes boys too.' Then she collapsed in a heap of giggles as the boy added in.

'And who just likes sex!' The pair looked up at us, all innocent eyes and curly blonde ringlets.

'Changelings?' Zora crouched down, eager to speak to them. 'Can you show me how you do it?'

The girl looked at Zora, and after a moment, her skin tone shifted to match Zora's deep, dark skin, her curls grew tighter and denser and her eyes darkened. She smiled at Zora.

'May I touch you?' Zora asked. The girl nodded. Zora felt the changeling's hair and turned to me. 'It's not like your glamour. She feels *right*. If you keep practicing, could you?'

I shook my head. 'No, it's all an illusion. They can physically change.' I looked at them consideringly. 'You can't change into an adult, though, can you?'

'I *am* an adult!' the girl replied. I hadn't meant to offend her, and she must have seen the concern in my face, because she laughed. 'But if you mean, can we look like an adult human? Not really, no.'

'That's a shame. Are we ready?' I asked the others. Môr nodded at me, Ivy smiled, and Zora curled her hand into a fist, then opened it to reveal an ice ball. I took it as a yes. 'Then, lead on, changelings.'

'Call me Daisy and him Thistle,' she replied.

'Lead on, Daisy and Thistle,' Môr replied, and our party wound up the hill towards the town.

The roofs shone in the evening sun, and the sounds of humans reached my ears at the same time as their scent hit my nose, the stench of cooked meat and spices turning my stomach.

Môr and the other selkies followed Thistle as he led them towards a sea-level path, while we hung back. A hubbub of noise rose as the selkies, un-glamoured, aside from their teeth, walked into town. Rushing feet were swiftly followed by whistles of appreciation.

'We are here to entertain you,' Môr shouted. 'At the request of your queen.' A cheer rang out as music filled the air. It wasn't subtle, but I trusted them to do what was needed. A wall of mist gently crept towards the shore, and from our vantage, I spotted masts moving out to sea. Y Plant had begun their part.

Singed roofs grew more common as we walked through rapidly emptying streets. The evidence of Lord Flame's wrath was marked on the islands for any to see. With any luck, it meant that most of the humans had moved further towards the water, and we'd have a clear run to the tower. With light fading in the sky and the sun sinking like a punctured buoy – turning the misty sea into a beautiful distraction – we headed for the tower.

Once the way was obvious, Daisy left us to return to the harbour and help the others, leaving the four of us to continue. I looked at my companions. Ivy's slight form stuck to the shadows, sliding along the walls. Zora strode by my side, powerful and strong; she left the shadows to Ivy, sticking close to my side instead. The gwyllion hobbled behind. I noticed that no matter how fast we went, she kept up with us, despite the appearance of frailty.

'Can you do what Ria could?' I asked as we paused to let her catch up. I could feel nerves bunching in my stomach, coiling like an eel into a writhing ball of uncertainty.

'Can I kill? Not with magic. Can I steal a spirit from the dead so the Irrlicht doesn't get its life force? Yes. But once she has it, I cannot do any more. I cannot split it like she does, nor would I want to.' She grimaced. 'Pickings have been slim for a long time. If you kill, I will take. Beyond that, I can hide you in darkness or produce a gentle ball of light.'

'If I kill someone, will it make you stronger if you can take one in?' Ivy asked, so close behind me I jumped. I hadn't even heard her move from the shadows.

Zora put a steadying hand on my arm. 'We can do this.'

'Oh, I know that,' I replied. 'I just want to do it without causing more problems for Anard or Maddoc's Pact. It isn't quite the snap and swim we were expecting.'

The short hedge was guarded by a small group of humans. From where we stopped, they smelt of smoke and nerves, acidic and tangy. Strains of joyful music carried on the wind. Without exception, they appeared to be focused on the area of town where it came from, and a boatload of selkies were putting sailors to sleep.

We were too far away to return them to the water and too close to risk them alerting Diana. 'Be ready then, gwyllion.'

Zora went first, stepping fully into the light. She swayed her hips – and oceans, but she exuded sex with every step. I'd never seen her like that, and I wasn't the only one mesmerised by her performance.

'Now, that's a hard act to follow,' Ivy muttered. She pulled her top low, exposing her chest, and winked at me.

'Gotta use all my skills,' she said, and to my amusement, she sprang into a series of acrobatic manoeuvres, landing in a strange position with one leg directly out to either side at the feet of the group.

'No one wanted you to miss out,' Zora purred. 'So we thought we'd come up to see if anyone else needed ... entertaining. She ran a finger down the closest man's chest as she spoke, but he paid her little attention.

'You're barking up the wrong tree there, my lovely,'

another man said. 'You've the wrong kit between your legs for that one. Now, I, on the other hand ...'

Zora turned her attention his way and giggled.

'Well then, my handsome, shall we find somewhere a little quieter and let him guard the hedge from the rabbits?'

Ivy rolled herself up from the floor. 'Who else wants some fun?' she asked. As the closest man stepped forward, she leaned in as though to kiss him, then pulled back. He grabbed her wrist, and she tensed – a split second and no more.

'Over there,' he said, gesturing to the silhouette of a nearby building. Ivy let him lead her by the hand. I suspected the gwyllion might be taking that spirit shortly. She clearly thought the same, as she hobbled in the same direction, away from the ring of light and out of human vision.

I readied the needles in my left hand and steadied myself with a breath. Just two remained. I peered at them, trying to work out what the last looked like, but all I could make out was a silhouette. I drew the young man's form around me – the same one I'd used in Orange. Familiar and comfortable to maintain, it took less effort than creating a new one. I strode out into the light, pausing at the gateway as the fourth became visible. She was slight and lithe, reminding me of Ivy, and I suspected she might be every bit as dangerous. The man looked at me intently.

'I don't know you.' He rested a hand on the gun case at his hip. I hid a sigh. I hated guns.

I started to unbutton my top. It was harder to pull off as an illusion than I realised, and I struggled with concentration, trying to project a masculine chest beneath it. His breathing quickened, and he glanced at his companion. She appeared entirely disinterested. She'd be left for the others. I needed to get him away and keep his attention for long enough to needle him. I backed out of the light, circling around the hedge –

trying to pull him with my eyes. I let just enough glamour drop to try and increase my hold on him. He muttered something to her, and she shrugged as he practically ran after me, his hands already unbuckling his belt.

'Not so fast,' I whispered, using the darkness to my advantage. I pushed him back against the hedge, using the opportunity to spike him as the hedge dug into his back. He was panting as I took his hands from his belt.

'Let me do it,' I murmured, slowly opening his trousers and dropping to my knees at his feet, both to keep him from making too much contact with me and keep my own genitals from his grasp. There shouldn't be too long to wait. I pulled his trousers down, whispering lewd suggestions all the while. His knees were starting to wobble.

'How do you like it?' I whispered, tempted to stick a needle in the erect cock a hand span from my face, but why waste the poison we had? He'd pass out very soon, and do so believing he was about to be very happy.

He reached down for my head. 'What the fuck?' he mumbled, as his hands found long hair instead of the short glamour. I stood back up and dropped the glamour fully.

'I'm so sorry. Tonight does not appear to be your night.'

He fumbled for his gun.

I held it up. 'Missing something?'

He opened his mouth to shout, and I clamped my hand over it. 'Not tonight.'

His knees finally gave way, and his breathing slowed as I lowered him to the floor. For a moment, I considered reclothing him, but given that he had willingly joined their force to usurp Anard, I had little sympathy. He could die half undressed, much like the prince he'd likely supported.

I slipped back to the path, where Ivy crouched over a body, accompanied by a middle-aged woman.

'I take it that you feel a little better?' I asked, and the unmistakable voice of the gwyllion replied.

'Quite a lot better, actually.'

Zora reappeared moments later. 'Are we all done? Let's do this.'

My heart pounded against my ribs so hard that I was certain had it been daylight, the others could have seen my chest moving to its frenetic pace. My hands grew clammy as we drew closer to the tower door. Last time we met Diana, she'd proven too much for me. With no water on hand for Zora to access easily, it would be far from a fair fight. Still, with as many of her shrieking ghoulish spirits removed as Ria had managed, maybe we stood a chance.

The door was closed. I stared at it blankly, my brain empty of logical thought. Ivy gently moved me aside. 'Here, let me.' She pulled something from her pocket and crouched by the door with her ear pressed tightly against it. 'All done.' She rose smoothly and opened the door. 'I'll see you up there. Good luck.'

With that, she took off up the side of the tower, climbing like a spider. There was no magic in her, but Oceans above, she was good. It just showed what humans were capable of when they tried.

I drew my magic around me, trying to resist the temptation to fiddle with my cuffs as we climbed the stairs. A window part way up gave a view over the gardens and the slope leading down to the water. I hoped Môr's plan was working. I exhaled slowly, pausing to gather my nerves, to calm the whirlpool of emotions. We stood together in silence, listening for movement anywhere above us. Voices carried down the stairs, the words unclear, but at least three people spoke. Urchin's arse, four soldiers were one thing, but four including the Irrlicht...

I pushed the tide down, steadied myself, and let the reassuring calmness of my companions soothe me. Zora appeared entirely unruffled – a goddess in her own skin.

'Let me go first,' the gwyllion said. 'That way, you can perhaps sneak in behind me.'

She passed without waiting on a response, and we crept up the remaining stairs. As she reached the doorway, she stopped, staring into the room. I heard a sharp intake of breath and a whispered, 'No' before she stood tall and marched in.

'I knew you were a sly, double-crossing, self-serving annwn, but this takes the flowers from the hills.'

Zora glanced at me. That meant trouble – one of the annwn in there too? I recalled the blonde hair retreating into the woodland and held back the shiver. They were working against their own kind? I knew the Tylwyth Teg were as varied as any group of Old Ones, but to realise that some were as sly as the *sidhe* was disappointing.

'What are you doing in my tower, hag? Was it you who stole my spirits?' Her heavily accented voice pulsed through my body, with the discomfort of a hundred crabs nipping at my skin.

'What if it was?' the gwyllion replied. 'What reason could you possibly have to need those poor spirits ensnared?'

'You wouldn't know, would you? Living in this fertile land filled with all the strength you could possibly need.' Diana's voice rose. 'Those of us who were abandoned in The Barren lost our everything because of mankind … our EVERYTHING. While you sit here, cosy and content in your pretty land, they wipe my land out. So, will I wipe theirs clean of their stinking stain. We will sail south to ransack the lands of the Terranian Sea to return it to its rightful queen. And when she has the lands back—' Her voice grew louder as she closed on the doorway. Zora and I crouched lower on the stairs, and

Zora raised her hands in readiness, drawing a trail of water from behind us into her hands.

'When she has them back, so many of these humans will have died in the attempt. They will have given their spirits for her, and I will take them, and she will remain on the throne as long as I choose to keep her there!'

The gwyllion made a strangled noise as something happened beyond our line of sight. 'Join us,' Diana hissed.

A Terranian bird called from outside.

I drew the glamour around me, looking out from sea-grey eyes with a practiced sneer. Zora followed at my heels as I strode into the room, carrying myself with all the poise and haughtiness Dottrine had worn in life.

'Thank you for the most informative chat,' I said as I brushed past the gwyllion. I narrowed my eyes at Diana. 'You told her I was dead? You use my daughter to ruin a country I spent my whole life waiting to run – having to play mistress when that old bitch sat at his side as queen.'

I stalked closer to her, careful not to make contact in any way, remembering the sting of our last touch. 'I played madness to escape, to travel north, and here I find you plotting to put my daughter on the throne. That much I approve of. Our gift was well received, and the dragon's egg a notable prize. But the plan was never to ruin the land.'

Diana's voice had a slight waver as she looked at me. 'You were dead. I watched you rave and rant. I called on the blood witch to draw you back, but she was gone.'

I ignored her. Dottrine would have. I closed on the teenage girl, sat alongside a tall, handsome annwn. That was our supposed queen. I hoped she had no hidden secrets, though I saw the annwn's eyes narrow as I drew closer. Again, the bird called. Ivy would be just outside. Neither the queen nor Diana appeared to notice, but the annwn stood abruptly and moved to the window. Of course, he'd know what he expected to hear.

I took the moment to quickly check around the room. Zora stood square in the doorway, lit from behind by a lamp, her hood covering her face and keeping her features buried in its shadowy depths.

Hidden in a dark corner was a heap of blankets. It was out of place for a room so overtly ostentatious. I flicked my hand towards it, and Zora moved across, pulling them off to reveal Maddoc and another individual who I didn't recognise.

'Alive,' she mouthed at me, then kicked them.

'What scum are these?' she asked. 'Do you not clean your mess as you go along?' She shook her head as she raised her hands as though in exasperation. From the stairwell, a snake of water rose into the air.

Diana stared at the water. 'YOU!' she shrieked, turning toward me. I was already in reach of the queen.

I lunged for her. To my shock, the annwn split in two, and instead of the queen, I found him in front of me, growing a glowing blue dagger from his right hand.

If it was like my lens, I had a few moments before he could use it. I reached for his long hair with one hand, pulled his head backwards, and Zora filled his lungs with the water. I let my needle sink into the back of his head. He spluttered in anger and lashed out at me with the dagger. It grazed my arm, slicing through my clothes completely. The one stood at the window turned to face me, fury writ across both of their beautiful faces. The closest one doubled over, trying to expel the water from his lungs as the dagger shrank back into his body. I searched for the queen, who'd slipped further from me. Motion caught my eye near the window. Ivy would have that one dealt with in moments.

Diana stood central to the room, screeching, with her arm

outstretched toward Zora. None of her spirits would come to help. They were all well and truly in the Otherworld. Except … two did. One headed directly for Zora, shrieking at high volume. It hurt, but nothing like the level we'd endured on *Black Hind*. The one targeting Zora swiped at her uselessly as it circled overhead – the man she had killed but a few minutes ago, back for revenge. Their volume grew louder, shrieks of terror and fear echoing around the gilded room.

'What can your ghosts do to me?' Zora narrowed her eyes as she closed on Diana. I'd trust her to deal with the Irrlicht. Ivy would drop the one by the window any moment. I clasped my hand over my arm. I could have done without that, but at least it was the left. Motion from the dark corner, and the man I didn't know rose to his feet.

'Witch, use this,' he called weakly and filled the room with mist.

Zora drew it into a solid shard of ice and threw it at Diana.

It must have hit, as the sound of her cry hurt so badly that it made me want to vomit.

The glowing dagger cut through the mist as it condensed into his hands, and my attacker approached again while I struggled for control of my stomach.

'Slimy selkie. Stinking selkie. You think I do not know what you are?' he taunted. 'I will get myself a selkie bitch like the humans do.'

I circled round, keeping my eye on his hand, reaching behind me for the weapon I'd stolen earlier. Why wasn't it working? Why wasn't he dropping to the floor? Was he slowing? I'd never shot a gun – it was the one skill that I had truly not wanted to learn. Sal's insistence rang in my memories. I should have listened.

'I see the confusion in your eyes. This silly venom trick isn't going to hurt me.'

Urchin arse, of course it wouldn't. I'd got so used to using it on humans I hadn't considered that he'd heal before it hurt him, exactly the same as I would. I backed away, waiting, hoping that Ivy would drop the other one soon. A blur shot through from the window, and it was done. She wiped her dagger clean on his body as the one facing me span in her direction.

'Stop dancing and shoot the bastard,' Maddoc's groggy voice came from behind me.

'I don't know how,' I hissed. A hand reached for the weapon in my belt as he propped himself up against the wall. Ivy was dancing under the blue blade, once inside it, then out again. Her effortless ability to climb made it almost impossible for the annwn to land a strike on her as he still battled the living, choking water.

'She went up,' Maddoc muttered, gesturing to the staircase in the corner. I ran after the queen. After all, that was why we were there.

39
MESSY BUSINESS

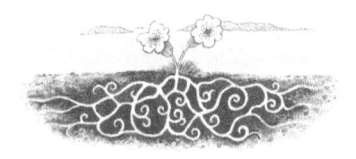

MADDOC

It was the kick that woke him ... that or the incessant screaming. Maddoc cracked his eyes open. Had he been that tired that he'd fallen asleep on Queen Maria's floor? The grunts of fighting interspersed with choking sounds roused him further.

There was fighting, and the room stank of magic. Before he opened his eyes, he tried to work out what was going on and who was there. The Sea Witch and Diana. The selkie, Tellin. A pulse of annwn magic ripped through the room – *the twins.* He forced his eyes open.

Zora there, the gwyllion in a crumpled heap near the door. A tall unfamiliar woman his senses told him was Tellin danced as she tried to avoid the annwn blade of a twin.

The twins! The double-crossing, sly, conniving twins. He tried to shuffle upright, moving slowly so as not to draw attention to himself as he took in the scene. Gwyn stirred. The howling spirits circling the ceiling must be cutting through his drug-addled sleep too.

Maddoc elbowed Gwyn. 'Make thick mist for the witch. Help her.'

He rolled over. 'Mist for the witch,' he murmured. Maddoc elbowed him again.

Gwyn slowly raised his hands and filled the room with dense mist. 'Witch, use this,' he croaked, then flopped back down, snoring gently.

The mist coalesced into an ice shard. Zora wielded it at Diana, and the queen slipped up the stairs, unnoticed by those engaged in the fight. Maddoc tried to persuade his legs to cooperate and follow her, but they were still useless.

Tellin backed towards him, and he spotted the gun in her belt. Why was she using tiny needles against an annwn? Whatever poison she used would be pointless – the twins' healing power would outmatch it comfortably. A small woman appeared through the window, and within moments, she was astride the body of the twin, wiping her dagger clean.

'Stop dancing and shoot the bastard,' he called to her. Gods, he sounded drunk. When she replied that she didn't know how to use it, Maddoc wrestled his body into action, reached for the gun, and braced himself against the wall. He sent Tellin after the queen, and as the twin turned to attack the shorter woman, Maddoc pulled the trigger. The recoil smashed his shoulder into the wall, and pain lanced through his body, but the annwn dropped.

The crack of the gun paused the battle for a moment, these magical creatures all so unused to the human weapon, despite its lingering presence and all The Old Ones guns had killed. He struggled to his feet.

Zora had Diana pinned with a rapidly melting shard of ice, so he left her to it.

The twin he'd shot opened his palm, exposing the small shard of blue regrowing. Maddoc wobbled towards him and swiped his hand through the blue light, shattering it. 'You traitor. Had my mother been here, you'd have died while she laughed.'

'You are not your mother.'

'No,' Maddoc replied, 'I have human blood too. But my mother's blood – that will let me kill you.' He reached into his pocket and pulled out the lump of iron from his bracelet. The twin's wound closed fast as he healed and his sneer widened as he pushed himself from the ground.

Maddoc lunged forward and thrust the iron into the open wound. The twin screamed, coiling in on himself. Maddoc raised the gun once more and shot him; the annwn ceased moving.

Maddoc laughed, his mother's instincts bubbling to the fore. He quashed it quickly. If killing brought that instinct from somewhere deep inside, he never wanted to kill again.

The gwyllion stared with utter hatred at the Irrlicht. Shrieking spirits dived past Zora, coiling around her. Occasionally, she shook her head as though shaking away a fly while she hurled tiny shards of ice at the Irrlicht. Diana's voice blended with the noise, and she summoned a ball of light. The room lit up to a blinding brilliance as she hurled it towards Zora.

Almost as soon as it left her hands, it began to shrink. The gwyllion pulled it towards herself, reducing it to a highly concentrated prick of light, then swallowed it.

While Diana was distracted, Zora wove her arms up and down the Irrlicht's body. Maddoc found himself staring in confusion. There was no ice or water coming from her hands, and nothing could reach them quickly so far from the water's edge.

Zora stopped, her hands clasped tightly around each other as Diana stared down at her own body in shock. Pain etched her beautiful features.

'No, you can't do this,' she said. 'You don't—'

'Blood is not pure water.' Zora said and opened her hand, fully splaying her fingers. Shards of frozen blood flew from inside Diana, daggers of death scattering around the room. Individually tiny, but their combined effect was enough to shred her body to pieces. 'Huh, it worked,' Zora said before collapsing to the floor.

It was done.

The queen was not his responsibility, and Tellin would shortly have that under control. He needed to save the Pact and, judging by the willingness of the twins to push and break it, it needed resetting as soon as possible. He looked around the blood-spattered room as the scent of blood, urine, and all that death brings filled his nostrils. Yes, very soon.

'I need to fix this,' he muttered.

'You've done enough,' Gwyn replied. 'The mess is easy to clean if we can get the army off the islands.'

Ivy wove through splattered chunks of Diana and the dead twins to crouch in front of Maddoc.

'We have the sailors under control. What we really need now is a reliable' – she kicked one of the twins' bodies – 'Tylwyth Teg. One who can make the sailors forget what they are doing here or who they are.' She turned the twin over, exposing his beautiful face. 'Why did he turn traitor?'

'Some of their kind like to hunt. I know my kind lure the unwitting to their death, but the sheer joy in death, the fascination with endings, is very much an annwn trait.' The gwyllion stared across the room at Maddoc. 'What I can't understand is why they helped you to escape and free the tibicena?'

Maddoc put the gun on the floor – foul thing. He hated that he'd had to use it, and hated that killing the twins had brought out the primal Tylwyth Teg in him. It made him no better than his mother. He focused his attention on the gwyllion.

'Where are all our black dogs? When did you last hear of one roaming the lands? The Barren was the end of most of them. Maybe the tibicena was their main aim? Maybe it was purely to see me suffer their betrayal. That would be a very Tylwyth Teg thing to do.' He gestured at Zora. 'Will she recover?'

The small woman reached for Zora, moving her slightly so she could breathe more freely. 'Yes, given rest.'

'Do you know who could help us end this?' Gwyn asked Maddoc.

'My mam.'

'Then let's find you a mist-ride off the islands. There's no way I can do it just yet.'

The short woman glanced at the stairs. 'She went that way?' Maddoc wasn't sure if she meant Tellin or the queen, so he nodded. She ran off, light-footed, blood-spattered, and cold-eyed.

'Not a woman to cross, that one.' Gwyn stared after her.

'I'll keep any stray humans out.' The gwyllion smiled with rather more energy than her body looked as though it could produce.

Maddoc needed to get to the mainland fast. If the twins had turned, it was only a matter of time before others found the Pact's bonds too weak to stay their hand.

They leant on each other as they walked onto the cove where they'd left the others.

A boat bobbed in the middle of the bay. 'I thought you might be needing a lift home.' Julia's voice carried through the mist.

'Yes, an urgent one. I need Lewis,' Gwyn replied. Within moments, Lewis had appeared at his side.

'I'm at your service. Maddoc, let's go.'

Maddoc held out his hand falteringly, and Lewis took it. Within the space of a breath, they were above the water, flying on a cloud of mist toward the mainland. Maddoc decided it was a lot like the Path – high, unstable, and he was petrified.

'Wait for us here.' He hopped onto the grassy clifftop, and Lewis backed his mist away. His small cloud hung unnaturally over the sea as Maddoc flung his cloak around himself and stepped onto the Path.

Before he had taken four steps, Maddoc knew he wasn't alone. His drug-addled body struggled with balance as he took faster and longer steps. Laughter carried to his ears.

'Another traveller who shouldn't be here. Your blood cannot protect you much longer. Soon, I will chase you from the Path and watch you fall. I can feel the hold weakening…'

Maddoc reached the Black Mountain and leapt off, skidding to a halt at the top of the escarpment. Descending the invisible stairs to his mother's realm would make him vulnerable once again. With no choice but speed, he lowered the hood and gripped his feather charm even tighter. Never had he run down the stairs so fast.

He didn't slow as he entered the water, landing on the mossy cushion. Without waiting for an escort, he ran into the town, trying to hide panting gasps for breath.

The Tylwyth Teg gathered in groups, and whispers and distrust permeated the air. Was he too late?

'Where is The Lady?' he asked a passing changeling.

'At the flame, obviously!' they replied.

Maddoc drew a few deep breaths, resting against a door frame before rushing toward the cave. He stifled a yawn as he entered. The sooner this sleeping potion's effects fully wore off, the better.

The flame was a mere flicker, a tiny tongue of power, and his mother sat vigil over it. Maddoc knelt next to her.

'It is done. We have traitors in our midst.'

'I know. Did you kill them?'

'I killed the ones you sent with me, yes.' Maddoc replied, aware of the potential for listening ears. 'I need your help. To make the invaders go away, we need their minds blanked.'

'I need to reseal the Pact.' She looked at him. 'How do I leave this, knowing that the moment I go, others will extinguish it?'

'Leave me here, and I will guard it in your absence. Just get this stupid sleeping potion or whatever it is out of my system before you go.'

She laid her hands on his head and sighed. 'So primitive! There, all done. I thought he'd be more efficient than that.'

'You expected them to try to kill me?'

His mam rose to her feet and offered him a long, silver sword. 'I've been working on this while you were away, worried I may have to use it myself. Use it on any who come close, Guardian,' she said, ignoring his question. She drew her shimmering dress around her and paused for a second at the doorway. Maddoc could feel the air humming with power as she left him alone to guard the flame.

40
A NEW WIND BLOWS

TELLIN

'When the sky falls and the land swallows the sea, that's when you'll be the Queen of Terrania. Born to a mistress, hidden from the world ... why would you ever dream they would accept you?' I stalked toward the young woman I'd backed into the corner, still wearing her mother's face.

'I am the face she saw as she died. I am the one who killed her.' It didn't matter if she knew. She wasn't leaving this tower as a queen. Her army slept, and I trusted that both those who had whispered poison in her ears – the belief that she could rule a land she'd never seen – would be dead.

'You play with toys you cannot comprehend. There are more people ready to fight on a single one of King Anard's ships than you have on this entire group of islands. It's pitiful.' I moved closer, raising my chin in imitation of the haughty attitude her mother had worn. 'Your gifts have been returned, the lands you stole them from once again able to flourish. Did you even know what you did? Did you want to rule over nothing but another Barren?'

She trembled like a poked jellyfish, shaking her head in panic. I could see none of the malice that Dottrine wore so proudly in this girl. She was either a great actress or easily manipulated. I dropped my glamour.

'This is the face your mother looked on as she died. It was the last face seen by the leader of the pirates you dragged up here too. You took on the flotsam left after they were ejected from Terrania. Do you seek the same fate?' I bared my teeth at her.

She whimpered.

Damn it, but I missed Rialta. She'd have known what to do – whether it was an act or the child needed to be removed.

'They told me I'd be welcomed. That the people of Terrania would open their lives to me. They told me that my brother was unloved and that the men who came to find me spoke for them all.' My gut said she was telling the truth, that she was led as easily as a hooked fish. I trusted my instincts, but needed more.

'The annwn? Why did you let him influence you? What was he offering, and what did he want from you?'

A tiny smile quirked the corner of her mouth. 'Didn't you see him?' Yearning filled her voice. 'He is beautiful. Show me a woman who wouldn't be under his spell.'

I pointed at myself and sighed. 'Any woman with a brain! Everyone knows you don't bargain with his kind.'

'I didn't bargain. I was going to marry him.' She had the grace to blush.

'You'd have lasted as long as it took to get you crowned. Then, he'd have killed you, too, and installed himself in your place. His kind would have hunted humans, returning the favour for what your kind did to us over thousands of years until the Pact.' I'd heard enough.

'This won't hurt a bit,' I murmured and leant to scratch her with my left hand. I may have killed to get to her, but something deep inside me said she'd be more use to us alive – somewhere far from Anard.

'What did you do?' Her hand flew to her neck and scratched the place I'd stabbed her.

'You'll sleep soon. When you awake, we'll see what happens next.' I held her still as she struggled to break free, her slender body and youthful strength no match for my sailing-toned arms. She flailed uselessly. Eventually, she flopped to the floor as Ivy pounded up the steps into the room.

'Dead?' she asked. I shook my head. 'I don't know why, but I feel certain she will cause us less trouble alive.'

'She'll need watching like a hawk.'

'I know.'

'Can you keep her asleep until we decide that?'

I nodded and picked the girl up in my arms, and then we returned to the room below. Zora had passed out on the floor, and the gwyllion sat over her. The entire room was splattered in blood, and viscera dripped down the walls.

'What on the ocean floor did this?' I asked.

'Zora.' Ivy shook her head, but there was more admiration in that single word than fear.

'What did she do?'

'She froze Diana from the inside out, then shredded her. It was bloody impressive.'

'That sounds like something she'd do.' It explained how entirely wiped out she was. The concentration needed to perform something so complex must have been immense. I was well used to the results of Zora's exertions, but getting her down those steps was going to be as difficult as pushing the tide back.

'What happened to the spirits and Maddoc?' I asked, their absence dawning on me as I took in the mess. The queen was getting heavy, so I lowered her to the floor and sat next to her, trying to work out what to do next.

Shouts and the sound of running feet carried up the stairs.

Ivy sprang to her feet, slipping alongside the door frame, and I moved to stand between Zora's prone form and the doorway. I changed back into Dottrine's form, as being most recently used, it was fastest to apply. I bound it tightly to myself just as the runners came into sight.

I made a 'hold' gesture to Ivy. She froze her knife hand as Môr appeared at the doorway, followed by another two selkies.

'Salt and blood, what happened here?'

I pointed at Zora.

'After seeing how much ice she could make, her power isn't in question, but this is a massacre.' Môr shook his head.

'It needed to be,' the gwyllion chipped in. 'Only one was killed in breach of Pact, and the Guardian did it.'

Môr looked at the blood pooling from the fallen annwn and shrugged. 'He would be the only one who could bypass the Pact to do it. Therefore, if he did, they deserved it. Y Plant sent someone called Gwyn to find us. He said you might need some help.'

'Can you carry Zora and the small woman over there down to the north cove where we came ashore? I need to heal this arm properly. Then I'll follow.' My arm was sore, but nothing I couldn't handle with a little concentration.

'We've loaded most of the humans into boats, and they are sleeping the night away. It was easy enough to draw them into the dance and needle them as we went. I'm impressed with the effectiveness of these.' He gestured at his sleeve before scooping Zora up in his arms.

'She's heavier than I expected.'

'Don't worry – the other woman is lighter. And she won't wake soon.'

'Who is she?' the selkie carrying her asked.

'Just some servant girl. Maria is her name.'

The gwyllion stared at me. 'It's your business,' she said from under furrowed brows.

'That it is,' I replied as the selkies left the room, carrying the two sleeping women.

Once I had pushed some healing into my arm, the gwyllion and I followed. 'I took their spirits,' she confessed as we walked.

'I thought you'd recovered well. From what a good friend told me,' I continued, trying to ignore the pang of loss for Ria, 'it is a good thing to take in bad spirits and stop them causing trouble.'

The gwyllion stood a little taller at that, her stride easier, and I hid a smile.

'I won't need to find more for a long time. If the Pact is reset, I will not be able to lift a hand against others if they are bound by blood to Mynyw.'

'That's quite an eddy of a hole in the bond,' I said, gesturing around us at the burnt houses and the general situation we walked from. 'None of these were from Mynyw.'

'It is. But it's as it should be,' she replied. 'Else you could never have helped us.'

'Old One problem solver at your service,' I joked, and she laughed. It felt good.

We arrived at the small cove as a misty cloud came in to hover over the sand, and The Lady of the Lake appeared from it.

'Maddoc?' I asked

'His part here is done,' she replied. 'Where are these people whose memories need wiping?'

I pointed at the queen. 'That one there, and the rest are on the misted isle where their vessels are tied up.'

She leant over the young woman, murmuring quiet words, then rose to her feet. 'Is this one going out to the isle too?'

Lewis stared at the sleeping queen, then looked up at me and nodded. 'No, I think this one can make a fresh start. I know someone who could use a set of young hands in their old age. That way, I can keep an eye on them too.' He picked up Maria and carried her to the boat in the bay.

'What in the name of the old gods am I supposed to do with a girl?' the woman's voice drifted over the water.

'Take me to the others,' The Lady demanded. Lewis rushed back to collect her, and then they disappeared over the water. I waded into the sea, swimming out to Julia and emerging alongside her boat.

'May I speak to you?' I asked.

'Seems you already are.'

'You have the false queen there – keep her safe and keep her close. Never let her know who she is. Do not let the annwn find her,' I whispered.

'Fine. She harmed my home, and she un-homed my friend. She will work for her food and board. Don't you people start thinking you can ask more of me, though. I want a quiet life.'

I suspected The Lady might have one more ask of her, but I said nothing, swimming back to the cove instead. Washing the blood from my clothes felt good.

It wasn't much later when The Lady reappeared. She stared at Môr for a while. 'You are very handsome. I can almost feel your pull. Who represents your community these days? Is it still that boring old bull?'

Maddoc tensed but kept his cool. 'I lead the bachelor pack, but the main pack is still led by Sgomer, yes.'

'Then you'll do. Who leads Y Plant Rhys Ddwfn these days?' she asked of Lewis. He pointed at the still-resting Gwyn. 'Excellent, that's three out of five. Now we need a human who knows we exist and is a leader in her community.' She said it louder than the rest and faced the boat.

'I'm no leader. You'd better not be looking at me, Lady of the Lake!' Julia's voice floated back over the water, and I had to hold down laughter.

'Oh, but you are. You could be, and you understand the commitment you make.'

I sat on the cove, glad to be out of that particular problem. Given my pack's range was so far north of Mynyw, there would be no need of my help.

'Gwyn, use as many of your people as you need. Get the selkie, the human, and yourself to the Pact stone at the arch, but avoid the Path. I'll deal with Lord Flame. The Pact will be resealed today.'

'Selkie.' She turned to me. 'Thank you for your help. I can take it from here. Go home.'

Part of me wanted to see it to the end, to travel with them and watch the resealing of the Pact, to bear witness. But it wasn't my land, and if the Lady of The Lake said she had it under control, who was I to doubt her?

So we did as she said. When Zora woke enough to board, we rejoined Theo and Ventios to return to *Barge*. Ventios sat with Zora in the cabin, and Theo and I sailed us back towards Haven. Wet spring rain drenched the deck, and the grey sea and sky reminded me of Erin's pelt safely on *Barge.*

As we drew close to the selkie isle later that day, I realised there would be one way that we could see if the Pact had been fixed. Theo pulled us alongside the remains of the steps, and Zora and I rushed onto the island, followed closely by Ventios. We didn't wait for a welcome or invite, but headed straight to the blow hole.

We heard it before we saw it. A huge standing wave almost crested the top of the hole. Several selkies stood around it, staring in.

'Môr has re-bonded the Pact on behalf of your pack.' I gasped for air as I joined them in staring downwards. It was amazing. Puffins dotted the island, and their beautiful striped beaks added even more cheer to the moment.

Sal's mother saw us and walked around the blow hole. I braced myself for whatever came next, and was entirely shocked when it was a hug.

'Thank you. Tell my son he may visit before he leaves. I would swim with him once more. He promised you would fix it, and you did. We are safe again.' She smiled at Ventios, and he quivered. 'Oh, my dear,' she said and reached for his arm. 'You couldn't handle me.'

Then, she turned and dived gracefully off the cliff into the water below.

We returned to *Barge* then, tying *Black Hind* alongside for the night. Theo took himself off to see Aline and check his hand. Murmurs followed him as he boarded; his dragon-scale eyepatch attracted attention from all who saw him. I suspected a new legend of Timothee Maritim would be born as a result.

Zora and Ventios headed for the Ocean Bar. The residents' food was good, but I couldn't blame them for wanting something a little more indulgent. I preferred to eat there anyway as I knew Seren kept the most selkie-suitable food in those kitchens.

I headed up to Sal's rooms, hoping to find him and deliver the usual debrief. With my Georgie face applied, I wound through the decks and took the staircase up from *Petrel's* berth. I was tired and forgot to knock, bursting in to flop immediately in one of his chairs.

A surprised squeal came from the bed that I'd passed in my exhausted haze. I looked up to find Seren, naked.

'I see you made up your differences,' I said, trying to hide my embarrassment at intruding on them. Clearly, I'd have to knock in the future. I didn't mind at all. In fact, I struggled to hold the grin from my face as Sal wandered in to see what the noise was.

'You're back then,' he said.

'I came to, umm, debrief you,' I replied, still fighting the growing smile on my face.

'Stop grinning like a shark!' Sal returned my smile, his pointed teeth showing in his own wide grin. 'Get on with it.'

'One queen has been removed from power, her memory wiped and placed with a safe human guardian. One evil Irrlicht was killed, a turncoat annwn dealt with – twice.' He raised an eyebrow at that, but I pushed on. 'The Pact is resealed by The Lady and appropriate others. All Guardians are presumably back in place. Mynyw's Old Ones are saved from both themselves and others.'

'Good. The selkies?'

'Môr was a good leader. I'm sure Ivy and Ash will be returning with him. Your mother says you can go home. She would like to swim with you before you leave. Oh, and there's a tibicena we left in a cave on the islands of Y Plant. It will need taking home by one of our crews at some point.'

Seren sat up in the bed with the covers around her waist, relaxed in my presence once the surprise was over. 'You've done well,' she said.

'Thank you, Seren. Can you arrange supplies for *Black Hind* to sail north? Sal, can you retrieve Eryn's pelt when you return the others to your pack? It's time I took it home. There's a selkie pup waiting to meet a mother who wears the wrong skin.'

With that, I bowed deeply to them and retreated the way I'd arrived to join the others for food, happiness filling each step until I felt as though I would overflow. Sal deserved the love of Seren. I was glad she'd been able to see he was still the same person.

We relaxed in the gentle light of the Ocean Bar as creatures swam round us. We had just finished our meal when Theo joined us, his hand freshly dressed and splinted.

'How is it all looking?' I asked as I sipped yet another alcohol-free, rainbow concoction the bar had created for me. Zora was drinking something rather plainer. It was a tiny volume of liquid and was coloured like a wood-stained tide pool It smelt strong, and my eyes watered when I stuck my nose in it for a sniff.

'The hand is good, but Aline can't see under the scale.' He stroked his beard. 'It will have to stay as it is. It's not hot, and she's happy with the skin around it.'

'Can you see anything at all from it?' Zora asked. She sat on the same side as his scale and waved her hands near it.

'I can see perfectly well with the other one.' He laughed, and it was relaxed – happy. He sounded like his old self. Although the shade of the Theo whose finger had to be amputated would ever haunt me, I felt certain it would fade in time. 'Aline does want me to rest and relax for a bit when we return to Terrania. Apparently, focus on recovery rather than survival will give me the best chance of a mobile hand.'

'It's a fair request,' Ventios replied. 'Where will you recuperate? I'm sure your mother would love to have you.'

Theo looked into the distance, once again stroking his beard. 'My beard might need re-dying,' he murmured. 'Maybe I could visit Jena and get some help with that.'

Ventios looked puzzled as Zora and I traded smiles.

'I think that sounds like a wonderful plan,' I said. 'Before you rest for a little while, could I request all your company for a short voyage north?'

Zora beamed at me, and Theo threw his arms around me. 'I'm not missing the chance to see you swim in your own skin,' he replied. 'When are we leaving?'

'As soon as Môr's boat returns. I've asked Seren to ready our supplies, but I'd like to be sure that Môr can take Sal home before we leave them.'

'Can I come with you?' Ventios leant forwards expectantly.

'To my home? Of course. We need your help to sail *Black Hind*.'

Ventios swirled the drink in his glass as he stared into it. He looked up hopefully at me. 'Actually, I wondered if I could stay aboard more permanently.'

I glanced at Theo, and he nodded. Zora reached across the table and placed her hand over the closest of his.

'As long as you promise to take lessons from Driftwood when we get back to Terrania. I don't know where Sal will send us next, but if we hadn't had your help, we couldn't have achieved what we just did,' she said.

'Ria may be back one day.' Ventios's gaze followed the fish behind me as he said it.

'She might, and we have room for you both if that happens.'

Ventios maintained his own boat, so clearly was able to deal with some of the basic technical aspects of *Black Hind*. It wasn't just him who needed to work on their contribution to the crew, I decided. While Theo was resting, I needed to split my own time between being Lady Gina and learning to helm *Black Hind* solo. The more we could all do, the better for the future.

Lady Gina without an aide – that was another problem. I knew who I wanted around, but would she stay with me?

'As Ria isn't back, would you like to share Lady Gina's quarters with me?' I asked Zora.

She almost choked on her drink. 'No way can I get you dressed into that fancy gear. Nor would I want to slink around after you.'

'Gods, Zora! I would never ask you to. It's just that her bed is way comfier than the ones in the residences, and I thought you might still need some decent sleep.'

'I'll sleep just fine in my room.' She smiled, and I held down the sigh. It would have been good to have her company. I toyed with rejoining them down in the residences, but since I'd said I was staying in Gina's room, it might make it look like I was after something else. Oh, puffin burrows and cockle shells. I sighed deeply, and Theo shot me a sympathetic look.

'What about Ivy?' he asked. 'She's as subtle as Ria and just as tough, in her own way. You'd just be taking your own part of Driftwood.'

It was a good suggestion, and I'd already trusted her with my secret. I'd ask her when they came back. I said goodnight and left the rest to return to their rooms in the residences as I returned to Gina's rooms alone. Oceans, but I needed some rest.

41
GUARDIAN OF THE FLAME

MADDOC

The first few hours Maddoc paced back and forth across the archway, his body full of energy, thanks to his mam's healing. He felt tough, strong, and ready; he'd cut down anyone who tried to take him on. He was the Guardian.

Maddoc swung the long blade experimentally. It was far lighter than he expected, and the flared ends of the hilt and pommel looked vaguely familiar to him. After studying them more closely, he realised it was the same shape as the sword in the Pact stone.

Had his mam done it on purpose? He looked more carefully at the blade; she'd recreated her legendary sword. Maddoc's eyes widened as he realised what he carried.

If that couldn't protect the flame, he supposed nothing would. He shrugged and returned to his watch, kneeling with his back to the flame and the sword across his lap. Each time his legs grew numb, he readjusted his position but always kept the archway in his eye-line.

He was hungry, his stomach always a more accurate timer than his eyes or other senses down there. When had he last eaten? Maddoc couldn't remember. He was exhausted once the effects of the healing had worn off, desperate for food or drink, and a little light-headed.

A crackling noise drew his attention back to the flame. It had dimmed even further, the tallest flame no taller than his palm. Maddoc barely dared to breathe as he studied it for fear of blowing it out.

A growing commotion swelled outside the cave, drawing his focus back to the task he'd accepted. Voices raised in anger, and fear echoed around the cavern. He gripped the sword hilt tightly and stood ready to defend the tiny flicker of hope that so many Old Ones were relying on.

'Where is he?'

A shiver of fear rippled through Maddoc. He gripped the handle tighter and held the sword out in front of him.

He'd use it to protect himself. Protect the flame? What was he thinking? It'd been decades since he'd wielded a sword. His stomach knotted as the voice called again.

'I told you I'd get you, Guardian.' It was the annwn who had taunted him on the Path.

She stood at the head of a small group of others. To either side clustered smaller Tylwyth Teg.

'Do you want us all to die?' a coblynau screamed at her from the closest group.

'Death? To die would be an adventure. To travel and hunt, an even bigger one. The Lady is gone, and the Pact is in such trouble she was called to the Islands of the Lost with those sanctimonious, human-loving creatures that we tried to rid ourselves of once already. I will douse this flame, free us from its confines. Any day now, the twins will return victorious.

The Lady will be defeated, and we will travel afar with new lands to hunt.'

'You'll have to get past me first.' Maddoc lifted the sword, his body finding a muscle memory that his brain had lost.

'You?' sneered the annwn. 'You? Who came running home to your mam like the human weakling you are?'

Maddoc noticed the other annwn carrying a container. He moved slowly, trying to sneak through the edge of the arch from behind the main group, while the one leading them tried to draw Maddoc's attention. A blue knife began to grow in her hands. He'd let them think he hadn't seen.

He stood as tall as he could, which was still fairly short compared to the annwn, and let a wide smile grow on his face. Maddoc would deal with the ramifications of letting his mother's nature loose afterwards.

'They died horribly.' He laughed. 'I killed the twins, took their precious queen, and watched the Irrlicht explode.' He lowered the sword tip. 'So, if you think you can do better than they did ... be my guest.'

He opened his arms wide and walked towards the group. 'Because you don't actually know what I can do – none of you. I am the Guardian. Maddoc, sat in a cottage staring at a tree, was born to defend the Pact and trained to fight you.' He passed the sword to his other hand as he continued to advance. 'You see, I'm both human and Tylwyth Teg. I can kill my own kind. Even when that flame blazes to the cavern roof – when you cannot lay a hand on me – I can rip you limb from limb.'

The blue blade was only half the length of his sword so far, and the annwn tried to goad him forward by directing it his way.

Maddoc took one more pace, then span and leapt towards the annwn sneaking close to the flame. As he swung his blade, a small blur shot past him, and water went flying against the wall of the cave.

Ddôl stood square in its place. 'Now you have two guardians to contend with.'

'A human with a big mouth and a child. You are hardly a challenge.'

Maddoc returned his focus to the leader. He'd not wanted to kill, but there was little choice left to him. He wasn't confident of winning, and his bluster and bravado had not scared the annwn off. Maddoc would buy as much time as he could. He prepared to fight.

The annwn behind the leader moved forward, and before Maddoc could react, threw a knife directly at him. It hit him in the shoulder. Pain lanced through the joint, and Maddoc struggled to hold his sword level. He moved it to his weaker hand and charged toward them, screaming as he swung for the almost solidified blade. His sword sliced through it, shattering the magic and breaking the illusion. The annwn flew at him, her fingers growing clawed nails, short and sharp.

She raked his face in passing, and he backed towards the flame, trying to stay between it and the crowd. The annwn with the container was still struggling with Ddôl. The changeling was impressively dextrous and was attacking the annwn from all angles with flying punches.

Maddoc lost sight of his opponent for a moment. He span around trying to find her. A laugh from the far side of the flame crawled across his skin. She leapt onto the surrounding wall and jumped onto the flame.

'I'll stamp it out!' she screamed.

It blazed. The fire immolated the annwn, and the stench of her burning flesh filled the cavern with rancid smoke.

A clattering noise came from near his feet. Maddoc turned to find a second dagger fallen to the floor. Another was thrown, and again it stopped before it made contact, dropping harmlessly at his feet.

Maddoc stalked towards them.

'Who wants to die today?' he growled. 'The Pact has been re-bonded. You are bound. I am not.'

'You're Her son. Of course, you are.'

Maddoc laughed. 'I wasn't born here, but in the green hills across the sea to the west. I've never been bound. Now, who wants to go back to their beautiful homes and accept their future, and who wants to be hunted? I have more than enough of my lifetime left to find you.'

He lifted the sword and tried to hold back the pain, fixing his grin to avoid giving away how weak he was. Maddoc knew he'd lost blood; he should be on the floor. The annwn turned and fled as a howling mass of smaller Tylwyth Teg pursued them from the cave.

Once they had left, a ring of coblynau arrayed themselves across its open archway.

Maddoc sat on the ground clutching at his shoulder.

Ddôl stood over him with a frown on his face. 'Is that true? Are you really unbound?' he asked.

'They'll never know for sure,' Maddoc replied.

The changeling burst out laughing. 'That was the best deception I've ever seen. You had me believing you, and deceit is what I do!'

Maddoc managed a weak grin. 'Do you think that fixing my shoulder is something you could do too? Or could you find me someone who can?'

Ddôl gestured for one of the coblynau, and they ran off.

It was nightfall by the time his mam returned. Nightfall in the under-lake was star-spangled and entirely beautiful, one of the true joys of being down there. Maddoc's shoulder was stable, and the bleeding had stopped.

His mam crouched by his side.

'Every time I leave you alone, you get injured,' she said, unwinding the bandage and placing her hands over his wound. Warmth flowed through his body as the pain subsided.

His hunger and thirst did not. His mam studied the flame for a moment before calling Ddôl over. The sword was almost as tall as he was, and his eyes widened as The Lady gestured for Maddoc to pass it over to him.

'You showed yourself to be a true guardian today, Ddôl.'

He bowed deeply, his curls almost grazing the floor before retreating to stand in front of the flame with it.

'Maddoc, it's time for you to go home. I need you back at the old yew. Your work here is done.' His mam helped him to his feet.

That was it? He saved the Pact, and all he got was to return to his tree? Maddoc smiled. There was nothing he wanted more. He was hungry, and a rest would be wonderful.

'If Rialta reappears, would you send her to me before she leaves?' he asked. His mam nodded. 'She's earned her rest too. If you still live when she returns, I'll send her to you. Don't leave it so long between visits next time.'

Maddoc smiled. 'You could always come for tea at mine? Just food, no entrapment.'

'Maybe I will.'

Maddoc walked through the beauty of the under-lake in a trance, so light-headed that he could barely walk. His mam helped him up the stairs. 'I'll be off then,' he muttered.

His mother embraced him briefly. 'Thank you,' she whispered. 'I'll come and see you soon. Here, take this.' She pointed at a flask and a wrapped packet. 'It's a cheese sandwich. You always used to love them when you were small.'

Maddoc picked them up gratefully and drank deeply. When he turned to say a last farewell, she'd vanished.

He wandered along the stream bed, enjoying the birdsong and spring flowers as he munched the small, dry roll. A tiny wren hopped across his path on the outskirts of the village, and he watched it vanish into the ivy on a hedge. He had no idea what day it was or how long he had been away. Maddoc took off his cloak and stuffed it into his pocket, tucked the feather charm inside his top, and strolled into the village. The scent of freshly baked bread wafted up the road.

He stopped at the shop door, enjoying the smell.

'Daddy, daddy! The tree man is back!' A small girl ran to the doorway and pointed at him.

Her father rushed out. 'We've been worried sick. My Ffion has been looking for you every day since you vanished. Mair, Maddoc is here! The baker's wife popped her head around a door with flour streaking her hair.

'You look exhausted. Are you okay?' She frowned at her husband. 'Why are you just staring at him? He's clearly had a long journey. Those old boots have carried him far this time – oh, Maddoc, those are fancy new ones! Give him a loaf and some of the nicest cheese. We can catch up tomorrow. You'll come for tea and tell us all about where you've been, won't you?'

Maddoc shuffled his feet. 'It was only a family emergency. I'd still love to drop round for tea if that's okay?'

'Of course! We'll see you then. Ffion, get off his sleeve and let poor Maddoc get home.'

He took the warm loaf and cheese. It would be that delicious crumbly one with the extra tang – he could tell by the smell. He stopped at his cottage to bury his cloak at the bottom of the chest and thought about putting the charm in too. As he lifted it over his head, he stopped. Having worn it for so long, it felt odd to remove it. Maddoc locked the chest and hid the key.

He made his supper and left the house. As the sun went down, Maddoc sat in the hollow of his yew tree, eating his warm cheese sandwich. He'd had enough adventure to last for the rest of his life. All he wanted was regular meals and a bed.

42

ELLIN SILVER SKIN

TELLIN

Spring was in full bloom as we left Haven. We sailed between the headlands for the last time, accompanied by Môr's boat. I wondered what he would rename her once it was refitted in Safe Harbour. Sal stood in the bow, much as Zora stood in ours, reclaiming her customary position from Ventios.

We'd eaten on *Barge*, but the scents of something being prepared drifted up from below deck as Ventios experimented with their next meal. Theo and Zora passed appreciative encouragement to him, and I left them to enjoy the – frankly sickly – smell.

The swell was low, and the crisp breeze was a reminder that summer had not prepared her entrance yet. Frost had graced the hillsides overnight, and they wore their white coats with grace. A boat I didn't recognise passed us slowly. Two women and a man crewed it.

'May you explore new lands and fly freely on faraway

winds,' Lewis called. Julia appeared to be instructing the younger woman in how to set nets. Maria looked across at us – there wasn't a flicker of recognition.

As we came into the waters around the island, I heard another familiar voice.

'Tellin, Sal! You came back!' Gar was sunning himself on the rocks. He was rounded and sleek, finally as healthy as he should always have been.

'Sal is swimming with you today,' I called across, and Gar dived into the water to surface near us.

'I love swimming with Sal. Are you joining us?' His bark even sounded healthier.

I leant over *Black Hind's* railing and whispered, 'I'm going to go and get my skin back.' Gar flicked water at me then, playing alongside as we sailed past.

'Go back. Sal needs a guide. I'll come and see you again one day.' I waved farewell as we pulled away.

'One day, I'm going to sail with you!' he called after us.

'I'll miss that pup,' Zora said.

'We all will.' Theo turned us towards the North, and I watched with a lump in my throat as Môr's boat anchored up, and a sleek, black seal dived from the deck to play with a small pup.

It took several days to make it to the furthest reaches of the Territories, and we turned towards the north east as we rounded them, heading to the islands I had once called home.

'Can we stop before we get there?' I needed a chance to gather my thoughts, to sit with my new family – Zora and Theo. Ventios belonged there too. The longer we sailed with him, the more I recognised it. His instincts on the water were strong. He spotted surface changes and winds better than I did, and he could climb the rig almost as fast as Eden had.

The holes in my being where Eden and Ria should be nipped at me with their incessant crab claws of pain, but I'd learn to live with it. And it was a shared pain. Sometimes I caught Zora staring at the bunk where Eden had slept or at Theo's fading, green beard. Theo stroked it more often as we travelled away from *Barge*. With no urgency or mission driving us, it left time for our own thoughts to surface. Mine were filled with too many lost friends and family. Soon, I'd fix one of those.

I needed to know that my sacrifice hadn't been in vain – that Eryn's pup would arrive soon and that her bonding had gone as well as we'd danced for it.

Theo tilted his head, studying me. 'I think we should stop for the night. That way, you can arrive in the morning, and we won't scare your pack by arriving at night.' He called to Zora, and she stopped her ocean-gazing for long enough to help him drop the anchor in a small bay on the south of the first island we reached.

We sat on the deck that evening, watching the stars and talking about missing friends. Theo had Ventios tell us all the story that his mother had left with the storyteller.

Ventios told it beautifully, and for a moment, we were transported to a mother's view of her child, into a tale of sirens, dragons, and loss.

'So, you really might be part dragon?' Zora studied the scale. 'It explains why you survived the arctic water.'

'And, why you have the patience of an Old One and the skill to read the winds too,' I added. It certainly made sense. Theo reached up self-consciously.

'I don't know. I can't understand the sirens or Ocean. They still allure me.'

'It wouldn't be much of a tactic to attract a mate if they didn't.' Ventios' eyes crinkled at the corners.

'True. Maybe while I'm on the fringes of the southern barren, I might see a dragon there.'

'The golds are much smaller than Lord Flame. You're going to feel let down after riding on his back.' Zora's hand fluttered, gliding across the table as she spoke.

I soaked the chat up with my new pack. I loved my sister, but I knew in a similar situation, Theo and Zora would have found a way to free me – not flee, never to return. I couldn't blame my selkie family, but I realised I was growing a new home. Sal and Gar were part of my new selkie pack.

The sun sank over the horizon as we went to our bunks that night, and my heart was calm, my spirit happy. No matter what the dawn brought, I was ready.

The next morning, I took Eryn's pelt from the locked box in the hold. I brought it on deck and held it on my lap as we sailed directly for the islands.

'That one was where I was taken,' I said, pointing at the small lump of Stone Island. The harbour wall wasn't visible from there.

'Do you need to visit there?' Zora placed her hand gently on my arm. I shook my head.

'No, the stones sing at Midsummer, but we're a little early for that. I don't have any desire to relive the experience.' I held down the rising tide of hatred that grew as we passed it and sailed onward towards the distant lump on the horizon, where Eryn should be.

I joined Zora at the bow as we closed in.

'Would you like a dramatic entrance?' She held her arms

out and gathered water to either side of us. The waves were small and choppy today, so the rolling wave travelling with us certainly stood out. 'I just thought it might help if they can see there's someone on the boat who isn't a human.'

She had a point, but I decided that a magical wave wasn't the way to make it. 'Theo, can you slow the boat. I need to get off.'

'We're nowhere near!'

'I know, but I need to let them know we're coming now we're close enough.'

Theo turned our bow and slowed us so that the sails flapped. I slipped over the side, holding onto the rope ladder, then dived beneath the water and called out in Ocean.

I called of home and sadness; I called of love and of excitement. I poured all my emotions at coming home into my call. Then, I waited.

I was starting to think that the pack had moved, or maybe all been caught. The chill and fear began to fill my every bone as it occurred to me, making it hard to distinguish the source of my shivering.

'Get out! You'll be too cold to do anything.' Zora reached over the side, extending a helping hand. At that moment, I heard it – a song of welcome from a multitude of selkie voices.

'Quickly,' I said, clambering back aboard. 'They are calling me home.'

Zora rolled her eyes. 'One minute you are lounging in the sea, the next it's rush, rush, rush.'

Ventios sprang into action; excited muttering about stories drifted across the deck. Zora winked at me. 'There's nothing like having someone aboard who will record your entire life story.' She tweaked another sail and stood back to check it was filling as she wanted.

'As long as he doesn't share it with the world.'

'The world should hear your stories,' Ventios called back, almost bouncing. He couldn't sit in one spot, and his gaze flickered to the ever-growing island.

'He is so eager,' Theo said.

'Someone has to be,' I replied as the mix of emotions threatened to overwhelm me again. We drew as close to the beach as we could get, given the entire pack of selkies surrounding us. Silver heads bobbed in the water all around. But nowhere could I see my own pelt, worn by Eryn.

I jumped in, and holding the pelt as far out of the water as I could, I swam for shore. I sat on the sand, her pelt across my lap, overwhelmed by the number of voices, the excuses, and the surprise at my return.

'Did you have any children? Are they selkies?' one youngster asked.

'Did he do horrific things to you? Are you unharmed?' another asked. I folded my arms around my body to hide the scars from my run-in with the rocks and the more recent knife attack.

'I have no children. I've been to the Arctic and the Everstorm, and I've met selkies who live amongst humans, helping Old Ones.' I poured my stories out to them, missing those that involved my own justice and skimming over how we actually killed anyone.

By the time I'd finished, a handsome bull seal had swam into the bay. The rest parted for him, deferring to his presence. He still shone – that could only mean my sister was alive. He hauled out onto the sand, removing his skin to sit on the beach belegged with me.

'She did want to come,' he said quietly. 'But she cannot leave Ellin yet.' I looked up at him as a broad smile grew across his face.

'She pupped just a few days ago.' He ran his hand over her

pelt, and much as I had, he buried his face in it. 'Come,' he called back as he sprang to his feet and ran over the hill.

Eryn must be in the small cobbled bay on the far side – the very beach we had been born on ourselves. I grabbed Eryn's pelt, waved at the crew of *Black Hind*, and ran after him.

Down in the small bay, a lone black seal lay with a silver-white pup. It was fluffy and, oh so tiny, snuggled alongside her.

I ran – faster than a surfing dolphin, faster than I ever had before. Joy bubbled up, leaking from my eyes as streams of tears. When I fell to the sand beside her, Eryn opened her huge, brown eyes wide.

'I was starting to think – to fear ...' she said. Her own eyes leaked too. Her mate refitted his skin and shuffled himself alongside the pup.

'Go on,' he encouraged. Eryn needed no more.

She had slipped out of my skin in moments. The pup still dozed and didn't see the switch as Eryn wriggled into her own silver skin.

'There's a small, cold patch,' she said.

'Yes. *He* did it.'

'But he didn't hurt you? Thank you for finding my skin. It's wonderful to have you home.'

I almost put my own skin on then. I held it in my hands, feeling its soft familiarity, the way it wanted to seal around me, to warm me. It was part of me, and I was finally whole.

'I'll be back in a moment,' I said, crouching to touch my belegged nose against hers. 'I have to do something.'

Eryn's whiskers twitched a little. 'Do what you need to. We have all the time in the world. Nothing needs to be rushed.'

Part of me missed that idea. The slow, easy pace of life that I had enjoyed, where food was the biggest worry, and every day was for sunning and playing. But the innocence had been stripped from me.

I ran back over the hill, waving my skin aloft. Out in the bay, three friends watched from the deck of my boat as I slipped into it and headed directly out to them. I swam round and round the boat, barking my joy. Eryn had taken great care of my skin, and bubbles streamed from my fur as I dived. A fish tried to hide in a crevice and I pursued it, reaching for it with my flipper for a moment before snapping at it with my jaws. Cold, juicy fish – it was delicious. Others joined me.

I was surrounded by my pack as they played. We chased each other across the sea bed, where I grabbed a piece of kelp, and another selkie took it from my flipper. We chased each other over the soft sponge mountains and past the entrance to the only sea-cave on the island. I carried on around the coast and hauled myself out on the cobbles next to Eryn and Ellin.

'Nice name,' I said to the pup.

'She can't speak yet, Tellin,' Eryn said.

'I'll come and see you as you get bigger.' I nuzzled the small pup. Love and pride intermingled – tidal eddies without restraint.

That selkie pup was the reason for everything I'd been through. Without her, I'd never have gone south, never have met Sal, nor saved Sirena or the white hind. As a crew, we'd never have found and returned the dragon egg or been in the right place to help with the Pact or save Gar.

Without that little pup, I'd be sat on a beach, eating and sunning myself all day, and the magic would still be fading. I would be happy, unknowing, and self-centred. Instead, we were making a stand – changing things and bringing balance back.

'You have changed the world.' I told her.

ACKNOWLEDGMENTS

As the world of Black Hind's Wake is our world, so the folklore is ours too. In The Pact I wanted to bring more of my own folklore to the foreground. Not just the big, symbolic characters – although they do appear – but smaller folklore less frequently talked about, such as the *coblynau* and *y Plant Rhys Ddwfn*. To allow the integration of these groups I have taken some liberties with grammar, both with Welsh and English to hopefully allow the story to flow. My apologies to my editor, Diana James, for the additional headaches this caused and thank you again for your support and encouragement. The source links to some of the folklore tales I have been inspired by are on my website.

It takes a crew to make these books work, and I have the best, even Lord Sal would agree. Asa and Elis, you both cheer me on and motivate me. For everything and all the love, whisky and cups of late-night tea, for all the mountains of mini-eggs as I create that first draft, for the motivational hugs, thank you. I am sorry I broke the car getting photographs for the cover.

Alex Bradshaw, once again, you gave epic sized support with motivation, checking in to make sure I was still writing, plot wrestling and taking on the first read, thank you. To my beta readers, Damo, Peter and Rowena, your critique has helped polish this book, and add extra sparkle. Carina has once again produced beautiful artwork and Paul at Trif book design has brought my sketch to life.

For making every Friday night an adventure, thank you to 'The Gang,' we never did choose an alternative name. And, thank you as ever to Tom, Lee, Julia, Andrew, Timy, and everyone I promised I'd come and visit but got distracted by the characters in The Pact! I promised name checks - Some of you got them in a bigger way than you might have expected.

Lastly, thank you to everyone of the readers and bloggers who picked up The Skin and took a chance on it. I hope you enjoy your return voyage just as much. The new crews cannot wait to meet you.

As for those tales that Ventios tells within the pages of this book…

You can read them too. The first, 'Sirencall' – Theo's tale, can be read for free when you sign up for my newsletter. Ria's story from beyond the arch, will follow for subscribers later this autumn.

ALSO BY J E HANNAFORD

<u>Black Hind's Wake</u>

The Skin

<u>Black Hind Short Stories.</u>

Sirencall

<u>Anthologies</u>

Through Shadows - So Alone
A story from the world of the Aulirean Gates.

Skybreaker - Darkwhale

Lightning Source UK Ltd.
Milton Keynes UK
UKHW010228101022
410220UK00004B/70

9 781739 921330